Keepers Weepers

***

Keepers Weepers

An Unacceptably Faulty, Unreasonably Embellished,
Inaccurately Reconstructed, Overly Dramatized,
Hopelessly Exaggerated and Barely Believable
Recollection of One Individual's Brief
Childhood Existential Excursion

A Novel

by

Spencer Islo

Keepers Weepers

Published By:

CreateSpace
(an Amazon Company)

for the Author

Spencer Islo
755 Keup Road,
Cedarburg, Wisconsin USA
53012-1627
(e-mail: sislofilm@yahoo.com)

*

1st Print Edition - August, 2016
(Trade Paperback)

(Also available as an E-Book)

*

ISBN-13: 978-1523630844
ISBN-10: 1523630841

Keepers Weepers

Copyright, 2016, by Spencer Islo
(Print Edition)
All Rights Reserved

No part of this book may be reproduced in any form or manner, by any electronic or mechanical means, including information storage and retrieval systems, without the express written consent, permission and agreement with the author, except by reviewer, who may quote brief passages in a review. Scanning, uploading and electronic distribution of this book or the facilitation of such without the express written consent, permission and agreement with the author is prohibited. Please purchase only authorized electronic and/or hard copy paper editions and do not personally undertake, participate in, cooperate in or encourage others to engage in electronic or unauthorized hard copy piracy of this copyrighted work or other copyrighted materials. Your support, understanding and respect of the author's rights are greatly appreciated. Any member of educational institutions wishing to photocopy and/or printout part or all of the work for classroom use, or anthology, should send written inquiries directly to the author;
Spencer Islo,
755 Keup Road,
Cedarburg, Wisconsin USA 53012-1627
or, email requests to *sislofilm@yahoo.com*.

Disclaimer

All characters appearing in this work are fictitious. Any resemblance to real persons, living or dead, is purely coincidental.

***

Dedication:

For Ann, Erik, Angela & Kristina with Love and Affection Always and Forever.

***

Acknowledgments:

For her love, patience, encouragement and support, my wife Ann who understands that when I sit for hours staring at the wall or gazing out the window that I'm actually writing. To my son Erik and his wife Angie for their patience and understanding as they've embraced my countless assurances that "I'm almost there, it's almost done." For her editorial observations, suggestions, unending technical assistance and encouragement my daughter Kristina. For Daniel and his friendship and great conversation. For Liz and her objectivity, insight and clarity. To S.K.. To Paris for everything it has been, for everything it is and for everything it will continue to be. To all readers of this work in the hope that they find something of value to enjoy, appreciate and hang onto. To the authors, famous and obscure, whose work I read and reread every day, week after week, month in and month out, for years on end. To those writers whose combinations of brilliant flaws and damning faults, their life's great accomplishments and equally great personal tragedies and failures, were/are able, as necessary, to stand apart from their emotional struggles and varied endearing-to-maddening idiosyncrasies and produce literary efforts past, present and into the future that continue to delight, teach, entertain, provoke and inspire. To the books that from the opening words to the closing sentence hold you firmly in their grasp. To the books of hundreds, even thousands of pages that you read through by sheer will and determination that seemed to have been written for you to find that one page, to discover a lone paragraph out of hundreds, to read, again and again, that single sentence out of thousands, that can open a window, unlock a door, free a mind and change a life.

***

Brief Aside Regarding Book Title Derivation:

First there was; **"Finders Keepers"**

Old English Adage most commonly used in reference to Maritime Wreck and Cargo Salvage. Old English Usage was derived from and based upon an original cultural and legal concept in Ancient Roman Law. Essentially refers to making a Legal Claim of Ownership upon unclaimed, surrendered, lost or abandoned property. Modern Uses have included Titles for Motion Pictures, Stage Plays, Books, Songs and Television Drama, Game & Situation Comedy Shows.

Next there was; **"Finders Keepers, Losers Weepers"**

Children's Nursery Rhyme based upon the Old English Adage "Finders Keepers" (see above). Modern Uses have included, but not limited to, the Title and repeated Line of Lyrics to an *Elvis Presley* Rock-'n'-Roll Song, Recorded and Released in 1965. Music & Lyrics composed by *Day Jones & Ollie Jones*.

Now there is; **"Keepers Weepers"**

Late Twentieth Century Fictitious Linguistic and Grammatical Invention based upon the Old English Adage "Finders Keepers" (see above and above the above; sorry, not Ancient Roman Law or the *Elvis Presley* song but most definitely the likely association with and influence of a salvaged wreck). Only known Usage, Older or Modern, is the current use by the Author as a Title for this early Twenty-First Century Linguistic and Grammatical Contrivance of a Novel.

***

Table of Contents

Prelude: "...we are all" *1.*

Prologue: The Cat's-Eye Nebula *5.*

Chapter One: "It" Starts *9.*
Chapter Two: A Mother's Faith *45.*
Chapter Three: A Father's Ordeal *87.*
Chapter Four: Defeat *103.*
Chapter Five: The Temptation, The Burden, & Warren 'Rusty' Axlerod *121.*

Intermission: Uncle Dave *167.*

Chapter Six: Opening Moves *177.*
Chapter Seven: False Start *235.*
Chapter Eight: Limbo *293.*
Chapter Nine: Marble Madness *337.*
Chapter Ten: "It" Finishes *395.*

Epilogue: Swimming Trunks *409.*

***

Prelude:
"...we are all"

"...WE ARE ALL, unknowingly, born into this life and onto this world as existentialists. We all, consciously aware or unknowingly and unaware, will with certainty and without exception meet our mortal end as such. Death, the final arbiter of all life's resolved or unresolved philosophical questions and arguments settles the matter, before or after the fact, as it presses us all, willingly or unwillingly, up against and then through the existential door from temporary mortal existence to eternal nonexistence as we join the billions who have disappeared before and precede the billions who, hopeless of any reprieve, are certain to follow...

...no matter how dutifully, how painstakingly, we construct and doggedly, reverently, maintain our fabricated belief structures, the illusion of the thick solid walls, sturdy unyielding plank floors, beamed protective ceilings, shuttered and sealed black glass windows and locked and barricaded impenetrable doors that house our fiercely defended and dearly held ideas, opinions and beliefs are no greater barrier to the ever-sharp penetrating edge of the universe's soulless indifference than sheets of wet tissue paper or drifting wafts of translucent smoke. There is no fault or error in embracing, enjoying, finding comfort and meaning in our mortal interests, diversions and illusions. The only error, the only fault, is in believing, in trusting, that somehow they will save us from the inevitable result of the simple absence of oxygen atoms and glucose molecules which fuel and maintain the function of the organ in our head (not the one in in our chest) that built and houses our diverse but limited understandings of our own and others' human existence...

...the question of whether or not the universe will ever cease to exist is answered on an individual basis hundreds of thousands of times every single day as the expression's terminal phase brushes across the face of the planet with those left standing having been only temporarily spared. The eventual and unavoidable end of conscious sentient life emphatically punctuates and defines the

very meaning and implication of the term...

...the 'one' of our physical existence added to, combined with, the 'one' of our psychological and emotion existence can give the idea, the impression, of a magical mathematics of a third component (where one plus one equals three); a soul. The soul being the expectation, the hope, the wish of a familiar ongoing conscious and aware personal presence that survives and carries on in some unseen, some undetectable, some manifestation of an after death – afterlife existence the proof of which remains as unseen, as undetectable and frustratingly illusive as the number of souls lining up to report back with the good news which to date inexplicably, mysteriously, remarkably, remains at – zero...

...most importantly it is how we use, how we invest, all the time between our mortal beginning and our mortal end, either denying and running from the inevitable or affirming and accepting it, that defines us as either culturally conditioned, culturally burdened, prisoners of life or unencumbered open thinkers and free actors in life. It is, undeniably, more desirable, more life affirming but far more emotionally and intellectually strenuous to embrace the simultaneously bleak and beautiful, the tightly woven and synchronized order up against and then giving in to the relentless push and pull of entropy, the side by side coexistence of the absurdly simple and yet absurdly complex and the unavoidable and inescapable irony of the existential dilemma, while you're still able to breathe deeply and, with an open mind, to see and think clearly...

...the insight, the understanding, the acceptance, empowers the only logical response, the only meaningful and mountable, albeit doomed to fail, temporary defense we as individual human beings will have when the grim reaper finally comes calling, to freely, without doubt or hesitation, to earnestly and wholeheartedly laugh in its face, no matter how long or short, how good or bad, how deceptively significant or insignificant or how fallaciously meaningful or meaningless the beginning, middle and end of the simultaneously greatest gift ever and grandest joke of all may have been..."

(Summarized snippets from a conversation that took place between the Author and an adjacently seated (soundly sleeping) fellow passenger during a late evening bus ride between Milwaukee and Madison, Wisconsin, in mid-April, 1978, regarding the then recent and, within certain philosophical circles, controversial, but nonetheless Ph.D.-granting successful, Philosophy graduate student's doctoral thesis wherein there was an imagined [lively, and at times rancorous] Classical Western Philosophy round table discussion between Plato, Aristotle, and Socrates titled "Infinite Turtles; Physics, Philosophy, Fantasy or Fallacy")

*

***

Prologue:
The Cat's-Eye Nebula

IT'S A PLANETARY Nebula located in the Constellation Draco (the Dragon). In the night sky of the northern hemisphere it lurks in the vicinity of Polaris, the North Star. It is 3,300 light-years from Earth and far enough away, you'd think, not to have caused any problems. But, there it was, and still is, apparently distant enough as not to be dangerous but close enough to screw with us now and again. A gigantic cosmic feline eyeball staring at Earth across the interstellar frontier like our planet was a plaything, a toy to be pounced upon and batted around on the living room carpet until it is lost under the sofa. A multicolored hypnotic pendant, shooting out potentially lethal cosmic rays near the speed of light in all directions, including towards Earth, and, more specifically, directly into my backyard on a late summer's evening in August, 1958.

Cosmic Rays travel in a combination of direct straight lines and curved, twisted, convoluted paths, steered by strong gravitational fields from some point of origin in the cosmos to some point of final destination. They silently race through ions of time and endless billions of trillions of miles of dark space, passing through massive clouds of galactic gas and dust, picking up and leaving behind who knows what kind of quantum flotsam and schmutz.

The path, at least the last several hundred feet, of one particular clump of cosmic bullets indicated a final destination generally as my backyard, but more specifically, my head. To be even more precise and personal, the little permanent swirl of hair on the back of my head. It was the cosmic coincidence of a million human lifetimes, the random intersection of Destiny, General Relativity and the type of unbelievable luck you have when you hold a grand prize winning lottery ticket. For just an infinitesimal fraction of a second they'd all converged and then met at the algebraic x-y-z coordinates of an exact single point in gravitationally curved space and a precise single nanosecond moment on our universe's infinite time line continuum.

My six-year-old brain participated in this intersection of Quantum Physics, the Probability Law of Extremely Large Numbers and random Fate as I stuck my noggin out of my second story bedroom window and called out to my brother who, at the time, was sitting in his backyard tree house. I don't recall if at the moment of collision I blinked, sneezed, coughed, farted, shuttered, felt an itch, lost an eyelash, registered a tickle or if my head momentarily bobbed down and then gently recoiled back up from the impact. I am certain that if the right instrumentation had been in place one could have witnessed the flash of the ionization trail curving down from the evening sky as the lepton cascade proceeded to the point of contact.

What I do remember is at that moment I could not recall what I was going to ask my brother. I'd gone all sort of numb-and-dumb. Frozen in place, my little kid's muddled and befuddled head hung out the window as I vacantly, absentmindedly, stared down into and then through the backyard lawn.

It was a foggy but momentous couple of seconds. Those little space intruders zipped into my head and bounced around inside my skull flipping, crunching, turning-off, disconnecting, redirecting, reconstructing, reconnecting and then turning back on countless neural switches and pathways before exiting my cranium through the tip of my tongue, having departed with the slightest 'snap' of static electricity. It was only the briefest wink of star light but it had skipped and rolled around inside of my brain as if it had a plan, a will and mind of its own; a mind of its own inside of my own mind.

Whether the seed had already been there and just needed a spark to grow or whether the whole thing had been a fresh external galactic implant, it initiated a personal evolutionary transformation. The windows of my mind had been forced open, the place aired out and all the furniture rearranged. I still recognized the room but it had been...redecorated. Something new had definitely opened the door, slipped inside and began to hang out in the dark shadows of a far corner. Instinctively, my gaze turned upward and my eyes searched the star-filled sky and I listened, as if I'd unmistakably heard a color, I licked my lips, as if I'd unexpectedly tasted a sound and, most certainly, that I'd gently touched a thought, an idea of – something.

Where those little galactic strays ricocheted off to and what stuff they'd left behind in my head or had picked up and carried out and away with them I never completely figured out. But true and certain was the lingering afterthought that I'd experienced and survived some sort of 'brain blitzkrieg'. It was an undeniable, overwhelming feeling that something had grabbed hold of me and wasn't going to let go – ever.

As dramatic as it all might sound, as traumatic as it all may have been, after contemplating any and all actual science (from modern physics to psychiatry to exoplanet geology), applicable abstract philosophy (both eastern and western, classical and modern, pure thought or chemically induced) and highly unlikely but remotely possible metaphysics (from old-aged medium-managed séances to new-aged power from pointy little pyramids), it must be remembered that I'd simply stuck my head out the bedroom window! Hundreds, maybe thousands of kids had stuck their heads out of their bedroom windows just like I had on that warm and beautiful late summer evening and yet, it had been my six-year-old hairy noodle that got the subatomic particle shotgun blast right in the brain box!

Everything considered, after all had been said and done, with all speculation and guessing about possible or actual earthly and cosmic events aside, it has to be remembered that at the time I was just a little boy. So, the big question was, just because of all that, what could have possibly happened?

*

***

Chapter One:
"It" Starts

I WAS JUST a little boy – when it all happened.

Nine months before the unfolding of final momentous events, I'd begun my public school education at the Fifty-First Street Elementary School. During those initial and formative months of school attendance, yours truly, Michael Archer, patiently observed and experienced the subtle but gentle forced feeding and guardedly absorbed the soft and slow bludgeoning blows about the head and shoulders of the ever pervasive cultural drum beat of the *American Creed* that the elements of success, in any endeavor, were the unquestioned imperatives of hard work and focused, unwavering persistence. If you were able to creatively, even accidentally, combine any of that with the random good luck of an innate natural (or unnatural) ability, a personal driving ambition and then neatly (or not so neatly) wrap everything up inside of a driving obsession, an unstoppable idea that held it all together, you just might have had a good shot at ending up with something meaningful and worth your while.

Although I was initially an eager and focused student, something which drew encouragement from my teacher, I soon realized that my academic talents were common and uninspired. Yet, in my desire to be successful, to find meaning in my young life, in one form or another, I resolved not to let my average academic abilities be a hindrance. "I would," I simply told myself, "seek a truer path." So, not unlike earlier generations of young boys, I staked my future success, reputation and fortune on the landscapes of my childhood, confining my "search for meaning" to the last untamed urban frontier of the wide-open dirt, grass and asphalt of the school's playground.

After weeks of quiet and studied recess observations of fellow students and their varied, amusing, weird and frequently distressful playground hobbies, efforts and avocations, I organized and reviewed my thoughts. The catharsis, the moment of absolute clarity of purpose, was instigated almost by accident. As I wandered across the schoolyard deep in thought, I noticed movement in a distant corner of the playground. Behind the baseball backstop there was a small gathering with two of the group lying on the ground. As I walked closer to investigate the mysterious going's on, I saw that the two bodies on the ground were, in fact, on hands and knees, each intently focused on the ground between them. The ground, the field of play, was a finger-inscribed circle in the dirt randomly populated by an assortment of multicolored round glass crystals.

It started as a faint lightheaded dizziness accompanied by the internal sound of muffled clicks, tiny ringing bells and soft vibrating buzzing. Then, an unstoppable thought wave rippled through my mind. All of those reconfigured neural pathways from that August evening jerked and jolted to life. The stranger that had slipped into the dark corner of my rearranged mind weeks before had stepped forward, full figure, into the light. The great unstoppable idea, the obsession, had a face.

Possessed, I'd walked right up to the edge of the hand-drawn ring. With eyes as big as *Eisenhower* dollar coins and my mouth hanging open with drool on my lower lip, I was the picture of the local village idiot. My unblinking, hard-focused stare drew matching looks of surprise and fear as the assembled spectators cautiously backed away at my approach. That was it. There it was. The search was over. I stared down right at it and it stared right back up at me, like it had been waiting impatiently for me to finally show up. The 'It', the answer, was my future and it lay at my feet in the dirt. The scattered glass crystals were...irresistible. The 'It' was marbles.

The game of marbles was so different from everything else that played-out in the schoolyard. It was, without a doubt, the most demanding playground sport of the time. The self-reliance, the independence required by the game struck a resounding, reverberating chord. The other games I'd observed such as shoulder-punch suicide tag, four-square, kickball, head-shot dodgeball, baseball and the forbidden-but-played-anyway tackle football were all very popular. But to one degree or another they'd all been subject to and hampered by the equalizing aspects of adult input and supervision complete with all the accompanying cautions, unwarranted inclusions, intrusions and weight of moral baggage. In effect, this meant that just when things started to get interesting all of the participants were dutifully reminded and cautioned that "winning is not as important as how you played the game" and "everyone, regardless of ability or desire, should have a chance to participate."

Marbles was not a game that lent itself to such oversight, such niceties. In marbles, winning was the only thing that counted and losers were not only scorned for their lack of ability but were also punished by leaving the contest poorer for their failing efforts. I'd soon discovered that marbles was a complex game. The social realities disguised in the give and take, the winning and losing of marbles in a match could be overwhelming. However, at the time the gleam of a newly acquired Cat's-Eye boulder had much more significance than any social milieu that played out on the school playground.

The game had its unwritten rules, all right, but their implementation never subverted the true nature of the game or clouded the crystal clear motives of the players. We were all out for each other's marbles and we all knew it. Thus, with a goal in sight and a firm understanding of the rules, I took the truer path that my gut instinct had dictated. The clouds parted and I was willingly and without reservation drawn through the portal and into the 'marble world', into the 'marble state of mind'.

Without hesitation I immediately propelled myself into the thick of recess competitions with a resulting and fortunate blend of beginner's luck and amazing skill-inspired success. As the early weeks of autumn rolled by, my growing confidence in my natural abilities allowed me to refine and hone my individual style of play.

Hugging the dirt on hands and knees, my shooting-hand knuckles glued to the ground, I learned and improved with every shot. I'd rapidly built an expanding reputation pushed along by an unstoppable momentum. I quickly graduated to the school's elite marble-playing circles. Thereafter it was not uncommon for me to be seen taking on sneering brutes and intimidating hulks called fourth-and-fifth graders and walking away with their best marbles. However, participating in the highest levels of playground marble competition was not without its risks. I was a short, precocious first grader whose presence and winning ways did not gain immediate acceptance or gracious tolerance.

The first inevitable altercation threatened an early end to my blossoming marble-playing career. Being so young and a beginner at many more things than just playing marbles, I naively took it for granted that when a marble match concluded, the better boy would win out and losers would willingly submit to their fate and abide by the competitive conclusion. Theoretically accurate, but in practice, well-off the mark. I would learn, more than once, that risk at all levels and in all of its implications was a big part of the game. It was where the smooth rubber of the imagined ideal game met the rough reality of the well-traveled road.

Rodney Strong, the fourth grade champ, was the first lesson in risk and the biggest threat I faced in my early marble career. His friends and colleagues just called him "The Rod." I discovered that his nickname was a fitting description and well-earned tribute. You don't call someone "The Rod" because of his big heart. He was built like a baby slug of cast iron and just as dense. Rodney's nickname assignment was no accident. We all had nicknames that reflected who we were. You couldn't give yourself a nickname; it had to come from your friends and classmates. Nicknames could and would change overtime as a kid changed. They covered the whole range from cute-to-cool-to-unflattering but were always pretty accurate as to the individual's publicly presented and perceived 'persona'.

"The Rod" at nine years old, pretty much presented who and what he'd grow up to be. He was a large, poorly designed and carelessly conceived four-piece jigsaw puzzle where none of the pieces fit exactly with any of the other pieces, not to mention the multiple inconveniently placed never-to-be-filled empty spaces in between. Rodney's 'persona' left little creative wiggle room to come up with a more complimentary nickname. Rodney was a hulking little human organism who, some thirty years down the road, would simply transition into a larger hulking human organism. He'd still be the same physically and intellectually 'thick' kid doing his part as a member of the *American Space Program*, that is, taking up more than his fair share of space in America because he'd be at least two feet taller, a likely hundred-plus pounds heavier and consuming valuable "better used and more needed elsewhere" resources at a rate commensurate with his increased bulk and intake capacity.

Inevitably, Rodney and I met in a marble match showdown during a noon hour recess. For all of his buildup and reputation he was a sloppy and clumsy player. How he stumbled across and then fell into the marble game was one of the unanswered questions, one of the big schoolyard mysteries, of the time. He seemed so distantly related, so remotely in touch with the game, that "marble-playing skill and finesse" was not in his vocabulary nor within his reach as a player. His ascension to fourth grade marble champ was just one of those evolutionary quirks, a naturally occurring failed genetic experiment, a random accidental flip of a biological probability coin that resulted in a mutated human dead end.

My methodical and meticulous style of play was relentless and unmerciful as I claimed all of his best Cat's-Eye boulders. Rodney was stunned. "The Rod," as you may have guessed, was not known for his clear and capable thinking. What he'd been known for, apparently, was his expertise as a bully and his willingness to express and unleash his brutish anger when circumstances turned against him. As I took marble after marble in the competition the relentless taunting by many of Rodney's classmates and detractors did not help matters in the least. Rodney just knelt there smoldering in the dirt. His empty dirty marble sock lay on the ground next to him stinking from the disgrace of having lost to a lowly, but inspired, first grader.

Realizing that all had been lost, to save face and potentially reclaim his lost marbles, Rodney bolted to his feet and growled that I'd cheated. I assured him in a calm, steady, and unwisely dismissive tone, that I had not cheated. I further volunteered the equally unwise elaboration that he was a sloppy player and a poor loser. The fuse had been lit. By referring to Rodney as a poor sport I had unwittingly tried to drown his flaring anger with a bucket of inexperience and poor-judgment-inspired emotional gasoline. Rodney's face ignited in a crimson flush as he repeated, evermore forcefully, that I'd done him out of his marbles unfairly.

Glancing at the surrounding faces in the gathered crowd, I quickly ascertained that no one was volunteering to intercede on my behalf. I slowly stepped back, pulled my full marble sock tight to my waist, and prepared to make a rapid exit from the situation. As I turned to walk away with his marbles, which by then were my marbles, Rodney exploded into action and lunged forwards and caught hold of me by the back of my shirt. He roughly spun me around and stepped up to me with his chest up against my nose. Looking down at me he threatened to do terrible things unless, right then and there, I publicly confessed to cheating. He not only wanted his lost marbles back, he demanded that I should surrender mine as well, as a penalty and punishment for my supposedly unfair play.

It became ever clearer, in those terror-stricken moments, that Rodney had become the fourth grade champ through his ability to intimidate and his willingness to demand submission from his opponents. He was an unskilled marble pretender. My winning efforts had simply allowed him to discover that fact and had assisted in revealing, for all present to see, his true skill and ability level; all very logical in a brutally honest sort of way. However, as much as I might have wanted it to be true, logic had not emerged as the topic at hand. Rodney was all too ready, willing and able to send his two tightly balled-up, pudgy, pugilistic little punchers on a mission to non-therapeutically massage the various contours of my face.

We all have our own ways of coping with difficult situations; even as kids we managed somehow. "The Rod," however, wasn't coping or managing at all. He was falling apart, melting away in big gloppy chunks from the heat of his own anger. The grass and dirt around his feet had begun to smoke and char. Either Rodney was going to explode and take everyone within twenty yards with him or he was going to simply vaporize right before our eyes with nothing left but his shoes, the burnt remnants of his empty marble sock and a sooty cloud of smoke hanging in the air just above where he once stood.

All the 'situation critical' warning lights were flashing and the sirens screaming. *"Duck and Cover"* was not going to do it for me. I had to think of something fast when such rapid thought processing was out of reach as my mind was in 'marble mode', not in 'run-for-my-life mode'. Then, the recess bell rang loud and shrill as the noon hour break ended with a clanging echo. As the recess teachers called for everyone to line up I left 'marble mode' behind and twisted loose from Rodney's loosened grip, darting for the school doors. Fortunately, Rodney and I had to report to different sets of doors after recess. Although Rodney receded into the distance, his shouted words that he would "deal with me later" followed right behind like a bothersome buzzing bee. I'd escaped and probably missed out on a painful and embarrassing beating. As I ran for the door I kept asking myself, "the game was marbles, right?" Where exactly did "painful and embarrassing beatings" fit into that scenario?

He would "deal with me later." I could only imagine that what he had in mind would probably be the worst deal of my young life. I had a full three hours from the ended midday recess until school let out for that day. Three hours to think things over and devise a plan. There would be an intervening afternoon recess but fourth graders and first graders were out on the playground at different times. The main part of the plan was to put the impending threat out of mind, the 'denial defense'. For the most part, due to actually having concentrated on my schoolwork, I successfully ignored the fear that lingered and the uncertainty that loitered side by side in the darkest shadows of my deepest thoughts as the school day afternoon passed to the final bell.

Walking out of school at the end of the day I had Rodney squarely placed on the back burner. I had hoped, I had wished, I had convinced myself that Rodney had sufficient time to reconsider his threats and graciously accept the outcome of the match. Besides, it was Friday and I wouldn't have to deal with him until the noon recess on the following Monday. By Monday certainly, by Monday at least, Rodney would have surrendered his anger to the winds of time.

What I failed to consider accurately was how much time and wind it really took for a glowing, burning and smoldering white and blue hot cast iron rod to cool off. There is a type of hot created by very high voltage. A type of electric hot that takes forever to cool down. Rodney's vibrating electrons were still humming away, the result of my noon-hour lightning strike on his marble sock. At the end of the noon recess he glowed a white-hot hot. By the end of the school day he'd become that searing blue-hot, hot enough to start forest fires or cook slabs of raw meat hanging on racks twenty feet away. I guessed that Rod had to be wearing asbestos clothes and underwear, that's how hot he was.

Exiting the school that Friday afternoon I comforted myself with the thought that if trouble came my way I was a scant five blocks from home and safe haven. Rodney was a big fourth grader all right, but I could run with the best of them regardless of age and size. I stepped into the schoolyard completely on my own. My older brother Robert, my fall back protection, had walked home a few blocks ahead of me with his friends. I'd swiveled my head around on my neck like an owl on the lookout for pestering crows. Any sign, the slightest hint that Rodney was in the area would be the signal to 'light-up-the-engines'.

I'd just walked through the school gate onto the sidewalk partially hidden within a covering group of friends. My moment of relief and partial concealment was shattered by the sound of my name being screamed from across the schoolyard. Rage on a bicycle raced across the playground as a blazing and sparking Rodney Strong closed in. "The Rod" had two accomplices, one on either side, most likely riding along to witness and certify the planned capture, cruel interrogation and brutal punishment. My pals scattered and not too calmly called back to me during their hasty exits that I should do the same. For one awful moment I froze in place on the sidewalk as my escape engines flamed out. I gave up valuable seconds before, mercifully, the personally harmful potential of the situation completed the circuit between brain, kidneys and muscles as my adrenaline reserves initiated a restart and ignited the rocket boosters. I launched for home.

The free flowing adrenalin blasted through my body. There was so much extra pressing to get into my muscles that a significant portion spilled over into my imagination, which took full advantage of the overflow. All the repressed fears of my young life came to life and to the surface of awareness. The racing Rodney and accomplices bore down on me like screaming, wild-horse-mounted Cossacks, waving and swinging razor sharp sabers above their heads that glinted in the afternoon sun as they'd charged across the rolling Russian playground steppe.

My body pulsed and shook from the shock of impending doom. I'd never been that frightened in my young life as three older toughs were bearing down on me intending serious physical harm. In the panic of running so hard while being painfully aware that the distance between myself and my rapidly closing assailants was shrinking, buckets of mud inexplicably materialized on my feet and would not relinquish their hold. I came to the realization that my only chance was to take a diversionary route home by running where bikes could not follow. I would make up for their advantage in speed by being more maneuverable.

The path home was not a straight five blocks but rather a zig-zag stair step pattern. Instead of running my walking route home I ducked into the first alley I came to and hid behind the second garage in. Rodney's two pals followed first and rode right past. But, as I stuck my head around the corner to see if the coast was clear, Rodney saw me and came on strong. "The Rod" wasn't going to miss out on any chance of avenging his bruised ego. I pulled back from the garage corner and waited until he was almost upon me. Then I burst from my concealment and ran right in front of him along the length of the overhead garage door, across the alley and over a white picket fence into an adjoining backyard. My dart in front of Rodney had left him piled-up against the garage door.

With my books and marbles in tow I ran down alleys, through backyards and past barking dogs and snarling property owners as Rodney and his gang recovered and managed to keep pace. As I broke back onto the sidewalk a block from home they came back onto me like a pack of hounds on a fleeing fox. It was home or havoc in one final mad dash for safe ground. Rodney was only three screaming feet behind me when I leaped over the white wood picket fence and fell sprawling and crawling head first into my front yard. My rubber legs barely carried me forward as I flopped with a THUD onto our front porch.

Skidding to a halt on the sidewalk in front of the house Rodney and his two thugs shook their fists and shouted dares and double-dares as I lay half-dead and face-up on the porch deck. Pulling myself up onto my elbows, I breathlessly shouted back that they'd better stuff it somewhere really personal and shove off or I'd call in reinforcements. Rodney dismounted and was about to come through the front gate into the yard when, on cue, the front screen door squeaked open and then swung closed with a loud door against door frame CLAP! I threw my head back and got the upside-down view of my older brother Robert, calmly chewing on a big, thick, raisin-oatmeal cookie.

"What's going on?" Robert calmly stated as he casually chewed his mouthful of cookie, all the while staring a hole into the bridge of Rodney's nose.

Stepping past me and slowly walking up to the porch railing, Robert mockingly followed up, "You guys want something? Hey, wait a minute, you guys aren't trying to sell *Girl Scout* cookies again!"

Rodney had stopped in his tracks and slowly retreated back onto the sidewalk without saying a word. His two accomplices quickly backpedaled to the street side of the sidewalk. The idea of any intervention on my behalf that would have evened the odds was all it took. The three bullies on bikes were just cowards in disguise as they rolled away without a sound. Robert then bent down and calmly looked me in the eye and stopped chewing his cookie.

"Rodney's kind of a poor loser," he casually informed me.

He turned and walked back into the house letting the screen door bounce closed as he did. I lay back down on the porch and stared up at the ceiling boards with my chest heaving, heart pounding, legs aching, languishing in my pain and breathlessly whispered my response to my brother's observation, "Geez, I never would have guessed," having realized that I'd just experienced, firsthand, the meaning and implication of risk. Marbles, it turned out, could be...dangerous.

Chances, big and small, risks, major and minor are part of any successful venture and I encountered my share in the early days of my marble-playing career (amazing, just six years old and I had a career). Challenges and difficulties included, my victories continued to accumulate and with them, as an undeniable measure of my success, so did the weight of the old cardboard boot box which housed my expanding marble collection. Everyday after school I pulled the box out from under my bed, hefted it up onto the bed, opened the lid and poured the sparkling contents out onto the bedspread. Grabbing that day's newly filled marble sock by the big toe, I suspended it upside down above the bed and pulled off the restraining sock-knot as that day's spoils of battle flowed out into and mixed with the victories of previous matches. It wasn't uncommon for me to spend an hour or more sorting through my growing collection, dividing them by type, size, quality and color. I was continually refreshed and amazed at the variety of rewards that success could bestow.

Frequently assisting me in the admiration of my daily conquests was Kit Cat, a big, gentle, playful and curious black and white bi-color family house cat who honored me with his presence when so inclined. We were best pals. When he wasn't sleeping, eating, napping, visiting the litter box, yawning, stretching, cleaning himself, sitting in an open window, curled up on a chair, stretched out on a bed or holding court on the living room sofa, he would be busy running from one end of the house to the other at top speed, pawing, scratching and rubbing up against things and us (did I mention the napping, snacking and yawning?).

He'd run at paw-thumping full speed into my room and hop up onto the bed to the sound of my marbles being dumped and spread on my bed quilt. No matter where he was in the house and no matter what he was doing there, that sound of pouring marbles had become his cue. His uninhibited playfulness actually inspired an early form of rapid-fire practice session. Kit Cat would layout full-form across my marbles, then start rolling around on top of them, batting them all around with his big front paws.

As the marbles rolled, bounced and flew off the bed in all directions, randomly rolling to all the near spaces and far corners of my room, I'd jump and crawl around in time as fast as I could and take up shooting positions wherever the marbles came to rest, taking aim at one of the bedpost feet. When finished on the bed, he'd jump down to the floor and try to intercept my shots before they found their target. When he was done he'd just stop, sit down, lick his chest and then hop back up on the covers and wait for me to kneel down next to the bed and scratch him behind the ears as he purred his approval. That was the routine. It was great practice and a real bonding moment between me and the *real* Mr. Cat's-Eyes.

When success came to stay fame was soon to follow. I found that matches were much harder to come by. It seemed that my reputation had grown in direct proportion to my marble collection. Eventually the displaying, sorting and admiring of my growing fortune began to take up a greater portion of my free time. Wherever I went, I always carried a select few of my collection along with me. It was a constant reminder of what I'd become, what I'd accomplished and what I would try to attain in the future. Walking home from school at the end of the day with a marble sock full to the ankle band with fresh conquests was like coming home from school daily with a fresh set of straight-A's on a report card.

I was never far from my marbles. While suffering through homework there were three Cat's-Eye boulders studying along with me. During the family dinner five clean and bright Cat's-Eyes stood watch around the base of my water glass. Sick in bed with some or another childhood malady a clutch of Cat's-Eyes would watch over me from the bedside night table. Watching Friday and Saturday night scary science fiction and horror movies ten small Cat's-Eyes peeked out from under the blanket right along with me.

My devotion to the game and resulting good fortune were measured in ways other than a bulging marble sock at the end of a school day. To maintain my level of play demanded total dedication and complete application of all of my conscious and unconscious abilities towards the chosen goal. My obsession not only expressed itself by regular intense practice sessions but also through all the intensive thought and directed motivational skills that a six-year-old boy could muster. Certainly arithmetic, reading and spelling all had their places, as they should have, in the mind of a new student, but they were only allowed the time and space required to be kept in the minimal flow of classroom academic proceedings. I programmed myself, I brainwashed myself, to funnel and focus all of the energy possible into the effort necessary to achieve and maintain an exceptional level of play.

What better way for a schoolyard marble champ, aspiring to even greater competitive heights, to focus and direct a single purpose of mind and body than through concentrated, intense and vivid dreaming. Both daydreaming and night dreaming were extensively employed and enjoyed. Reality of gratifying victory after stunning triumph in the schoolyard was nothing when compared to the expanse, suspense and color of imagined competitions. Much more was at stake during such dreamy matches than could ever be experienced on the school playground. As I settled down for a night's rest from a day's activities it was as if my real marble life was about to begin. Absent in such a sleepy state of mind were all of the frivolous and complicating factors of everyday reality. My dream life was free and clear to live out every marble fantasy unencombered.

There was one special dream I would summon night after night as I drifted away into the twilight regions of sleep unconsciousness. More often than not, after such REM sleep adventures, I woke the following morning ready, renewed and refreshed, eager with nervous anticipation for the coming school day's three recess periods.

The premise of the dream was the simplicity of basic organization and essential event logistics. The list was short. It started with the largest enclosed marble match arena in the world. Moving down the list it included a crowd of thousands, colorful programs listing the evenings minor and major events, decorative amenities such as ushers, security guards, photographers, domestic and foreign broadcast radio and television, snack and souvenir vendors and other assorted public spectacle necessities. It was the world's largest and most prestigious marble competition: *The Golden Sock.*

After many months of preliminary matches, the brackets had narrowed and the pretenders to the throne had been cleared away as the whole giant sock of marbles was up for grabs in one final action-packed roll-off. The spectators' anticipation, the tension, rolled through the crowd like shallow waves of thick clinging mud; the kind of tension thick mud that went all the way up to your knees and permanently ruined any pair of new white sneakers it touched.

It was time for the evening's main event. The arena lights surged brightly and then rapidly softened to a faint glow accompanied by a breathy hush from the capacity crowd. Above the stage a single overhead spotlight sparked to life with an audible 'snap' as soft, scattered screams of shock and surprise snapped from the audience in response. The focused light burned a brilliant circle onto the stage at the center of the auditorium revealing the official regulation competition Olympic size five-foot diameter marble ring. The Referee stepped from the surrounding shadows into the cone of light and synchronized a rendezvous with a microphone being lowered on a cord from the dark regions above the stage. The crowd started to scream, clap, shout and stamp their feet as the Ref raised his arms, microphone in hand, and slowly turned in a slow circle under the light as he addressed the crowd.

"Ladies and gentlemen, boys and girls, young and old alike, THIS - IS - IT! The match you all have been waiting for! The match to end all matches!" the Ref shouted into the microphone. His words echoed and reverberated back and forth and across and into every close and distant and every bright and dark corner of the auditorium. There was no escaping the cosmic magnitude of the event. I'd dreamed of everything! At this point in the nocturnal sequence I'd start to sweat for real as my pillowcase and bed sheets would become warm and tacky. Yet, in the dream, the challenger, me, was as cool and frosty as a Cherry *Dreamsicle* straight from the freezer.

My opponent on such occasions, the defending champion, was never an equal in marble skills, marble know-how, marrble finesse, physical size or coolness of marble temperament. He was always just above adequate as player, the biggest ignorant goon one could imagine and would always fall apart under the sure and certain aim of my superior abilities. It wasn't *David and Goliath*. It was much older, more primordial than that story. It was the Nordic pagan myth that *David and Goliath* were based upon. It was the mythic *Marble Mountain Michael* verses the *Swamp Bog Marble Dragon*! It was the most ancient of contests brought forward in time.

The Ref introduced the reigning champion first. The ugly brute would emerge from the surrounding darkness and lumber up to the marble circle shuffling his feet as he came to a stop at the edge of the cone of light. The crowd greeted his appearance with the usual assortment of groans, boos, nose holding, *Bronx Cheers*, hisses and shouts of "get outta here." He was just that type of guy, the type of guy who invited derision. He was a book that could, in fact, be judged by its cover.

It was immediately apparent, just by his unsettled appearance, that the guy had muscled his way to the top of the game by brute force and threat and not by any type of marble playing prowess. From his place at the edge of the lighted playing circle the champ growled, spit and snarled back at the hoots and catcalls from the jeering crowd. To intimidate the hecklers he crushed a fistful of Cat's-Eye boulders between his bare hands. It usually worked.

I'd dreamed up one tough guy in all respects. He was tough looking and he was tough to look at. He acted tough and it was tough for him to find clothes that fit. It was tough for him to tie his shoes and button his shirt. It was *as* tough for him to hold a thought as it was for him to even have one in the first place. When you got close to him it was painfully apparent that it was really tough for him to shower and brush his teeth. I'd given the guy the distinctive but disturbing amalgamated appearance of an oversized nine-year-old fourth grader combined with an unshaven, angry, forty year old homeless drunk. As long as I had control of the ol' dream screen, that poor slob wasn't ever going to have a break come his way.

I, on the other hand, was always the young, confident, daring upstart challenger, eager to conquer the hearts and minds of the gathered throng and claim the marbles of the beast. As the challenger was introduced, the youngest player to ever make it to the championship match by the way, the spectators exploded into screaming cheers. The anticipation of seeing the old champ dethroned and a new champion crowned beamed from every face in the auditorium. As I emerged from the dark and took my place at the edge of the lighted circle the adulation transformed into gasps of disbelief that such a small and young player would even dare to attempt what had proved to be impossible for so many before. The gravity of the situation was, without a doubt, elemental.

The crowd quieted and settled into their seats. I slowly turned in place and glanced out across the darkened arena. My face beamed and radiated a confidence that reflected onto and illuminated the faces of the closest spectators. I turned back to the competition circle and focused a concentrated gaze toward my opponent and fired off a penetrating stare in his direction. I scored a direct unblinking hit squarely between his crazy eyes. The champ's head snapped back from the impact as he let loose a muffled growl. We matched flying dagger stares. The closer I looked, the more certain I became that the lug's only possible connection to the game was that he ate crushed marbles on his breakfast cereal.

The Ref motioned us to join him at the center of the ring to start the proceedings by reviewing the rules of the match. The champ and I stepped right up to each other, toe to toe, silent. Our eyes met as I stared upward, bright and confident, and he stared downward, dark and menacing. The Ref forcibly elbowed his way between us and with chin up explained the match rules in a loud, clear and matter of fact manor. He presented a large wooden box which he slowly opened, revealing the marbles for the match, like a dutiful second offering loaded pistols to the principals of a dual.

"Gentlemen, choose your marbles!" the Ref instructed.

The champ got to choose first as was match protocol. He grunted, leaned over the box and grabbed one of the two commemorative leather sock pouches, each containing twenty-five brand new pristine Cat's-Eye boulders. As the Ref swung the box my way I lifted out the remaining sock just before the champ lunged forward and grabbed the empty wooden case. He crushed it with his free hand right in front of my face while snorting like a wild hog. The Ref got all upset and admonished 'Bruno' that he'd have to pay for the box, which was just the excuse the champ needed to let out another disgusting snort. The Ref boldly held his ground while 'Bruno' growled and gnashed his teeth. What a show-off!

Besides the twenty-five match marbles we were each presented with a small velvet lined jeweler's case which contained one commemorative engraved steely boulder; a memento of our participation in the championship match. I picked up my steely case from the presentation tray and jauntily gave it a couple of quick short tosses into the air to the delight and applause from the fans. In response the champ grabbed his cased steely, and shoved the whole thing right into his big mouth. Two chews later the package, steely and all, had been crushed between his teeth. With a long breathy spit-wad the champ launched the wreckage out towards the crowd.

Undaunted, I removed my steely from its case and confidently gave it a short toss and popped it right into my mouth. With disdain emanating from every square millimeter of my face, I leaned in towards the champ and stuck the steely out at him from between my lips like it was my tongue. What I lacked in size I more than made up for by being fiercely tenacious. I showed-off a bit myself.

The outsmarted champ took a threatening step in my direction accompanied by the gasps and squeals from the crowd as the Ref pressed his way back between us and pushed each of us back to our respective sides of the circle. The match announcer called for order and instructed the players to take their playing positions. The Ref collected the ante marbles and tossed them into the middle of the ring. The match began.

The contest rolled on for hours. All the combined nervous sweat expended by the growling champ and all of the spectators and other associated attendees combined could have filled a small swimming pool. The air inside of the arena would start to get pretty tropical as the structure's air conditioning system strained to keep up. The cutting edge drama, the violent back and forth, the surging and retreating competitive ebb and flow, blew across the arena and swirled around the match ring like counter-rotating storm winds. The led grudgingly changed hands by the minute as the match advantage or disadvantage wildly fluctuated with every shot.

The champ's style was disturbingly unorthodox. The hamfisted way in which he held and launched each shot defied marble logic and about seven or eight theorized, tested, established and accepted rules of *Newtonian Physics*. As big, dumb, stinky, mean, ugly and stupid as he was, the champ could still shoot a marble. It just proved how democratic the game was: it did not discriminate, it took in any and all kinds.

At his turn he grabbed a shooting marble and shoved it into the confines of his clenched fat-finger fist like he was ramrodding a musket ball down into the barrel of a rifled musket. Then, when he took a shot, you had no idea were the hell the marble would exactly exit from his wadded-up shooting hand. The marble would sort of be squeezed and then come flying out from between his fingers like a marble dart blasted from the barrel of a sawed-off marble cannon. His marble style was equivalent to the flight dynamics of the bumble bee; impossible, but still, there it was, right in front of your amazed, disbelieving and dumbfounded eyes. The champ's crude match etiquette also showed as he grunted, cursed and pawed at the stage floor like a caged animal when he fell behind in the match. My role in the match alternated between marble competitor and whip-snapping circus animal trainer.

But, as it was my dream and I controlled how the big drama

played out, the ending to one degree or another was always similar and always satisfying. The match of the century, hours old, was back to dead even when I decided to stop fooling around (besides, I reached the point in the evening where I tried to get some much needed sleep). The champ's geometry-challenged style finally caught up with him resulting in a miss and the match came back to my shot, and then my shot again, and then again and again. I took a deep breath, refocused, fine tuned the geometry, and in a few short minutes ripped-off twenty-five consecutive hard and true solid hits.

As the last shot cleared the circle the resounding shock wave from the bursting roar of the crowd's approving cheers blasted across the stage. I knelt before an empty marble ring with fifty match-nicked and match-scratched Cat's-Eye boulders gathered together at my knees. Handful at a time, I stuffed my winnings slowly and steadily into my leather marble sock as I claimed final victory over the shell-shocked loser. The stunned Dragon lay at my feet as I triumphantly swung my loaded marble sock over my shoulder. The conquest was always devastatingly complete.

The crowd went wild right along with the dethroned champ who had to be physically restrained and dragged from the stage. My parents, relatives, neighbors, friends, classmates, reporters and fans alike would rush the stage and hoist me up onto their shoulders accompanied by the strobe effect of hundreds of POPPING photographer flash bulbs. With my arms triumphantly held high, the Referee would struggle through the jostling crowd and press into my hands the winner's prize: *The Golden Sock*.

The glory of the moment would echo and abruptly fade from view, chased back into dreamland by the glaring bell of the alarm clock. The mechanical intruder rudely jarred me awake and shoved me into the starting gate of another ordinary day. I half-slid-half-fell out of bed and sort of let my body's directional momentum propel me coasting towards the bathroom. During those drowsy morning moments, standing in front of the toilet for my morning pee, I puzzled over how to reconcile the reality of my daily marble life with the perfectly conceived world of my marble dream life. However, I have to admit that, despite numerous attempts, the 'Unified Marble Theory' remained...elusive.

Whatever 'Standard Model of Marble Theory' may have or may not have existed, the gravitational momentum of the dream process would effortlessly transition from the dark and nocturnal to the brightness of daylight. Daydreaming, every kid's daily diversion, took its rightful and prominent place in my conscious thought process. The many hours between recesses were not only breaks in the competitive action but also served as periods for psyching-up and serious imagination enhancement.

Out of necessity, like breathing air and drinking water, I put certain limited, guided and strategically placed efforts into academic endeavors as the school day situations and circumstances required. But, as far as I was concerned, my imaginative abilities far exceeded anything schoolwork had to offer as an alternative. I did not stray from the illuminated path my mind had created and my heart directed me to follow.

Whereas night dreaming involved the winning of the crown, daydreaming centered on the rewards that came as a consequence of the ultimate victory. Often during arithmetic instruction I was no longer seated in the third row, fourth seat, Room 107. The small wooden chairs in a semicircle for arithmetic group by the chalkboard at the front of the class were often left far behind. I was the new champ, invited to demonstrate his winning form at an open round robin marble marathon. Like the *Chess Master* who plays dozens of simultaneous matches, walking from chessboard to chessboard, I was the young *Marble Master* walking from match-circle to match-circle. I played multiple simultaneous matches against all comers, amateurs and professionals alike, as any and all were invited and challenged to test their own skills against the best. Such public displays would be staged in large department stores, state fair pavilions and the expanse of sports arenas to the delight of hundreds of strolling shoppers, eager spectators and other assorted passersby.

It was not uncommon for one spectacular daydream to pick up where another left off in a logical and rapid fashion. While addition and subtraction filled the board or *Dick* chased *Jane* up and down the hill as they spilled buckets of water in Reading Group, I was whisked away from the multi-match marathon by limousine on my way to a personally guided tour of the world's largest marble manufacturing plant. The company big shots would spare nothing in giving me the red carpet treatment in hopes of getting the newest and youngest marble champ to sign-onto an endorsement deal promoting their line of marbles and marble-related accessories. They just about offered me the world and anything and everything in it for the exclusive use of my name and likeness for the promotion of their marbles. If I agreed, a photo of my bright beaming face would have been on every bag of marbles sold by the *Perfect Marble Company International Incorporated* for years to come. But my signature on the dotted line was no shoe-in. There is being easily bought and then there is paying the price. My price always had to be paid.

The company's top management and I walked the factory floor stopping at the main conveyor belt loaded with unblemished, crystal clear, production fresh, brand new Cat's-Eye boulders. Untold riches rode that belt from one end of the building where the marbles were forged to the other end where they were bagged and boxed for shipping. I stopped midway along the belt and removed a custom made marble case from the inside breast pocket of my jacket. I snapped open the cover, revealing six of my personal all time best Cat's-Eye boulders, all polished and bright. The *Perfect Marble* execs crowded around so close I would feel and smell their hot nervous breath fill the air around me. I sensed every pair of beady, greedy little eyes following, inspecting and trying to interpret and anticipate my every move and thought. Leaning slightly forward over the rapidly passing marbles I purposefully and decisively plucked one of their new and freshly cooled best right off the belt. I had one of my own boulders between the thumb and index finger of my left hand and one of theirs between the thumb and index finger of my right as I raised them both up to the light streaming in through the factory skylight, side by side, for the critical comparison.

As the prismatic light from both marbles spread and rolled across my face I squinted with a hard, focused and inquisitive stare, all the while humming and grunting to myself just like a doctor analyzing an x-ray film. The suits would start sweating, straining to see what I was seeing, sense what I was sensing. I was an enigma, a conundrum, all wrapped up inside the body of a mysterious little kid. Some would take notes, others hummed and grunted right along with me, while others unbuttoned their suit jackets and patted perspiring foreheads with monogrammed hankies.

As a precondition to considering any contractual agreement, I requested the opportunity to test out their goods before I made any final decision to sign on the dotted line. Eager to meet any reasonable or unreasonable request I might make, they invited me to grab as many finished marbles as I thought necessary right off the production line. "Fair enough," I said as I filled my pockets with brand new Cat's-Eye boulders.

Then it was time to put their marbles through a series of tough conventional and unnervingly unconventional durability and reliability performance tests personally devised by me. The company execs led me off the factory floor and directed me to a private room which had been reserved and prepared in accordance with a prearranged, previously communicated and agreed-to set of prior specifications. A sparse, barren, windowless room, one-hundred feet square, with a single door locking on the inside, overhead florescent light, low pile carpet and a single hardbacked wooden chair met all the prearranged conditions.

We all marched our way through company offices and back storerooms; high and open warehouse space and past active loading and receiving docks. Eventually the entire entourage would arrive at the door to the designated testing room. All the while, unobtrusively trailing at the back of the group as a personal assistant, bodyguard and majordomo was my older brother Robert. Stopping at the closed door I signaled for my big brother to step forward through the crowd. He'd firmly but politely weave his way forward through the gathering with a quiet "excuse me" here and a "pardon me" there as he carried my testing implement and equipment bag. The worn leather bag had an intimidating personality all its own as all sorts of strange and unsettling sounds, weird smells and odd protrusions were evident with every step

Robert took. My brother passed the strapped bag from his shoulder to my shoulder as I'd open the door and then stand in the doorway of the dark testing room.

The executive group as a whole moved forward, incorrectly assuming they would be invited inside to witness and take notes on my testing procedures. But Robert turned and sternly took up a rock-solid blocking position just outside the door, preventing any such occurrence. Flicking on the light switch, with door open, I strolled to the center of the room and dropped my equipment bag, which made the loudest and most incredibly disturbing noise of metal on metal as it impacted the carpeted floor. I turned and walked slowly back to the open door and with a look of quiet and determined contemplation, looked past my brother as he blocked the still open door. I politely but firmly expressed and reiterated the condition that I be allowed to work on their marbles alone and unobserved.

Of course they mumbled their assent as they were in no position to do otherwise. I slowly closed the testing room door on two-dozen very nervously smiling men and women. They all leaned in real close around Robert, trying to catch any last glimpse, any final indication of what I might do all alone with their marbles in that big empty room. The hope, the chance, of a final reprieve to witness the proceedings was smeared across their faces like they all just participated in a no-hands-allowed blueberry pie eating contest. No such luck! Not a chance! If witnessed, what I planned to do to their marbles would've resulted in a mixed and varied selection of heart attacks, strokes, panic attacks and a wide range of general-to-specific degrees of fainting and other various forms of emotional shock, stress and anxiety related collapse.

With the door closed and locked I walked to the center of the room where I stopped and casually emptied my pockets of all of the brand new marbles I'd collected. Tossing those little gems into the air, I flipped them up and about, randomly scattering them, gently spreading them around with my foot as I strolled around the room. I slowly made my way to the single wooden hardbacked chair at the center of the room, removed my jacket and carefully hung it over the back of the chair.

From the other side of the closed door to the room I would hear the muffled verbal expressions of fear and concern emanating from the excluded company execs in response to the brief moments of nerve-racking silence inside the room. Just to shake them up a bit I picked up a single marble and threw it hard against my side of the closed door. A muffled explosion of bodies flying back and falling on the floor and against the wall opposite the door along with more than a few shrieks and groans filtered through the closed door and adjacent walls. It was cruel, I admit, but it got me all fired up for the task at hand.

Facing the open windowless expanse of the testing room I opened my implement bag and calmly started tossing the array of personally selected, task-specific testing tools around the room. I could not help but hear the corresponding groans from the other side of the closed door in response to the sound of every tool that hit the floor. I rolled up my shirtsleeves and unbuttoned my top shirt buttons and prepared to really go at it. With Robert standing guard against the outside of the testing room door, all the company men and women gathered and tried to orderly compose themselves. But, it was no use. They were all once again piled up around my brother as they tried to peek under the door, peer through the keyhole and listen with ears pressed against adjacent walls, desperate to see, hear or register in any way the nature and the progress of the testing.

Cracking my knuckles, I selected the first tool and began. The testing was merciless, ruthlessly thorough and thoroughly ruthless. I put their best marble goods to the ultimate skill and abuse tests. As the testing proceeded, the noises that made it through the testing room door and walls sent many of the execs running for and repeatedly returning to the lavatory. The rubber mallet, the hammer, the pliers, the screwdrivers, the portable propane torch and the slingshot were just a brief list of the tools and devices that the situation had called for.

The marble layperson should remember that kids didn't just collect and play competitive marbles. Marbles were just as often and likely to be used in a myriad of unconventional and unexpected play scenarios. I conventionally cradled, aimed and shot their marbles with the gentle finesse necessary for a match-winning shot. Then, I shot, crushed, kicked, smashed, stepped on, sat on, stomped on, jumped up and down on, pounded, threw, launched and torched their marbles, anything a kid might intentionally and unintentionally do to their marbles. There were nicked and scratched marbles, crushed marbles, cracked and scorched and melted marbles. There were marbles shot so hard out of a slingshot that they penetrated and disappeared inside walls, through and above ceiling tiles and burrowed into and under the carpeting.

   The testing was exhaustive and stopped just short of putting their marbles through a garbage disposal, setting them on the rails in front of an oncoming one-hundred ton diesel electric freight train engine or firing them out of a homemade Napoleon eight pound field gun artillery piece (with adjoining, marble loaded, ammunition caisson - but no horses 'cause I was scared of horses) and all that would have been done as well if such equipment and opportunities had been readily available in the testing room. To sum up and more to the point it was a balance between use and abuse. I made their marbles do things they should always have to do and then I made their marbles do things that they should never have do because the 'marble game' was not always...pretty.

   Finally, mercifully, after an hour of sweat-soaked effort testing and torturing their marbles, I decided that their stuff was good enough for any regular kid to play, collect, keep or abuse. As the smoke and dust in the room gently drifted in the air I calmly rolled down my shirtsleeves, re-buttoned my shirt, combed my hair and then collected my jacket from the chair-back and slung it over my shoulder. I left behind a testing room with damaged walls, wrecked ceiling tiles and destroyed carpeting along with the mixed residual odor of sweat and smoke, all of which bore solemn testament to the determined physical intensity of my efforts.

   Opening the door released a thick cloud of dusty smoke which wafted out over a multi-layered frozen human sculpture formed by the company bodies pressing against any available door and wall space around my guarding brother Robert. They presented a marvel of stacked, contorted and sculpted human engineering. As I emerged from the testing room the company guys and gals abruptly collected and rearranged themselves in respectable fashion as they formed a shoulder to shoulder semicircle in the hallway around the open door. Bathed in the floating remains of the smoky testing dust that had followed me out the door, anxiously rubbing his hands together, the head guy stepped forward, leaned down real close and whispered: "Well, Mr. Archer, how'd we do?"

I knew that they'd been sweating it out. The odor of fear, shock and nervous anticipation permeated everything within the vicinity of the test room. I looked each one of them directly in the eyes in turn, straight-faced, without emotion, then, settled my gaze on the main man. I gave him the thumbs-up with a little half-smile. They all cheered and jumped up and down like a bunch of *Pom-Pom Girls* at a junior high basketball game. The company president put his arm around my shoulders, promising no regrets on my part, as the company photographer with his *Leicas* and the rest of the junior execs with their *Kodaks* snapped away.

I was led away to the main office to discuss royalties, advertising campaigns and other fine points of our blossoming business relationship. A few of the office personnel stayed behind and dared a look or ventured a step or two into the aftermath of the testing room; they would never be the same for the experience. The champ had to have style, class, courage, confidence and a fine-tuned sense of timing. Believe me, I properly equipped my daydream-self with an abundance of all the necessary attributes.

There was something about daydreaming in class. It involved a rapidly, randomly, rotating screen. It either made you totally invisible, gone, completely out of sight and mind, or, ten times bigger than physically possible with big fat puffy white four-finger cartoon hands which you waved around frantically begging to be called upon, ready or not. On that day, just as I was giving the thumbs-up to the marble company president in day-dreamland my screen changed and got stuck with a loud BONK at the reality setting.

The previously invisible little boy sitting right in front of the teacher magically rematerialized into a baby elephant who'd just parachuted through the ceiling tiles and crash landed with a car-horn-honking THUD wearing a big sign that screamed "Me, me, oh-oh me, please, oh-please, me, me!" As the fog of imagined marble fame evaporated I discovered myself sitting in one of those tiny wooden chairs made special just for little students like me. My little chair and a bunch others just like it with other little people just like me sitting in them were at the front of the classroom right in front of the main chalkboard.

It was Arithmetic Group Two and I'd been staring off into some vacant space in the upper front left corner of the room near where the top of the windows, the ceiling tiles and the front chalkboard wall all met, with glazed-over eyeballs, a big goofy smile and my big white cartoon thumbs bobbing up and down pointed towards the roof. Mrs. Goodchaulks, my first grade teacher, responding to my surprising and unexpected reappearance from thin air right in front of her, had taken the opportunity to call upon me to demonstrate my arithmetic expertise. She had tried in vain for several seconds to get my attention and co-operation in solving an addition problem written on the board.

As the final traces of cloudy haze cleared the situation snapped back into painfully clear focus. I didn't have the slightest idea of what was going on, where it was going on or what was expected of me in those going's on. Not more than six inches from the front of my face was the front of Mrs. Goodchaulk's face. Face to face and eyeball-to-eyeball, she firmly but patiently repeated her request that I step up to the board and take on the beckoning addition problem.

I didn't have a clue. Even the most confused and foggiest idea of what I was supposed to do would have been light-years away from where I was at that moment. What I needed was a different deep dark hole to fall into other than the one I found myself in at that moment. The arithmetic problem on the board might as well have been a sentence in *Old Icelandic* that I was being asked to translate into *Mandarin Chinese*. Heck, I'd just spent the past several minutes in a dimly lit room using assorted hand tools and a selection of low yield explosives testing brand new marbles, not concerned in the least with arithmetic except how it might have translated into dollars and cents on an endorsement contract.

   I had no choice. I slowly, reluctantly, rose to my feet in front of my seat, hoping and praying that in those few seconds I could recover enough of my real world faculties to grasp, understand and solve the problem. Instead, I found myself taking a mental detour and concentrated on conjuring up any lame excuse I could use to get myself off the hook. If I'd had the time to secure that endorsement deal back at the marble factory my agent would have been handling my difficult situation for me. Instead, I was caught red-handed and red-faced on my way back from fantasy land without a signed contract and without a valid written excuse for being absent.

   Standing in front of my little wooden chair, shaking and shivering in my little shoes, I took my first hesitant steps towards the chalkboard. I was dealing with the threat of what I thought to be imminent nervous physical and psychological collapse when my already embarrassing predicament precipitously dropped down to the basement level of emotional injury. At my first footfall of my first step the sock full of marbles that I'd, apparently, insufficiently, tied to my belt slipped loose and hit the hard tile floor. Marbles boinged, bounced, rolled and scattered across the breath and width of the front of the classroom. Fate poured suffocating mounds of black dirt down on top of me at the bottom of that deep dark hole I was in.

   My teacher stood as stiff, hard and cold as a stone statue in mid-winter. With her arms folded, Mrs. Goodchaulk's electric blue eyes, glowing and unblinking, stared a smoking hole right through the center of my forehead. It was a "just let me die now" moment. I was not supposed to be carrying my marbles on my person during class time. In fact, she had even helped me clear a space inside of my desk to safely keep them squirreled away during class. In my defense, to me, carrying my marbles at all times was a form of dedication and commitment to my sport. To Mrs.

Goodchaulks it was taboo, like running with scissors or eating too much of that really tasty peppermint-smelling white school paste. Somehow she felt that she was better situated to determine, more able to decide how, when, where and to what extent my marbles were to be handled inside of school.

I came to a bone snapping halt, frozen in place by the icy stare of my teacher. From somewhere I summoned the resolve to try to save the situation. Momentarily, I'd thawed just enough to make the very slightest of slow motion moves and bent down ever so cautiously in a feeble attempt to corral and collect the closest of my unruly marbles. Mrs. Goodhaulks would have none of it. Asserting total control, in the clearest and sharpest diction, she instructed me to leave my marbles be and as requested, proceed to the chalkboard without delay and begin work on the pestering addition problem.

All of my classmates were staring, giggling and whispering as I felt all the blood in my body rush to the surface of my face to see what was going on. If the humiliation of my situation could be measured in depth, I was at forty fathoms with no air or light in sight and sinking into the crushing cold at the bottom which was at some indeterminate depth far below. I was a carefree child in the garden of fantasy land who stepped right into a time warp and wound up in front of Mrs. Goodchaulk's first grade class naked as a new born. I discovered that Rodney Strong wasn't going to be the only hazard on the road I'd chosen to travel. Marbles, as it turned out, could be...embarrassing.

All seekers of great goals in past, present and future times have found, and will find, the roadblocks, diversions, distractions and temptations to be many. Faith and doubt, failure and success go hand in hand; the two opposite sides of the same coin as it has often been said. You cannot understand, appreciate, survive and embrace this duality of life without experiencing both the joyous outcomes and the tragic moments of that life. It is rough enough when, in darker moments, you doubt yourself, your goals and your abilities. We've all gone off the road into that ditch at sometime or another. Somehow, even as a little boy all those years ago I managed to come through such dark moments of doubt and confusion with refreshed vigor and renewed confidence. Doubts, second-guessing and other uncertainties projected onto one's skills and ambitions from the outside, especially family, were always the toughest for me to handle. For me, during my earliest days of marble-playing, doubt came in the form of one Harold Archer, my father.

I practiced all the time; really practiced hard. I practiced until my shooting hand started to cramp up. At school during recess if there were no match to be had, I'd slink off to a quiet corner of the playground, draw my circle in the dirt and go at it. Whenever I practiced I always practiced alone, the sole exception to this hard-and-fast rule being Kit Cat's slap-the-marbles-around-off-the-bed sessions. Like I said, we were pals, an inner circle of two.

Toward the end of each practice session I tried to stretch the ability boundaries of my game. For example, shooting southpaw (lefty) instead of my standard right-handed or sighting my target marble, cocking my thumb for the shot, then closing my eyes as I tried to make the shot blind. I put my shooting hand out to the side and tried to make the shot on an angle by the feel and estimation of triangulation rather than direct sight aiming. On hands and knees I faced the shooting circle butt-first, and shoot backwards between my legs. It was all about translating the geometry in my head and transferring it to the actual physical lining-up and execution of the shot. I wasn't always successful with my experimentation but I was convinced that the unconventional practices made my conventional game that much better.

As the cold and snowy winter months settled in, playground marble competition and related activities went into hibernation. Being the dedicated marble champ that I was, I continued to practice diligently nightly, honing my skills, keeping my edge sharp and clean. In the early evening hours after supper the clear space on the living room carpet became my practice field. Cold winter wind drifted the snow outside as marble practice time inside heated up. Pulling out a selection from my collection I'd go at it for at least an hour per night.

During those sessions my father often took up a familiar position in his favorite living room easy chair with legs and feet resting straight out onto the ottoman. He was all but completely hidden behind the evening newspaper, as only his feet, lower legs and the knuckles of his hands would be visible. Reading the newspaper was my father's effort at a daily intellectual workout. The sounds emanating from his direction were the crinkly sound of the newspaper pages being turned and the mumbled, blurted and mostly indistinguishable comments to himself on that day's newsworthy events, which were all testament to his mental exercise.

From my vantage point it wasn't so much that he made recognizable comments as much as he made sort of, well, sounds. Grunts, coughs, snorts, mumbles, paper shaking and various single word pronouncements were all common parts of the evening newspaper reading vocabulary. This included, but not particularly in this order, approving and disapproving grunting, ahhaaing, yesssing, nooooing, what's, who's, ughs, "who would've thought's," "unbelieveable's," and "I'll be damned" in various unpredictable combinations of length, rising and falling crescendos and emotional concern, indifference or intensity.

As my regular practice sessions wore on through the dark winter nights, it became increasing common for Dad to peek around from the back of his newspaper to checkout what exactly I was up to. My father, sad to say, did not always fully comprehend or understand the unwavering dedication that I was able to sustain day after day for my marble obsession. Occasionally the sharp little cracking and slapping 'music' of one marble kissing another disturbed his reading concentration. Often after a rapid sucession of several dirrect clean hits, Dad would bend down his paper and ask one, all or any number of the following four questions. Mind you, the questions were not asked in anger or with any discernible or consciously contrived malicious intent but they would slip out during the course of the evening just the same.

"Don't you have something more important to do?"

I rarely dignified that question with an answer.

"Is your homework done?"

I WAS working on my homework, right before his eyes.

"Does your mother need help with anything?"

No, but if she did she would have asked him, not me.

"Is there something interesting to watch on the television?" (Something more interesting than marbles?) There usually wasn't but if there had been it would have willingly been missed.

It was my dad's off-the-cuff remarks that I should have been spending my time doing something else that got on my nerves from time to time. However, my mom's more positive interest and understanding of my passionate attachment to my marbles more than compensated for my father's...uncertainty.

To his credit my dad did occasionally make the big effort to understand his youngest son's obsession. It was a weekend evening in early March with the spring competitions not far off when Dad made the big move from his chair to the living room carpet. I had put my evening practice sessions into high gear, as the spring was the high season for all the school's players. My father decided to investigate firsthand my attraction to the game. Putting aside his newspaper he crawled from his chair to a hands-and-knees position next to me on the living room carpet. I was one very surprised, you might even say pleasantly shocked, little boy as Dad sidled up.

"Mike, mind if I take a few tries? Yeah know, I wasn't too bad at this myself when I was your age."

I made a one-time exception to practicing alone because, well, come on, he was my dad. I wasn't going to say no. But the clue was that as soon as he left his chair and got down on the floor Kit Cat left the room. He knew. It was his special cat sense. He jogged for the kitchen and crawled up onto the seat of a chair that was slid in against the table and covered by the tabletop. Like I said, he knew.

I had slowly but steadily learned in my young life that there was the truth and then there was what actually happened despite the truth as told. The truth as told was that my dad was a real marble rabble-rouser in his youth. If what actually happened were to be known my dad wasn't a big marble guy at all in his youth. In fact, all those years ago my father's childhood obsession was rocks. He studied them, searched for them, collected

Keepers Weepers

them, saved them, washed them, identified them and, on occasion, threw them and lost them in inconvenient places. Dad would go anywhere at anytime to get his hands on a rock specimen he coveted for his massive collection. His interest and dedication was so intense that for a few brief moments he ran the risk of becoming a permanent part of the concrete pavement for a section of state highway.

My grandfather, my dad's Dad, had operated a large gravel shovel for a living near my father's childhood home in the country. The gravel pit had afforded my young dad all the opportunities that an eager young rock hound dreamed of. It was an almost daily ritual during the summer months of his youth for Dad to accompany Grandpa to work at the pit and spend the long day digging around for rocks while his father put in his eight hours. When Grandpa and the guys would break for lunch my dad would join in and put on display what he'd collected that morning. After the noon break Grandpa would go back to work and Dad would go back to his own digging around the quarry.

Grandpa, during one of his stories from the past sessions, recalled a July day from years before when my dad was his little boy. While digging into the side of a fresh gravel deposit Grandpa's shovel had uncovered a large, gleaming, virgin deposit of sparkling quartz stone. Dad, being a scant lad of seven, standing nearby, unbeknownst to Grandpa, caught sight of the uncovered quartz glinting in the morning sunlight and blindly rushed up the gravel slope to investigate. Dad was as oblivious to the large equipment operating right next to him as Grandpa was to his son's immediate proximity.

Young Harold scampered up the gravel slope and was face to face with the mesmerizing quartz just a second ahead of Grandpa's shovel scoop which followed up the slope right behind my dad. Grandpa was not thinking "watch out for Harold" because Harold was supposed to be hunting for rocks a long ways away from the work site, not standing on the slope from which the next shovel of gravel was to be taken.

Unaware of his son's presence, his view partially blocked by the shovel's large metal box-like scoop, Grandpa dug into the side of the gravel hill. Simultaneously, he'd scooped up his very surprised little boy right along with several cubic yards of cool, damp and shimmering quartz infused gravel. Following the typical loading pattern, Grandpa rotated the shovel scoop to his left and hit the trip lever when squarely centered above the gravel truck dump box. The gravel SWOOSHED out of the scoop right along with my screaming dad.

Grandpa thought he saw a momentary flash of something unexpected pass with the gravel into the truck's bin. It was his son, my father, as clear and sure as you see these words, screaming and blubbering bloody murder as he had none too daintily been deposited with the quartz gravel into the box of the dump truck. Grandpa shutdown the shovel and rushed up the side of the dump box along with the truck driver who'd also heard the commotion. There, half-buried in the load of gravel, with head, hands and feet sticking out, bruised but not broken, dazed and teary-eyed but still smiling was my father, triumphantly grasping two large chunks of beautiful quartz crystal, one in each hand.

So, at the time, my dad and I weren't really far apart in terms of a mutual understanding. The dedication had been the same, only the obsessions were different. What I had in unbridled ambition had been lost to the preoccupations of my father's adult life. Anyway, Dad grabbed a few stray marbles at the edge of the circle and started flinging away. Maybe it was his glasses, maybe a child's coordination lost years before, but Dad was, well, all over the place. He'd shoot and marbles would disappear under furniture, roll down hallways and into the kitchen. That caught both my Mom's attention and Kit Cat's who was still holding fast on the chair under the table.

Having retrieved one of Dad's wayward attempts, my mother strolled into the living room, tossed the marble into the ring and with arms gently folded marveled at the playful companionship of a father and his youngest son. Just as her admiration reached its peak, Dad lost control and launched one really hard, almost like throwing a small rock. It flew straight for my head but I ducked as the marble-bullet whizzed past my ear. I turned my head and looked back up just in time to witness the flying marble glide through the air and score a direct guided missile hit on a small flower vase resting on an end table. The vase took it right in the neck. The ceramic was no match for the hard speeding marble. The decoration's delicate structure disintegrated into dozens of splintered pieces.

"Harold!" my mother gasped as she rushed to rescue what could not be saved.

"Sorry Dear," my father cowered as he sheepishly crawled back into his chair on hands and knees and sought refuge and safe haven behind his newspaper, all the while muttering something to the effect that I should find a safer place than the living to play with hard glass projectiles.

Later, after the fractured vase had been laid to rest, my mother and I conferred and agreed that in the future I could still hold my practice sessions in the living room as long as I made every effort to restrain and discourage my father's active participation. As I drifted off to sleep that night, I wondered how many vases and other easily smashed objects of art had fallen victim to my dad's rock collecting days.

Rocks plus my dad, holy cow, it must have really added up! It turned out that marbles, like rocks, were not always...safe.

*

***

Chapter Two:

A Mother's Faith

THE WINTER LIVING room practice session was not the only time that my mother came to my aid as I faced the ongoing trials and tribulations of being a first grade marble phenomenon. All true greats, whatever their goal, at one time or another, on their way to the top, have crossed paths with a true benefactor. Whether a rich relative willing to share a bit of the wealth to get things started, a best friend brimming with patience and encouragement, or even the good luck of crossing paths with a kind and understanding stranger recognizing and willing to see an honest, driven, hardworking individual get their chance.

Through all of my struggles, good times and bad, my most faithful and unwavering supporter was my own mom, Margret Archer. Don't get me wrong; she could get as quirky, irritable, impatient, distracted, frustrated, absent-minded, angry, lost-in-thought, creative, understanding and thoughtful as any kid's mom or any adult for that matter. But when she focused she was as attentive, interested and patient with my endeavor as any true benefactor could be.

It was my mother, during the early weeks of the school year, who took note of the sparkle in my eyes for the glint in the marbles. It was her suggestion that I join her on an expedition to the local *Five & Ten* Store to pick out some brand new marbles to start off my collection. Prior to my mother's invitation, I'd been using the remnants of my older brother's abandoned attempt at the game. Robert, three years my elder, had given the game a disappointing, half-hearted try a few years before. Robert had the touch all right, it just wasn't for marbles.

Robert left marbles behind and turned his full and undivided attention to the trading, winning and collecting of baseball cards. The switch had paid off. He was by far the best in the fourth grade and most likely the best in the entire school. He could flip a baseball card end over end and tell each time, while it was still in the air, whether the card would land face up or face down. He could flick a card sideways through the air into an upside down baseball cap twenty feet away on the other side of the room. He had all the technique, finesse and control of a major league pitcher on the mound. If not the best he was as close as one could get and he was an inspiration.

It had also occurred to me at the time that there was something about the men in our family that centered on, well, throwing things. My dad primarily collected rocks as a kid but could, on occasion, when circumstances required, launch one with the accuracy of a rifled bullet. My brother could launch a baseball card across the room so precisely the card slicing through the air could extinguish a burning candle if so aimed. For me, the expertise of putting a marble along the ground or through the air anywhere I'd wanted it to end up had rapidly developed. Mom wasn't exactly a launcher or a thrower but she could work miracles in the kitchen and Dad often said, "she could flip the best pancakes and sling the best hash he'd ever had", so I guessed that her "flipping" and "slinging" was her contribution to the family Archer reputation. In the wider constellation of family relatives I often overheard Mom and Dad converse about how such-and-such aunts, uncles and cousins who could really "fling the bull." So, skillfully throwing things about, including, apparently, large male bovine farm animals, appeared to be a much wider inherited family trait.

When Robert unceremoniously presented me with what was left of his tattered old marbles, thirty of them to be exact, he encouraged me to put them to good use and give it my best shot. He elaborated that I could really count on Mom for backing because even after he'd aborted his marble-playing she still had the faith and confidence in his decision to reinvest in his newfound interest. The rest, he'd pointed out, was history.

Although it was generous of Robert to hand over what was left of his small marble collection, I soon determined that it was no great personal sacrifice. The marbles were in the worst possible condition, like they'd been put through a meat grinder. They were so nicked and scratched that only a few of them would roll true over our linoleum kitchen floor. As the most seriously wounded of the thirty marbles rolled, they would hop, skip, jump up, jump left, jump right and generally zigzag across the floor like soldiers serpentining their way across open fields of enemy fire; hardly conducive to accurate marble play.

As Robert witnessed this futile exercise he confided that, in fact, he had literally jammed his marbles through a mill. When Robert threw in the towel on the marble game for good he was so discouraged and disgusted by his lack of success that he expressed his frustration by, until then, untold acts of marble abuse and cruelty. His disappointment was so complete and his desire for revenge on the little glass balls was so overpowering that he jammed several of the little innocent crystals through the hand-cranked kitchen meat grinder (as Robert was relating this story our mother, listening in the background, without comment went directly to the kitchen cabinet and retrieved the same meat grinder for a close inspection, all the while directing a silent, distressed and disapproving glare in Robert's direction).

What Robert wasn't able to destroy in the kitchen he maliciously crushed in the vise attached to Dad's basement workbench. The thirty that managed to escape total obliteration were the same thirty that he handed down to me. They bore the bruises, scratches and gaping wounds of his marble meltdown. He also passed along two medium sized steely boulders that were not usable owing to Robert's partially successful attempt to flatten them with Dad's sledgehammer. He wasn't able to shatter or completely flatten them but he did manage to make them both a sort of rounded oblong like two miniature lawn bowling *Boccie Balls*. A fitting homage, I thought, to his failed mastery of marble management, and a fitting reminder as well of how things could have turned out for me if I wasn't careful and properly focused.

So it was Mom and me off to the *Five & Ten* for fresh marbles and new start. The marbles occupied a large section of display space between miniature construction equipment and plastic model airplane kits. The available selection was overwhelming, immense, which made it all that more difficult to choose between the many sizes, styles and types. I wasn't alone in my admiration and confusion. There were three other kids, all about my age and size, gawking wide-eyed and slack-jawed at the glowing crystal treasure trove. As we all gently nudged and jostled for position to admire the objects of our mutual desire my turn came to stand directly in front of the largest part of the marble display.

As sunlight came in through the store windows the reflecting marble colors hit me full force as the rays of prismed marble light passed right through me, simultaneously creating a burning heat and freezing chill that made me sweat and shiver. I could not blink, I could not turn my head to look away, I could not move; I could only stand fast and stare. I was locked in place by the beams of reflected light that made my entire body feel translucent, like holding your hand tightly over the beam of a powerful flashlight in the dark. That was it, the mother lode, my calling and my destiny. Few things purer had happened to me in my young life. As I came to, back to the world, I noticed that the other three kids standing nearby were all staring at me. They saw it too. They sensed it. They felt the heat and the cold and saw my glowing body under my clothes. But it wasn't the marbles they sensed, it was me.

Coming to, I realized that one of the other three kids was a girl with very distinctive features; braided blond pigtails, the face of a bulldog and the build of light infantry vehicle. It was unexpected to see a girl checking out the marbles as intently as the other two guys because marbles at school was generally regarded as a man's sport in those days. I bit down on my tongue and fought the urge to say that the dolls and doll accessories were in the next aisle and the weight lifting equipment was at the back of the store. As if I'd telepathically shouted the suggestion wouldn't yeah know it if one of the other guys brazenly suggested pretty much exactly that out loud. The moment the words left his mouth you could almost hear the rubble of a distant explosion. 'Pigtails' did not take kindly to the suggestion and walked right up to the guy. As she made a tight balled-up fist she contorted her face into a combined sneer and manic smile that looked like her mouth was about to suck in and swallow her entire face. With her lower lip jutting out like a bulldozer scoop, she shoved her rock hard fist right up under the guy's nose.

"Make me," she dared.

"Dumb girl," was his careless response.

With the speed and accuracy of a trained boxer 'Pigtails' responded by depositing her tight little fat fist directly into the guy's midsection, doubling him over breathless, a reward for his chauvinistic impertinence. The very idea of being punched in the gut by that girl was almost as abhorrent as the thought of being beaten by her in a marble match; a disturbing passing thought. I couldn't take my eyes off the poor kid who was still bent over and sucking air from the fierce blow. I didn't recognize the girl as anyone from my school as she slowly walked away towards the other side of the store (right past the dolls and right up to the weight lifting equipment).

The kid who'd gotten punched was still bent over; trying to catch his breath, as barely audible moans of pain, anguish and embarrassment leaked out from between his clinched teeth and quivering lower lip. Mom walked up and asked how I was doing. She couldn't help but notice the gagging kid next to me whose mouth was then opening and closing like a dying fish left in the hot sun on a boat dock. I returned my attention to the marbles on display as the victim of the unknown girl's assault slowly bent upright enough to slowly walk, with hesitant, halting baby steps, past the cash register and out the front door. Mom's perplexed stare followed his staggering progress all the way out of the store as did the cashier at the front checkout counter who wished him a "good day and come back soon" which he acknowledged with a painfully pathetic half-wave of his hand and a fit of coughing.

There were so many marbles that would have fit the bill that I had trouble even starting to make up my mind. I didn't want to be greedy and ask for too much and yet I didn't want to be too timid and stingy and cheat myself out of a great chance to start my competitive collection. As I saw it at the time about half of what was displayed in front of me would be just about right; about two-thousand marbles. I was all ready to bring up the wheelbarrow and start loadin' 'em up! As generous as Mom could be, she would never go for such over enthusiasm, such extravagance, for what might have been a total cash outlay of thirty or forty bucks, not to mention the cost of the wheel barrow.

Exercising restraint and focusing on just getting my beginner's foot inside the competitive marble door I cast a look of confusion and concern up at my mother who responded in kind and helped me make the final decision. Picking up on her cue, Mom suggested that a varied selection and quantities enough to effectively compete and cover any losses incurred in the beginning would be a wise plan. She made her point really business-like, like a banker or the lunch lady at school who always reminded kids to buy only a week's worth of hot lunch tickets at a time. With her help I chose five bags of the most beautiful marbles that I'd ever laid my eyes or hands upon. I was on my way. Like my brother would have said, the rest is history.

Instances too numerous to list and describe here provided ample opportunity to discover just how understanding and supportive my mother could be. It wasn't that I was intentionally, conciously or unconsciously, putting her to the test. Rather, it was all of the unavoidable circumstances of everyday marble life that collided, head-on, with the unwavering devotion to my newfound love. This devotion, this desire, was nothing so transient and fleeting as some overnight short-lived infatuation. It was the real thing; it was as forever as forever could be for a six-year-old kid.

In a small way I began to understand and appreciate why my dad didn't take as deep an interest in my abilities and goals as my mother. First off, my mother's protective instinct was pervasive. Dad wouldn't have been able to get a negative word in edgewise. Second, she didn't want me to pick up any of Dad's former bad habits associated with his rock collecting, i.e., his rock throwing. Thirdly, I concluded that my health would be adversely affected; I don't think I could have survived all of the excess positive attention.

My mother commented to me, years later, that the most trying situations during my first year of school were those moments when I somehow managed to lose control of my marbles to her consternation and embarrassment. For a kid who was as greedy and protective of the spoils of victory and conquest as I was, I sure figured out a way, unintentionally, to precipitate my participation in several unforeseen situations in which significant portions of my hard-won treasure could've been lost to me forever. A string of just such incidents had their beginning at the local supermarket. But, in my own defense, I maintained from the first episode to the very last that I was strictly an unwilling victim in a series of unfortunate and unforeseen circumstances. Mom always countered any such assertion by pointing out that the two main ingredients necessary for any of the "surprising and unexpected situations" were always present; me along with my full marble sock.

Most supermarkets not only sold the expected food and food related items but also carried an array and varied selection of school supplies, magazines, hardware and often, a small selection of cheap but interesting toys, including, bags of marbles. During one particular trip to the local *Always Save Food Market* on a Saturday afternoon with Mom, I nobly volunteered to help by picking out the family's weekly supply of breakfast cereal. Luckily for me the sugar-loaded breakfast cereals were displayed right next to the store's toy selection (and not by accident either). Prominently displayed with other various interesting looking goodies were several clear plastic bags filled with bright new marbles. I never missed any chance to checkout any marbles that crossed my path.

I took it upon myself to bring some needed snap and zest to the family's breakfast table. So instead of the normal boring selection of assorted bran, wheat and corn flakes I decided it was time to truly awaken the family taste buds with a four-box supply of *Super Crunchy, Chocolate Flavored, Captain Moon Ball's Space Bombs, The Best Breakfast Cereal to Land on Earth since the Discovery of Breakfast Cereals in the Galaxy.* Who could go wrong with that? No one, that's who! So, weighed down with four boxes of chocolate space bombs, two boxes under each arm, I casually slid three paces to my right and started to checkout the bags of marbles.

The marbles were displayed just above my eye level so I had to stand on tiptoe to get a good look. In doing so the sock full of marbles that I'd tied to my belt jiggled and bounced reassuringly against my right thigh. At the time most guys my age would have walked around in public with a pair of holstered six-guns belted to their waist. Not me. For me a sock full of clean, hard marbles bouncing against my hip was as comforting as any matching set of imitation *Colts* with a full ammo belt.

As I trained my discerning eye on the bags of crystal boulders, one aisle over a supermarket renegade had broken away from his mom and was trying in vain to tame a wild runaway shopping cart. The shopping cart 'Chief', armed with twin cap-fired rubber dart pistols and wearing a fully feathered *Plains Indian* head-dress, struggled to cling onto and control his rolling empty shopping cart mount which, with his help, was rolling along at maximum speed towards the meat counter at the back of the store. The 'Chief' had his hands full of dart pistols and unruly cart as he careened out of control toward the waiting meat counter.

There was no chance of stopping as the kid and the cart slammed head-on into the solidly anchored meat counter just where the "thickest-cut maple smoked bacon in town" met up with the "thickest-cut chops in town." Simultaneously the kid flipped head first over the handlebar, landing butt-first inside the cart basket and involuntarily fired both dart pistols. One dart, with a small popping noise, pegged the surprised butcher right in the center of his forehead as the other bull's-eyed a five pound stuffed pork roast that was cradled in the arms of a nearby customer.

The cart-riding kid quickly recovered before the wounded butcher could restrain him. 'Kid Chief', undeterred and undaunted, reloaded his pistols and remounted his unsteady steed for another ride despite the protests of the angry butcher. Once again not holding a tight rein on the unruly cart, the 'Chief', with dart pistols cocked and reloaded, was off and rolling. Unfortunately for me even a wild-eyed, dart-firing *Indian Chief* could be distracted from a raid in progress as, from the corner of his eye, he caught sight of the toy section. Leaning into the unsteady shopping cart as he made the precarious sharp left turn into my aisle, he headed straight for the authentic imitation plastic lever-action *Winchester* rifles displayed right next to the bags of marbles.

The 'Cheif" lost control of his untrustworthy mount one more time as he came skidding around the corner on two wheels. With the screaming kid barely hanging onto the cart handlebar, the shopping cart slammed right into me. I took it right in the marble sock as the two boxes of *Captain Moon Balls* clasped between my right forearm and rib cage exploded into a shower of box tops, torn wax paper, shredded cardboard and hundreds of chocolate space bombs. The crushing and crashing impact was heard throughout the store as the howling 'Chief', the charging cart and yours truly went flying into and brought down the almost ceiling-high display of *Captain Moon Balls Space Bombs.* The falling and tumbling boxes of cereal completely buried the 'Chief', the cart and me with the exception of my feet, which were sticking out of the pile of cereal boxes at an upward and awkward forty-five degree angle.

Trapped under dozens of king-sized boxes of cereal, slowly coming to my senses, I realized that my marble sock had taken the brunt of the charge as dozens of my treasured marbles were forcefully freed from their then torn and ripped sock sanctuary and were rolling free down the aisle on their way to the far end of the store by the checkout counters. Meanwhile, Mom, who'd been one aisle over trying to decide between 'Fancy French Cut' and 'Regular Cut' canned green beans, rounded the far end of her aisle by the checkout lanes to see for herself what all the commotion was about. Just as she stepped into the open end of the aisle, she was greeted by a wave, a rushing tide, of rolling, bouncing marbles.

She looked toward the scene of the disaster and recognized the feet sticking out of the pile of cereal boxes as mine and rushed to my rescue, stopping here and there on her way to pick up my wayward marbles.

Whereas my mother tried to save me, the 'Chief's' mom tried to kill him. It seemed that the 'Chief' had been on the warpath for sometime, creating fear, havoc and various degrees of disturbance and general unrest all along the supermarket frontier. His mother, screaming louder than he was crying, dragged him from the store by his pistol belt while vowing to bring him before final tribal and territorial justice, his father. With Mom's help I emerged from the pile dazed, my shirt pockets full of space bombs and one of the 'Chief's' rubber suction darts firmly attached to my right temple; a hundred-to-one lucky shot.

With every little marble mishap I unintentionally pushed Mom just a little bit closer to the limit of her patience and goodwill. The supermarket collision was forgivable; it hadn't been my fault so I got a free pass on that one. But, the first giant step I took away from a "no fault" to a "your fault" incident occurred on a bus trip to the country.

My grandparents, on my father's side, lived in a small country township some miles to the north. It was customary, on occasion, for my mother on her own, or with either Robert or me or both of us in tow, to hop aboard the local bus service and spend a few days in the country visiting Grandma and Grandpa. They looked forward to our visits as they tolerated our city ways and we tolerated their country ways, all for the sheer joy of one another's company. Besides, as stated earlier, Grandpa was a great storyteller and in me he had one great listener, especially when it came to the tales of the family Archer.

It happened on the bus. That trip it was just Mom and I heading into the country. Not to be caught unprepared, I had a full sock of marbles with me as I used the hour-long bus ride as a chance to inspect and admire my abbreviated travel selection. Mom was lost between her magazine and the passing countryside as I quietly emptied the contents of the marble sock into my waiting lap.

The bus ride was swift and smooth so I anticipated no surprises or problems. What I didn't anticipate was a two-mile stretch of road renovation and construction. The bus slowed to a crawl as the highway changed from a ribbon of flawless concrete to a bumpy gravel pothole-riddled obstacle course with a six-inch drop-off where the road construction began. The front wheels of the bus navigated the drop slowly and carefully without any on board mishaps. It was when the back wheels went over the edge, dropped and landed hard that I bounced high off my seat. That promptly turned my lap into a launch pad as my marbles rocketed into the air. A marble bomb had gone off right in my face as the marbles left the safety of my control and landed all about the surrounding seats, passengers and floor of the bus. The moving bouncing bus helped spread the already scattered marbles to all of the accessible and remotely accessible nooks and crannies of the vehicle. The main aisle of the bus became a marble freeway way as the little loose crystal balls rolled and frolicked back to front and back again at will.

At first Mom acted surprised, then slightly annoyed and then, finally, fully agitated. Despite my repeated and ongoing attempts to retrieve as many of my marbles as possible as they rolled back and forth past my aisle seat, several still rattled and rolled freely along the floor of the bus for the duration of the trip, endearing me forever to the driver, fellow passengers and one unfortunate slightly intoxicated regular rider who'd found quiet refuge at the rear of the bus.

Jake Duncan would always take a few drinks before his weekly bus trip home in an effort to ease his persistent motion sickness. He'd been using the tiny on board bus bathroom when the rear wheels entered the construction zone. We could hear Jake calling out with a string of muffled cuss words as the sudden loss of bus axle altitude caught him unawares as well. Several of my free rolling marbles had managed to find and settle in a small depression in the bus floor just outside of the little washroom door. A bit tipsy and still cursing under his breath, the unsuspecting Jake opened the washroom door and firmly placed his first footfall squarely on the waiting marbles. Placing his out-of-balance weight fully onto the jostling marbles, he not to gracefully lost his already questionable balance and flew backwards back into the tiny john. He gave out a sort of deep-throated "Yeeeooo" as his faltering feet kicked the washroom door that flew open hard and ricocheted back off the side of the rear seat. The door recoiled shut with a loud slam. The lock jammed, trapping the dazed, bewildered and only partially conscious Jake in the bus toilet.

When we arrived at the next stop, our final destination, the bus driver, with the help of the local station attendant, freed the trapped Jake from the bus bathroom and carried him from the vehicle. The attendant had him under the arms while the driver had him by the ankles as they carried him stretcher style. Mom and I stood waiting just outside the bus door as the driver and attendant walked by with the sagging Jake suspended between them. They stopped in front of us just for a moment as the driver released Jake's left ankle (his foot dropped to the ground) and reached into his right pants pocket. He returned a large handful of my wayward marbles that he'd collected as they'd rolled around his seat and feet during the course of the trip. My mother gave me the "be more careful next time" look as she apologized to the driver and to Jake for the inconvenience. Halfheartedly, the driver grumbled his acceptance of the apology as Jake slowly came to for a moment.

"Now this is service!" he exclaimed before slipping back into semi-consciousness.

Jake was unceremoniously carried off into the bus depot. Then, as other passengers exited the bus they simply handed back to me small, medium and large handfuls of marbles that had come their way during the trip. I didn't lose a single marble. Dumb luck.

It was more than 'necessary', it had been, in fact, an 'absolute necessity' that my marbles be with me every moment, everywhere I was, without fail. The sock of marbles held in my hand, the sock of marbles safely tucked into my jacket pocket or the sock of marbles tied to my belt and bouncing against my thigh became as much a part of me as my arms and legs. So it stood to reason that my mom's marble tolerance level would be tested on a regular basis.

The next such test was a Saturday *Moon Monster Triple Feature* at the local movie house. Despite our halfhearted protests our mother insisted upon joining my brother and me as she was quite the fan of the moon series herself and in fact had not missed a single episode. Robert and I had plans to meet up and sit with buddies so we made Mom promise to respect certain predetermined seating arrangements. She agreed as she dutifully reminded us that it would be her who'd awaken and comfort us at three a.m. from our screaming nightmares fueled by such science fiction extravaganzas. Walking into the theater I, naturally, was loaded to bear with a extra full bulging sock of marbles hitched to my belt as a precaution, just in case the triple feature did not live up to its billing and a more entertaining diversion was called for. Besides, a lot of kids from school would be there and I never knew when a marble challenge might be issued and a match would break out.

It was midway through the second feature, *Attack of the Crater Crawler,* just when the non-air breathing *Giant Toad* surprised the *Moon Princess* by eating the *King of Mars* right in front of her. I shrieked right along with the Princess and the three-hundred other spectators of the tragedy and jumped the requisite one-foot off my seat. The marbles I'd removed from my sock and had been nervously fondling in my lap launched into the air like of covey of wild quail flushed from cover. The flying marbles momentarily flashed through the projector beam as the prismed image light flashed and sparkled across the screen, over the theater walls, ceiling and across the faces of all the patrons present (it accidentally turned out to be a pretty cool unanticipated visual special effect).

The marbles' arc of trajectory brought them down randomly over the next several rows to my front, bouncing off seat backs, audience member's heads and seat arm rests. Most made their way down to the floor. The sound of the scattered gems rolling away from me on the slanted concrete theater floor was pure agonizing torture, far worse than the fate of the *Mars King* was suffering in the slimy maw of the *Giant Toad* on the big screen. They were lost in the dark, rolling and bouncing off shoes and seat legs as they methodically worked their way to the front of the theater underneath the big screen.

I insisted upon trying to find every last lost marble immediately regardless of the perils faced by the *Moon Princess,* but, from the seat behind me my mother's hands had extended over the back of my seat and were firmly locked onto the tops of my shoulders.

"Stay put," she loudly whispered into my ear.

She was trying to make a point, to teach me a lesson. But her efforts at a down-the-road teaching point had definitely strained our mother-son relationship. I was literally ready to lift the proverbial overturned car up off the trapped baby all by myself in any effort to reclaim my marbles. I arrived at the bursting point from adrenaline-fueled frustration and anxiety. I just had to sit when all of my instincts were screaming "now or never-get-moving!" But sit and mumble and smolder I did, as I had no choice in the matter. Not only was I forced to stay put until the end of the second feature, Mom also made me sit through the entirety of the third installment as well. The third feature's torture of the *Moon Maiden*, daughter of the *Moon Princess*, at the tentacles of the *Venusian Slime People* was laughable, a picnic on a nice day, compared to the torment I'd endured for two hours that Saturday afternoon.

As the third and final feature ended, I sprang to my feet as though I could make the twenty-row distance to the front of the theater in one giant flying leap. The flying, landing and rolling marbles had created quite the distraction during the film as several ushers had already collected a greater portion of my lost marbles.

Mom, Robert and I waited expectantly in the lobby as the show house crowd made its way out. The ushers emerged one at a time, each with paper popcorn bags or paper soda pop cups holding the collected marbles. Almost all of the wayward marbles had been recovered but they did not resemble the clean crystal balls that I'd brought. As they'd rolled and bounced their way along the theater floor each of the once beautiful little spheres had collected its share of soda syrup, popcorn butter and salt, melted chocolate and other assorted and not necessarily recognizable goodies. I immediately reached to reclaim and return my trophies to the warm and protective cover of my marble sock and back into the company of their brethren who had not joined them on their theater floor adventure. But Mom interceded once again, insisting that I keep the recovered marbles in their respective bags and cups until they could be washed and dried.

My mother thoughtfully thanked every single one of the ushers

Keepers Weepers

and rewarded their efforts with a twenty-five cent tip each. With the bags and cups of marbles cradled in my arms, we headed for the exit, when from behind, Toby "Tubby" Wilson, a second grader who had the distinction of being one of the "huskier" kids in school came bouncing and skipping after us, calling out my name. Toby waddled up and, out of breath, offered his pudgy left hand.

"Archer, you forgot these!"

There in Toby's butter and chocolate smeared hand were three more of my lost marbles. It just so happened that Toby was sitting two rows to my front when my marbles leaped into the air. Four of the flying escapees landed directly into Toby's king-size tub of double-buttered double-salted popcorn. Being engrossed in the plight of the *Martian Monkeys'* fight for control of the *Great Northern Volcano,* Toby unknowingly shoveled the marbles into his ample mouth along with a sticky clump of popcorn. Since Toby more typically inhaled his food as opposed to chewing it, he'd actually swallowed one of the marbles before discovering the other three in his mouth. Owing to Toby's ferocious appetite, it seemed that he'd swallowed, quite by accident, other non-food, indigestible items in his culinary past. Thus, being more aware of nature's course in such matters, Toby offered to keep watch, as it were, and return said fourth marble to me at school within the next day or two depending upon how long it took for such things to work out.

My mom, not too pleased at hearing this, thanked Toby but insisted that he not trouble himself any further and that it wouldn't be necessary to 'keep watch'. Robert started to laugh to Mom's dismay. I took a more practical point of view and said that as far as I was concerned it would be great for him to 'keep watch' anyway just in case he happened to come across it. Mom groaned in frustration.

"Sure thing Archer!" Toby called out.

"Ugh," Mom sighed.

"It's my marble," I quietly countered.

Taking into account all of the emotional and practical considerations that swirled around any event which involved me being involuntarily separated from my marbles, my mom had taken it all in stride with good amounts of measured patience and reasonably good humor. They were all relatively minor incidents that fell well within the range and boundaries of motherly understanding. However, once a speeding vehicle is out of control it becomes increasingly more difficult to keep it between the curbs. Likewise, once I started dropping my marbles it was only a matter of time before I rolled that vehicle over and landed upside-down in the ditch. There were only two possible options at that point; stop and regain control or run out of marbles. Having demonstrated to that point that regaining control was really unlikely and owing to my marble match skill and success all indications pointed to my supply of marbles to be approaching infinity, so the possibility, the probability, of some sort of marble catastrophe was distinctly imminent. The glint and sparkle of flying marbles in the movie projector beam was just the flash image in the rear view mirror as the six-year-old marble-playing machine was taking the corner too fast, too hard and on only two wheels with the curb and ditch coming up fast.

My mother's patience, the limits of her gracious understanding, was like a large, flexible but resilient single pane of window glass, and I, having no block wall to bounce my tennis ball off of, decided to use the expanse of that transparency as my backstop. Then, as if my arm had a mind and purpose separate from my own, it decided to sneak in a fastball and catch everybody by surprise, including me.

The occasion was my parents' wedding anniversary. The evening's plans called for Mom, Dad, Robert and myself to meet up with the usual assortment of aunts and uncles at a high-class steak house for an evening of good food, drink and recognition of their years of married and family bliss. It meant Sunday suits with ties, haircuts with fancy hair cream, brushed teeth and just a touch of Dad's after shave cologne; all top notch.

Befitting the special occasion, I decided that my carry along marble sock would have to be just as special as would the marbles I'd take to dinner. I picked out twenty of my cleanest, clearest, best looking Cat's-Eye boulders and ceremoniously dropped them one at a time into the dark blue dress sock that perfectly matched and blended in with the color of my suit. I didn't want the fact that I was carrying to be known so I firmly secured the tightly packed marble sock to my belt, double-knotted and well concealed. As an added measure of security, to ensure they would not give their presence away by rattling around against each other, I snapped one of those really big, thick, strong rubber bands around the neck of the sock. "No problem tonight you guys," I thought to myself.

Everything seemed to be perfectly in place. Robert was spying on my preparations from the bedroom door with visible apprehension. Without speaking, Robert had the same look on his face as he did when we were at the circus and the high wire act was performing without a net. I stared back at him and confidently patted my tight marble sock, which did not make a sound. Besides, as Robert was putting on his suit coat, I detected him placing a stack of rubber-banded baseball cards into his coat's inner breast pocket. One thing was for certain: neither my brother nor I would be without entertainment if the party started to drag.

The ride to the restaurant was uneventful except for Robert, who enjoyed the quiet luxury of leafing through his selection of *National League* shortstop cards, and Mom, who slid over and was sitting right next to Dad in the middle of the front seat like it was a high school date night. We entered the steakhouse and were escorted by the headwaiter to a large oval dining table with seating for twelve in the center of a reserved dining area. With great difficulty and a patience and tolerance we'd never known possible, Robert and I endured and ultimately survived the unrelenting barrage of bear hugs and sloppy wet red lipstick kisses bestowed upon us by our large loving aunts who'd arrived earlier and were already seated with our uncles. The seating arrangements called for Robert and me to sit across from each other at the large table with each of us intentionally placed between a set of our aunts.

These were large aunts, big women! Broad-waisted, big-armed, large-legged, wide-bottomed, giant-bosomed, old-world European Grandma type women! Big oversized pots of whole potatoes could be found boiling away on their kitchen stoves twenty-four hours a day 365 days a year. It could be observed and argued that carbohydrate starch was the glue that held the extended family together, not bloodlines. Food, of all kinds and in all forms, had a disturbingly prominent place in the lives of our elder relations and it showed. Then, as if the seating arrangements weren't imposing enough, our four large, loving aunts were unable and unwilling to keep their hands off of us. Apparently the ordering, serving and consuming of cocktails before we arrived only fueled the uninhibited demonstrations of affection.

If they weren't hugging and kissing us, they were mussing then straightening our hair or making us stand up by our chairs so they could compliment us on our rapid growth and our well-appointed attire. But the worst were the big, loud, wet, sloppy, juicy kisses that left big smeared red lip marks all over our mugs. Robert and I would signal to one another from across the table when we spotted the glowing red lip brands on each other's faces. We pointed out the location of the offending marks on the other guy's face by pointing to the same spot on our own. It got to the point where we just pointed to our own faces and made a circle with our fingers that meant that both of our faces had become nothing but big red spots each with eyes, a nose and a mouth.

By the time dinner arrived, my once clean white napkin looked as if it had been used to stem the flow of a couple of bloody noses. The lingering red rouge glow on our faces was impossible to simply wipe off. We finally realized that we'd been overrun and gave up. It was not possible to keep up and pointless to try to do anything about it at the table. It only stopped when the food started to arrive and the full attention of our aunts turned to molesting the food on their plates instead of us. Despite the reputation of great food if Robert and I would have known beforehand that all the mushy stuff was going to get out of hand we would have requested that Mom and Dad make it an all-adult night and left my brother and I to the TV and the cold pizza pie leftovers in the fridge.

When the drinking water and the baskets of bread and dinner rolls arrived, I took advantage of the distraction and looked around. I discovered it was a pretty nice place. It was very different than *Dottie's Drive-In* where all the food was delivered to your car by teenage girls wearing sneakers and your food was served on metal trays that hung on the half-rolled-down car windows. The only girl I saw working in this place was the hat and coat check girl who was politely chewing bubble gum. The thought occurred to me that Robert should talk to her because it might have been the type of bubble gum that came inside a pack of baseball cards. Maybe they could compare collections and work out a few trades.

Shortly thereafter the menus arrived and I immediately started to search for the section where I'd find the burgers, hot dogs, fries and malted milk shakes. All I found were paragraphs of prose describing foods that I didn't recognize much less ever imagined existed. Being stuck between Aunt Wilma and Aunt Alice was bad enough, but not having any food that would reward me for my pain and suffering was unthinkable. Mom noticed my disappointed look as I closed the menu and laid it on the table.

Taking heed of my dilemma, she asked the waiter if the establishment offered a children's menu. He nodded his assent and soon returned with a little white paper menu that had little pink and blue construction paper balloons glued to the cover. I felt like a total jerk. I was afraid to even open and look inside the delicate menu, certain that if I did, a two-fisted baby's rattle would fall out on the table right in front of me. It didn't help that Aunts Wilma and Alice commented out loud what an adorable little menu it was. The indignities of childhood, even for a childhood marble champion, a minor celebrity like myself, could be almost unbearable. But, out of desperate hunger, bear it I did as with squinting eyes I slowly opened the menu ready to catch and rapidly conceal and dispose of any baby's toy that might appear. No rattle, no rubber nipple pacifier or teething ring with giant plastic play keys attached materialized as I discovered, to my relief, that a selection of food more tuned to my palette was available.

During my menu embarrassment and resulting lonely suffering my brother had been yucking it up under his breath. He wisely concealed his own confusion and disappointment with the adult fare menu, thus sparing himself the arrival and presentation of the children's menu. When ordering he simply looked across the table at me and told the waiter that he would have what I was having. That dog! I reached into my suit jacket pocket and gave my secured marbles a good hard reassuring squeeze. I told myself that it would all be over in just a few hours. Another round of drinks was ordered for the table from the bar, which was a good thing because if anybody at our table really needed a drink, it was me! I took four fingers and a thumb of cherry soda, neat – my third.

At this point in the festivities, Robert and I exchanged the pre-determined signal and simultaneously requested to be excused from the table for a bathroom break. Once safely inside the confines of the men's room we both sighed with relief as he bent over a wash sink basin and I leaned against a wall with my feet splayed-out, having made it, albeit temporarily, to a safe and neutral area.

It was like a break between rounds of a combination wrestling and boxing match. We'd just gone a full round with our aunts and it had been exhausting. The only thing missing in the bathroom were a pair of little four-legged wooden stools to sit on and some crusty old boxing guys chewing on stubby stogies to put towels over our heads and throw cold water in our faces while yelling at us to led with our rights, keep up our lefts and don't stop dodging and weaving.

Robert pulled out his baseball cards as I checked and re-secured my marble sock. We compared notes and complaints as to who had it the worst, Robert between Aunts Lucy and Jane or me between Aunts Wilma and Alice. We agreed that it was too close to call.

After several attempts, we concluded that the rouge affect of the lipstick kisses would not just wash or rub off and that it would probably take days of sun, rain and dirt exposure to just wear off. Reasonably composed and ready, the bell sounded and it was back to the table for another round.

Upon returning to the table the atmosphere of the occasion had decidedly changed. The earlier giggles, loose and foolish behavior had intensified as a result of two more rounds of drinks ordered and consumed in the short time Robert and I had been on break in the john. Squeezing back into our respective seats between our respective pairs of aunts resulted in renewed greetings and assaults of affection as if we'd been gone for two months instead of ten minutes. All the alcohol-fueled inhibition-lowered cheek-pinching, forced-puckering, hair-mussing and squeezing-the-breath-out-of-you hugs bordered on nephew cruelty. It took another three rounds of drinks before Robert and I could free our hands and point out the fresh lipstick marks on each of our faces. I even had red kiss marks in my hair, oh man!

Good ol' Mom and Dad, normally quiet, reserved and well within respectable control were downing their share of the booze right along with everyone else. It was bizarre to see the spreading glow of inebriation on their faces as they loosened up in a fashion that my brother and I were unaccustomed to witnessing. Mom was all giddy and giggly while our usually reserved, mumle-under-his-breath father was talking, talking, talking!

The festivities just kept moving along at a steadily accelerating rate. The Archer party had developed and maintained a definite momentum that would be hard to break. Another round of drinks arrived and with them three guys dressed in leather bib shorts and funny hats accompanied by singing twin sisters in garb that matched each other and the violin guys. The sometimes romantic, sometimes lively musical interludes were a surprise, by special arrangement with the restaurant owner, just for Mom and Dad on their special day: a gift from the aunts and uncles at the table. Dad gave Mom a big loud kiss on the lips as everyone at the table cheered and applauded.

All through the toasting, the drinking and the funny-dressed singers and musicians, Mom hugging and kissing Dad and Dad hugging and kissing Mom, Aunt Wilma on my right had her large heavy left arm around my shoulders, as she laughed and sang and drank along with my Aunt Alice seated to my left who put her very large and heavy right arm over Aunt Wilma left arm around my shoulders. As they pulled towards each other, as they rocked back and forth their respective and equally very large medium-to-soft spongy breasts pushed against both sides of my head and face. As they swayed left then right then back left again to the music I had no choice but to sway right along with them.

While I was being kneaded like bread dough to the music by my pair of fat aunts, I looked across the table to Robert for a lifeline only to discover that he was likewise helplessly trapped between the swaying and singing Aunts Jane and Lucy. It was the mirror image of what was happening to me. Robert's head and face would appear and then momentarily disappear and then reappear to varying degrees as the flabby-armed big-soft-breasted press was working him over the same as me. Robert and I both tried, in vain, to join in the celebration by reaching for our drinks on the table in front of us. Just as Robert's outstretched hand was an inch from grasping his glass his aunts swayed to one side as his arm lifted up and swayed back and forth repeatedly four inches above his glass as his head and face continued to appear and disappear between his set of aunts.

I momentarily gained successful access to my drink as I forcibly pressed my way forward against the table and took a mouthful of soda. Aunt Wilma and Aunt Alice momentarily altered their rhythm as they separated away from me only to simultaneously come crashing back together in the middle, on me. The giant-breasts-flesh-press almost squeezed the bubbling sweet cherry soda right out of my mouth. It took all of my pressing lip and cheek strength to keep the red soda from shooting out all over the table.

I struggled to work free and create some necessary breathing room but it would not work. The thought had occurred to me that my suffering was serving some sort of preventative benefit to everyone at the table. If I managed to completely free myself from the fleshy enclosure, Aunt Wilma and Aunt Alice just might have fallen in toward one another and crashed together face to face like two avalanches roaring down facing hillsides, meeting head on in the valley below. I surmised that neither of them would be able to halt their forward momentum as their individual and considerable moving masses would rush to fill the gap created by my destabilizing absence. The resulting shock wave of crashing loose middle-aged flesh would have reverberated across the table and around the room with devastating results.

While these disturbing thoughts and images raced wildly through my mind, I became aware that Aunt Wilma's leg was bouncing up and down, left and right, keeping time to the upbeat music. Her left leg and all of its random undulations were pressing really hard against my marble sock and putting quite the strain on the sock knot and the rubber band holding that knot fast. The violins and the twin sisters were singing and Aunt Wilma was rocking back and forth in her chair like she was manning the oars in the final leg of a rowboat race.

Aunt Alice on the other side wasn't exactly asleep at the oars either as she sped up her rocking to match the music. It was no longer just my head and face that were being pressed, pushed and squeezed. My entire body was being lifted up and down and back and forth in my chair! My situation approached critical mass when Aunt Wilma's moving body fell out of sync with Aunt Alice's counter-rotating moving body. One would lunge forward as the other would lurch backwards with several random rapidly repeating combinations thereof. Their opposite flowing inertias had me suspended completely off my seat and almost rubbed and ripped the clothes off my tiny body. I found myself on the verge of being roughly kneaded right into involuntary public nudity.

The pace of the music picked up and in turn so did the seated chair dancing of all the adults at the table. Unable to keep up with the music, my two aunts were completely out of control like two giant cams on a giant fly wheel inside of a giant engine, running way above safe and acceptable tolerances and about to throw a giant rod! I was drowning, sinking, disappearing in the tidal wave and backwash of clothed rubbery flesh.

An unexpected moment of respite ensued as the violins stopped. Wilma and Alice slammed on the brakes with me caught under the tires. The restaurant owner ceremoniously approached the table with a complimentary magnum of champagne. He poured everyone's glass full and proposed a toast to the honor of Mom and Dad. The violins played a melodic overture as I tried in vain, still suspended off my chair between my two aunts, to reach my cherry soda to join in the toast. No way, it wasn't going to happen. There was just too much of my aunts holding me fast. I didn't even get close. I was reduced to a bodiless little arm and hand, sticking out in an odd direction from between Wilma and Alice, which randomly and aimlessly waved around just above the table. The same thing had happened to Robert except whereas my outstretched arm and hand waved in the air above the table his outstretched arm and hand had gotten stuck under the table. I could just barely hear his hand thumping and bumping upward against the wood of the bottom of the table in a futile effort to reach his drink.

Aunt Wilma came to an abrupt halt completely out of balance. As she started to lean she awkwardly lurched forward to catch her balance. To keep her weight from getting the best of her and sending her face first into the tabletop, her left leg pushed out hard and fast against my already-straining marble sock. It barely held. I tried to reach my marbles through my suit coat pocket but Wilma's leg was fat, flat and heavy against my own which prevented me from even touching my marbles let alone affecting a rescue. I broke out in a real soaking sweat as Wilma pressed towards Alice and Alice leaned towards Wilma.

The building pressure proved to be too much of a burden for the rubber band holding my marble sock in place. It snapped in half and slapped hard against my upper thigh. I winced in muffled pain. Panic flooded my eyes, as I pleadingly looked to Robert for help only to see him being crushed and mangled as he disappeared into the ample arm and breast folds of Aunts Jane and Lucy.

The music stopped again as the owner stepped up to the table and flamboyantly commanded everyone's attention and proposed "a toast to Mr. and Mrs. Archer on their many wonderful years of marriage!" At that moment I briefly pondered the thought of not surviving the celebration to see the end of the evening. I accidentally found and raised my glass for the toast but I was still just an arm and hand sticking out from between my aunts holding a glass of cherry soda. Robert's still empty drink hand still randomly bumped against the bottom of the table. The final toast proved to be the last straw. Wilma and Alice, caught in the climactic drunken emotion of the moment, put the final big squeeze on me. The owner raised his glass and called out the toast.

"Salute!"

Wilma and Alice were goners as they cried their response with the rest of the table and other nearby restaurant patrons as well with a resounding toast.

"Salute!"

The struggle had ended. I'd been mauled like a soft plastic whiffle ball being rolled around between two expanding bags of densely packed foam rubber. The simultaneous inward and downward pressure of Aunt Wilma's leg was just too much to endure. In the seconds of silence of the last toast, as everyone downed their champagne, my marble sock gave up and exploded at the seams. Twenty of my best, chosen just for the occasion, flew down onto the waxed hardwood plank floor like twelve gauge buckshot fired from a shotgun at pointblank range, shattering the sanctity of the moment.

I was held helpless and hapless as Wilma and Alice knocked back their drinks and pressed in on me like I was a lone piece of thin cut salami sliding between two giant loaves of bread. Dad finished his drink without a clue but Mom, even after all of the alcohol, registered instant recognition of the all-too-familiar sound. She hesitated just long enough for me to notice and then finished her drink. My arm was still aimlessly waving around in the air. Robert's hand had stopped bumping against the bottom of the table. It was still blocked under the table but he'd given up trying.

Putting her glass down along with everyone else (except me, because I could not) she glanced at me from the corner of her eye. I wasn't able to avoid Mom's brief stare as her focused gaze burned a pinpoint hole right between my eyes. My rotund aunts, unknowingly, held me firmly in place like a target nailed to the wall. The only sound to be heard throughout the entire restaurant was the twenty lost marbles bouncing and rolling their own celebration of freedom to all the far corners of the dining room. The headwaiter, caught unaware, saved the moment and broke the awkward silence.

"Dinner is served!" he proudly and timely announced.

A dinner served was a dinner to be eaten so Aunts Wilma and Alice centered themselves on their chairs and on the plates of food in front of them. It was relief at last as I sat back, unmolested, and took long deep breaths, wiped my face with my handkerchief and glanced around the room trying to get a fix on the last known position of each of the twenty wayward marbles. I halfheartedly picked at my food during dinner as Mom threw cautionary and sometimes threatening glances in my direction, just daring me to get up from the table and start crawling around on the floor to collect my lost treasures. For the remainder of the evening she managed to say only three words to me.

"Eat your dinner."

I did.

As the evening progressed and first the salad course was consumed, then the soup course, then main courses and then dessert with coffee, Mom's anger had finally subsided, probably due to the lingering aftereffects of that night's alcohol consumption. Dad, for his part, remained blissfully ignorant, having never really comprehended what had actually happened. Robert, also freed from his pressing fleshy restraints, offered his unspoken sympathies from across the table. He patted the baseball cards through his suit jacket as if to suggest that I might consider a quieter, less disruptive avocation.

When the meal drew to a close and we prepared to leave for home, our waiter delivered all of the requested doggy bags to family and relatives. Fortunately, during the short wait between getting up from the table and the delivery of the assigned leftovers, our loving aunts and uncles were just too full, too tired and too drunk to re-indulge in unbridled expressions of affection. Still low in spirits over losing my marbles, the headwaiter approached me with a small white doggy bag. I'd nervously finished my entire meal, thinking it might be my last, so I wasn't expecting any leftovers. Formally and politely, he approached and bent forward.

"I believe these are yours young sir," he said as he lightly jiggled the small white paper bag.

To my elation and relief all twenty of my marbles had been recovered. The evening wasn't a total loss after all. It wasn't necessary for Mom to do any of the apologizing and thanking this time as, all on my own, without prodding or prompting, I did so most profusely and sincerely. The headwaiter managed a slight smile as he lightly patted me on the head. Dad watched all this with an expression of mild bewilderment.

During the drive home Mom sat snug and tight right next to Dad in the front seat like a couple of kids on their way home from the *Junior Prom*. Robert and I spread out and lounged in the back seat, with the rear windows down just a bit letting in the cool night air as we savored all of the unrestricted breathing room. Dad had consumed several cups of strong black coffee with his dessert before getting behind the wheel for the drive home, ensuring that he was wide-awake during his somewhat impaired driving. Cruising through the dark cool night, headed for home, Robert once again sorted through his baseball cards while I possessively fondled my reclaimed treasures. He looked across the back seat, recognizing the familiar sound of rolling marbles and with a sigh, shook his head.

"Geez, you were lucky this time," he whispered.

It is often said that to forgive is divine. Luckily for me, my parents' inclinations towards forgiveness, divine or otherwise, took a back seat to the necessary preoccupation of recouping from hangovers the following day. Nagging headaches and slightly sour stomachs took precedence over pursuing and rehashing the events of the night before. I spent that day lying low, remaining almost invisible as I planned and practiced future marble-playing strategies. It was just a scant two weeks later, that I put my mother, unintentionally, to the final test. She, justifiably, almost lost the faith – in me, that is.

It was the ten a.m. Sunday morning service at *Light of the Lord Lutheran Church.* Pastor Crossmann was plowing (and I mean whipping the horses) his way through one of his hour-long "fire and damnation" sermons. Pastor, normally a calm, quiet, pleasant man of the cloth, would really let his hair down when it came to getting out the word on "hell and damnation." Mom, Robert and I were sitting in the family's usual location, a centrally located pew on the right side of the church just off the center aisle. Mom was sitting on the aisle, Robert was next, and then me; the rest of the pew was empty.

As was usual, Robert brought to church a small, concealed stack of baseball cards and I carried a Sunday quality doubled-up dress sock of marbles double-knotted to my belt. This was our normal Sunday church service routine. There was no history of or any anticipated issues as several past church services had been attended so outfitted without incident. Just another Sunday morning to get through before heading home to comfortable clothes, a plate of jelly filled frosted pastry and then a late, leisurely Sunday lunch.

Seated right behind us on that particular Sunday was the sporadically church-attending Snuezzer family. They were notorious in the congregation for living up to their name and regularly having six of their seven family members fall asleep during the sermon. That Sunday service was no exception as the only wakeful Snuezzer was the baby of the family, Rebecca. Rebecca was always wide awake and raring to go. She wasn't actually a baby. She was a rambunctious four-year-old who came to life as the rest of her family napped. While the Snuezzers slept away the sermon, Rebecca would play away the sermon. She crawled around at will; uncorrected and unescorted, roaming freely wherever her little legs would carry her. The sleeping Snuezzers all sort of leaned in on one another as they drifted off into Sunday morning dreamland. Miraculously, the rest of the Snuezzer family, in unison, would routinely awaken right on cue as the sermon would end with a final "Amen." Rebecca, immune to the sleep dust that drenched her family, freely walked, talked and visited about the church as she saw fit.

On previous Sundays Rebecca undertook all sorts of exploratory adventures that included discovering her mother's makeup and altering her appearance with liberally applied layers of powder, rouge and lipstick, which resulted in her looking like she'd been standing too near a cosmetics factory explosion. The church service would always include a choral interlude in which Rebecca frequently demonstrated her exuberance in assisting the choir by singing along and wavering her arms about while standing next to the director. Luckily for Rebecca and the Snuezzer family, most of the regularly attending congregation understood the circumstances that allowed Rebecca her church service freedom and would, as the situation required, go out of their way to assist and keep tabs on the wandering and energetic little girl.

It was not at all unusual for Rebecca to go visiting some of the other nice people in church as her family slept and the Pastor preached. One of her favorite rituals was to go sneaking away by crawling around on all fours on the church floor under the pews, popping up here and there between peoples' legs and the like. You could hear the toes of her hard-soled shoes as they tapped and bumped the floor. It was during one of the Pastor's sermons where he took a respite from the "hell and damnation" tract and spoke of Jesus' call to the children to come unto him. As Crossmann spread his arms and lowered his gaze from on high down onto the congregation before him, with the smile of grace and continence upon his face, Rebecca obliged, right on cue, by popping out from under the front pew right in front of the pulpit.

"Here I am!" she giggled and waved.

On that particular Sunday morning the Snuezzer family awoke, right on cue, only to discover the youngest Snuezzer waving and calling to them from the arms of old Mrs. Frunkstadt fifteen pews to the front.

On the Sunday morning in question, Rebecca was juggling and tossing objects around the back of the church. As the remainder of the Snuezzer family sleepily piled up against one another Rebecca discovered that she greatly enjoyed the heft and feel of the church hymnals. She seemed to especially like the way the book felt as she swung it back and forth in the air in front of her. This was all going on right behind us in the next pew back. If I'd paid closer attention, I would have felt the slight breeze as the waving hymnal wafted past the back of my head.

Pastor Crossmann was in his element, really going at it. He

was leading the charge, shouting into the church's PA system with all the enthusiasm of a General from heaven calling his holy troops forward into battle against the undead hordes of hell! His zeal for the subject transformed him from a gentle man into an unapologetic raving madman who literally spit his words out over everyone sitting in the first two pews. You'd sort of hunker down and cringe as he worked his way to the finish.

Mom was paying her proper and respectful attention, cringing a bit herself at the onslaught, despite her familiarity with the Pastor's loud devotion to the subject. It wasn't uncommon during such self-righteous harangues for Robert and I to retreat and contract terminal cases of "we've heard this all before" boredom-induced sleepiness. The materialization of Satan himself along with hordes of evil unknowns, right there in church, couldn't have brought either of us back to full alert consciousness. Looking toward Robert I noticed that his left hand closely held his *Milwaukee Brave Warren Spahn* card that he'd slipped from concealment in his suit coat sleeve. With a hymnal cleverly covering his activities he was reading the major league history of that esteemed player.

Trying to decide between various distracting and entertaining diversions of my own, I reached beneath my suit coat and very cautiously grabbed hold of my marble sock. My eyelids started their heavy downward slide to a complete close when Pastor Crossmann boomed out, shouting full force into the PA system, that "the Devil, that Evil, could enter into our lives at any moment!" For effect, he stretched out the pronunciation of the words "at – any – moment." Just as the letter "t" on the end of "moment" left his lips, Rebecca dropped her hymnal flat on the floor. The resounding BANG was like a gunshot that echoed throughout the church. Everyone bolted upright in their seats, including Pastor Crossmann, who stood rigid with his complexion having gone white as school paste. Crossmann froze in the pulpit with a terrified look on his face as though he suspected, just for a moment, that his over-exuberance had in fact caused the Devil himself to materialize right then and there in the Church to accept the challenge for holy vs. unholy battle.

I was not spared as the bang of the falling book hitting the tile floor went off right behind me. My eyes popped wide-open at the moment of book-floor impact. I could not help but notice the Pastor's shocked white face with mouth agape and eyes wide-open as well. I thought for sure that if I turned around at that moment a leering slimy serpent from hell would be preparing to snap me up in its claws and take a big bite out of me for almost falling asleep in church, a minor but always believed-to-be-forgivable breach of faith.

   During those tense, silent moments that followed the only sounds to be heard were Rebecca's cooing as she crawled down onto the floor, her shoes banging against the hardwood pew, as she reclaimed the dropped hymnal. The sleeping members of the Snuezzer family rested unaffected. The instantly accumulated tension slowly dissipated. Everyone in the church relaxed with a series of little sighs and under-the-breath chuckles as the color of a living person returned to Pastor Crossmann's face. The image of a toothy dragon faded from my mind. I reassured myself that even if it were so, the Devil would have his grasping claws and fanged maw more than full devouring the more deserving Snuezzer family for all their unrepentant during-the-sermon napping.

   To bring a final, settled calm to my shaking body, I again turned to my marbles and gave them a quick reassuring squeeze. But after a few seconds the conclusion was clear that the "quick squeeze" solution just wasn't going to do the trick. Daringly, but ever so carefully, I untied the two knots which held the marble sock closed and to my belt and daintily placed it in the space between my legs, resting it quietly on the wooden pew beneath my own copy of the church hymnal. Robert spied my move and gave me a hefty elbow jab in the ribs, looking at me as if I'd gone completely nuts! I elbowed him back and gave him my best "mind your own business" stare. I congratulated myself for having kept the situation well in hand.

   Working as unobtrusively as possible, I managed to get three of my marbles out of the sock and into my right hand, well hidden under the hymnal on my lap.

   "Oh, though I walk through the Valley of Death..." Pastor

Crossmann was letting it all out as he closed in on the really gutsy part of the sermon.

He became so animated, so agitated, that I cringed from the sheer force of his voice. His unceasing torrent of pious words also stirred Rebecca into a religious fervor of her own. She stood on the pew directly behind me. Using both of her little hands she swung her copy of the hymnal back and forth in the air in front of her and just behind my head. Crossmann's words blasted out from his ever-widening mouth like verbal mortar shells. I grabbed my marble sock and lifted it closer to my chest, still hidden behind the hymnal.

The Pastor was reaching a deafening crescendo; the artillery shells of salvation landed and exploded all around us causing the stained glass windows to shake-and-rattle in their frames. As I squinted through my eye slits at Pastor Crossmann, my face and body absorbing the verbal shock waves, I expected at any moment that Crossmann's head would fly off into the air with a resounding POP! Pastor's face became a deep crimson as in one final all-powerful God-fearing gesture he pounded the podium of the pulpit.

"The material greediness of mankind is the root of all evil in the world!" was his shouted admonition to all the parishioners.

Just as Crossmann pounded the pulpit Rebecca responded in kind with a wordless shriek of her own. Simultaneous to the Preacher's shout and the yell of the kid, Rebecca's swinging hymnal cracked me one square across the back of the head. With the loud WHACK all I saw were tiny balls of light bouncing and bursting before my eyes as I involuntarily relinquished the firm grip I'd had on my marbles. Hell's fires licked at my feet. My sock of marbles completely emptied itself over the hardwood pew and then down onto the hard tile floor. Blinking, tiny little stars ridden by even tinier sparkling little angels shimmered before my eyes with every bounce and crack of a marble hitting the floor. Mom, unable to convince me on her own, had called upon God himself for assistance in delivering the final blow. The slimy dragon devil that waited to devour the Snuezzer family as the main course would have, no doubt, appeared with an updated menu that listed me as a very recently added dessert.

Pastor Crossmann stopped dead in his verbal tracks. The silence in church was only interrupted by the bouncing, rolling marbles and the squeals of delight coming from Rebecca who scrambled around on the floor chasing and collecting the beautiful crystal balls. Half-blind, cross-eyed and my ears still ringing from the blow, I slowly gathered the presence of mind to chance a sideways glance towards Mom. Ice. She looked straight ahead. Her face was as cold, solid and expressionless as the gravestones in the churchyard cemetery. Her eyes were a dead blank gray with little red streaky veins.

Robert, I sensed, did not appreciate for a moment his precarious position. He found himself, through no fault of his own, helplessly stuck between a ton of explosives and the detonating device that had just sent the charge to the powder. Pastor Crossmann recovered with a rousing "Amen." The congregation responded in kind with an "Amen" of their own; Rebecca repeatedly giggled several "Amens" in a row as she crawled along the floor chasing, collecting and then re-dropping as many of my lost marbles as she could possibly get her hands-on to the strains of the closing hymn organ music.

The service came to a close and the Snuezzer family awoke in unison refreshed from an hour's deep sleep. Mom still hadn't acknowledged that anything had happened except for her ominous silence. Wiping the sleep from their eyes, everyone unpiling from leaning against and on top of one another, the Snuezzers were astonished to discover their very own little Rebecca sitting in her place in the pew with her hands and lap full of marbles. As the service ended and the usher excused the Snuezzer family from their pew, Rebecca, from her father's arms, re-dropped several of my marbles back onto the floor in the main aisle.

It was our turn next as the usher stepped up to our pew. While slowly walking from the church hall proper, I tried to bend down and retrieve a few of the rolling strays that Rebecca was leaving behind, only to discover that I was unable to execute such movement. Mom's left hand was firmly in place around the back of my neck just under my suit coat collar, holding me stiffly erect, almost on my tiptoes. The only voluntary movement available to me was upright and straight-forward.

I'd really "stepped in it" and that was tough to do because you wouldn't think that anyone, especially a little kid, could ever find something like "it" to step into inside of a church. But I miraculously not only found "it" in the most unlikely of places, I found a whole bunch of holy "it" and I managed to hit the bull's-eye and land right in the center of the biggest pile of "it" ever, right up to my neck! There was always the definite possibility that all the "it" I found myself in was not really "native" to the church environment but had been something I was inadvertently and unknowingly dragging around behind me for sometime. On that Sunday, unfortunately, "it" had been innocently dragged into church by me and my marble sock and came to rest right under the pew where I was sitting. So – come to think of it, that might have had something to do with the deep "it" mess I found myself in at that moment.

We exited the church hall and stepped to the side in the entrance-exit foyer and waited for the rest of the departing congregation to file out. During the wait I was put on public disgrace display for all the passersby. Several of the exiting parishioners cast looks in my direction, some in sympathy and some with mild rebuke. We were the last to leave as we most humbly approached Pastor Crossmann who'd taken up his end-of-service position wishing all of his departing flock a pleasant day with handshakes and pats on the shoulders. The whole time we spent waiting and watching the others pass, Mom hadn't utter a single solitary word. She stepped up to the good Pastor with me in tow by the collar. Mom complimented him on another rousing and inspiring sermon. Then, pausing for a moment, Mom gathered her thoughts and shifted her icy gaze down to me. She calmly apologized and asked forgiveness on my behalf for the disturbance I'd created during the service.

Crossmann was an understanding man. He lowered himself to one knee before me and gently grasped me by the shoulders with his large hands. He graciously used the opportunity to suggest, in a most Fatherly tone, that I take the words of the sermon (less all the shouting and spitting, I assumed) to heart and not put too much stock into material possessions, within or without the confines of the church walls. I felt like a losing investor in the afterlife receiving an inside tip from my personal soul broker.

As the Pastor rose to stand, that Sunday's head usher came forward and returned to me several marbles he'd managed to collect from Rebecca and retrieve off of the floor. He returned them to me by offering them up in one of the Church's collection plates. He apologized for not being able to return them all as little Rebecca refused, with some amount of fuss, to give up most of the little treasures that she'd managed to collect. A compromise had been negotiated and Rebecca walked away with seven of my best to keep as her very own. I thanked the kind usher for his efforts and then, with head bowed, thanked Pastor Crossmann for his understanding and his kind words of advice and wisdom.

Even after the dispensation of reprieve granted by Pastor Crossmann, the situation between Mom and me was touchy, unresolved. She didn't offer up a single word in my direction. The drive home was dead silent. Even the car somehow managed to not make its normal moving car noises. Creepy. Mom was at the wheel, Robert rode shotgun and I sat firmly and quietly in the back seat against the door directly behind my brother. I'd momentarily contemplated concealing my shame by covering my head and shoulders with the small car blanket we kept folded on the back seat. But I decided against it as I felt it too obvious an act of contrition which would have invited further and unnecessarily angry rebuke. Mom's temporary vow of silence had all of the earmarks of a ticking time bomb. I nervously contemplated, much like an explosives expert, risking an attempt to defuse the explosive device. Which was it, the red wire or the green wire? Who knew which one to cut? Not me! When would somebody just shout, "FORGET IT, RUN?" I suspected that if I made one false move, the resulting blast would've separated me from my marbles for sometime well into the future.

We pulled into the driveway and I swung my door open fast and wide, even before the car had come to a full stop. I leapt out and ran for the house. I figured that I was going to catch it from

Mom for certain and then probably from Dad as well. I burst into the house through the back door ready to make the twenty odd steps up the stairs and to my room in ten or less long bounding strides, only to come across Dad's legs and feet sticking out from under the kitchen sink blocking my way. Scattered around on the floor was an array of wrenches, hammers, screwdrivers and an uncoiled plumber's snake that sprawled out and over the kitchen floor like a giant sprung watch spring.

To appease Mom for not joining us at church that morning (good thing), he'd volunteered to wash the morning's breakfast dishes and generally tidy up about the house. Unfortunately, Dad's good intentions were rewarded with a clogged kitchen drain as the dirty dish water stood motionless, greasy and cold in the sink. His efforts to figure out and remove the clog had been unsuccessful up to the point of my entering the kitchen. I bent down and stuck my head in under the sink to see how things were progressing as Mom and Robert entered through the back door. The stern face Mom had been steadfastly modeling and her reasons for maintaining it were momentarily forgotten when she found Dad hard at work under the sink. All the assorted cans and boxes of stuff normally stored in the cabinet under the sink were stacked and scattered on the floor among the tools and uncoiled metal drain snake. Dad used his automotive troubleshooting light-on-a-cord for the job that when combined with all the other stuff on the floor, made the space under the sink look like the opening to a mine shaft. I took the opportunity to slink away to my room to collect my thoughts and change clothes.

The time alone in my room afforded a break in the tension and allowed me the time to consider a plan of action, a good defense, an appropriate response to all of the probing, hostile and accusatory questions that I was certain would soon be at hand. To be more honest and more to the point, I used the time to dream up as many cockeyed excuses and reasonable sounding reasons as to why I should be forgiven and not dealt with to severely. Heck, if Pastor Crossmann was willing to let bygones be bygones and he'd forgiven me right there in church where it had all happened right in front of God and everybody else, well, hey, problem solved, right? Besides, I'd suffered the pain and sacrifice of watching as some little girl walked away with seven of my best after smacking me across the back of the head with a church book! I'd been marble mugged right there in church! However, reluctantly, with all things considered, I concluded that reprieve was not likely. Realizing that there would be no easy way out I resolved to ride out the coming storm and get back into marble action as soon as able, as soon as allowed.

Feeling confident and self-assured, convinced that I could handle the whole mess and anticipated likely outcomes as well as could be expected, I left the quiet confines of my room and descended the stairs, ready for anything except for that which awaited me. As I reentered the kitchen, Dad grunted from under the sink that he'd most likely located the troublesome clog and that everything would be back to proper plumbing working order in a minute or two.

Robert and I dropped to our hands and knees to get a better look and in the process almost fell over each other right onto Dad's unprotected stomach. We were each vying for the best possible position so as to not miss seeing any of the neat glop that was sure to come slipping, sliding and plopping out of the clogged pipe. Mom stood by just the same out of a sense of duty and loyalty to her husband's hard work and aggravation. Fixing the plumbing would have been Dad's job anyway but doing the dishes and cleaning up in the kitchen was not. It was a real unexpected effort on Dad's part deserving of my mother's gratitude and continued presence, despite her aversion to the possible presence and display of any kind of slippery slime covered glop.

Dad was huffing and puffing that one more turn of the monkey wrench would do the trick as he asked Robert for the empty metal bucket from the top of the sink. Dad placed the pail under the pipe joint and backed out from under the sink to a kneeling position on the floor between Robert and myself. Mom bent down over Dad's right shoulder with a frightful wince on her face in anticipation of witnessing something really disgusting falling from the open drainpipe and slopping into the waiting bucket.

Dad cranked the pipe's restraining nut the final turn, the pipe seal popped and, sure enough, some of the meanest looking slop I'd ever seen came gurgling out of the pipe. Mom gave a sigh and turned her head as the dirty water poured and splashed into the bucket. Then, suddenly, disgustingly, unbelievably, it wasn't just greasy water falling out of the drainpipe. For the next agonizing seconds, with the help of the cold dirty water reservoir in the sink above, several (forgotten? misplaced?) Cat's-Eye marbles from my collection passed through the refracting beams of light from the trouble-shooting lamp.

My initial reaction was of total mind-numbing disbelief and body-freezing shock, sure in that moment that my eyes were playing terrible tricks on me, possibly a lingering adverse aftereffect of the whack on the head in church. But the telltale sound of marbles banging into each other and bouncing off the rounded interior sides of the metal pail was conclusive proof that that Sunday was not going to be one of my better days. I sensed, I felt the quizzical (Dad), shocked (Robert) and disappointed (guess who) stares from three pairs of eyes as I fought the temptation, the urge, to just end it all right then and there, under the sink, by sticking my head into the bucket of glop; marbles, dirty dishwater and all – and drowning myself.

"I should have guessed," Mom sighed.

The look on her face was, well – indescribable.

Much to my dismay and bewilderment, all of that "it" I'd inadvertently brought along with me to church just a short time before hadn't been all of the total "it" I'd had available to drag around. As I and the rest of my family discovered, apparently, I had sufficient amounts of extra "it" to have left one big invisible chunk of "it" behind in the kitchen that morning which had just become visible in the bucket under the sink. Unfortunately, my unprepared and unsuspecting father had spent the good part of a Sunday morning sorting out the resulting complications of my residual "it" which had found its way into the kitchen plumbing.

The drainpipe was down to just dripping one drop at a time when Dad reached in under the sink for the collection bucket. There, mixed in with the glop, slime and dirty water the marbles responsible for the clog could be plainly seen. They all pointed their little Cat's-Eyes right at me. The water in the bucket made them look as if they'd been crying unconsoled, drowning in their own tears of disappointment and rage. They were members of the same batch that I'd scattered in the movie house a few months before. I'd washed them in the kitchen sink in accordance with Mom's wishes along with several others from my collection that also needed a good bath at the time. Obviously, and much to my personal embarrassment and consternation, I'd missed retrieving more than a few from the soapy water and they'd ended up going down the drain with the leftover suds.

 The wet marbles leered at me from the bottom of the bucket as they had their revenge for having spent several weeks in the dark dirty drain. It was as if they found out what had happened in church an hour before and decided to take advantage of the situation and piled on to finish me off. I reached the point of wondering exactly how much more Sunday morning "it" one little boy could handle! "It" had become as insidious and as dangerous as a communicable disease which had already, in one morning and within a matter of minutes, infected both my mother and my father and had rendered my innocent bystander brother speechless and suffering all the detectable effects of shell-shock.

 Those same little marbles had more than played their part and taken their share of nicks and scratches while making me the school's youngest marble champ and first grade celebrity. They repaid me for the shabby treatment they endured due to my carelessness. It momentarily occurred to me that maybe that was how my mother felt when my marbles started bouncing around in church. She'd gotten me started, helped me along and stood by me through some tough marble times. It struck me square in the face that I'd repaid her kindness, patience and understanding by letting her faith and trust in me slip into a dark and gloppy drain.

 It wasn't until the next morning at breakfast, after a very restless night, with Mom at her end of the table and me in my regular place that she finally decided to clear the air. Dad and Robert sat in their regular spots as well and each hid behind sections of the morning newspaper. Both had taken protective refuge in anticipation of the approaching storm front that by the look of the dark clouds had dangerous potential indeed. But if Mom "went-off", hiding behind thin newspaper as close as they were to the potential epicenter of the explosion would have been useless. The only other living-breathing member of the family was our cat and he'd taken-off and was hiding somewhere as far from the kitchen as possible with at least three solid walls and two partially closed hardwood paneled doors protecting his secluded position.

Mom's face took on, unexpectedly, a more familiar and recognizable tone, maybe a little warmer and compassionate than I expected or deserved but then again, maybe not. What I expected, deserved and hoped for, in matching order were; marble confiscation, forty lashes or a total pardon with a large serving of loving forgiveness tossed in.

The kitchen was quieter that morning than it would have been if no one were there. It was as if even the various kitchen appliances sensed impending conflict and doom and had voluntarily shutdown and retreated into their respective piping, compressors and circuitry. If the toaster on the kitchen counter had little arms and legs it would have unplugged itself and climbed up into the cupboard, closed the cabinet door and hid in the back behind a stack of dinner plates. The strained and intense silence clung to everything and everybody like the egg yolk that clung to the bacon on my plate. I knew that Mom was going to start in on me momentarily as I listlessly picked at my breakfast. Who could've eaten at a time like this? Well, maybe Toby "Tubby" Wilson could've, but not me, that was for certain.

"Mike, let's talk," Mom started.

"Okay," I whispered back as I put my fork down and picked a yolk-covered piece of toast from its resting place on my school pants.

Dad and Robert, suspecting that the moment was at hand, raised their respective sections of newspaper a little higher and a little closer to their faces in an effort to remain as invisible and as uninvolved as possible. Only their knuckles were showing. "What a couple of chickens," I thought to myself. I redirected my eyes back to my mother for our mom-to-boy talk. Her facial expression was...puzzling. She looked like she was either going to break down and cry or leap across the length of the table and grab me by the throat. It was the look of a person who was undecided, at an emotional crossroad, still making up her mind, waiting for one impulse to win out over the other. Decision made, she spoke (and didn't leap).

"Mikey, please, when we have places to go, like church, eating out, do not bring your marbles with you. You can have them in the car, but leave them there. Look, I know it's going to be hard, a big sacrifice, but believe me, you and your marbles will be all right even though they are not tied to your belt twenty-four hours a day. To me, to your father (Dad pulled his paper aside and winked at me) and to your brother (Robert pulled his paper aside so only I could see and made a really stupid face) you're the best. To us you're the champ. Okay?"

"Okay," was my response with a slight cracking in my voice.

That was it. That's all she said. No yelling, no screaming, crying, ranting, raving, no name calling, threats, hitting or anything of the like. Just a calm, correct and reasonable request presented as loving advice. The menacing storm front had dissipated into a steady and refreshing cool clean breeze. All the kitchen equipment had come back to a quiet, just under the noise radar, normal humming operation. Even Kit Cat had run back into the kitchen at a paw thumping gallop and took a familiar position at his food dish. Stability had been reestablished. Dad and Robert were as pleasantly surprised as I was. Marbles, surprisingly, in the most trying and difficult of circumstances could invite understanding and inspire...compassion.

It worked. Any and all leftover situational "it" that could have circumstantially materialized over time in the presence of my mother had dispersed and evaporated. I never dropped my marbles to the bother or embarrassment of my mother ever again. Dad, on the other hand, well – that was something else altogether.

*

***

Chapter Three:
A Father's Ordeal

MY DAD WAS next. Neither one of us had and inkling, the slightest clue, of what he was in for. It must be understood and remembered that there was no list, no plan on my part, as to whom, when or where anyone would find themselves speeding down hill toward the cliff's edge on a sheet of rolling marbles. I was just a little six-year-old kid living his life, day in and day out, whose obsession had this unfortunate side effect of ensnaring and then dropping those closest to me, unwillingly, dead centered, up to their eyeballs, into one big pile of difficult, albeit unforeseen, inconvenient circumstances.

Dad liked nothing better than to get up extra early on a warm spring Saturday morning, pack up the gear, and head out to his favorite nearby lake for a day of fishing. He'd rent a small boat, pack an "all guys" picnic lunch and make a day of it on the small water. It was sort of a family tradition that Dad would take each of his sons, when he thought they were old enough, on their first Father-and-Son fishing trip. Robert had gone first a few years before and then it was my turn. So, one Saturday, not long after the fishing season had opened, it was Dad and I, just the two of us, hitting the water for a day of nonstop fast fishing action!

We were up at five a.m. and to the lake by six a.m. for a day of eating sandwiches, catching fish, eating Danish and sweet rolls, catching fish, drinking soda pop and catching even more of the big ones! Dad was dressed in all of the latest fisherman's fashions. Rocks may have been his childhood passion but fishing was his adulthood escape. It seemed like he had everything necessary to catch, clean, package, freeze, market, sell and ship a small whale from a rowboat. Thus prepared, we launched our rented ride on the water from an old wooden dock and glided silently through the morning mist and out over the glass-smooth surface of the lake.

All day long we cast spinners and spoons, soaked with floating bobbers with night crawlers and minnows on hooks three feet down, trolled diving plugs and then some more casting with only a modicum of success. By late afternoon we counted five bites, three fish landed and two snags with two lost lures, one gone for good and one recovered. The combined weight of the catch wasn't enough to fill a sardine can. It wasn't exactly minute-by-minute action. By four p.m. that afternoon the sandwiches, Danish, soda pop and candy bars were gone, along with my enthusiasm which dissipated along with the last bag of corn chips. Dad kept up an unceasing flow of encouragement. He refused to give up hope that the elusive "big one" was just one more cast of a lure away just waiting to bite. Boredom overtook me like a spreading, speeding tidal wave.

The bright afternoon sunlight sparkling and dancing off the lake's rippling surface, combined with the gentle, almost imperceptible rocking of the boat, was slowly hypnotizing me to sleep. The excitement of just me and my dad alone together, fighting the big fish on the favorite lake, had taken on water and sunk to the bottom. As the passing shadows of the puffy white clouds drifted over the boat, I decided, in quiet desperation, that I'd have to entertain myself as best I could.

Out came my sock of marbles which, for the occasion, were wrapped inside of a clear plastic bag and hidden in my raincoat pocket. Dad concentrated on unsnagging his bait lure from the oar lock which he'd accidentally hooked for something like the tenth time that day as I unobtrusively rolled a couple of Cat's-Eye boulders into my hand with a murmured sigh of relief. Admittedly, I was an unapologetic marble junkie, a confessed but unrepentant crystal ball-a-hol-ic. Thus fixed, I quietly sat back, enjoyed the balmy weather, the nice lake and sky views and the feel of the lightly rolling marbles in my hand. My boredom blew out and away over the surface of the lake with the light afternoon breeze. But Dad wasn't giving up. He intently and accurately cast around a group of promising looking lily pads just offshore.

It was just my bad luck and Dad's good luck that he finally connected with the ever-elusive "big one" right off the edge of the weeds in shallow water. Dad jerked back hard on his rod to set the hook.

"FISH ON," he called out in an excited, rising, three octave yelp.

To keep us from being pushed by the breeze and drifting out into deeper water Dad quickly ordered the anchor over the side to hold the boat close in to shore. If there was another boat within shouting distance and they heard Dad's surprised, almost panicked call they might have expected to see a father and his son beating off a giant pike that had risen from the depths and was trying to destroy the boat and eat the occupants.

The anchor that came with the boat was of the homemade variety, consisting of a healthy and heavy wad of cured cement in an old metal lard bucket with rope wrapped and knotted around it. It rested in a rat's nest of anchor rope which was piled and tangled on the floor of the boat beneath my feet. When Dad shouted, "anchors away" I jumped to a sitting attention from my reclined resting position. That caused my bag of marbles to fall into the mess of uncoiled anchor rope at my feet. I was fully aware that I'd dropped my marbles into the bottom of the boat but in the excitement their exact location and circumstances were unknown to me. Like a good sailor I hurried to obey the Captain's order and grabbed the heavy bulky anchor and with a grunt of exertion tossed it over the side. The cement-filled lard bucket and knotted rope broke the water's surface with a resounding KER-PLUNK as the explosion of splashing lake water came straight-up and hit me square in the face and soaked the front of my shirt and pants.

The anchor rope swiftly flipped out over the side after the rapidly sinking anchor as I fell back onto the boat seat and quickly lifted my feet to avoid getting tangled up in the whirling rope and going out over the side myself. Although the water we were in at the time was only three to four feet deep and the amount of rope needed for the anchor to reach the bottom was not extreme, it was just enough for trouble. As the five to six feet of anchor rope uncoiled out over the side into the water, along with it catapulted my clear plastic bag of marbles.

I caught the initial stages of the disaster only from my peripheral vision, gaining full frame focus just in time to witness my marbles flying from the open bag, glistening ever so beautifully in the afternoon sun against the blue water backdrop.

"PLOP, PLOP, PLOP" – into the lake they went and dropped towards the sandy bottom. Dad was much too busy and excited, fighting the catch of the day at the end of his line, to have noticed the tragedy that had transpired at my end of the boat. During the man versus fish struggle, I was sure that Dad would, at any moment, lose his balance and either fall headfirst or backwards out of the boat to join my marbles at the bottom of the lake.

In one final grunting acclamation of conquest, Dad brought the exhausted fish to bear and hoisted it from the lake with the landing net. It was a very large small mouth bass. But I'd only been able to catch a glimpse of the closing drama from the corner of my eye. Bent over the side of the boat with my forearms restting on the gunwale and my chin resting on my forearms, I stared into the water, trying to raise my lost treasures from the depths by the power of my mind alone.

Dad was bubbling, burbling and boasting with self-satisfaction for finally having landed the big fish after the big fight! He proudly pulled his prize catch from the net.

"Not bad, eh Mike! Not bad at all! I'd say it was well worth the wait, Yesss-Sirrr, wouldn't you Mike?"

He let loose with a hefty and hearty laugh and admired the large fish. He removed it from the net and held it up by its lower lip for me to admire as well. I glanced back over my shoulder and tried to give my Dad the attention and recognition that he rightfully deserved. Having given the catch the quick once over, my attention was unavoidably drawn to the fish's eyes, glassy and pleading, begging for release, just like the marbles four feet below, also pleading, begging to be rescued as well.

Dad sensed that all was not well at the front of the boat. Not sharing in the excitement of the moment, I slowly replaced my chin to its resting place on my forearm and stared back into the water from the boat rail. Dad's first thought was that all the rich food, bright sun and rocking boat had caught up with me and was taking it toll. The sun was starting to glare down and off the water but my *Red Racer* plastic sunglasses were doing the job intended. True, I'd eaten more junk in the boat that day than I normally would have eaten in a month, but my stomach was keeping it all down without stuff coming up. So I answered Dad's inquiries that I wasn't sick, at least not sick in the way he meant it.

With his waist high rubber waiters belted securely, with fishing hat and multi-pocket fishing vest secured in place, fishing rod in one hand and half-dead bass in the other, Dad walked towards my position at the front of the boat. Dad's sense of balance on dry land was sometimes questionable, but when he walked in a small wobbly rowboat he lurched, leaned and swayed with each tentatively placed step. He went to one knee along side of me as he put down his fishing rod. Still holding the bass with his left hand, Dad leaned forward over the side of the boat and out over the water and tried to locate and ascertain exactly what it was that I was so intently focused on. He stuck his nose right down to the surface of the water as the boat heeled over towards the shore while adjusting his sunglasses to compensate for the glare.

His squinting expression went flat when he recognized the scattered marbles on the sandy bottom. He gave a little grunt, unsteadily stood back up, and mumbled something to the effect that I'd agreed not to be so careless with my marbles. I mumbled back something to the effect that how did he even know they were mine. Maybe I was just looking over the side and spotted them, found them, discovered them lying there under the water on the sand.

Dad sat back down on the boat's middle bench seat, attached the bass to the tied off stringer and tossed the near lifeless fish back into the water for fresh keeping. I started to get a really bad, uneasy feeling about the unfolding situation. A numbing paralysis started at my feet and slowly crept its way up through my body as I continued to stare down into the lake. Dad mumbled again that it was too bad but he wasn't going to take the chance of wading into the lake to collect the lost marbles, whether they were mine or not.

Tired of all the mumbling I responded.

"Why do you have your waders on if you weren't gonna walk in the lake?"

"Losing a few marbles isn't the end of the world. Besides, you've got hundreds more at home just as good if not better than those. I've lost more than a few prize rocks in my day, it's hard, but you'll get over it. Believe me, you can afford to lose a few without the world coming to an end," was my father's insensitive response.

Boy, was he wrong. With marbles, there was no such thing as a small loss. Any loss was big, too big. So he'd lost a few of his prize rocks in his day, so what. If he'd lost some prize rocks in the lake it would have been no big deal. The lake was full of rocks, thousands of rocks. Any lost rocks would have just blended in, felt right at home. No one rowed around the lake and looked down into the water to see thousands of marbles just stacked-up lying around with weeds growing between them and fish swimming over them. Marbles, especially my marbles, didn't belong in the lake, didn't deserve to be left behind. Dad instructed me to cheer up and raise the anchor so we could steam for home. Dad was to have his prize and I was to lose mine? So, that was it? Some rotten deal! I wasn't going to cheer up for him or anyone else ever again, period.

That bad feeling, the paralysis, spread across my entire body and quickly took total control. In fact, I had so much extra bad feeling that the excess was overflowing through my watering eyes and runny nose. With tears streaming out from behind my sunglasses and down my cheeks, dripping from my face into the water and onto my already soaked shirt, I lifted the anchor back into the boat and in the process, unintentionally (intentionally) banged it several times against the side of the boat. All the while I was recalling, believe it or not, one of Pastor Crossmann's sermons about the shepherd who could not rest until he found the one lost lamb from his flock of hundreds.

Dad took up a rowing position and started for open water as I cried a quiet goodbye to my disappearing marbles. I was really getting choked up as Dad continued to make light of the situation which only made it far worse. Every word, every stroke of the oars was another arrow through my heart. We were ten yards out into the lake when I started to sob out loud. It was like we were leaving my brother behind beneath four feet of water without even trying to save him. If it had been my left foot that had fallen off and sank to the bottom of the lake instead of my marbles, Dad's attitude would have been just as cavalier, "don't worry kid, you'll learn to get along without it. Besides, you hav'a good one left so you got nothing to worry about. You'll get a really great set of crutches and after a couple of months, before you know it, you won't even know it's gone. Trust me, you won't even miss it."

At that moment I would have traded my left foot to have my lost marbles safely back in the boat with me. I momentarily fought the urge to just jump out of the boat and go stand in the lake by my marbles until a more sympathetic passerby helped me affect a rescue. I'd never felt worse. Dad just kept rowing until I finally broke. My crying became uncontrollable. All the sniffling, sobbing and choking had become unbearable for my father as well. I wasn't trying to manipulate or guilt my father into helping. I was losing it and falling apart for real.

Dad eventually stopped rowing and sat silently as the boat drifted and coasted over the water for about a minute. Unable to cope with my blubbering emotional disintegration, Dad slowly turned us around and headed back towards the shore. He called out to me over his shoulder to keep watch as we neared our original anchorage. I eagerly hung out over the front of the boat like a bowsprit on a two-masted schooner. My relief was instantaneous as I searched forward to determine the exact spot while my teary eyes and drippy nose started to dry in the breeze.

All during the return trip Dad grumbled and muttered something that I probably didn't want or need to hear, just so much indistinguishable garble that fortunately drifted away from me and out over the back of the boat towards the center of the lake. As we closed in on the shore a cloud crossed in front of the sun making the entire shallow sandy bottom under the boat visible as my sunken marble bag and scattered gems came into clear view. I shouted the find back to Dad who just mumbled and signaled with his hand to once again drop anchor. The cement filled lard bucket went over the side like an explosive launched depth charge. This time the water splash exploding back up into my face felt cool and refreshing on my reddened and puffy eyes and nose.

My father wasn't pleased in the least with the prospect of walking around in the water to find my marbles. Walking around in the lake with a fishing rod in hand while scouting out and casting for fish was one thing, but what he was about to undertake was not exactly that same enjoyable adventure. His aggravation plainly evident, he adjusted and tightened his waders and prepared to disembark from our vessel by sliding over to the side of the boat nearest the shore.

Resolved to get the job done, he resolutely stood up and immediately caught his wader boot toe and almost made a head first entry into the lake. He quickly jerked to a straight-up stance while flapping and waving his arms in his struggling effort to regain his balance. No sir, my dad was none too happy with the turn of events. I had doubts about my dad's ability to rescue anything, including himself if that became necessary. The original idea of a few moments before, where I jumped out of the boat and stood in the lake by my marbles suddenly seemed a plausible and less risky solution. I pictured my dad rowing away as I stood in the lake up to my neck in the water reassuring him not to worry, being certain that something or somebody would have turned up or come along and I would eventually make it out of the lake and safely back home in one piece, marbles and all. Finally stabilized, Dad reached forward and pulled the anchor rope snug and tied it off tightly at the boat rail. Leaning out over the side of the boat he almost stuck his face down into the water in an effort to accurately judge the depth.

Satisfied that the only thing left to do was to get into the water and get it done, Dad rolled up his sleeves and prepared to put his left leg out of the boat and down into the water. Simple enough. Dad ordered me to slide over on my seat to the opposite side of the boat and act as a balancing counterweight. Simple enough. Dad swung his wader covered left leg out over the side and into the water. Simple enough. Ever so slowly and carefully, he searched for the bottom with his left foot. Still pretty simple.

Dad wore glasses which, when combined with the visual distortion created by the water, contributed to his miscalculation of the water's depth. With his wader covered left leg bobbing up and down and around in the lake and his right leg still hooked over the side of the boat, Dad hung in limbo. Suddenly – not so simple.

Confident that the elusive bottom of the lake was only a fraction of an inch blow his probing foot, he'd lowered his left leg just enough for several gallons of cool lake water to rush over the top lip of the boot and into the warm dry wader. Dad yelped in surprise. With a shiver he found himself precariously stuck half-in and half-out, half-wet and half-dry. Suddenly, it all became very...complicated. He clung to the side of the boat momentarily at a loss as to what his next move should be. He dangled there for a while as he looked at me, then looked into the water, then looked back at me again. Helpless to lend a hand, I had to stay put on the opposite side of the boat for balance and to keep us from taking on water.

Summoning the resolve to carry on and finish what he'd started, both of his white knuckled hands gripping the side of the boat, he forced his right leg over the side and into the water as well. But, not having his right wader full of water like the left proved to be another frustrating turn of events as the more buoyant right leg kept trying to float to the surface. First it floated up in back of him, then it floated up to his right and then it floated up under the boat to his front as the toe of the air-bloated wader boot knocked on the bottom of the boat. Feeling giddy, light headed, due to the pending marble rescue, I fought the cruel urge to look down at the floor of the boat and say "come in." If that had slipped out the matter at hand would have no doubt been decided and I definitely would have found myself out of the boat, standing in the lake by my marbles, with the likelihood of rescue dependent upon the benevolence of passing strangers with me eventually making my own way back home some indeterminate number of hours or days into the future.

Dad looked like some modern dancer doing his warm up exercises. All the time this was going on he was "oooing", "eeeing" and "aahhhing" as he tried in vain to gain control of his bobbing right leg. Listing hard to the left, with one final effort, he forced his right leg down into the lake as it also immediately took on water and rapidly filled to the top. It sounded like bath water going down the bathtub drain as my father cringed with chilled discomfort. Both of his water-logged waders went to the bottom as cold water flowed up-and-over his waist soaking his regular pants.

Determined to complete the unplanned excursion into the lake, with both water weighted feet planted firmly on the sandy bottom; Dad endured the cool water gently rippling up against his wet clothing at bellybutton height as he let go of the side of the boat. I immediately shifted my position back to the shore side of the boat and put my face down to the surface of the water and timidly started pointing out the locations of my submerged marbles. Simultaneously Dad waded through the lake with his face an inch or so above the water, his hands cupped around his eyes to reduce the sun glare as he approached the rescue site. The scattered marbles rested within a condensed two square yard area. Dad slowly tracked down, reached for and recovered my lost marbles, one at a time. To add to his considerable discomfort, every time he'd reach down into the lake the water would soak through his rolled up shirt and jacket sleeves and leak down his sides.

It took a full fifteen minutes and one wet, physically and mentally exhausted father to affect a total recovery. I could not disguise or restrain my relief despite Dad's misery as he returned to the side of the boat and handed over all of the lost marbles and the marble bag as well. I was one sad shepherd made happy again as the flock was safe and complete. I thanked my dad for his help. With obvious effort he managed one of those "if you weren't my kid" type smiles.

Mission accomplished, Dad had to get back into the boat. Still smoldering under the by-then soaking wet collar about the whole wet rescue situation, he wasn't thinking to clearly when he grabbed the side of the boat and tried to dead lift himself up and over the side and back into the boat. It wasn't going to happen, at least not that way. The problem was his water filled waders. As soon as they were even partially above the lake surface his legs looked like bulging balloons from the weight of the trapped water. Discouraged and disgusted that the ordeal continued, he slipped back into the lake and prepared for another try. I thought I saw steam forming just above the water around my dad. He was really miffed. He wanted to be done and back in the boat. If a giant musky had mistakenly swum by and accidentally bumped into him he would have grabbed it by its big back fin, lifted it out of the water, punched it in the snout and then thrown the knocked out fish up onto shore.

    For his next try Dad gave it all he had with one big lurching pull. He propelled himself out of the water and flopped belly first into the boat with his legs still hanging out over the side and his feet dangling in the lake. I leaned out over the other side of the boat as far as I dared without falling in myself and struggled to keep us from listing too far and taking on more water than we already had sloshing around in the bottom of the boat. Dad's face was bright red, flushed from exertion as he fought to maintain the position he'd gained on the boat rail.

    With an angry BARK he whipped his legs up out of the water and into the air and went directly into a momentary handstand in the center of the boat. The small water craft rocked and rolled as his full waders emptied in a rushing gush all over my acrobatic, upside down father and into the bottom of the boat. He gasped for air as water poured down over his face and into his mouth and nose. Dad lost his balance as the swaying boat shifted his momentum backwards. With another loud BARK, Dad flipped from his handstand right out and over the other side of the boat and back into the lake, completing his unanticipated and far-from-Olympic quality somersault.

    It was bad for my Dad. I sat there with mouth agape as the situation unraveled right before my eyes, a situation for which I was prepared to accept full responsibility, as if that would've actually meant something. Fortunately the water was not deep enough to be dangerous to the well being of my father. He was much more dangerous to himself at that moment. I pictured myself, after several unsuccessful reentry attempts, rowing us back to the boat landing out across the lake with my Dad securely nestled in a life preserver ring at the end of a long towrope.

Dad popped right back up to the surface, gasping for air, and angrily thrashed his way through the water and back around to the shore side of the boat. The previous milder sounds of discontent and discomfort had transformed into indiscernible vocalizations the likes of which I never heard him (or anyone else) ever make then or since. The thought of suggesting that he should simply consider grabbing hold of the boat's anchor rope and walking the boat to shore just feet away occurred to me. He could've climbed back in from there, pushed off and we'd have been on our way, simple enough, problem solved. That wasn't going to happen either because "simple enough" would not do. He wordlessly motioned to me to stay put in my seat and keep still and most certainly keep silent. I did.

Determined as ever, my father was going to get back into the boat his way, on his terms, regardless of the consequences or other, more logically available options. Once again he firmly grasped the side of the boat and decided to re-enter the same way he'd originally exited, one leg at a time. I ventured to offer my hand to help but he barked out his order to stay back as he lifted his water-logged right leg up onto the boat rail. The trapped water poured from his boot with half going back into the lake as the other half joined the already several gallons in the boat.

Why my dad persisted going at it the hard way, I couldn't understand, at first. Even I could plainly see that he wasn't using his head. But how do you tell someone, especially your father, who just did you the biggest favor of your life, to stop being a hard-head, come to his senses and pull the boat twenty feet to shore and just walk in? In fact, it occurred to me that he could have gotten out of the boat the same way and avoided all of the splashing, falling, flipping, BARKING and general-to-specific misery and wetness. But I sensed, by the look of hardened determination etched into the lines of his face, that Dad wasn't just trying to get back into the boat, he was at war with the lake! He was in no mood whatsoever to listen to reason and call a cease-fire. It was going to be a fight to the finish. How could his all-time favorite fishing lake treat him so badly? It had developed into a real "Man versus Nature" thing just like the stories in his favorite sports magazine, *Outdoor Man*.

As Dad hung on, suspended between being in the boat and in the lake simultaneously, the strangest expression took possession of his face. This new look on his face – well, I'd never witnessed anything quite like it before and I'd seen my dad come up with some real hilarious, goofy, frightening and puzzling doozies. I'd known my dad for just over six years and I can remember seeing his grown-man-grinning-mug as he leaned in over my baby crib and coochie-cooed me under the chin and his distressed and disturbed look the time I'd experimented at the dinner table by eating my entire supper with the non-business ends of my eating utensils (you could eat mashed potatoes with anything [including a stick you'd found lying in the yard], forget gelatin except with a oversized serving spoon that fit inside your mouth and using the handle end of your knife to cut meat, well, let's just say that ripping your pork chop apart with your bare hands would be a better idea). This face, this look, was from the far, far, furthest end of the list, well outside of his normally expansive and expressive facial expression repertoire. With his left hand he desperately reached down into his left wader boot that was still completely submerged in the lake.

He jumped and jiggled around as if he'd grabbed hold of a live electrical wire. Dad vaulted out of the water and back into the boat in one swift gravity-defying motion. Water was pouring from his left wader as his left hand and arm repeatedly thrashed about inside the draining boot. It was an act of sheer desperation as Dad frantically searched for whatever was down inside of his boot. It was then that I noticed that the stringer which held Dad's prize bass led right down into the very same wader. Dad's face contorted in unexpected pain as he extracted his left hand from the wader with the large, ferocious, small mouth bass vigorously biting down on the four long fingers of his left hand. In the final flopping attempt to get back into the boat Dad had sufficiently agitated the revived bass to the point that it swam down into his bloated wader and then proceeded to attack his probing fingers.

There he sat, my father, a soggy lump in the back of the boat, soaking wet from head to toe, his left wader boot half-full of water and his favorite fishing hat slowly sinking twelve feet out to starboard. Adding further insult and injury to his already substantial insult and injury, his prize five-pound-eighteen-inch bass had attached itself to his left hand. He looked...lost.

He glanced up into the sky, then out over the lake and then down to his left hand where the fish still wiggled and gnawed on his fingers. Then, suddenly, unexpectedly, in an outburst of frustration and anger, my dad growled like a mean dog and grabbed the flopping fish with his right hand and wrestled with it until it relinquished its painful biting grip. He was well beyond all help as he stood up in the boat, unclipped the bass from the stringer and threw the offending fish a good thirty feet through the air out toward the center of the lake, all the while fighting to maintain his balance and not fall back into the lake.

Dad sat back down with a loud and soggy SQUISH!

Exhausted, wet and with four very sore fingers, my father stared past me towards some distant vanishing point far out on the horizon.

"We should head for home," he whispered.

I thought that Dad was going to give up the ship for good and, at any moment, silently slip from the boat and back into the lake where he would randomly drift around, through the seasons and through the years, forever. All the joy, anger, frustration and mad determination, the spirit, was gone. Dad was a tired and beaten shell of a fisherman.

I pulled the anchor in without being asked as Dad slowly crawled along the bottom of the boat back to the middle seat and took up a rowing position. It was a long journey; a lot of oar pulls to get back across the lake to the boat landing. He didn't say a word. Dad slowly rowed as I steadily bailed. The gallons of water in the bottom of the boat swished back and forth in time with his pulling of the oars. I bailed in time with the water sloshing towards the front end of the boat.

Several times during the course of the trip across the lake, Dad stopped rowing and we silently drifted for a while under the sun and the billowy white-top gray-bottom clouds. After a few minutes of such respite and reflective thought he came back to the world of the living and started rowing again. During one such episode he mumbled something and then waved his arm as if throwing something out and away from the boat. That fish would haunt him. It was part of the pattern. After running the gauntlet of one of my marble-dropping experiences, most people were left in shock and either speechless or mumbling incoherently.

Dad robotically drove the car home, in silence. With both hands firmly at ten-and-two on the steering wheel, his unblinking eyes stared straight ahead as he dripped little puddles of lake water onto the front seat and floor mats. One moment my dad was safe and sound above it all and the next moment he was up to his neck and then just as suddenly he found himself below the surface. It took a bright beautiful dry day to discover that marbles could leave you all wet. It became evident, repeatedly, that for those closest to me, marbles could be...inconvenient.

It was a while – a really long while – before Dad offered to take me fishing again. I didn't ask either because, well, I just couldn't. As I remember, the "while" lasted just past two years and, admittedly, I never blamed him.

*

***

Chapter Four:
Defeat

A RELIABLE AND predictable pattern had emerged. I played marbles all the time and I won, all the time. Pretty simple. In competitive situations I always managed to walk away with the pot. Sure, I lost a game or two here and there but it was always close and in the end I always came out on top and ahead in the overall match. Like tennis, lose a game or two but still win the set, lose a set here and there but still win the match. To sum up, I always walked away from a marble circle with more marbles than I started with, and, usually, a lot more than I started with. My equipment needs were simple; marbles and socks to hold my marbles to my belt. I went through a lot of socks. My marbles wore out more socks than my feet did.

When it came to competitive marbles I always found myself in the driver's seat. Properly studying, judging and carefully selecting all of my shots had become second nature. It wasn't just focus, it was hyper-focus. I learned that each and every individual shot in each and every individual game needed to be understood as a separate and unique set of circumstances. The previously made or missed shot was in the distant past just as the shot after next was some related but unforeseen distant forthcoming event. It was not the proverbial "one shot at a time." It was more of a momentarily fixed point of intense focus on a continually unfolding, multi-dimensional, event horizon; yeah – that's what it was!

Conversely, in direct contrast, were the lapses in my razor sharp focus outside the boundaries of competitive play, when unforeseen circumstances randomly, even maliciously, combined with unanticipated, wholly unpredictable, moments within those circumstances that my marble dedication and priorities came into direct conflict and stood at odds with the purposes and intentions of those around me which resulted, unfortunately, in unreliable, untrustworthy control of my marbles; yeah – and that's what that was! Either way, regardless, I'd created a very special, very unusual "world of my very own" as my father, mother and brother all used to say each in their own way, time and turn.

It wasn't long after the eventful fishing trip that spring came to stay (it took awhile but Dad finally and completely dried out, not to mention that the story of the big bass he'd caught and then "released?" had grown an additional three inches and put on an extra two pounds). With the longer days and warmer weather came the really meaty part of the school year's marble competition. Autumn was not to be mistaken for a slouch or slack time by any means, but the fall brought out all of the new school year marble wannabes. The spring, conversely, brought back all those with practiced marble skills; those who'd survived and were ready and hungry for the action. As I'd cleaned up big-time the autumn before, all the more pressure was on to repeat the performance in the spring when everyone who turned out to play was match-hardened and experienced, determined and reloaded with bags of fresh marbles.

It was the last day of school before the Easter break. There'd been a solid week of intense competition with match after match during all three recesses. The last recess of the last day of school before *Good Friday* rolled up. All of the winter practice sessions bore fruit as my reputation resumed its invincible stature of the previous September and October. I picked up right where I left off with an unbroken string of consecutive and convincing match victories. I successfully faced all of the week's serious and not so serious challenges that the first through sixth grades had to offer. As a result of my torrid winning streak, a good match was virtually impossible to find during that final recess. I was just too sharp, just too "on my game" and everybody either heard about it or experienced it first hand. It was lonely at the top. I put out the word that I would be willing to take on any comers in a thirty marble, best Cat's-Eye boulders only, winner take all shoot out.

Having assumed a comfortable leaning position against the baseball diamond backstop I patiently bided my time. The flat dirt area by the baseball field included some of the best marble-playing turf in the entire neighborhood. It was hallowed marble ground. As I reclined against the cyclone fence backstop, caually watching the ball game in progress, I unexpectedly absorbed two very hard finger pokes into my right shoulder. I turned quickly, ready to respond and return the favor in kind only to find myself face to face with the braided bruiser, "Pigtails" herself, in person. It was the same redheaded bully who'd knocked the wind out of the kid in the *Five & Ten* several months before. It was Priscilla 'Babes' Hanrahan. Her piercing green eyes were firmly set in a rough featured, freckle-covered face. With her nose not more than three inches from mine, she enunciated, in no uncertain terms, what seemed to be more of a threat than a challenge.

"You the kid lookin' for a match; well, are ya or aren't ya? What, can't yeah talk? How 'bout an answer, shrimpy!" was Babes' way of introducing herself.

She seemed...angry, really, really mad about – something.

At first I looked around, suspecting that I'd been set up for some kind of practical joke, expecting to see a bunch of my goofy friends off in a corner laughing, snorting and choking back uncontrollable giggles. Nope, there was nobody else around but the 'Babes' and me. That was when, after I stopped looking around, Priscilla swung from behind her back and over her shoulder a giant white sock loaded with marbles. The sound and sight of that loaded sock convinced me that at least the marbles were real enough but was the challenge just as certain?

Dubious of Babes' intentions, looking her straight in the eye (which was a challenge all its own) I repeated the rules of the offer in order to avoid any unfortunate or uncomfortable misunderstandings. I had no desire to walk away from the match bent over, eyes bulging out of my head, hands holding my stomach as I staggered around gasping to catch my breath. No thank you. So I laid it all out one final time; each player puts up thirty Cat's-Eye boulders; first one to win fifteen marbles wins the match and all sixty marbles. During the rules explanation Babes blew huge shimmering and shivering pink bubblegum bubbles. At the conclusion of the ground rules explanation, she bit right into one especially large bubble she'd been holding for sometime with a resounding loud juicy POP!

"So let's play already yeah little creep," was Babes' way of saying she understood and agreed to the rules.

"Oooo-kay," I'd cautiously responded.

Even though Babes wasn't one of your ordinary third grade girls she was still a girl and I didn't feel good about playing girls for anything other than funzies. There was nothing better than separating a serious challenger from his best marbles but at that time, on the playground, competitive marbles was still predominantly a man's sport. I'd never taken a challenge from a girl seriously because one had never been seriously offered, until that moment. Some guys referred to my chivalrous attitude as "sappy" for missing out on some easy wins. I saw it more of a budding sense of discretion and fair play. But Babes seemed serious enough and, owing to her poor attitude, I changed my mind. The thought of quickly picking up thirty Cat's-Eye boulders didn't seem such a bad way to spend the afternoon recess. I bent down and drew the playing circle in the dirt. As I rose to my feet, Babes stepped in real close and shoved her tight balled-up fist right up under my nose to set the tone of the match.

"Listen booger face. I don't want you pulling any funny stuff, GOT IT?"

The only funny stuff that would happen would be all the laughing I'd be doing when I dropped her thirty Cat's-Eye boulders into my marble sock.

Babes took a position on her side of the circle with a sneer on her face that I couldn't wait to wipe off with a quick and decisive victory. Word had gotten around that Babes and I were getting ready for the marble match showdown of the year. A mixed crowd quickly gathered around to witness, firsthand, the weird unfolding spectacle. It was shaping up to be a real battle of the elementary school sexes as the girls started cheering for Babes and the guys stood staunchly behind the champ. I hadn't seen anything like it since the kickball game in gym class when the girls surprised us fatheaded guys, beating us seven-to-six in extra innings. Half the guys on the losing side of that one nursed the psychic scars for months.

This was the first time I'd seen Babes since the memorable incident in the *Five & Ten*. I found out later that she'd been attending a different school in the area. She'd recently been transferred to my school. It seemed that Babes saw the inside of a new school pretty frequently as a result of some rumored adjustment problems. Her last "adjustment" problem at her previous school had something to do with "adjusting" a badminton racket to fit down over the head of a fourth grader: some sort of disagreement over a disputed in-or-out line call.

Babes' physical build and appearance was a dimension of her personality, which contributed to the fear and mistrust exhibited by her classmates. Unfortunately it made Babes the target of many verbal barbs, taunts, and insults which she'd learned to ably defend against. Maybe it was just a case of mistaken identity. Kids could be so cruel, such primitive little primates. But, asking a bunch of kids to take Babes on as a friend, on face value, was asking an awful lot. It is unfair, unjust to presume to judge a person by the appearance of their physical person, especially a child. But Babes pushed the limit of first, second and even third impression understanding. She was, well, different. Not many third grade girls were a muscle-bound female humunculus shoved into little girls clothing with bows in her hair and then told to act like any other eight-year-old little girl. It doesn't work. You end up with Babes Hanrahan. As sure as I saw it, Babes had seen it too, every morning when she looked in the mirror. Babes fluctuated between tolerating and hating the world and everyone in it including herself as we prepared to play.

Maybe, just maybe, it was the unusually large boisterous crowd. I usually only played in front of big energetic crowds in my dreams. It could have been the continuous and unrelenting threats that Babes shouted at me throughout the match. Her chunky fists and sneering grin could have brought a smooth idling V-8 truck engine to a sputtering, coughing halt. Even when she launched a marble and it made contact, it didn't just hit my marble with a sharp clean snap. It was like her marbles were grabbing my marbles by their shirt collars just under their chins, lifting them up off the ground and then punching my marbles in the face, knocking them out of the ring and flat onto their backs! It wasn't a marble match as much as it was a bad marble mugging; a one-sided marble-gang-fight with my guys coming up short and getting pounded. But maybe, just maybe, my time had come and in a grand and embarrassing fashion as well. The quick pickup match that was supposed to be a breeze, a walk in the park, me ripping off a fast one against an arrogant sucker, ended in eight short minutes with a totally unexpected result – I lost.

My sharpshooter's eye had completely failed me. The usually clean, clear shooting geometry in my head had dissolved into a rat's nest of tangled, hopelessly knotted string. Babes Hanrahan, vicariously seeking revenge through me, avenged herself against all of the people and experiences in her life that made her world such a hurtful place. It wasn't the dream brute 'Bruno' who dethroned the champ, it was the real world dwarf woman wrestler who pinned my marbles to the mat. I was Babes' victim just as she, in all likelihood, was victimized countless times before. If I had a choice I would have preferred to keep my marbles and taken that badminton racket over the head.

All understanding, all of the desperate, on the spot, amateur self-psychoanalysis, any and all wild emotional rationalizations rushed to the open wound and tried to stem the flow of my profusely bleeding self-esteem. All of the structural components of my self-image along with all the other integral 'selfs' (respect, confidence) were breaking down and leaking out. I'd taken one right in the ego-artery and I began to uncontrollably, psychically, hemorrhage and bleed-out.

I hadn't the foggiest idea of what had exactly happened, nor could I precisely pinpoint the exact moment that whatever happened had happened, but I could not escape the gnawing sensation that I'd just been struck by lightning. I was so used to being the source of the blinding flash and thundering bang of the lightning strike on an opponent's marble sock that it took me sometime to come to my senses and discover that I was the smoldering source of all the smelly smoke which hung in the surrounding air. My entire body had the feeling of being pressed asleep then slowly reawakened with that tingling, needle-pricks-on-the-skin, unable-to-move sensation. I had no voluntary muscle control. I tried to move but none of my body parts were responding to the commands being sent out from my brain. It took all I had just to keep from tipping over front first into the dirt.

In eight short miserable, unbelievable minutes I lost everything I worked so hard for over the previous seven months. To make the situation even worse I lost to a girl, or at least to a reasonable facsimile of one, who had the beginner's luck of a lifetime. But even worse, I wasn't just beaten; I was beaten to death, killed, creamed, annihilated and humiliated. I didn't even have the excuse of having lost a long, hard-fought close match. I was wiped out. Custer never had it that bad. At least he died after his defeat. Actual death wasn't part of the marble game but its moral equivalent was and I feared that I'd just suffered the passing into marble afterlife.

I always went wherever my marbles took me. Most of the time that meant right to the top of the mountain. But this time they'd led me down a dark blind alley and right into a brick wall. I suffered in stupefied silence for the remainder of that school day afternoon. The thought of the upcoming long spring break seemed dark and bleak indeed. Sitting in class at my desk I became indisguishable from the inanimate lifeless components that made up that desk. I wanted, I longed, but unsuccessfully fought, to summon any remaining fortitude and strength to get up and stumble if possible, crawl if necessary, into Mrs. Goodchaulk's classroom coat closet, close the door, turnoff the light and just sit in the quiet dark with an especially thick brown paper bag over my head.

The last hour of the school day passed as quickly as seven days and six nights locked in the trunk of an abandoned car. As I made my way home after the final bell, the shock started to wear off only to be replaced by a deepening disappointment which flowed in cold and damp to fill the void. I was only six years old and the uncertainty; the unpredictability of life had hold of my head between its cold uncaring hands and stared me straight in the face.

Pre-defeat, during the walks home from school, looking skyward, I was always amazed and inspired by the magical imaginary figures appearing and disappearing in the clouds.

Post-defeat, all I saw were lifeless floating lumps of water vapor. It took everything, all I had left, burning all of my reserves of mental toughness, just to make the walk home and open the back door. Robert passed me on his way out to the tree house. He noticed my condition and took just a moment to ask if I'd gotten the license number of the truck. I responded that, no, I hadn't but I was pretty certain I could pick out the driver from a police lineup.

My fragile dignity, my sense of accomplishment was in critical condition from the deadly, almost fatal cut as what little was left of my self-worth slowly oozed out through the gaping wound. A freckle-faced, redheaded storm had roared through, blowing in several of the windows in that rearranged, redecorated room in my head. I made it, barely, to the kitchen table. The tears that rolled down my shell-shocked face only added to the deep unfamiliar waters in which I was floundering. I took a seat behind the table in the darkest corner of the kitchen, my head resting in my hands, and waited to die, documented by the sound of my head dropping down onto the tabletop with a solid, lifeless THUD!

Mom came waltzing into the kitchen from the living room cradling a large mixing bowl as she hummed along with a song that played on the radio. She was in the middle of preparing supper and was so involved in whipping up that evening's dessert that she did not notice my presence. Mom was mixing some sort of batter so hard and fast that her entire body was caught up in the mixing spoon rotation as her hair had fallen down across her face. With the mixing bowl firmly locked in place against her left side and her right hand working the wooden mixing spoon her shaking voiced sounded like someone was thumping her on the back as she hummed along to the music. Mom stopped her mixing motion long enough to blow and brush her fallen hair from her face when she finally noticed my huddled figure in the corner. She took a few steps towards me just to make certain that it was her youngest that she was seeing. Satisfied that I was in fact one of her own, she acknowledged my presence.

"Hi Hon!" She went onto inform me that we'd be having something special for supper.

It must have been my lack of an enthusiastic response that caused Mom to step a little closer and take a better look. Noticing the redness of my eyes and the dripping nose, she put her bowl down on the table. Tilting my head back with the tip of her finger under my chin, she asked if I was okay as she placed the back of her hand on my forehead.

"No, I feel terrible," I blubbered as I let my face fall back down into my hands.

Somehow the world seemed much more manageable, less bleak and dreary when I covered my eyes. Mom sat down at the table and ran her hand over all the surfaces of my head with momentary stops at my temples, cheeks and both sides of my neck. It was the motherly instinct of fever and swollen glands check, an automatic unconditioned evolutionary reflex like a mother cat licking the fur of its young. She'd continued to investigate. Sour stomach-no, headache-no, trouble going to the bathroom-NO, bad trip and fall-yes (in a manner of speaking) – she was closer. Satisfied that I wasn't suffering from a high temperature, sore throat, sore head, constipation or cuts and bruises from a fall, she was at a loss to explain or understand the nature of my morbid state.

Sobbing and slobbering, Mom's nervous attention not helping, I exclaimed that I'd been "wiped out!" That was all I could get out as any further explanation and elaboration would have caused me to spit and dribble all over myself even more than I already had. Overreacting, Mom deduced that I'd gotten into a fight and had been beaten up. She gently yanked me out from behind the kitchen table to inspect my physical person for any signs of a struggle. Finding no such obvious indications, she remained baffled.

Realizing that Mom's questions would just keep on coming until she forced me to answer, I finally gained a semblance of control and the limited ability to speak.

"I lost!" I blurted out.

"Lost what?"

"Thirty of my best, that's what," I sniffled back.

Mom, rather cruelly I thought, considering the magnitude of the situation, jumped to an incorrect conclusion.

"Where'd you drop them this time?" she'd sarcastically remarked.

Talk about being kicked when you're down, and right in the teeth, too!

"I lost them in a match. I was slaughtered!" I cried in response, making it clear that her last comment had been uncalled for.

I tearfully highlighted the low lights of the match. I went on to explain that it was as if I'd never even seen a marble much less ever held one in my hand or ever once played the game.

Mom put her hand on my shoulder and quietly contemplated the situation at hand. I was running out of water to manufacture tears so I slowly stopped crying and settled into what was certain to be a long term, possibly crippling depression. Grasping the seriousness of my setback at last, Mom pulled me close and started to pour on dose after dose of hugs, sympathy, empathy and reassuring words of comfort and encouragement. Her kind words and warm gentle gestures were having the desired effects, when, through no fault of her own she unintentionally blew it!

"Come on Mikey, Honey, cheer up. You can't win them all," was her well meant but devastating motherly advice.

I plummeted back into the void as my lifeline had been cut. Telling me that I couldn't win them all, when for months on end I'd won them all, was like a head-on car crash in my head. Mom had become the nervous, first-day-on-the-job, lifeguard at the local pool who, in her excitement to save the drowning boy, got confused and threw a bag of cement into his pleading arms instead of a life preserver.

Sinking to the bottom of the pool with a bag of *Redi-Mix* cradled in my arms, Dad could not help but notice the crying and whining commotion coming from the kitchen. With newspaper in hand Dad walked up to the table to get the story firsthand. Mom repeated the basics as Dad took a seat at the far end of the table. He nodded his head "yes" and then shook it "no" as he equally divided his glances between Mom and myself throughout the explanation. In an honest and well-intentioned effort to do his part to ease the pain and suffering of his sorrowful youngest son, Dad offered his condolences and attempted to lighten and lift my deflated disposition with a tragic childhood story of his own.

Some years before, quite by accident, Dad dropped one of his favorite quartz rocks into the toilet. His mother caught him trying to reach into the bowl to retrieve his prize rock. The complicating factor was that he just finished using the facility and hadn't yet flushed. The beautiful quartz crystal resided at the bottom of the toilet bowl and shared the water with the number one-two punch he'd just delivered. His mom was not amused.

Hypnotized by his own recollection Dad slowly rose from the table, unfolded his newspaper and walked back towards the living room and his easy chair. On the way, he mumbled under his breath something to the effect that he'd been forced, helplessly, to witness the premature water burial of his rock as his mother flushed it into oblivion. The lost quartz rock was part of the same mother lode that Dad had grasped and held onto when he'd been scooped up and deposited into the back of the dump truck.

My father resumed his reading seat in the living room. As Dad slipped back behind his evening paper it became clear that he'd succeeded in making himself as miserable as I was. I stared at my father from the kitchen in empathetic disbelief. My mother looked at me, shook her head, and then looked towards her husband with a mixed expression of kindness and impatience, wondering when the biggest and kindest kid in the house would finally find adulthood.

Fortunately, Dad's little painful anecdote diverted my attention long enough to soften the biting edge of my own sadness. Consequently, my depression didn't seem to hold its earlier fatal possibilities. Dad served as living proof that such childhood tragedies could be survived; although he left me with the distinct impression that the traumatic and painful memory would haunt me for the rest of my life.

Meanwhile, Mom quietly came to the conclusion that there

was little more she could say or do. Sitting back in her chair, arms folded across her chest, biting down on her lower lip, deep in thought, she carefully contemplated her next words. Leaning forward, with a relieved tone of voice, she suggested that I talk things over with my older (wiser) brother Robert.

I doubted whether Robert was capable of the serious mood required by my distressed state of mind. Looking out of the kitchen windows across the backyard up towards Robert's tree house, I floated in boundless empty space, appearing and disappearing and reappearing, fluctuating back and forth between past, present and future time. It made me sick to my stomach. I struggled to keep the fine tether of my emotions from breaking and sending me off into the limbo of empty space-time forever. I pictured Dad reading all about it in the next day's paper; headline - *"MARBLE CHAMP LOSES BIG! LITTLE HOPE FOR MENTAL OR MARBLE RECOVERY!"*

A bruised, beaten, cut, scratched, chipped, thawing hockey puck after the big game with two overtime periods along with a sudden death shootout would've been in better condition than I was as I dragged myself from the kitchen, out the door and into the backyard towards the big maple tree that held suspended, fifteen feet above the ground, Robert's favorite place on the planet; his tree house.

There are moments when your life hangs by the thinnest, the barest, of threads. Sometimes you know it and other times you don't. When you're lucky enough to know you only pull on that thread with the slightest of touch, leaving plenty of soft looping slack to safely absorb any unforeseen and sudden shocks until such time as you can carefully rewind and strengthen safe and secure ties to the outside world. When you don't know you inadvertently pull with all of your might, putting all of your weight onto the stretched slender thread with every careless yank, thoughtless tug and neglectful pull.

The walk across the backyard to the base of the big maple tree was no small feat for a little boy in my condition. At any moment during the journey the earth could've cracked open and swallowed me whole. Why not? It wouldn't have surprised me one bit. In fact, I was expecting it! I saw to it that there was plenty of gentle twirling and swirling slack in my threadbare lifeline as I crossed the backyard lawn. Without my continued care and attention it might have all wrapped around my unsteady wobbling legs and shuffling feet and then tripped me as it broke! I reached the rough bark of the tree trunk without life threatening mishap; just incredibly good "dumb luck," I concluded.

I grabbed one of the makeshift two-by-four ladder rungs nailed into the tree trunk and called up to my brother. Robert stuck his head out of the tree house door and looked down at me like I was some pesky door-to-door salesman who was bothering him while he was in the shower. He asked what I wanted. I whimpered back that Mom said I should talk to him about something. He motioned for me to climb up.

The tree house was Robert's private sanctuary, his hide-away. It was his place and nobody else's. It was only the second time I'd seen the inside since it was built but the first time since Robert had completed the interior decorating. Robert left my room and all the stuff in it alone so I returned the favor and respected his wishes that no one mess around in his tree house.

Once inside, allowing time for my eyes to adjust to the dimmer light, I realized that I'd entered a miniature tree-suspended *Baseball Hall of Fame*. For a few minutes I completely forgot my own problems. My astonished gaze traveled from wall-to-wall-to-ceiling. Every inch of wall and ceiling space was covered with overlapping posters, magazine covers, team photos and team pennants. When it came to big fan baseball stuff, name it and Robert had it or knew where to get it. Old baseballs, baseball bats, team hats, old and new fielder's mitts and his hard-won *Little League Championship* trophies. It should be known that Robert was just as good at playing baseball as he was at collecting and playing baseball cards.

Our dad saw to it that the tree house was very sturdily constructed. It was strong, weather-tight and well secured to a large healthy tree. It had four windows and a door, each with a canvas curtain for privacy. The tree house even had electricity provided by an all-weather extension cord from a garage outlet. A single overhead shaded light bulb provided more than adequate illumination. Robert sat against the south wall as I crawled to sit against the opposite wall right in front of a magazine cover photo of *Henry 'Hank' Aaron*.

My temporarily sidelined sadness returned with a tight grip around my throat as I struggled to hold back another wave of tears. I whispered, with head down, talking into my lap instead across to Robert, that during the afternoon recess I'd been "hammered in a thirty marble take all match." I looked up and studied my brother's initial reaction from under my eyebrows and paused, before deciding it was safe to continue. Reluctantly, I added that I didn't even win a single marble. I'd been cleaned out in eight short pathetic minutes.

Robert put down his baseball cards as the impact of my story sank in. I was relieved to discover that he knew the feeling, in his own way, firsthand. It had been at a different time, at a different place, under different circumstances, but he got what I was going through. Robert asked who I'd lost to. Instantly a large lump materialized in my throat; a total blockage. Either I was going to get it out or I was going to choke on it. I hadn't even told Mom or Dad who'd done me in. I wasn't even sure that I should tell Robert. But I realized that it would be all over school after the spring break anyway, so I got it off my chest. Looking up at the team picture of the 1958 *Chicago Cubs*, searching for the courage, I blurted it out.

"Babes Hanrahan!"

I shivered as I said it as if saying her name would bring it all back like it had happened just a few seconds before. Either not hearing what I said or not believing what I said, Robert asked.

"Who?"

"Babes Hanrahan!" I loudly repeated, more from embarrassment and shame than anger.

"You mean the redhead with pigtails and forearms like *Louisville Sluggers*?"

"Yeah, her," I exhaled.

Robert, a fourth grader, had heard of her from friends in her class. In her short time at school Babes had developed a reputation for fighting with the world and its human inhabitants. She worked hard at smashing other kids hopes and dreams whenever and wherever the opportunity presented itself. The word was that if she couldn't beat you at your game, she'd just beat you up, period. In hindsight I considered myself lucky in light of the new information; I'd only lost some marbles. Memories of the doubled-over kid in the *Five & Ten* rematerialized. If I'd won I would've been thirty marbles richer and ten teeth poorer. Yikes!

It was Babes' private little game. She'd find out who was good at what and then launch a campaign to threaten, coerce and intimidate them into proving it. If she won, she left her intended victim defeated and suffering from a badly bruised ego. If she lost, she just left her intended target badly bruised!

Robert proved to be understanding, empathetic but equally philosophical about my unenviable circumstance. He spoke plainly and directly. He started off by acknowledging that it was most unfortunate to lose so decisively and to be assaulted by someone not interested in playing good marbles but only interested in being the bad person. A champion in his own right, Robert had suffered through his first major baseball card defeat none to gracefully. His journey through the dark cavern of self-doubt had run it course some years before. The passage of time had allowed him the breathing space, the time necessary to sort through and reflect upon his own misfortune. It had helped him and it allowed him to be of aid to me in my sadness. I listened intently. Where Mom's stumbling but well-intentioned sympathy was kind and soothing, my brother Robert's calm and insightful reasoning was the perfect medicine.

Many of my brother's insights jabbed and poked like sharp pins, each word finding a vulnerable spot. But the more Robert talked the closer I listened until slowly, I afforded myself an entirely different perspective on my situation. Wild horses, giants, alligator heads and sailing ships returned to the cloud-filled sky for everyone to see. Robert concluded his advice with a short speech that threw me at first, but, as I ran the words round and round in my head, they made more and more sense.

Recollecting and paraphrasing it went something like this:

"Yeah know little brother, yeah gotta learn to take the hard hits, the losses. They are just as much a part of the game as any of the wins. Being beaten out of your marbles now and then gives you the chance to think things over, adjust, clear the air and start fresh. Besides, do you just like winning or do you like playing the game too? When winning becomes everything, they're not just marbles anymore. When you forget it's just a game, the wins and losses take on a meaning and significance they don't deserve. The point is, either you go with the flow of win and lose and accept the good and bad of the game, or else your marbles, which were never supposed to be in charge, start running your life. If you let that happen, suddenly one day when you really lose big, you'll feel as if you've lost everything, when in fact, you haven't lost them at all because you'll have given them away. Your marbles are part of your life; they are not your whole life. Don't let your marbles assume a position and responsibility in your life that they shouldn't have had in the first place and could have never handled anyway."

I sat there, my mouth half-open, my lips slightly trembling, as wisdom, belying Robert's years, washed over me like ice water pouring off a glacier. It became apparent that Robert had really gone over it from start-to-finish, backwards-and-forwards and inside-and-out, thought it all the way through. He really helped me out that spring day all those years ago. I'm not sure what could be attributed as the cause, but my brother's baseball and other life experiences had made him pretty savvy at a tender age. His view of life was "precocious" as my father used to say; "wonderful" as my mother used to say.

It became clear to me over the years why Robert spent so much time in that tree house. It wasn't just his baseball hideaway: it was his think tank. What had been stuck to the walls was interesting yet totally incidental when compared to what had gone on in my brother's mind. His two or three hours per day suspended up in that tree were well spent. When he was sorting and shuffling through his baseball cards, he was really shuffling and sorting through his head.

What he said to me that afternoon made sense on every level. I didn't fathom it all at once, but its impact was emotional as well as intellectual. Robert's calm reasoning illuminated that I'd lost because I'd lost my way. I'd strayed from the truer path I'd set out to follow and I'd paid the price. What my intellect didn't fully grasp, my emotions had completely embraced. I'd faced marble death and, with help, walked away, scarred but alive. It became painfully evident that marbles could be psychologically complicated and emotionally...exhausting.

Relieved but drained from hours of emotional turmoil, I descended from my brother's sanctuary a new boy, who, at the very least, would be willing to try and put Robert's suggestions, his clear and insightful philosophy, into practice. Even though not all of my future efforts in that direction were to be successful, my brother's sound ideas and insightful advice held up well and got me through many a tough match, the toughest of which would not be far off.

**

Chapter Five:
The Temptation, The Burden & Warren 'Rusty' Axlerod

The Temptation

ROBERT'S UNIQUE AND thoughtful view of the world had put me squarely back on the right track and sped my recovery. I actually enjoyed the spring break rather than dreading and suffering through it. I did my best to put the loss to Babes into proper, non-world-ending, perspective. When I returned to school the following week the disastrous day seemed months in the past, not just days. Any remarks that came my way, positive or negative, well-intentioned or not, were acknowledged or dismissed out of hand, respectively. Soon I was back to my winning ways as my tarnished reputation regained its former brilliance.

In accordance with my brother's advice, I put more effort into enjoying the finesse and skill of the game and less into pressuring myself to win. There were many would-be-vulture-like challengers who heard of my single match demise and swooped in to claim and fight for their share of the scraps, to pick over and clean up the remains. But they were sorely disappointed. I couldn't have set a better baited trap if I'd tried. The pretenders to the throne greedily lined up for their chances at the leftovers only to be beaten back, beaten down and thoroughly thrashed to within inches of their marble lives. I was clear headed, freshly focused and had reclaimed a clean unconfused shooting geometry for every shot. The results were phenomenal. My newly adopted easier and more relaxed style of play brought me near effortless victory after victory. I was back after being lost. The jagged and scattered line of empty lifeless marble socks in my wake stretched from one end of the school playground to the other.

I soon discovered that spring heralded many other renewed aspects of life other than marble matches. That particular time of year meant many different things to many different people. A few of those different people with the different and unfortunately confused understandings were classmates of mine. Most of the new growth that was popping up out of the ground that spring had been sewn as seeds and scattered by the winds of the autumn months before. They'd remained dormant through the winter, patiently waiting, biding their time for the arrival of the warm sunlight and showers of the new season. But one had to be careful because the new growth of spring's smothering vines frequently had such visually stunning and breathtakingly perfumed flowers. I was oblivious, at that tender age, to any type of wind-blown seed lying under the snow that waited to sneak up out of the ground with the spring thaw, grab you by the ankles, grow spiraling up your legs, creep inch by inch up your torso and then swirl tightly around your throat.

Gentle thoughts, strong emotions and uncontrolled devious motivations have been known to invade and overtake the body and mind of the most innocent and unsuspecting of those among us. As a matter of course during a normal school day, just like everybody else, I had daily contact with a wide variety of kids who exhibited an equally wide variety of different personalities, some of whom, unfortunately, were not as immune as me to the psychological ravages of the heart. Brought on by the annual rite of spring, *Cupid* had awakened with a vim and vigor previously unknown to man and woman alike. Having overslept from his long winter's nap and arriving late to the party, he panicked. To make up for lost time he double-dosed his love arrows and started rapidly firing away indiscriminately in all directions until his quiver was empty.

He intended, in his careless haste, to only score hits on primed and ready soon-to-be-love-sick, age appropriate, adult targets. But just at the wrong moment Melissa Williams unwittingly stepped right into the path of one of the misguided arrows and took it square in the temple. She stumbled and stuttered in her tracks and went completely cross-eyed as the arrow stuck there in her head and quivered as it delivered its lethal dose of what could only be described as the "cupids-stupids."

Melissa sat in the desk in front of me and I have to say she wasn't a bad sort in any way. She ran, played dodgeball and kickball with the rest and best of us. Melissa and I shared a mutual but cordial indifference to one another. One day, not long after spring break, it all very suddenly, unexpectedly changed. Previously friendly, indifferent and all around "good Joe" Melissa became, well...overly attentive – in my direction.

If I looked close enough I could have probably spotted the tiny little arrow sticking out of the side of her head. Getting too close to Melissa in her condition would've been unwise. At the time I could only imagine that it was similar to sticking a big nail into a live electrical outlet and hanging on for two or three seconds. Parts of one's brain would get all charged up and over stimulated resulting in all kinds of personality damage and resulting aberrant behavior. So charged up, Melissa had been let loose out onto the school landscape.

If Rodney Strong had been the risk, my mother the faith, my father the doubt, then Melissa Williams was definitely the temptation. Overnight, the girl I hardly noticed was suddenly everywhere to be noticed. She turned up at almost all of my matches and embarrassed me by clapping and cheering me on during the competitions.

Every time I turned around there she was. Sometimes alone and sometimes with a group of her girl friends, with love and adoration in her eyes, my name was written in tiny neon that blinked on and off across her pupils. I tried, in vain, to understand and reason with Melissa and get to the bottom of her all-too-sudden personality shift. All she did was wink, giggle, blow kisses and tell me how cute and wonderful I was. She asked me to walk with her and hold her hand, all while being in wide-open public view, on the school playground. Some nerve! I almost lost my lunch. It was that disgusting.

The Melissa I'd once known had died and in her place had risen a precocious young woman with an entirely new set of priorities, one of which was me. I wondered if Melissa had eaten from a bad batch of macaroni and cheese from the school lunchroom and instead of getting regular everyday variety food poisoning had contracted a rare case of botulism of the brain. It must be understood that I did nothing to invite or encourage this change in her behavior. The affection that radiated unchecked from the big brown eyed Miss Williams had a hidden and endless source all its own. I did more than my share of providing polite and tactful discouragement but she became as relentless in the pursuit of my affections as I'd been in the pursuit of marbles.

Six-year-old girls at that time had a myriad of strange ways of communicating their intentions and affections. Melissa's favorite was to repeatedly and at every available opportunity, kick me in the shins. When I turned on her and told her face to face to stop kicking me, to stop following me and to stop bothering me, my directness, honesty and heart-felt sincerity would be promptly rewarded with several more rapid-fire kicks to those same shins. There was a lesson for life in there somewhere, I knew it, just couldn't put my finger on it at the time.

I only guessed and then surmised that she thought that when I sat in bed at night, contemplating and tending to my sore and battered lower legs, that I smiled with longing sweet thoughts in anticipation of her next affectionate assault. There seemed to be a disturbing interpersonal dynamic emerging, an inverse sensibility about the relationship, wherein the more my legs hurt, the greater my pain and suffering, the better she felt. It was the reverse of the inverse-square law. The tighter I closed my eyes to shut out the light and pain the brighter and more wide-open her eyes became. That just couldn't be right. There was definitely something very wrong with that equation.

Grudgingly, I had to admit that Melissa was rather attractive for a girl. In first grade parlance that made her "cute." I had to further confess that there was something different, something almost special, about a girl who, running at full speed, would come up from behind you and shout, "I love you!" just as she tackled me face first onto the ground with a big bear hug (she had a lotta spunk). I lay there unable to move, the wind knocked out of me, the right side of my face pressed down into the dirt, as she planted one big loud wet kiss after another onto the left side of my face. And, if getting blindsided out on the playground wasn't bad enough, she blindsided me by hiding cards and love notes in my desk, my lunch box, my books and my jacket pockets. There was nothing worse than sitting down with the guys for lunch and opening my lunch box only to have been greeted by a copy of her school portrait photograph with "I love you" written all over it with dozens of those little X'ed kisses jumping out.

"Mel and Mikey sitting in a tree, k-i-s-s-i-n-g!" had become a familiar but unwelcome turn of phrase.

It was not, I repeat NOT, an easy time for me.

I also started to understand the familiar phrase "puppy love" as I heard it thrown in my direction often enough at the time. It was no different than being followed home by a lost and lonesome homeless animal that picked me out from a crowd and decided that I was its only salvation. Melissa had imprinted on me like a helpless and flightless baby duck. Wherever I went she skipped, hopped and waddled along right behind with little quacks of "mine, mine, he's all mine".

Melissa was proving harder to get rid of than a bad summer cold. Complicating the already over-complicated mess was the fact that what were once long brown braids had become flowing fluffy waves of auburn curls gently waving in slow motion in the breeze. If I were aimlessly floating through first grade life like many of my male classmates, Melissa would've been hard to resist. Owing to her good looks and her cave woman approach to expressing her affection, she started to get under my skin in a sort of unpleasant way, like a shallow wooden splinter that didn't hurt, at first.

The temptation was there all right and I struggled with it off and on for three weeks. In the end, what saved me were Melissa's own excesses. If I succumbed to any of her weird wishes or desires in any form or manner I would've been, without a doubt, the biggest jerk in school. My game concentration started to suffer under the onslaught of Melissa's wily ways no matter how ridiculous they seemed. The realization that I had to get back to my true priorities is what prevented me, saved me, from slipping into the charming swamp of love embraced in the all-encompassing arms of the big-eyed Miss Williams.

The whole affair came to a stormy conclusion one afternoon after school. My best friend Russell and I were having a first grader's bull session while having a friendly game for funzies behind the baseball diamond backstop before heading home. Russ and I played and talked and laughed as best friends and confidants are accustomed to. He mentioned that he couldn't help but notice my dilemma with Melissa. He offered his condolences which I gratefully accepted.

As I related to Russ one episode after another, all of the outrageous things Melissa had done and all of the corresponding trouble she'd caused in the name of love, the very subject of the discussion walked up and stopped at the edge of our playing circle. Melissa just stood there like she'd been invited. She refused to leave until I took the time to talk to her. Russ and I, on my cue, simply upped and moved our game as Melissa, undaunted, simply upped and followed right along, reimposing her presence. I started to feel...uncomfortable. I reached the conclusion that it had all gone beyond far enough. Something had to be done and then and there was the time and the place to do it.

I jumped to my feet and asked Russ if he wouldn't mind walking home on his own. Being the good friend that he was, he immediately grasped the magnitude of the situation, quickly collected his marbles, and respectfully resisted the temptation, with the help of my cold stare, to say something mushy and stupid when he departed. As soon as Russ had gone some distance away I turned to face the girl who'd become my uninvited second shadow over the previous three weeks.

Melissa's perception of the situation was so distorted and skewed that she actually thought that I sent Russ on his way so that we could be alone together and hold hands and other farfetched stuff like that. The look in her eyes sighed "alone at last." Melissa walked right up to me, flashed her big beautiful brown eyes and grabbed my hand. The certain anger and resolve that I felt just moments before started to melt into a confused mess around my shoes. I sensed myself slowly slipping under her spell, like the hypnotized victim of a vampire.

I came to with a shudder just before it was too late. I ripped my hand from her tender grasp. I must have had a really repulsive look on my face like she was infecting me with some sort of disease. My sudden change in demeanor infuriated Melissa. She immediately retaliated by kicking at the marbles that were still scattered on the ground and even tried to rip the marble sock off of my belt. She shouted and glared at me with eyes that instantly transformed from soft, moist reflecting pools into two rough chunks of broken jagged glass.

"All you care about are your stupid marbles!" she cried.

The truth, I'd felt, could not be more simply stated. She followed up by blurting out that when it came to love, one must leave their marbles behind. Well put again, I thought.

Firmly grasping and then roughly pulling her hand off of my marble sock I scampered around on the ground to collect my scattered marbles. That brought Melissa up to a full boil. She ran after me and continued to kick at any of my marbles her feet could find. A Melissa that had been hidden away, a Melissa I never would have guessed even existed, burst into full bold view before my eyes. The sweet, soft haired, glowing eyed first grader had become a raging, love-scorned wildcat, eager to tear the very object of her affections into little unrepairable pieces. Melissa no longer needed a boy friend; she needed a padded cage and a tranquilizer dart fired from a rifle.

Her uncontrolled anger, her escalating hysteria, pushed me to the limits of my patience and understanding. Standing on the very edge I realized it was either her or me as any residual compassion I harbored for the girl was flushed out to sea. I athletically jumped back up to my feet. With facial muscles strained, I unleashed a full verbal broadside, all guns simultaneously. I called her the ugliest thing I'd seen since the squashed rat I'd found in the alley behind my house. I scored a direct concentrated hit with all guns amidships. Her vanity went up in splinters as all her sails had come crashing down onto the deck all at once and she started to take on water.

She ran away frustrated, angry, hurt and crying. I hadn't meant to imply that she was that ugly: the heat of the moment and all that. She wasn't physically unattractive in the slightest. But, there was a certain ugliness in the way she wanted me to unconditionally respond to her clinging possessiveness. There was something wrong in the way that she wanted to be with me and wanted me to be with her. She backed me into a corner with her emotional pushing and shoving and tried to keep me there with her verbal kicks and punches. She forced me to decide, forced me to either give-up and give-in completely or to all out resist and defend myself. Ulysses had not only survived the call of the siren, but, in the process of pulling free, had destroyed her island base as well.

After a few minutes I calmed down and cooled off. I was truly saddened by the way things had ended between the two of us. Yet, I had to admit to being relived that it had finally been resolved and come to a conclusion, albeit a messy one. In the end I blamed basic incompatibility and fundamental irreconcilable differences.

Gathering up the last of the widely scattered marbles, I reflected back and recalled that Melissa's former skills at dodgeball and kickball would be missed. She changed so much that I doubted that she'd ever take the field again. Nobody ever said that the marble path would be painless for me or the people close to me. There were trade-offs required all along the way. Marbles, sadly, regrettably, could be...unkind.

The Burden

THE SPRING OF my first year in school not only proved to be a steady period of increasing marble success but also a time of increased personal conflict and aggravation as well. On the negative side there were Babes and Melissa. On the positive side, the rewards for a first grade marble sensation had been much more than a bulging marble sock at the end of every school day or the fearful respect of competitors on the school playground. The smaller, incidental, almost intangible honors and rewards were just as numerous and frequent. For instance, no matter how crowded the school's lunchroom, there was always a place for me to sit. If by chance there were no seats immediately available upon my arrival, one would always be swiftly provided, sometimes at the expense and inconvenience of lesser-known entities.

During gym class, I never suffered the humiliation of being the last chosen when teams were picked. It wasn't that I was particularly good at baseball, volleyball, dodgeball or whatever the game was. It was the prestige and novelty afforded the team that had the champ of the school's only unsupervised sport playing for their side. It was after I struck out for the third straight time or got the volleyball on top of my head instead of my fists or got plastered by the first volley of dodgeballs that the light went on. It finally occurred to me that my fellow students had made certain assumptions about my abilities in areas of athletic competition other than marble-playing. It was guilt by association, but altered. It was ability by association which was just as misguided. It had been this type of mistaken identity that led me to the burdensome part of my success. Many prices, it seemed, were to be paid.

Unknown to me at the time, a certain person was in the process of making me into something that I really wasn't. Playing marbles was one thing, but trying to instruct others in the art was not my forte. If somebody wanted to watch and pick up what they could from what I did they were welcome to try. The old saying those who can – do, and those who can't but wish they could teach instead, applied. I understood the saying to infer that being a good teacher required a different approach. Teaching was an art, an unstoppable inclination towards a subject along with an understanding, an acceptance of an on going responsibility to those who relied upon you to share that subject knowledge. I wasn't a practitioner of the teaching arts. I was an adherent of the player's art.

The certain person in question, the personality that was about to appear on the horizon and who, undoubtedly, became the greatest burden to my young career was the class enigma, Hector Hobart. Every school throughout the history of public schools has someone like Hector. His strange habits, seemingly limitless mental abilities and off-center appearance made him the school mystery. Hector was the kid who was always the object of the playground supervisor's pleadings and petitions that all kids, regardless of ability, should have the chance to participate.

Hector's physical abilities left a great deal to be desired. At times, in fact most times, letting Hector play was just plain dangerous. During volleyball games he always succeeded in creating pileups of bodies on the gym floor. When playing baseball, especially when at bat, he always, to one degree or another, let go of the bat when taking a swing at the ball.

One memorable game Hector, managed back-to-back mishaps, a sort of disaster-double-play. Hector fielding a batted ball was a journey into the purely unexpected. Whenever Hector took the field his teammates stuck him somewhere of little or no consequence to the game. Usually, he'd just end up wandering around like a lost kid, starting up conversations with any of his teammates that had been willing to listen. Just by chance, one game Hector was aimlessly floating between first and second base in the shallow outfield when Jerry Mueller hit a screaming grounder right at him. The crack of the bat connecting with the ball froze Hector in his tracks in shallow right field.

Stopping at the sound of a batted ball had become a cautionary habit he'd acquired the autumn before when, on the way to the shortstop position to tell a joke, he'd walked right into a hard hit line drive which he'd taken square on the shoulder. Even when Hector was ready and he'd attempt to make a catch, the ball would usually bounce off his glove, bounce off his knee or roll up his arm and smack him in the face. Hector did everything and anything other than catch the ball. As time went on and the ball was hit in his direction he'd either run in the opposite direction or fall flat to the ground to avoid contact with the hard white sphere which so often caused him physical pain and embarrassment. Hector had become sort of like a lab rat in a cage trying to avoid electric shocks in a conditioned response experiment.

Jerry's screaming hot grounder caught up to Hector before he could duck or run. The speeding bounding baseball, unbelievably, bounced right into Hector's fielding mitt with a resounding POP! Hector didn't believe he'd actually caught the ball and neither did anyone else. An eerie moment of silence descended upon the field as all of the available houseflies in the area headed for all of the wide-open gaping mouths. The shock wore off the rest of the team in time for them to shout at Hector to throw the ball to first base and into Harry Horn's waiting glove for the out.

Hector came to his senses, opened his clamped shut eyes, pulled the ball from his mitt and threw it as hard as he could in the general direction of first base. The problem was that in all the excitement of Hector's amazing catch he'd lost track of his relative proximity to first base. He failed to realize and recognize that Harry and first base were a scant twelve feet away. Hector's panicked hard throw went slamming into Harry's unprotected right kneecap and ricocheted into deep right field along the foul line. Jerry Mueller ended up with a stand-up triple. Harry Horn ended up sprawled on the ground clutching his knee and screaming in pain about three (maybe four) feet east of fair territory. Hector Hobart ended up fifty-five feet behind the center fielder Freddy Schmidt, where the farthest edge of the deep outfield grass met up with the asphalt of the school parking lot.

When it came time for Hector's turn at bat, after what had just happened to Harry, everyone took a few extra steps back. Hector's unsure grip on a swinging bat was well known. No one had been particularly concerned with Hector actually hitting the ball as they all kept their eyes wide-open for the direction his flying bat might take. Davey Hampstead was the pitcher on the mound and he, more than anyone, would remember Hector.

It was the bottom half of the same inning in which Hector deactivated Harry Horn when the impossible happened. Davey gave Hector a big, fat, slow strike right over the center of the plate when Hector, with eyes closed, swung his bat with all his limited might and connected, hitting a howling line drive right at Davey's head. Davey made a great catch as the ball slammed dead center into the webbing of his glove. A split second later, Davey caught Hector's flying bat right in the pit of his stomach. Hector's questionable grip on the bat had completely melted away at the shock of actually having hit the ball.

Davey collapsed in the dirt at the back of the pitcher's mound, gasping for air and holding his injured midsection. Hector didn't even try for first base and not because Davey caught the ball but because Davey caught the bat. He just stood at home plate figuring that he'd really gone and done it. First, it was Harry at first base, then Davey on the pitcher's mound; all on the same day, during the same game and in the very same inning. The casualties had started to pileup in the infield. That was it and Hector knew it. None of the other kids would ever let him play ball again no matter how much the playground supervisor protested. Hector was right, they never did.

Aside from Hector's shortcomings as an amateur athlete, there was something very different about him that was oddly indescribable, very distinct, in a special way. There were a few things you could put your finger on like the way he would solve an arithmetic problem the teacher kept getting wrong. But then there was the rest you couldn't put your finger on (or wouldn't want to even if you could) like the way he stared at girl classmates while picking his nose and eating the boogers.

Hector had a special talent, a unique ability of his own, a skill of being totally weird. When he grew up Hector was either going to be a very smart eccentric atomic scientist or a very smart eccentric flasher on some dingy street corner. There was always the distinct possibility that he'd end up doing both. The question then would have been which one would be his profession and which would be his hobby. Destiny and Fate were playing Ping-Pong for his soul and Hector's mortal existence was the ball.

Looking back, it didn't seem out of place in the scheme of things that one rainy noon hour in April, Hector made his move. Just minding my own business, quietly, privately sitting at my desk, I peacefully occupied myself by sorting through that day's marble selection. As was the practice on rainy school days our class had been confined indoors for the lunch hour recess. The games and other special activities saved for just such occasions were opened up and passed around as we all made the best of our captivity.

Unnoticed, Hector came walking up from behind as I sat at my desk. He quickly jumped into the vacant seat right in front of me and leaned over the front of my desk.

"ARCHER, WILL YOU TEACH ME HOW TO PLAY MARBLES?" he blurted out loud enough for everyone in the classroom to hear.

Keepers Weepers

I was about to tell Hector to go look at girls and have some nose candy when Mrs. Goodchaulks, having heard snippets of the short verbal exchange, stepped up to my desk barely able to control her excitement and commented how nice it was that I was going to be spending time with Hector. Dumbfounded, with a look on my face to match, I sat with mouth wide-open wondering what had just exactly transpired. It had to have been some sort of brain seizure induced wide-awake nightmare. Without any initiative of my own, my immediate future had been yanked from my hands. I shifted my wide-open, disbelieving eyeballs from Hector up to Mrs. Goodchaulks and then back down to Hector. A big weird smile was plastered across his big weird face.

It was no coincidence, no random confluence of circumstances. I'd been conned. I'd been had, big time. Hector had it all figured out well in advance. The mathematics, the personal and social probability factors had all been worked out and woven into the fabric of the trap. A *Swedish Social Scientist* could not have designed it better. If I asked he probably would have proudly shown me the diagram along with all of the supporting slide rule calculations of when (down to the second) and where (down to within a few inches) to drop his ensnaring net.

I wanted, really wanted, as matter of indisputable fact, to categorically, to emphatically state, in no uncertain terms that there had been one giant whopper of a mistake, a monumental misunderstanding, and that I wasn't going to teach Hector anything except how to stay as far away from me as humanly possible. However, thoughts in the mind of a six-year-old do not always find their way from the brain down to the vocal cords. Red faced, intimidated and back on my heels, my clear concise thoughts on the matter were very poorly translated into a stammering, stuttering and mumbled response along the lines of "sure – sounds great?" I was such an idiot!

Mrs. Goodchaulks continued on her way around the classroom (with her own style of weird smile on her face) relieved that Hector's social isolation from his classmates was, at least temporarily, no longer a front burner concern of hers. If she only knew that a heinous crime had been committed right under her nose and that she, unknowingly, had been an accessory before, during and after the fact. If she only understood that she'd been an unwitting accomplice, maybe things would have turned out differently. But maybe she would not have cared, being relieved that the responsibility of Hector's classroom socialization was no longer hers alone. Fair or unfair, just or unjust, I was stuck. I decided then and there, as Mrs. Goodchaulks walked away, that I'd set the ground rules in my favor. Hector sat at attention as I slashed through the webbing of his deception which hung all over me like a wet shredded blanket and enumerated the conditions of our relationship.

First, he'd have to provide all of his own marbles. Second, I'd practice with him only once a week and then only during the Monday afternoon recess as Monday afternoons were typically periods of diminished match play (most of the heavy hitting matches took place in the morning and midday recesses). As I was usually victorious in those early recesses the few marbles my competitors had left they didn't want to risk losing in an afternoon match and end up going home zeroed out with empty marble socks. Third, Hector could watch any of my marble matches as long as he didn't talk to me or call out my name. Fourth, and most importantly, he wasn't to tell anyone in the whole school that I was helping him with his marble game. All through the explanation of the ground rules Hector's head bobbed up and down and sideways like it was mounted on a big loose spring instead of his neck.

"Okay," Hector responded along with one of his big weird smiles. He jumped up out of his seat like a marionette whose controlling strings had just been yanked upwards and he departed for his desk at the far corner of the room walking like the same string controlled puppet. Geez, he was strange.

With my face buried in my hands, I wondered how on earth I'd gotten myself into such a mess when it occurred to me that I hadn't gotten myself into the mess. Hector had dug a hole in the ground and covered it with leaves and sticks and while on a casual stroll, I'd fallen right into it. I was ten feet down a hole and the only helping hand being offered for a lift out was Hector's. He'd stood at the top of the trap and promised to throw down a ladder only if I promised to play. I'd done my best to set things straight on the rules which made me feel better and more in control. I was forced into playing the game but I'd be the one calling the balls, strikes and the "you're outta here's."

The following Monday afternoon recess I prepared to give Hector his first lesson, to teach what I knew as a certainty to be unteachable. Lined up at the doors before going out onto the playground, I unobtrusively signaled Hector to collect his marbles and meet me at the far corner of the playground by the parking lot. On my way to the appointment with Hector, it occurred to me that a fifth and final rule would be prudent. If he was unable pick up a semblance of the game within a reasonable time period, I reserved the right to terminate his lessons and our relationship. I arrived at the designated spot a few minutes before Hector and sat down and quietly contemplated if it would even be possible to pass along any of my natural abilities and hard won working knowledge to someone as unusual as Hector. For a moment, just a fleeting unsettling moment, I fearfully envisioned that Hector might turn out to be a natural for the game, some sort of sleeping marble giant, just waiting for his chance to shine. The student teaches the teacher a few lessons of his own sort of thing.

I didn't wait long before Hector showed up, walking along like he was having a spastic attack. With his hands behind his back and one of his weird smiles rippling across his face he stopped a few feet away. The only other time I saw him smile like that was when Colleen Jacobs was standing at her desk answering a reading class question. Colleen sat two desks to the front of Hector and, halfway through her answer, Hector farted out loud. He really ripped a big one like he'd been saving it since breakfast. Colleen stopped her answer midsentence and put her fingers over her nose and pointed an accusing finger at Hector.

After Mrs. Goodchaulks ordered the guys in the back of the class to stop all the laughing, she made Hector stand and formally apologize to the entire class. Hector did not speak. All he did was slowly rise to a sheepish, slouching stand next to his desk with the exact same horrendous grin on his face. The guys at the back of the class couldn't contain themselves as the guffawing started all over again. Something told me that Hector knew something about Colleen and in the middle of her answer decided to make his thoughts known. Something having to do with payback, I suspected.

Hector came to a halt in front of me and snapped to attention with a salute like a new recruit reporting for duty. Grinning like a demented clown, from behind his back he swung around a huge clear plastic bag of marbles.

"How are these, Archer?" he asked.

My eyes must have bugged out of their sockets and then fell out of my head and rolled around in the dirt before snapping back up into place. I gazed upon the most beautiful bag of marbles I'd ever seen. The entire large clear bag was full, almost to overflowing, with nothing but brand new Cat's-Eye boulders and a few Aggie boulders thrown in almost as decorative accents.

"Where'd you get those?" I choked.

Hector explained that he told his mother that I was going to instruct him in the "fine art of marbles" (his exact words). Apparently overwhelmed at the prospect of Hector having a new friend, his parents went out over the weekend, got a bank loan, and bought Hector one gigantic bag of marbles. I got up to my feet, dusted off the seat of my pants, and adjusted to the fact that the crazy kid standing in front of me probably wasn't even aware of the riches in his possession. For Hector a big bag of dirty stones would have probably been more exciting.

Unable to avert my stare from Hector's bag of marbles, I haltingly explained the fundamentals of the game, the basic rules and the commonly practiced strategies then currently in use. I drew a circle in the dirt and started the first lesson. It rapidly became evident that Hector was not going to be any type of overnight marble-playing sensation. A marble savant he was not. In fact, I have to state that Hector was more skilled at baseball. The thought had occurred to me that if my dad and Hector had teamed up they could have pretty much destroyed the inside of a house with their combined marble skills. It also occurred to me that it was a good thing that baseball bats were not used in the game of marbles. Owing to Hector's inability to keep a firm grasp on large wooden clubs and the immediate proximity of players to one another during a match, it was a safe assumption that more than half of the marble players in school would have spent time on the disabled list.

Nevertheless, and to his credit, Hector tried and tried. Not only did he practice hard, with little improvement, he kept his end of the bargain by following all of the prior agreed conditions. Hector, on occasion and unobtrusively, helped me in return with my arithmetic, it being my worst subject after spelling. Hector was the only kid in school who knew what a slide rule was and how to use it. As I recall it worked pretty well on me. But even giving him credit for his efforts and his helping me with addition and subtraction, Hector was still one of the strangest people I'd met in my young life.

Sometimes, during class, he'd blurt out, completely unsolicited, all sorts of unusual things. After several months, during such occurrences, Mrs. Goodchaulks would just ignore Hector and carry-on as did most of the class. It was as if wires in his brain had gotten crossed and sent out unexpected involuntary signals. It wasn't hard, at any time during the school day, whether off by himself or mixed in the midst of a large group of kids, to catch a glimpse of Hector lost in deep thought, just staring off into space. It was anybody's guess as to what kind of crazy or sane, good or bad, brilliant or dumb, stuff was going on in that kid's head. At moments like that, completely unnoticed by Hector, you could have taken one of those really big cheerleader megaphones and put the wide-open end down over Hector's head and rested the rim on his shoulders then climbed up onto something tall and put your ear over the small end that you shouted into. All you would have heard was the collected distant muffled shouting of hundreds, maybe thousands, of loud calling and competing voices and ideas like listening to the echoing chaotic verbal commotion of a trading pit on the floor of a commodities exchange.

One of Hector's frequent and favorite theories was that all of the tiny dust particles floating around in the classroom (or any room for that matter) were actually tiny floating inhabited planets where time was a million tiny planet years to one of our seconds. Hector was "out there", right along with all the tiny dust worlds floating about. However, some of Hector's ideas, no matter how strange, once they'd gotten into your head, had a sort of mental "stickiness" about them. Consequently, for years I never looked at a spot of dust on a piece of furniture or a spec of dust floating in the air without flashing back to Hector's weird but somehow intriguing idea.

Hector's wide-ranging thoughts were not solely concerned with the origin and fate of the dust particle universe. His questions and mindful speculations spanned a wide and varied range across the entire spectrum of our existence. One afternoon as school let out, Hector raced up to me with a burning question. He wanted to know what I knew about girls. My first thought was that he was in love. That immediately led to the possibility that somewhere in school was a female Hector Hobart; a corresponding counterpart. The disturbing and unsettling image of Hector and a Miss Hector having found each other, together, as a couple – I shuddered.

Forcing the thought out of my mind, I came back to Hector's question. I quietly pulled him aside and told him that what I knew about girls couldn't help anybody, including myself. All I had to go on was the mess with Melissa Williams and, well, we all know how that turned out. But I felt obligated, on the spot, to tell Hector something. His craziness was sort of intimidating. I told him how I'd suggested that Melissa and a squashed rat could have been close relatives. I cringed with guilt after repeating the story but it was all I had, it just slipped out.

Hector stared off into the deep blue sky, in a trance, while he contemplated my answer. He came back to earth just long enough to say that he got it, my analogy that is. I really didn't think there had been much to get but, as I spent more time with Hector, I learned that he could invent and pull significant meaning from a discarded oily rag. As a reward for the information, Hector offered up half of his uneaten sandwich from lunch.

The half-sandwich was a perfect illustration of Hector's understanding and interaction with the world. It wasn't until after I accepted and taken delivery that I realized the contents and composition of the sandwich were of mostly indeterminable origin. Hector proudly proclaimed that the "food object" was of his own original design and one of his favorites. It was just as likely that the half-sandwich had fallen to earth inside some sort of large space rock, a geologic castoff from one of those tiny dust particle planets that Hector kept seeing floating around.

A brief visual inspection and physical analysis revealed recognizable peanut butter, mayo, cheese(s), pickles, different types of bread and three other mystery ingredients, two of which looked suspiciously like gum balls and red licorice whips. It wasn't just a sandwich but a *Frankenstein*-like invention bordering on being its own life form. Holding it in my hand it immediately became apparent that there was the chance that if I actually summoned the courage and took a bite out of the alien culinary concoction that the damn thing just might bite me back. "A man eating a sandwich" (man having lunch) was a completely different scenario than "A man eating sandwich" (man being lunch).

As I lifted the sandwich closer to my face for a more detailed inspection I'd sensed that "it" was looking back at me just as hard as I was looking at "it." For the one-hundredth time I had the creepy feeling that my association with Hector was the equivalent of slowly sinking into quicksand and the sloppy glop was starting to close in around my throat. Hector wasn't just "different", he was well beyond any meaning of the term, and I felt he was trying to drag me in there with him.

This conclusion was confirmed one Monday afternoon as I patiently waited for Hector in the usual place for his weekly lesson. I'd decided, with mixed feelings, we were about to have our last session together, bringing into effect the fifth and final condition of our agreement. What little progress he'd shown in the beginning had long since ceased; in fact, he had started to decline from that original low high point. He was the only kid I played marbles with who'd aim at his target to the front, shoot and have his marble fly back over his head and land in the dirt three feet behind him. Even during my planned periods of unconventional marble gymnastics practice, I never even came close, much less thought about trying a shot like that. He was an unintentional, accidental, expert at shooting a backwards curve ball with a marble. I waited and wondered how best to phrase the news of my decision. I hoped that Hector would remain calm and reasonable upon hearing the discouraging news. The fear that he might have "lost it" and tried to run me through with his slide rule was a lingering and disturbing thought.

I finally settled upon a direct but tactful approach, leaving plenty of room for a quick retreat to safer ground when my best friend Russell had come running across the playground in my direction with a chalk white face. Russ was one of the very few people who knew that I was attempting, through marbles, to normalize Hector. He stopped about thirty feet away, waving his arms and shouted that I should follow him right away. Russ was jumping up and down and yelling that Hector was cracking up.

Russell and I ran in that high-speed gear that leaves a dust trail in the air behind you. We rounded the corner of the school building and saw a crowd of screaming kids in a circle at the far corner of the asphalt-paved part of the playground. As we pushed our way through the crowd, I immediately comprehended the urgency of the situation. Kneeling directly over a storm sewer grate in that part of the playground, Hector quietly chanted, "sewers get hungry too," as he dropped, one at a time, all of his brand new Cat's-Eye boulders through the grate and into the dark wet bottom of the storm drain several invisible feet below.

I reached Hector just as the last beautiful Cat's-Eye boulder disappeared through the grate and into darkness. Hector's actions were madness, pure sacrilege. He'd sunk into deep dark waters and he'd taken his marbles with him. Hector just looked up at me with a blank face.

"As far as I can figure it Archer, it's just part of the game. Sewers get hungry too," Hector stated in an unnervingly calm and quiet voice.

"No," I thought to myself, "I didn't know," and I hoped I never would.

Hector was whisked away by the belligerent playground supervisor. They probably had rules about voluntarily dumping your marbles down the sewer; they had rules about everything else. I had the funny feeling that Hector sensed that either that day or sometime shortly thereafter I was going to terminate his lessons. As Hector was being dragged away he looked back at me with one of those big goofy full-face grins.

"Remember Archer, it's just a game. Sewers get hungry too!" he yelled back in my direction.

Creepy. His parting words left me with an uneasy feeling, like I was just exposed to an obvious but upsetting truth that I was strenuously avoiding. It was similar to the way I felt after talking to Robert about winning and losing and the meaning of games.

That same afternoon Hector did not return to class. The kids were still buzzing over Hector's playground antics at the end of the school day. Russ and I were still talking about it when we started for home from school. As we reached the gate that led off the school grounds onto the sidewalk who came running up to us from out of nowhere but the mystery man himself, Hector Hobart. Russ stepped away and headed for home and I did likewise, hoping that Hector would get the message and not follow. He followed anyway. I learned that Hector was never very good at picking up on culturally based, social behavioral hints like that. He was just too crazy inspired, awkward and honest. He caught up and grabbed me from behind by the shoulder and shouted for me to wait up. I stopped, spun around and, face to face, unloaded.

"You're nuts!" I shouted.

He stood silent, feet together, head down, looking down at his shoes (both of which were untied and he wore mismatched socks) with his hands stuffed into his front pants pockets. I just stood there as well not knowing what else to say. I thought I'd said it all. Suddenly, like someone had plugged his extension cord back into a wall socket, Hector came back to life as he pulled his righthand from his pants pocket.

"Here!"

In his extended right hand, palm up, were five of his new Cat's-Eye boulders. They'd never seen action, pristine. He told me in a halting voice that they were for me and all the rest had been fed to the sewer. Five beautiful marbles, each one representing one of the five practice sessions we'd had. I didn't know what to say or do. Hector stepped forward and forcibly grabbed my right wrist with his left hand and, holding my arm firmly in place, shoved the five marbles into my right hand and forced my fingers to close over the boulders. Barely able to speak, I choked out one last question.

"Why did you do it, Hector? Why did you go and drop all those great marbles into the sewer?"

He looked at me with that big ear-to-ear grin of his.

"Because Archer, it doesn't matter," he simply stated.

He turned and skipped his way back towards school.

I never saw Hector again. One day, not long after Hector disappeared, as class was being dismissed for lunch, I peeked into what used to be Hector's desk only to find that it was empty, completely cleaned out, not even a leftover sandwich-like thing. That same day, at the final bell, Mrs. Goodchaulks called me up to her desk. She opened her top desk drawer, reached in and pulled out an envelope with a card inside. I opened it where I stood. It was a little card with rabbits on the cover that had balloons tied to their tails with ribbons. It was a "Thank You" card from Hector's mother and father. "Thank You for being Hector's friend," signed, "Mr. and Mrs. Hobart." That was all.

My classmates and I often speculated as to the condition and whereabouts of Hector. The general consensus was that he'd finally and completely weirded out. I tended to agree but I also privately harbored the funny feeling that wherever Hector had disappeared to and whatever strange things he was thinking and doing, he was doing it all with that freaky clown grin on his face. Marbles could be a voyage into the...unknown.

I'd paid the toll and carried the burden. Once again I was a freeboy.

Warren 'Rusty' Axlerod

WITH THE BABES, Melissa's and Hector's of the season behind me, all of the emotionally taxing baggage that came along with them was willingly left behind at the roadside of rapidly receding and ever more distant memory. The reacquired invincibility of my game skills were unquestionably demonstrated across the expanse of the playground on a school-daily basis. However, there was a dimension of the marble game to which only the best players ever aspired, ever dared to reach. When competing against the best players one needed more than just a great winning record and a sterling reputation. Metal was required.

I'm not referring to the necessary fine 'mettle' of a resilient character, but literally, actual physical 'metal'. There was nothing that commanded unnerving attention and fearful respect more than a sock (really heavy-duty work type sock) full of ball bearing steelies. Steel marbles added a rarely attainable dimension of indestructibility to your game. When the steelies came out the regular crystal glass marbles weren't just put away, they ran and hid. If crystal Cat's-Eye boulders were the top-of-the-line ammunition of conventional marble warfare, steelies were the equivalent of the next giant step up: atomic.

You never mixed crystal glass and hardened steelies. The glass would be wounded beyond saving; it just wouldn't hold up against the overpowering and unyielding steel. The problem was securing a reliable source that would provide a readily available and ongoing adequate supply. Steelies weren't available at the normal marble outlets because they weren't really considered marbles. They were marble-like affectations that had been adopted into the darker, harder side of the competitive marble world. One could find small, insignificant peewee steelies at the hardware store but the really large boulder size ball bearings were used in industrial settings, in factories and in large pieces of machinery.

A shiny new steely was wondrous to behold, but they were most likely to come from dark, dirty, noisy, even dangerous places. When you had steelies, conventional marble players gave you a wide berth because maybe, just maybe, you were just as hard (or harder) than the metal marbles you carried and that meant you were trouble and that meant you were best left alone.

Having briefly reflected upon the Al Capone-like aspects of that part of the marble world, I talked my ideas over with best pal Russell, but he drew a blank as well on where or how to score the metal marbles. So once again I turned to my older brother Robert for his guidance and counsel in solving the problem. Late on a Friday afternoon Russell and I ascended, by invitation, the two-by-four ladder to Robert's private world. As ready and eager as I was to talk business, for Russell, it being his first (and only) visit to Robert's baseball world in the sky, he was allowed the requisite few minutes of mouth open amazement before he was ready to focus on the real issue at hand.

Robert lowered the canvas window and door shades with the pull of a solitary rope and turned on the single overhead light. I explained my plan and Robert agreed that a solid assortment of steelies would definitely make the desired impression, not to mention the resulting and desired competitive effects. I further explained that we didn't have a clue as to where to start our search. Robert asked if I'd checked out Dad's basement workbench and I responded that I had with the only unexpected find being an old double-walled cardboard box full of pretty rocks hidden behind the screwdriver rack.

Robert leaned back against the wall and reshuffled a stack of baseball cards. He stopped, put down his cards, leaned forward and started to whisper.

"Just how serious are you guys? I mean, how far are you willing to go, I – mean, just – how – far?"

I answered immediately that we'd stop just short of murder and insisted that he continue (Russell looked at me and silently mouthed, "murder?" I silently mouthed back "yeah, murder." Russ just shrugged his shoulders). Robert asked if either of us had ever heard of Axlerod's Salvage Yard near the edge of town. We hadn't because we were just two little kids who'd never been anywhere near the "edge of town." Robert went onto explain that if we wanted steelies by the car load the place to get them was Axlerod's junkyard.

Robert had never actually been inside the place but he'd walked by a couple of times with a group of friends. The catch was that the yard owner, Warren Axlerod, only traded his junk for money, better junk or both. A further complication was that Axlerod was kinda nuts, which was even further complicated by his hatred of kids of all sizes and ages. Those few times Robert and his friends just walked by the place had been enough to draw verbal fire as Axlerod, unprovoked except by their mere passing presence, shouted several warnings to stay out and stay away.

 Knowing well enough that neither Russell nor I had the money to buy anything, much less anything that was already classified as junk, we decided, out of necessity, to resort to other less than honorable means to achieve our goal. Russ and I agreed right then and there in the tree house that we'd actually venture, on our own, out to the "edge of town" and checkout Axlerod's Yard the very next morning. Robert produced pencil and paper and drew us a map. To the best of his recollection he sketched out how to get there, the layout of the yard and a big 'X' marking, as rumor had it, the spot where the steelies where piled three feet high, free and ready for the taking by those brave enough to try.

 As we descended from the tree house, Russ and I bubbled over with the nervous anticipation of not only the piles of free steelies but also the thought of having to pull off a caper to get at the goods. We planned to meet the next morning at nine o'clock and take a city bus to within a few blocks of Axlerod's place and plan our attack from there. We'd deluded ourselves and each other, in our state of blissful ignorance, that we were, in fact, both brave enough and daring enough to succeed. If we couldn't get at those steelies, nobody could.

 I couldn't have wished for a better partner than Russell to help me get at Axlerod's steelies. Russ could be a pretty daring guy who wasn't afraid to walk the narrow line between trouble and disaster now and then. Russ would try just about anything at least once. He was always experimenting with one idea or another and I was fortunate enough to be on hand for some of his more exclusive stunts. During spring break Russ had invited me over to his house where he demonstrated, first hand and up close, how quick and easy it was to mess up and find yourself in big trouble in no time at all.

After his birthday he invited me over to see his presents. His Uncle Chester knew just what Russ wanted and he'd delivered. Uncle Chester was his mom's younger brother and he had a reputation of being a bit of a rabble-rouser, which he proved by sending Russ one of those high powered rubber tube slingshots, along with a monster supply of hard cinder marble-sized pellets for ammunition. We had a great time shooting at weeds, clumps of dirt, tree trunks and a couple of low flying crows.

As the hours passed we longed for more challenging targets to test our aim. We even went so far as to shoot a couple of pellets straight-up into the air above and then stood with metal trash can covers over our heads in hopes of taking direct hits as the falling pellets returned to earth. What we finally decided upon was a form of slingshot skeet shooting. In the place of clay pigeons we used empty tin cans as our flying targets. Russ shot first as I tossed one metal bird after another into the air.

Where Russ lived, the houses were further apart but we still had to be careful when taking aim and firing away. There were a few close calls as several of Russ' misses bounced off roofs or slammed into house siding close to windows on neighboring houses. During our target practice Russ' nextdoor neighbor, Ella, was outside hanging her wet wash on the clothesline to dry when one of Russ' wayward shots whizzed past her ear. Luckily, she probably thought it was a passing honeybee and didn't take much notice because she waved to us as she walked back into her house. About a minute later another one of Russ' misses hit one of Ella's clean, drying, white pillowcases, leaving a black cinder streak down its entire length.

"Shit," Russ mumbled.

(Pause – up to the edge)

"Shit?" I mumbled back more as a question than a confirming comment.

(Another pause – then – over the edge)

Silence – (for one second) – then mouth wide-open, breathless, full body contortion, funny-punch to the solar plexus, convulsive gagging can't-get-it-out laughing. We laughed hard, really hard, choking, can-not-catch-your-breath, falling-down-on-the-ground holding-your-gut, drool dripping from your lower lip and eyes tearing with snot-bubbles-shooting-out-of-your-nose hard. "Shit" was the funniest one word joke we'd ever heard.

We'd both heard the word before. We were more than acquainted with the word's milder companions, "crap" and "poop." "Crap" was the middle of the road word used most commonly by the guys at school. It was a relatively mild expletive that could be serious or funny. "Poop," on the other hand, had never been taken seriously and was really considered one small vocabulary step above baby talk. But "shit" – that was a first rate, top drawer, front of the line expletive which covered a whole range of situations and circumstances. It could be downright mean and serious and yet, just about the funniest word you ever heard when used under the right conditions. I'd never said it before and if Russ had I never heard him. It was a word that had been there all along and all around us in our young lives without having been adopted for our own personal use. But on that day, in that place, at that moment, that particular species of swear-bird had been flying past overhead and couldn't help but notice all the tin cans and slingshot pellets flying around. It had dropped down onto Russ' shoulder at the most opportune, right-on-cue, masterly timed moment and whispered in his ear.

We both simultaneously understood the full breadth and implication of its many forms, uses and meanings. It was the perfect word, at the perfect time and we made it ours. From that instance on, when the conditions were right, when the circumstances called for it, my first serious four-letter word had become a permanent part of my vocabulary. It was a word that sat squarely at the center of an ever-expanding, ever-transforming constellation of expressive vocabulary.

There were numerous before and after adjoining words that could easily expand its use and definition into multiple directions and seemingly endless applications. But all that would come later. That simple core word stood ready and waiting on the sidelines, ready and willing to play its part, serious or funny, when called upon, forever.

I threw dozens of cans into the air as Russ correspondingly missed dozens of times. Along with the flying tin cans going in every direction and formation and slingshot pellets zipping through the sky like machine gun tracer bullets, our newfound word started flying around in every direction and formation too. The low altitude airspace immediately above Russ' backyard had become a mixed melee of airborne metal, cinder pellets and the often-repeated four-letter expletive. Every missed shot was another reason to let fly with another "oh shit!" or "what kinda shit?" or "that was shit!"

It was amazing how a word like that could be both an effective preluding prefix and/or a descriptive concluding suffix for something as simple as a flying tin can. We also discovered that both ideas could be employed simultaneously, like bracketing exclamation points or attached colorful bookends as the cans flew through the air. How a perfectly good word like that could have avoided our attention and use for so long had been baffling. But we both more than made up for months of previous lost opportunities in that single afternoon.

Russ' backyard started to look like a tin can reclamation center. Russ got pretty frustrated with his poor aim as he ordered one more tin can into the air for his last shot. He shouted to really whip it high and hard so I bent way down, cocked my throwing arm and sprang up and launched the can back over my head instead of straight-up. But "Dead-Eye Russ" kept it in his sights and fired away anyway. What he failed to grasp in those split seconds was that the can was headed right for the back of his house. His shot missed the can by a mile but found a bull's-eye on a kitchen window. That called for and resulted in a mumbled (and not as funny) "oh shit" in unison.

It turned out to be the last time that Russ was ever allowed to use his cool slingshot. It was also the last time that his Uncle Chester was ever allowed to send him a weapon as a gift. However, it wasn't the last time that either Russ or I used our favorite new word. The real rub was that I never got a chance at nailing even one of those "shit" flying tin "shit" cans (awkward, grammatically incorrect; but I was just a beginner and still needed practice).

Russ had that special knack for getting into trouble. He didn't always think things through before embarking on many of his misguided adventures. Not long after slingshot shutdown, we were playing highway construction with his fleet of toy construction rigs in the dirt behind his house. As the road crew clocked out for the day, Russ thought it would be a good idea to give the equipment a thorough after-the-job wash down. He wasn't allowed to use the garden hose any more because of an earlier incident involving an anthill. While using the powerful stream of water to attack, flood and destroy the large ant colony, he managed to inadvertently attack, flood and partially destroy the family living room through an unnoticed open window (that resulted in matching very big and loud "oh shits" from his mother and father). So Russ had to come up with a different plan as he ran into his house to search out a different solution.

Russ had come back with a large finger-pump spray bottle of purple glass cleaner. It took us just a few minutes with rags and the glass cleaner to have the fleet looking showroom floor new. When we finished, Russ let out a slow sick sort of "oh-shit" sigh (that word, it just worked everywhere). In our exuberance to clean the trucks we used almost the entire quart of his mother's favorite glass cleaner. Russ' eyes lit up like two car headlights as an idea had magically materialized. I followed Russ as he darted back into the kitchen.

He instructed me to get a glass drink pitcher from a lower cupboard. Russ stood on a kitchen chair while digging around inside the refrigerator's freezer. He found what he was looking for; a can of frozen grape juice concentrate. Russ moved his chair from in front of the fridge to in front of the kitchen sink where he mixed the grape juice to a drinking consistency. He opened a drawer and retrieved a metal funnel which he inserted into the top of the nearly empty glass cleaner bottle. He poured the bottle one-quarter full of grape juice. He filled the remainder of the bottle with a mixture of water, a little ammonia and a touch of dish washing liquid. Then with a little shaking, it looked and smelled just like the real glass cleaner. What a genius! We put the substitute glass cleaner concoction back under the sink. Russ then pulled two clean glasses from the dish drainer and poured each of us a tall cool glass of grape juice from the leftovers as we toasted his quick thinking and ingenuity.

I'd nearly forgotten our chemistry solution high jinx when some days later Russ came over and told me that he'd really caught hell from his mom. Our mixing job with the grape juice had been so convincing that his mom never noticed the difference as she used the entire mixture to clean all of the insides of the windows in the house. The problem became apparent when the warm spring air combined with the hot rays of sunlight had resulted in a thin syrupy light purple film forming on all of the windows. Hundreds of houseflies found their way to the windows to get their share of the fermenting grape cleaner. With every opening of a door more flies flew in searching for the grape sugar.

Poor Russ, it was just a simple miscalculation. The ammonia content was too low and wasn't enough to cover the grape juice sugar and repel the flies. His Mom made him re-clean all of the affected windows in the house and vacuum up all of the dead flies. In the end, however, Russ never suffered too severely at the hands of his concerned parents. They thought of grounding him but the idea of Russ cooped up in the house for hours or days at a time might have started him on all kinds of loony projects and experiments in an effort to keep himself occupied. So everything balanced out between Russ and me. I had the purpose and the plan and he had the daring and willingness to take just about any kind of chance. It was a perfect combination. What could possibly go wrong?

At twenty-one years of age, fat, stringy haired, greasy complexioned Warren 'Rusty' Axlerod had promised himself at a very early age that someday, some way, he would become the best, the most accomplished, junkyard owner-operator in the State. He really had his sights on being the best in the world but he resolved to be diligent and patient and proceed on his chosen path in small sure steps. If Warren had it his way he would have been on the job right out of the gate, so to speak, and been born in a junkyard. He considered it an unintentional innocent oversight on the part of his parents, a handicap and a deficiency at birth, that he gladly committed the rest of his life to correcting and overcoming.

Warren's dreams of a junkyard all his own came true one night when his Uncle Ralph's junkyard dreams and accomplishments abruptly ended. Ralph was Warren's favorite uncle and Warren was Ralph's favorite nephew. For all of his formative younger years Warren had spent every weekend, every day of every summer vacation helping his uncle buy, sell, collect, sort, inventory and generally control his world of junk. I guess one could say that from the very start Warren had junk in his blood. As much as marbles was my life, junk was Warren's life obsession.

Warren's Uncle Ralph was found peacefully deceased inside of one of his old junk freezers that still had the door in place; a real junkyard no-no (not the dying part but the leaving the door on a freezer part). Ralph often used the old appliance like a lounge sleeper that he'd outfitted with blankets and pillows. While dozing in his nap time hideaway one cool breezy afternoon the freezer had shifted as he turned in his sleep and the door slammed shut and jammed. Warren's uncle died of suffocation. It was not too swift a move for an experienced junk man like Ralph. Warren was the one that found his uncle on a Saturday morning three days after the fact when he showed the freezer to a young couple looking for a deal on the used appliance. Needless to say the unexpected gruesome discovery resulted in one very big "no sale!"

It was Ralph's wish that he be laid to rest along with the closest piece of junk in proximity to his remains upon his passing. Ralph was buried inside his lounge sleeper of a freezer coffin, a model *36A Great Northern Ultra Cool* (instead of flowers tossed into his grave, Ralph requested matching 1956 *Chevy* radiators, his head stone was an engraved weather-proofed under-the-kitchen-sink cabinet door). Out of his deeply-felt affection and appreciation for his nephew's loyalty and undivided interest, Ralph took all the necessary steps to provide for Warren's future including disclosing, for Warren's eyes only, multiple secret locations of buried junkyard cash. Warren would be more than amply rewarded for his years of enthusiastic help and friendly, unwavering loyalty and companionship.

As Uncle Ralph was the black sheep of Warren's extended family, many of the relatives were not too happy with the terms of his *Last Will and Testament*. Not one of those relatives, with the exception of Warren and Warren's parents (Ralph was Warren's Mom's older brother) had called upon him as a friend and relative for years, and, until his death hadn't given a damn anyway. While Ralph was still alive, he knew full well the arrogant and condescending attitude that his brothers, sisters, cousins, aunts and uncles had toward him for being a lowly junkyard guy. The only relatives who accepted Ralph's chosen profession and lifestyle were Warren's parents, who didn't judge so harshly the man that their son held in such high regard and esteem.

So it wasn't unusual, not unexpected, that one of the stipulations in Uncle Ralph's Will read that, when all the relatives gathered in his attorney's office for the *Reading of the Will*, everyone present except Warren and his parents, were required to wear farm animal costume masks. Those who refused to abide by the preliminary stipulation were denied entry to the *Reading of the Will* and excluded from any individual rewards that the Will might provide.

One might think that this final insult from the departed Ralph would result in no one attending. Oh, not true! The family rumor, yes, the odd old story whispered among the relatives over the years, the story that just wouldn't die and go away was that Ralph, despite his weird and nutty disposition, was one of those dressed down bum-like geniuses who'd quietly earned and squirreled away millions in junkyard profits. Every one of the relatives, in anticipation of the rumor being true and being potential recipients of large checks and/or grants of property from the eccentric Ralph, showed up with the best farm animal masks that money could buy.

Pigs, cows, sheep, chickens, horses, mules and roosters were more than adequately represented, like they all come straight from the State Fair, like they all just hopped off a Mardi Gras replica parade float of *Noah's* own *Ark*. If they'd also had guns, being so adequately disguised, and if so inclined, they could have attempted or even successfully pulled off a local bank heist (even though Ralph's least favorite cousin "Fred" – really cousin Fredericka, he'd called her "Fred" to just piss her off – and Ralph's second least favorite cousin "Alice" – really cousin Allen, he'd called him "Alice" just to piss him off too – both used rapid-getaway-hampering walking canes).

    The Attorney, uncomfortable yet necessarily tolerant of Uncle Ralph's unusual but legal nonetheless (paid for in advance) request, proceeded to read his *Last Will and Testament* to the assembled mixed herd. The first stipulation willed the entire junkyard enterprise to Warren. That included every broken lock, junked piece of metal stock and rusted barrel with the condition that every year he turned a profit twenty-five percent of said profit would go to his parents for their ongoing benefit and support. The second stipulation was that Warren and his parents were to leave the *Reading of the Will*, which both he and his parents did gladly. Warren's dream had come true.

    Warren, his parents and the Attorney could not see the faces behind the animal masks but various individual animal-like sounds, appropriate to each individual mask, started to leak out into the room, like a storm was coming and all the animals in the barnyard were getting nervous. After Warren and his parents departed that left the Attorney, the rest of Ralph's Will and all the agitated animals. The third stipulation was legally abrupt and unmistakably clear. There was nothing left for any other remaining relatives. Not one penny, crushed tin can, rusted wheel rim, old window frame, used tire or one single square inch of dusty rusty real estate. Nada. Nothing. The fourth stipulation was that he, Uncle Ralph, "knew exactly what they'd all thought of him during his life and that they were all just a selfish, mean spirited bunch of pigs, cows, sheep, chickens, horses, mules and roosters asses (and other unkind animal part references) and that they could all just drop dead and go to hell." That was it. Uncle Ralph had the final word fully knowing well in advance, while he was still alive, that he would someday make Warren's day, help Warren's parents and deservedly piss off everyone else. "So what?" was his scornful attitude, "I'll be dead." Everybody, respectively, good or bad, loved or hated, got exactly what they earned and deserved.

Several weeks later, the deprived relatives, en mass, minus the animal personas, approached Warren at the junkyard in hopes of negotiating a more even, equitable and amicable share the wealth settlement of Ralph's estate. It rapidly became apparent to the brothers, sisters, cousins, aunts and uncles of the deceased Uncle Ralph that he'd not only willed the junkyard business to Warren but most of his eccentricities, strange habits and family resentments as well. Warren not only refused to hear their complaints and renegotiation requests, he sent them all on their way stumbling, screaming, rushing for the exit and running to save their lives. He chased them all, with the greatest enthusiasm and sincerest contempt, from what was then, unmistakably and without question, HIS junkyard with a three foot long section of two inch diameter lead pipe which he'd astutely acquired in an even trade for a 1953 *Ford* Pickup carburetor.

Although Warren was only a young man with a whole life of limited possibilities before him, he felt certain that inheriting the junkyard was his Destiny. Dismissive of his parents' suggestions to keep his narrow options open Warren felt confident that he was on the right course for the rest of his life. Warren dove head first, with a goofy smile on his face, right into a six-plus acre pile of junk. He waded and waddled neck deep in the luxury of his newly acquired material wealth. It was well known among Axlerod family friends and confidants that, although Warren's parents were concerned for their son's future and welfare, they were nonetheless relieved that their son would no longer be using his bedroom, half the basement and two-thirds of their backyard for his own large, varied and growing collection of assorted "stuff."

Over the next few years it became apparent that Warren had listened and learned well from his Uncle Ralph. In fact, despite Warren's peculiarities, he ran his junkyard so efficiently that he received several awards in recognition of his astute proprietorship. He, reluctantly, belonged to all of the necessary, correct and important clubs, societies, organizations, associations and brotherhoods that had been created and were in existence solely for the membership and benefit of those who called a junkyard home and/or business. By the time Warren had lorded over and been master of his junkyard for two years he was well on his way to fulfilling his life long dream of becoming the best junk heap owner in the world.

Despite his rising star and status in the world of junk, Warren had that one problem that haunted his thoughts by day and his dreams by night. His limited prior experience with the feelings of power and control associated with the accumulation of wealth and physical (junk) possessions created by his rapid and bountiful success left a wide dark gap between the intellectual specifics of his expertise and the emotional implications of his material success.

Warren psychologically compensated. He didn't just manage his junkyard, he became the royal ruler and the yard was his kingdom. The very first day after legally acquiring the yard he started to "rearrange the furniture" so to speak. He towed his extensive collection of junked cars and trucks into three concentric semicircles, all centered on the yard office and connected workshop. Every morning, rain, shine, fog or snow he stepped out through the office door and paced back and forth in front of the rows of abandoned vehicles as if reviewing the palace guard. If it was an especially windy morning the air weaving through the gaps between the stacked kitchen and laundry room appliances sounded like the tribute of distant bugles. Old tires stacked twenty-five feet high with rusted axles as metal spines were stacked at the corners and other strategic locations in the yard like castle ramparts standing guard. The place looked creepy enough in the middle of a sunny day, but, at night, it looked downright frightening, like the junk might come to life and start moving around on its own in the dark.

The yard had become the external manifestation of the interior maze of Warren's mind. It was Warren against the world and it didn't matter whether you came as friend or foe, everyone was suspect. Warren's feelings of power over his possessions led to his feelings of inescapable, terrifying vulnerability. It was Warren's own special twisted version of the old "here today gone tomorrow" nightmare that all power-mad people have struggled with.

Warren harbored terrible fears of assorted solo and combined disasters that could befall his junk. To most people, a junkyard going up in flames, being washed away by a flood or blown all over the county by a tornado was not a major concern unless you lived next door or nearby. To Warren just the mere hint of any such calamity would start him shaking, trembling, stuttering, sweating and running for the toilet. All sorts of stories, rumors, lies, half-lies, half-truths and other mental inventions arose and floated about regarding Warren and his junk over the years including bio-mechanical junk monsters and a doomsday machine constructed from non-working car engines, washing machines without drive belts and petrified melon rinds.

Without a doubt, as bad as potential natural disasters could be, Warren's biggest fear was of people, all people; the very people he depended upon to achieve and maintain his ongoing success. It was people posing as customers, cheats, thieves and big and little kids that were intent upon getting something that was already worthless for nothing. Everybody in the world was out to steal him blind. Warren's recurring nightmare was of being tied up and gagged in his office by laughing masked crooks, as they'd make off with all of his awards, certificates of achievement, trophies and wheelbarrows full of all his best and most valuable junk. The only nightmare that was worse was when the masked thieves turned out to be little punky kids like Russell and myself.

The spreading fires of Warren's all-consuming paranoia were fueled by his bad dreams. After a while Warren had difficulty distinguishing between what actually happened in his daily life and what he dreamt happened in his daily life. Mornings after an especially bad night he skipped the ceremony of reviewing the troops and rushed out into the yard taking mental inventory, checking to see if the stuff he dreamt had been stolen had actually been taken. Warren was in rough mental shape and he was tumbling further down that hill every day and every night.

He spent entire days and nights in his dirty office-work-shop, sitting in front of a small portable black and white TV with a cracked screen and no sound, shoving handfuls of salted, greasy *Spanish Peanuts* from a five gallon metal tub into his mouth, as he kept watch over his yard with a pair of binoculars with cracked lenses that he peered through while wearing his glasses with cracked lenses while he looked out the office window which consisted of six panes of cracked glass. Warren's cracked and splintered kaleidoscopic visual world was an exact projection of his cracked and splintered kaleidoscopic psychic world. Warren was psychologically rotting and mentally festering.

Kids sneaking and messing around in his yard was Warren's single biggest fear, the great bane of his existence. Not because they might get hurt but because they'd just be messing around and stealing stuff. All kids were no good and up to no good, period. Kids topped the list of actual, potential and imaginary enemies list that Warren maintained in his fog shrouded mind. The next four on the list were stray dogs which always pooped in his yard (which the shoes he was wearing always managed to find), anybody who wanted something for nothing, pyromaniacs and any of his relatives with the exception of his parents and his dead Uncle Ralph's ghost who he frequently claimed to see and converse with at length.

On the particular Saturday in question Warren was in an especially foul mood. The combination of terrible dreams the night before, combined with the fact that it had been weeks since he'd chased any kids from his yard, left him feeling that the time was ripe – he felt due. His unceasing fearful vigilance was not always conducive to good customer relations. Any reasonable resemblance to a healthy mental disposition that Warren had remaining was steadily evaporating. He tried to reach out to people, to customers, in his own clumsy sort of way. For example, he insisted that people call him "Rusty", a self-given nickname. He even had it written on a handmade sign that hung on the fence at the main entrance to his junkyard, "Come on in and just call me Rusty!" It didn't work. Nobody ever "just called" him "Rusty." At a safe distance, everybody "just called" him "nuts!" All too often, perfectly honest, well-intentioned customers, with money to spend in their pockets, would hurry from the yard in fear and disgust, empty handed, another "no sale." To Warren everyone was a cheat and/or a thief or planning to be a cheat and/or a thief, all at his expense.

There he sat, leaning back in his broken office chair with his mismatched boots resting up on his cracked-top office desk, shoving load after load of peanuts into his bottomless chewing maw. The cracked silent television screen punched reflected image after image into and across his face as he surveyed his yard through his cracked glasses, cracked binoculars and cracked office window glass. Warren was a disturbing vision to behold. If he was only thirty inches tall, and sitting out in the yard by the car parts, Warren could have easily been mistaken for a discarded, nonfunctioning, oil-leaking, lots-of-parts-missing automatic transmission.

Russ and I got off the city bus one block from Axlerod's junk yard, pulled out the hand drawn map provided by Robert and planned our attack. Wanting to be safe and stealthy, we decided to sneak into the yard at a perimeter point furthest from Warren's office and then pick our way to the point in the yard where the sought after steelies were "just lying around for the taking."

We crawled underneath an unanchored spot in the cyclone fence by one of the corner tire towers and proceeded to dodge and weave towards the target area. The essence of any good caper (per the advice of the best crooks on TV's "all gangsters-all night" movie hours) was to get in and out with the goods and not have the theft discovered until the perpetrators were long gone, free and clear. Although we had to brave dangerously open ground in broad daylight, hiding as able, we were confident that everything would go without a hitch.

It was one-hundred yards from our target that Russ and I had to cross an especially large open area with minimal concealing cover that was directly visible from Axlerod's office. The complications started as soon as Russ and I made our move and darted across the open space headed for ground zero. Warren must have fallen right back out of his chair and onto the floor with glasses, peanuts and binoculars flying as our direction of motion coincided with his direction of stare as we unintentionally came into his unquestionably, unmistakenly, visually splintered view. Warren fumbled and stumbled to his feet, rushing to his broken office window mumbling cuss words accentuated by peanut fragments that flew from his mouth right along with all the expletives.

Russ and I dove behind several stacks of old tires just in time to see Warren bound from his office and stop just outside his office door with hands on his hips, spying in our general direction. We weren't sure if Warren had seen us or not because he stood motionless for just a few seconds and then put his hands in his pants pockets, slowly turned and casually walked back into his office. We held our ground, silent and still, certain that we'd remained undetected. As soon as Warren was out of sight back inside his office, we were back on the move slinking towards our intended goal.

Warren had seen us. Owing to his splintered, multiple-image view his first thoughts were that his yard had been invaded by a countless horde of rushing, surprise-attacking, evil thieving little rats. The second he stepped back into his office he sprinted for his workshop where he armed himself with his prepared-in-advance, ready-to-go, trespassing intruder defense kit. His weapons of deterrence consisted of a more than ample supply of a ready to deploy assortment of very specialized and dastardly, big and little, surprises he'd devised just for such emergency situations. His junkyard assault deterrence armaments package was designed to adequately handle single or multiple simultaneous intruders. Axlerod snuck out the back door of his shop and slowly crept along and circled in our direction.

Warren's well practiced and previously implemented plan of attack was to sneak up on unsuspecting intruders with twin hand held gas-powered nautical air horns and an assortment of bulging fluid filled water balloons. The balloons were inflated to almost bursting with a concoction of water, permanent fabric dye and a puree of rotten eggs. He'd creep up behind his intended victims and spring from concealment with a banshee scream, air horns blasting and staining stink bombs flying. Madman Axlerod would then pursue any offending trespassers from the yard, frequently following them for some distance out onto the public street before giving up the chase.

For Warren it was serious business all mixed in with some stress releasing sadistic psychotic fun. If his ambush was successful, which it usually was, the intruders ran for their lives badly shaken, badly stained, ears ringing, smelling like nobody ever wanted to smell and very unlikely ever to return as friendly customer or thieving foe. The rumor perpetuated by past victims was that it wasn't Warren that did the chasing but some fiendish contraption that he'd constructed to carry out the defensive assault. The dark vision, the nightmare of some twelve foot tall, rusty, bio-mechanical devil with an air horn for a mouth and the diabolical ability to manufacture, aim and launch staining stink bombs on demand was a commonly held and shared belief among the area's junkyard intrusion veterans and wannabes alike. On that Saturday, Russ and I discovered first hand that the only devilish fiend on the loose in that place was a solo human act, Warren 'Rusty' Axlerod himself.

"Two-Man Team Operation Steely Liberation" was a scant twenty-five yards from the objective when just by chance we saw Warren sneaking in our general direction. Axlerod had not reacquired us visually, but we then knew for certain that he knew we were somewhere about. The chase was on! It was the hunted verses the hunter. We scurried behind a wall of rusted wheel rims when we saw that Warren was armed to the teeth with air horns and jiggling balloons. Unable to make a run for it even if we wanted, we hunkered down and hid out until Warren walked past.

The plan was to slip in behind him after he passed, dash to the treasure, fill our pockets with free steelies and then run like hell for the exit. Russ and I, nervous, shaking and dripping with sweat, concealed in our hiding place, waited to see which way Warren would go. I was almost torn in half as the competing urges to run for the steelies or run for my life quaked and pulled at my center. When Axlerod reappeared, peering through gaps in the stacked metal wheel rims, I got a real good look at his face. Shit (I was with Russ), that guy looked scary! But instantly, I registered something completely unexpected.

In my fear I recognized that look, that crazy, focused and determined look. We may have been at the far opposite ends of the mental health spectrum but we were equals, dead center the same, in one important way. We were living obsessions about to meet – head-on. It was my fervent desire to get at his ball bearings to further my own ends and it was his equally fervent task to keep me from even getting close in order to protect and preserve his.

The first real difference between us was that Warren not only looked determined and obsessed, he looked dangerous. The second real difference was that I was a sane kid just temporarily acting nuts while Warren, conversely, was a full-time, always-on-the-job, permanently-seated First Class occupant of the crazy train, from start to finish, round trip all the way through, actual NUT! He sort of haltingly crept along, close to the ground, like a big, fat, greasy, hairy spider hunting down bugs for dinner.

Fortunately for us, the big fat spider fell into a sticky tangled web of his own making. Only twenty feet from our hiding place Warren tripped and fell front first into a pile of old, half-inflated rubber tire inner tubes. His charged air horns gave out two short sharp bursts like a giant clowns big red nose being squeezed. Adding to Warren's woes, as his horns fired off, the impact of his fall forced the unintentional detonation of one of his stink bombs all over the front of his already perpetually filthy coveralls. Warren angrily responded out loud to his predicament with an unending flow of words, many of which Russ and I never heard before and sincerely doubted actually existed in civil society. At the time we surmised that the unrecognizable vocabulary was some sort of technical junkyard lingo Warren saved for just such difficult junkyard situations.

We hastily agreed to retreat to a more distant, safer location as we darted out from our place of concealment and ran right in front of the floundering Axlerod. As Warren struggled to regain his footing, the under-inflated pile of bouncing inner tubes proved to be an almost insurmountable obstacle for him to escape from.

"I know you're in here you damn kids! You're not going to get away from me, yeah hear!" Warren shouted.

He could not regain his balance to save his life. He fell back in-to the pile of big, black, bouncy inner tube donuts with another series of unintended short air horn bursts along with a loud juicy POP as he was drenched by another self-inflicted stink bomb explosion.

Russ and I ran, terror-stricken and laughing hard at the same time. Our unexpected and out-of-place laughter could only be described as a stress-induced form of temporary situational madness, which proved to be impossible to avoid and made it difficult to catch our breath and run away fast enough. Deciding to exhaust our crazy laughing from a safer distance, we turned and sprinted straight into a pile of rusted hubcaps. Tripping and falling over each other like the panicked kids we were, the large rusted silver disks flipped into the air like giant, featherweight coins.

Warren somehow managed to roll out of his inner tube dilemma and struggled to his feet, as the sound of our collision was all he needed. He homed right back in on our position like a hungry weasel chasing noisy mice. Russ and I ran and scuttled between what seemed to be endless rows and stacks of old furniture, rusting cars and discarded appliances with Warren close behind howling like a rabid dog. Warren stuck to our trail like a wad of discarded chewing gum hanging onto the bottom of your shoe all the while blasting his air horns with one hand and the opposite arm held high, cocked and ready to fire a stinking balloon missile.

It was lucky for us that Warren was not in top physical condition. He was a tad bit fat, especially that part of his body from just below his triple chin, down across his belly tires to just above his thick bloated ankles. Fortunately, he tired pretty quickly. He still blew his horns but his howling and shrieking had given way to a wheezing squeak as Warren shuffled to an exhausted dead stop, completely out of breath. With his legs wobbly from the chase, with a short horn burst, Warren lost muscle control and fell backwards, butt-first, into a stack of soggy cardboard boxes which his bulky-butt instantly compressed into a form fitting lounge chair.

Keepers Weepers

Russ and I didn't stop. We kept on running, putting as much distance between Warren and us as we were able. We found a secluded cove in a valley of old washing machines where we caught our breath and decided our next move. We agreed, that if need be, Russ and I could just outrun Warren to any exit in the place. Based upon our superior speed and Warren's easily exhausted efforts at defense, we decided that one more try for the steelies was a go before we gave up and left Warren behind to play with his air horns and stink bombs by himself.

Russ volunteered to go topside to get a better lay of the land. I stayed grounded as Russ crawled to the top of a pyramid stack of old clothes dryers. Excitedly, Russ called down that we were right next to the old car and tractor axles where the steelies were supposed to be. Being as surprised and excited as Russ, I didn't fully grasp that my companion in crime had more shouted than whispered the news. We once again gave away our position to the wandering Warren.

I crawled along the ground to the side of the dryer pyramid where Russ had directed and there, sure enough, were the stacked and scattered axles. I felt like the weary African expedition leader, one of the last of the expedition explorers alive, to stumble and fall by dumb luck accidentally right into piles of ivory of the long lost secret elephant burial ground.

A quick survey of the immediate ground did not reveal any "stacks of steelies." There were only a few here and there, rusted, pitted and scattered about. A little panicked digging did reveal a stack of steelies which formed a small steely pyramid. When I tried to lift the point steely for a closer inspection the entire small pile came up with it. They'd all been welded together by some wise guy. Afterwards, if Russ and I made it out of Axlerod's junkyard alive, I made a point to have a talk with my brother.

Meanwhile, Russ was still perched atop the dryer mountain on his hands and knees, looking down and watching me on my hands and knees digging around in the dirt. With Russ' eyes on me and my eyes on the ground we had no eyes working on keeping track of the lurking Axlerod. Warren finally caught his breath and caught up to us as he peeked around the pile of dryers to my back and spotted me frantically scraping in the dirt. In his own excited anticipation of his long sought and impending surprise attack, Warren failed to notice that Russ was just above him atop the dryers.

Russ and I had become completely unaware of Warren's menacing presence as Axlerod prepared to pounce with horns blaring and stink bombs flying. If we'd taken the time and trouble to look up we might have noticed the turkey vultures beginning to congregate and circle above us in anticipation of the impending kill. Warren sprang from concealment into view with all of the physical effort that his energy reserves could produce coming to rest in a squatting stance with all the flare of a salvage yard *Samurai*. With feet spread, knees bent, mouth screaming, horns blaring and stink balloons armed and ready, Warren landed with a ground shaking THUMP!

His surprise reappearance and attack, as intended, was masterful in its shock and effect. I froze in abject terror as I waited for a quick number one-two combination to fill my pants. Russ, just as surprised and equally frightened, struggled to keep his balance atop the junk pile. Luckily for Russ and I, the shock effect of Warren's assault created a shock echo, a rebound effect. In his maneuvering to keep from falling Russ kicked an old metal washtub from the top of the pile. Before he was able to launch a single stink bomb, the falling washtub connected with the top of Warren's head with a deep dull metallic CLUNK!

Warren tipped, then rocked, then fell over, front first, into a pile of old newspapers like he was a freshly cut piece of tall timber falling to the forest floor. With his eyes half-open and his mouth fully agape Warren came to a dead rest on the stack of papers. He fell right on top of his stink balloons which burst in a shower of brilliant dye colors and rapidly spreading breathtaking stench. His limp body had also come to rest on the triggers of the air horns that continued to empty themselves, the sound muffled by his weight and clothes, until Russ and I got well out of hearing range. Appropriately, the washtub had come to rest, upside down, on the knocked-out Warren's back. He looked and smelled

Keepers Weepers

like a big, dead, stinky, decomposing snapping turtle.

Russ and I wasted no time in fleeing and putting a long and safe distance between ourselves and Axlerod's junkyard. We ran all the way to a bus stop several blocks further past the stop nearest the yard, certain that Warren would behave true to form and follow us for one last attack. We promised ourselves, out of breath and almost crawling up the stairs into the bus, that we'd never play hide-and-seek with Warren 'Rusty' Axlerod ever again.

During the bus ride back to our neighborhood, looking out the back window to see if Axlerod had recovered and run after us, the circling turkey buzzards were spiraling down lower and lower over the spot were we'd left Warren prostrate on the ground. It turned out that the daily persistent presence of buzzards circling above the junkyard was nothing new owing to the ever-present peculiar odor generated by Warren's equally peculiar personal hygiene habits. But the unusually large feathered crowd that had gathered at that moment was in response to all of the rotten egg smelling concoction, which by the end of our junkyard incursion, Warren had found himself amply bathed in. To the vultures, Axlerod lying on the ground smelling rotten, out cold and unmoving had justifiably, but mistakenly, been interpreted as dinner served! As Russ and I left Warren and the birds far behind to fight it out on their own, I reached into my pocket and pulled out the one and only rusted and pitted steely I'd managed to take from the yard.

Being the champ didn't make you immune to dangerously bad information or to the corresponding and equally misguided resulting advice. I was learning all along the way. Marbles – marbles would effortlessly roll you right up to the edge if you let them. If you let them they would roll you right over the edge just as easily.

The key seemed to be to roll up to the edge and stop, take in the whole view including, in their turn, the down-view over the edge, the out-view towards the expanse of the horizon and finally the up-view into endless space. That...that could be the most dangerous because you could loose all your referrence points and start to lean and lose your balance...forever.

Escaping Axlerod's junkyard and running to catch the bus for home was my way of a necessarily hasty but still careful and deliberate retreat; my stepping back from the edge after having taken in the whole view. Like I said, invading Warren's world may have been a crazy thing to do, but that didn't make me crazy. I decided then and there, bumping and bouncing along in the seat at the back of the bus, that in the future I'd confine any risky adventures to the edge of the one ring, the only ring that truly mattered – the marble ring.

*

Intermission:

Uncle Dave

FIRST, UNCLE DAVE wasn't really my uncle. He was a relative, all right – but a distant relative, some sort of cousin to my father three times removed, whatever that meant. He and my dad were close friends throughout their lives from little kids on into adulthood. My brother and I liked him a lot too so we called him Uncle and his wife Mary, who we liked just as much, we called Aunt Mary. He and Aunt Mary never had any kids of their own so they enjoyed their periodic stints as standby parents for Robert and me during our visits.

Uncle Dave was a great auto mechanic. He liked his work so much that he developed a sort of photographic memory when it came to car mechanic stuff. He'd read and study about a repair once, then do the repair just once, and then remember exactly everything he'd read and done forever without missing a single beat. But equal to his mechanical skills were his rare and unique abilities to swear and fart like nobody else I ever heard then or since.

My grandmother, on my dad's side, said that Dave was born swearing and farting. She claimed he'd cussed out the doctor who delivered him for having cold hands and farted while doing so. Mind you, Uncle Dave didn't just let loose with whatever dirty word that dropped into his mouth from his brain. He was a skilled, creative and emotive curser. He could tell a five minute long story about some "fat-faced bastard" that tried to cheat him on the price for a set of "four damn new tires" that used hardly any non-cuss words at all, making the story sound and flow like poetry. With a clever smile on his face he'd string together profanities in sentence after sentence that had a swaying singsong rhythm to it, like music. Uncle Dave's cursing was like other people's breathing; it had to happen all the time, or else.

Uncle Dave also shamelessly exhibited another trait, an unrestrained habit. He farted a lot, really a lot, like whenever and wherever bodily necessary and whenever and wherever the mood struck him. He rarely cared who was around or what the circumstances were. It was like his swearing; it just had to happen all the time, or else. Walking, sitting, talking, not talking, working on a car, not working on a car, awake, asleep (according to Aunt Mary) – flatulence was just part and parcel of Uncle Dave's vocabulary, an integral part of the "total Uncle Dave communicating experience" you might say. The mood and occasion didn't matter. Whether happy, frustrated, thoughtful or indifferent such circumstantial matters had no bearing on his mixed means of self-expression.

"It was always 'breezy' around your Uncle Dave," is how Aunt Mary used to put it.

We asked him if the lingering residual odor ever bothered him.

"Nope," he reassured us, "I never smell my own farts, that's what other people are for! Besides, I've always been told they sort smell like flowers, big colorful flowers and, if I'm not careful, my ass will start attracting bees and butterflies!"

His talent of weaving together his swearing and farting could be considered...artful. He was a gas-passer par excellence. Whether it was intentionally controlled or just a subconscious, built-in ability, his cussing and farting were synchronized, in tune as it were. There was a very basic, a very ordinary everyday, *Everyman* intellectual bent about his relentless and effortless blending of nice guy, skilled mechanic guy, profanity and flatulence habits guy that was, well, charming and endearing.

Uncle Dave also loved telling jokes to everyone and anyone and my brother and I were not spared as he not so subtly work his passing gas into the narrative. He had a favorite he saved just for us.

"Hey boys, have you heard this one?" he'd say and then instead of telling a joke he'd just rip a really big one, a blowout-the-back-of-his-pants big one.

Robert and I giggled and groaned even though we'd heard (and smelled) that one countless time's before. A good joke just never got old. He certainly had his fun with us but we had our fun with him too. It was always entertaining to get Uncle Dave all worked up, all riled up, about current events and politics. Local, state, national news, it didn't matter, as his cussing-farting combinations left no doubt as to his staunch positions and ardent views on any recent topic. When finished, he always concluded with a rousing summation, "...and that's what the damn hell (big fart) I think about that!"

Almost everyone who did business with Uncle Dave or socialized with him knew and surprisingly accepted, to varying degrees, his cussing and farting habits because he really was a most genuinely nice guy who also happened to be a great car mechanic who also just happened to swear and fart lot. For those who couldn't decide which was worse, his swearing or his farting, they decided to focus upon what was best for them, his ability to diagnosis and fix any car problem. They showed up, squinted and covered their ears or squinted and held their noses, depending upon which of the two 'presentations' bothered them the most, as they watched Uncle Dave perform his car fixing magic.

Uncle Dave wasn't all farts and swears. That is probably how some people in their town thought of him. It may have been a mystery to some how Uncle Dave and Auntie Mary met and stayed together but it wasn't a mystery to Dave and Mary. Dave was a good enough person to have originally attracted Mary in the first place and then did his part to keep their marriage and life together true and happy. Mom and Dad knew well enough and even Robert and I, just as young kids, sensed well enough the real care, deep regard and loving esteem that Dave and Mary had for one another.

Uncle Dave didn't smoke except for the occasional cigar, which he never finished because he never wanted to kiss Aunt Mary with an "ashtray mouth." He'd accept a cigar only to be gracious and polite when somebody gave it to him to celebrate a birth of a child or grandchild, that type of thing. He didn't really drink either, except for an occasional mixed drink or glass of beer when he and Aunt Mary had the treat of a dinner and movie night out alone together or with friends, because he figured having a husband who couldn't help all the swearing and farting was bad enough – he didn't want his dear wife putting up with a drinker as well.

For all his cussing and flatus he was always a gentle and understanding man in all of his family and friendly relationships. In his business dealings he was widely considered and regarded to be polite (despite his impolite habits), always direct, openly friendly, and scrupulously fair and honest, honest to a fault. Uncle Dave always said he never had any trouble sleeping at night as a result of his clear conscience. He may have carried certain past things that had always been with him, but he never had unresolved baggage dragging behind and holding him back. Although Aunt Mary didn't swear like her husband or pass gas (that we knew or heard of) like her husband, when they spoke to one another she said her piece and patiently listened to his, cuss words, farts and all, graciously taking it all in as a perfectly normal conversation between a loving but slightly flawed husband and his loving and very understanding wife.

When we visited Dave and Mary after a long absence his effusive, friendly and colorful greetings for my brother Robert and I could have melted the snow tires off a passing car in the middle of the coldest winter. He walked up to me and my brother with a smile on his face, farts in his pants, arms outstretched with true kindness, warmth and affection radiating from his whole persona while at the same time casually referring to each of us as something disgusting found stuck between the water-soaked moldy wood planks in the wet dank cargo hold of a Chinese junk. We just smiled and willingly, gratefully, accepted his firm but gentle bear hugs as the free flowing language and gas had the potential to cause any exposed green foliage nearby to smolder, smoke, turn brown and then wilt on the stem.

Mom and Dad liked Uncle Dave and Aunt Mary as much as my brother and I did. We all looked forward to and thoroughly enjoyed our stays with them. Before, during and after our visits our parents would only briefly mention, with kindness, good humor and without criticism, Uncle Dave's interesting habits and only asked that Robert and I not imitate his two most unique qualities during our visits or back at home. We were dutifully reminded that Uncle Dave was just being himself, being the guy we all loved to see and spend time with.

There were times, to his credit, that Uncle Dave was able to exercise appropriate restraint and self-control, like at church. He was a modestly religious man who attended church, not on a weekly basis, but on a regular every other month basis. On the way out of church he'd briskly and firmly shake the Pastor's hand with a big grin and (some would say "tongue in cheek") voice his encouragement and support for the good man's pious efforts.

"That was a helluva sermon Pastor. You sure know how to come down on those unrepentant heathen bastards out there that got it comin' to 'em. Yes-Sir-by-God, you got 'em on the run from the Devil's own Hell back on their ways' towards Heaven with their backsides smokin' for certain. Keep up the damn good work Reverend," all the while winking and smiling for emphasis.

Not only did he restrain his language, he held his ever-present gas supply at bay at least until he was in the car on the way home. Cruising down the highway for home with all the car windows rolled down the floodgates would open wide as the buildup exploded in a rhythmic, multi-movement, harmonized symphony of cussing-potty-mouth and farty-potty-pants.

One of the first things anyone learned about Uncle Dave was that when he was swearing a blue streak he was, in fact, smoothly cruising carefree, just being a normal, happy, in a good mood sorta guy. When the expletives and flatus were flying it was like fragrant songbirds filled the sky. But, when he stopped cussing that blue streak – that's when something would be up, something had gone wrong. When he got mad, when he got peeved and angry about something, he stopped swearing completely and started talking in an unnaturally (for him) calm voice with almost normal, near perfect, English vocabulary. He'd still fart but the tone and tenor changed from easy breezy to very short, sharp and angry. When that happened, everyone who knew him, including me, stayed quietly out of the way and at some distance until things calmed down and whatever it was that troubled him passed over, out and away. Admittedly, he was a lot more fun to be around when he was cussing and farting as he yanked and pulled on some rusted tail pipe that was obstinately stuck in the backside of a blown out muffler.

Our visits always included joining Uncle Dave in his garage for his lunch break. We sat around his shop office desk munching on plates of thick sandwiches, crunching on potato chips from a big red ceramic bowl and gulping down short-neck bottles of ice cold orange, grape and cherry soda, all of which Aunt Mary brought out from the house.

The conversation always got around to what us kids were doing, how school was going and all that other normal "catching up on your life so far" type stuff. When Uncle Dave learned that I was some sort of "sharp-shooting little marble bastard" he continued to chew his sandwich and held up his right forefinger as sign to pause the conversation. He asked me to put out my left hand, with open palm up and my eyes closed. He reached into and then pulled something from his right chest shirt pocket. Uncle Dave then dropped that same something into my hand from his palm down unclenched fist.

"Okay Mike, open 'em up," he said while still chewing his bite of sandwich.

There in my hand was a marble, a really old marble attached to some sort of thin circular chain, something you'd wear around your neck. I looked at it real close and then looked at Uncle Dave real close and he looked right back at me even closer while taking another bite of his sandwich with both his elbows resting on the desk.

"So kid, wha'da'ya think?" he asked as he washed down the most recent bite of his sandwich with a big gulp of cherry soda.

"What is it?" I asked with a puzzled look on my face.

"What is it; you kiddin' me? It's a marble yeah-dumb little turd! I thought you were supposed to be some sort of sharp-shooting little bastard that knew all about them damn things," he playfully chided with an affectionate laugh.

"Yeah, yeah Uncle Dave, I know it's a marble. I know what a marble is, okay? But it looks – it looks - really old and its got a chain – kinda' – stuck to it," I responded laughing as I closely inspected the curious looking relic.

"Not stuck to it Mike, mounted to it. That little shit marble is attached to that crappy old chain by a mount, like a piece of jew-

Keepers Weepers

elry," he clarified. "That little shit piece of glass saved my goddamn life back in the war - no lie, kids."

"Really?"

"Really," he answered back matter-of-factly.

The story was this. Uncle Dave was in the army during WWII in Europe, specifically at Normandy. He was in one of the follow-up waves of American infantry that came ashore over the several days immediately following the D-Day invasion. He was assigned to a small reconnaissance unit that worked its way inland somewhere in northern France. He and the other four soldiers in the patrol were searching for and reporting back on German forces in the area.

Late on a cloudy afternoon in mid-June 1944, he and the rest of the squad had taken up a position on the second floor of an abandoned, partially bombed-out farmhouse. They peered out over the glassless windowsills of an upper floor bedroom as they'd surveyed the surrounding French countryside. There were Germans visible in the distance but they felt safe, sure that their position in the farmhouse had not been spotted.

Uncle Dave was taking his turn at one of the windows when he knelt on something that dug into his left kneecap through his thick multi-pocketed army pants. He repositioned himself and bent over to brush away the debris when he discovered the dust covered little marble on a chain mixed in with all the scattered rubble; no doubt some little French farm kid's lost and left behind treasure, and, no doubt, Dave thought to himself at the time, some little French kid who, if still alive, probably had a lot more to worry about than a lost marble.

Just as he reached down to free the marble from the dust, the peaceful reflection of the moment was shattered by a burst of German 20mm light armored cannon fire that ripped through the stone house wall just above and around him. They'd been spotted after all. He survived physically unscathed but his four companion squad members were all gruesomely killed on the spot, instantly. The wounds Uncle Dave suffered that day were emotional and the resulting scars were permanent.

Later that day, when reinforcement relief arrived, he helped carry his dead comrades down out of that French farmhouse. He'd regularly swore a lot before, but that was the day he started to really cuss, all the time. The farting, however - that was not new, he'd always done that – that was the same. But, regardless, the truth was just as he said, some years before on that cloudy afternoon in June, in France, "that little shit piece of glass had saved his goddamn life...no lie."

After studying it for a minute I started to hand it back to Uncle Dave when he put up his hand in a stop motion and told me to keep it, it was mine. He said it had saved his life in the war and had also brought him great luck in the rest of his life to that day; a wonderful, understanding and good looking wife, a solid and sure business doing work he loved to do and reasonably good health. It was time to pass it on. It was mine to wear, or keep wherever I wanted to keep it. The only condition was that I had to take good care of it and if I ever didn't want it any more to give it back to him in the same condition in which I'd received it. We shook hands and he ruffled my hair with his hand and a big smile on his face.

"You're a good little shit bastard SOB," was his way of simultaneously complimenting me and sealing the deal. That Uncle Dave, day in and day out, he sure knew how to turn a phrase.

Then, sadly, in his turn and in his time, much sooner than anyone including him had a right or reason to expect, and not long after our last visit together, Uncle Dave died, just like we all do, like we all will. When he passed away I still had his gift safely tucked away in a dresser drawer, all in one piece and in as good a condition as the day he gave it to me. I'd worn it only a few times because, in many ways, I was still an unintentionally dumb and innocently careless little kid who stood a good chance of losing it or wrecking it by accident. I was just smart and careful enough to save wearing it for those very few times that I considered the most necessary and critically important in my young life.

Uncle Dave's funeral service and wake took place at his home, which was the custom at the time. His open casket rested upon two velvet shrouded saw horses in his living room. As people arrived to pay their respects and comfort our grieving Aunt Mary, they respectfully walked up to his coffin and in some instances privately, silently, recalled and in other instances quietly shared their best memories of him. Those who believed graciously forgave his unrepentant cussing and ceaseless farting as they wished him well in any afterlife journey that he might undertake. Those who did not believe silently thanked him for his friendship and the honest fair-priced deals they got on the trustworthy car repairs and equally forgave his frequently entertaining and only occasionally offensive profanity and flatus.

As the gathering started to spread out across the various first floor rooms of the house I walked up to Uncle Dave lying so unnaturally quiet and unrealistically still, engulfed by the equally unnatural pleasant aroma of all the funeral flower bouquets that surrounded his remains. I stepped up on a little footstool next to the coffin that was provided just so little kids like me could also see "how natural, how good he looked" lying there in his best suit.

I'd brought back the gift, the marble on a chain, that he'd given me to keep. I couldn't keep it any longer because it didn't feel right, nor could I pass it onto someone else because that wouldn't have been right either. My promise to him had been to take good care of it and give it back when I didn't need it any more. I figured that he needed it back, needed it more then than I did. It had first belonged to some unknown child in France, then it had belonged to him for several years, then it had belonged to me for a while and then it rightfully belonged back with him again for always, for any final journey he might make whether it was a trip to a life beyond his death or just the trip his remains would make to their final resting place underground in the church grave yard.

Wishing he could have reached over one more time, ruffled my hair and with a big grin and warm eyes called me a "good little shit bastard SOB" I unobtrusively slipped the memorable marble on a chain from my suit coat pocket and into his coffin. I gently pressed the keepsake down between his shirt and suit-coat-dressed lifeless right arm and the soft satin covered interior padding of the coffin that surrounded and comforted his inanimate remains. That way, I concluded, we'd both rest assured in always knowing exactly where it was, allowing both of us, as needed, to call and rely upon any and all favorable luck and good fortune it might be willing and able to bestow from that time forward.

*

Chapter Six:
Opening Moves

BEING AT THE top of the school's marble heap on occasion made me privy to information of a more spectacular nature. There were rumors and stories not commonly passed along to the less successful, less serious or recreational players. School would come to a close for the year as summer vacation stood waiting just five short weeks away. It was on a Monday morning that classmate Wilbur Hunt came running toward me and then only stopped by actually running into me in the hallway as I waited in line to use the boy's room. He'd been privy to a conversation the day before about a possible off-the-record, interschool marble match. The fine hairs on the back of my neck chilled and prickled to a stand. Wilbur's source was a kid in his neighborhood who attended the Catholic grade school in the vicinity. The rumored facts were, as best Wilbur could remember, that the parochial school champ was looking for a match with the best player from our school. The point being which of the two schools could claim the bragging rights for having the neighborhood's best player. The excitement, the possibility of an interschool challenge match was so intense that when it came time for me to step up and do my business I barely unzipped my pants in time.

Standing at an adjacent urinal, Wilbur went onto explain that the Catholic school champ was a fourth grader named Billy Schoutenlauder. Apparently, he was supposed to be the best marble player that Our Lord's Avenging Grace Catholic Grade School had produced in the past decade. This was no small achievement, considering that it was generally accepted back then that the students at Avenging Grace (AG) were an unhealthy mix of half-crazy religious zealots whose early life goals were to follow the path required to become saintly members of the church and not-so-saintly replacement members of the Catholic high school football team. AG's older sister school of higher education was named Brothers of Righteous Destruction Boys Catholic High School. It was a fitting description and tribute to the school's stature, function and place in the community. To help illustrate and further illuminate the reputation of the two schools as partners in social malfunction, Warren 'Rusty' Axlerod was an esteemed, graduated (by the skin of his teeth) and financially contributing alumni of both schools.

Through the years the unspoken but plainly evident primary reason for the existence of Righteous Destruction (RD) was the planned and methodical assault (psychological and physical) on other high schools, their student bodies (figuratively and literally) and especially against the members of opposing high school football teams. RD football games had all the color and pageantry of a head-on collision between two fast moving passenger trains. The Righteous Destruction football team's performance, on and off the field, resembled a series of poorly controlled riots. It was a commonly accepted fact that the referees at RD football games carried hardwood police 'billy clubs' along with their whistles and yellow penalty flags to help maintain order on the playing field and adjacent sidelines. The best background experience for a referee at a RD game was having been or currently employed as a maximum-security prison guard.

The team's name was the 'Crusaders' and their team emblem (worn on helmets, weather capes, letter sweaters and team jackets) was, appropriately, a crucifix with a jagged lightning bolt ripping through it. The team colors were crimson and black, which along with the lightning bolts earned the Crusaders the nickname "The Bloody Bolts." Crusader football games were more – a lot more – than just good adolescent sport. They were "public events" on the scale of a very localized natural disaster.

It wasn't at all uncommon for the violence perpetrated on the playing field to quickly spread and infect the RD fans who, in turn, like a battle front shock wave, launched several sorties and raiding parties of their own against the opposing team's cheering section. After such a game the opposing team and their supporters would resemble a tribe of badly outnumbered local natives who'd been "liberated" by God's chosen. Even the RD school band got into the action as they played military marching music and military bugle calls instead of school cheering and school spirit melodies. The schools sporting fight songs were intended, when played, to inspire and encourage actual fighting on and near the field! A more fitting name for the school might have been Outrageous Dysfunction, good ol' OD with a wild-haired, big-eyed crazy guy in a straitjacket as the team symbol.

Beside all the excitement, anticipation, trepidation, caution, worry and fear generated by upcoming RD football games, numerous opportunities were provided for various city and county agencies to get away from their normal work routines and get in some special preparedness training and practice of their own. For example, an RD football game was the only time that one-half of the City's Police force, one-half of the County's Sheriff deputies and fully one third of the emergency medical personnel and equipment force for the area were on special duty at the same time and the same location in anticipation of a problem.

All of the latest riot gear and transportable emergency medical equipment were on hand, standing by, just waiting to be tried out. It wasn't at all uncommon at the conclusion of such sporting events that the air was filled with toilet paper streamers, newspaper confetti and thick clouds of choking and drifting haze, the lingering residue of RD student-manufactured and deployed smoke bombs. It was customary practice that spectators at RD games came to see the sporting event fully equipped with sport blankets for the cold, seat cushions for the hard bleacher seats, helmets of varied types and sizes for head protection, army surplus gas masks for breathing protection and detailed maps of the immediate area to facilitate identifying safe escape routes for rapid retreat if that became necessary, which, more often than not, it did!

Such memorable events also provided experience for the emergency rooms and their medical staffs at the three closest hospitals. When a crisp Friday or Saturday autumn evening rolled around and an RD football was on tap, the hosting community prepared as if a terrible storm was going to blow through town and everybody knew days in advance exactly where and when the catastrophe was going to take place. Everybody concerned always hoped for the best, a miracle you might say (it being a

Catholic School and all) but always, as game time approached, expected the inevitable worst.

It was the spirit of the game, the friendly competition and good sportsmanship that always initially raised everyone's hopes, that kept people coming to the games with smiles. But unfortunately it was the sad reality of RD football that always had them running away with helmets on, blankets and seat cushions over their helmeted heads and tears pouring out from inside the gas masks with women and children running ahead and the men bringing up the rear in defensive formation.

When RD football was a home game the school's stadium was visible from a hill in a nearby park, about three blocks from the game field stadium. The hill's elevation was a great vantage point to get a general view and feel of the game from a safe distance. Robert and his friends would pack some snacks and sit on a picnic tabletop in the park and pretend that they were witnessing the re-enactment of famous battles in history.

The RD games' inevitable smoke, waving team pennants, echoing pops, bangs and explosions from student-fired fireworks and the waving of unfurled battle flags during RD spectator charges, RD marching band bugle calls and counterattacks on the visitors bleachers, all in the twilight of the setting sun combined with the flood lights of the stadium was a battle spectacle if there ever was one. The imagined famous moments from history included the battle of Waterloo, Belgium (RD vs. Holy Mother's Warriors) where Napoleon actually succeeded in turning the tide against Wellington, and Gettysburg, Pennsylvania (RD vs. Holy Father's Lancers) where Bobby Lee, despite his best efforts, lost again to the Union Blue and remained winless north of the Mason-Dixon line.

Another widely known and acknowledged fact was that the guys who played for RD were not always at the top of their game, academically speaking. Consequently, RD was the only high school in the State, public or private, that allowed their star athletes to get a graduation diploma by simply attaining a passing grade in Driver's Education. Almost the entire team took the Driver's-Ed option with a few squeaking by with questionably constructed wooden spice or hat racks made in woodworking class.

It was widely feared and acknowledged that RD Driver's-Ed diploma holders drove their cars just like they played football – with reckless abandon and total disregard for the rules. The result was, when walking near or riding bikes on the streets in our neighborhood, one always had to keep a tuned ear to and sharp eye out for Crusader drivers. Being on the sidewalk several feet from the street was no guarantee of free or safe passage.

One could always spot the RD Driver's-Ed grads, as their cars or trucks looked like they'd taken several hits from bazooka shells. The vehicles' steering wheels were always misshapen by the killer grip of the drivers and the exterior do-it-yourself paint jobs were the same shiny blood red or non-reflecting flat black, all applied by hand, literally, like massive finger paint jobs. But the real give-away was the cross with the lightening bolt charm on a chain that hung from the inside rear view mirror right along with the over sized fuzzy dice/furry dingle ball combination, all suspended just above the magnetic, but headless, Saint Christopher statue magnetically stuck to the top of the metal dash board.

After considering the background and influences that worked on the psyche of all Avenging Grace students, it only seemed logical that the AG marble champ would embark on a crusade of his own to conquer the local marble landscape. While quietly entertaining such thoughts, wondering over and over again what such a match would be like, I silently drifted through the rest of the school day.

I slipped unnoticed into my daydreams and became and remained totally immersed in that shroud, completely invisible to the searching eyes of my teacher, whose questioning gaze had passed me over and passed me by time and time again. I successfully disappeared while remaining in the quiet stillness of plain view. The secret was not to try. It had to happen naturally, like a sphere mathematically turning itself inside out without any breaks in the skin. I was learning, slowly but steadily, exploring all the time and then judiciously putting into practice what I discovered.

The last bell of that big-news Monday school day rang out just as our class finished viewing the last of several personal hygiene films brought in special by the school nurse. Although all of us were supposed to have benefited by such presentations, most of us in class knew who the films were really meant for. There were always a few kids in class who, each day, looked like they'd spent the night before sleeping on a park bench under a pile of newspapers. These were also the same few little kids in class who, for whatever reason, were finding themselves much more on their own in life than they should've been at such a young age.

The most exciting part of the movies was when we all thought for certain that we saw a naked kid, a totally naked kid, taking a bath in a segment on regular bathing. We all knew that when you took a bath you were naked. But all of us sharing the experience by seeing it together on the big screen was the absolute high point of that school day afternoon. As the film projector shutdown, the shades went up and the classroom lights flickered back on.

We all got up from our seats to leave the classroom for the day when Mrs. Goodchaulks did a confused double take, looked right at me like she was going to ask "where did you just come from and where have you been all day?" I returned her gaze with a slight but smirky sort of grin that plainly and clearly communicated "I don't think you'd understand my theory and practice of in-plain-view-invisibility and I'm not so inclined as to volunteer any insights I may or may not have on the matter at this time." Yep – exploring, learning and practicing all the time.

With all the excitement of the afternoon's "naked kid in the tub" flicks and rumors of a possible inter-school marble match, my enthusiasm engine was running out of steam. My after school energy tank level was indicating barely above empty. As I wearily stepped out of the school gate onto the sidewalk for the trip home, the last thing on my mind at that moment was Avenging Grace or Billy Schouten-what's-his-name. With my strapped schoolbooks slung over one shoulder and my full double marble sock slung over the other, I plodded towards home in anticipation of rest and food.

I hadn't gone ten steps from the school gate when I thought I heard someone call my name. There were dozens of kids everywhere walking and talking every which way and I wasn't able to identify or place the direction of the caller or even if there was one. I was tired and I was hungry and therefore subject and vulnerable to any variety of possible visual, olfactory and/or auditory hallucinations.

When I was a baby and got tired and hungry I just flopped down and cried. As I got older that changed to staying on my feet while seeing, smelling and/or hearing things that weren't actually there. Just before I decided to let it pass as my sugar and sleep deprived brain playing tricks on me, just the wind blowing through the tree branches above and swirling through the empty space between my ears, I definitely heard my last name being called sharp and clear.

I turned and looked to where I thought the call had originated from and there, fifteen feet away, was a kid, a stranger, who appeared to be a little bigger and a little older than me, leaning up against a big, metal, green painted, street lamp electrical control box located between the sidewalk and the street curb.

My eyes connected with his. He motioned with his right index finger to walk over to where he waited. I looked back over each shoulder, and then, pointed to myself with my right index finger in the chest.

"Me?"

"Yeah, you," came the answer.

Slowly and cautiously, I walked towards the stranger. I had no idea who he was, what to expect or the particular reason he had picked me out of the crowd walking by. One thing was certain, this guy, whoever he was, or whoever he thought he was, was playing it tough and cocky. He leaned back against the electrical box with his feet spread and legs extended. His hands were jammed into his jacket pockets with both elbows bent out and a tuft of black hair curled down across his forehead, which partially, secretively, covered his left eye. James Dean would have been proud of my earnest but awkward attempt at unruffled coolness. I stepped up and stopped with not more than three feet between us.

"Who are you?"

He slowly brought his left hand out of his jacket pocket and held up a Cat's-Eye boulder between his thumb and forefinger.

"I'm this," he stated matter-of-factly.

Big deal, I thought. So this strange kid thinks he's a marble. As far as I was concerned, if he thought that was funny, dramatic or something else, he was probably right; his head was full of marbles just like the one in his hand. That probably left little room on his top floor for anything else. I had a lot of experience with people thinking they were other things, especially Hector Hobart who on occasion waxed poetically aloud about what it would be like to be a rubber ball, or a grasshopper, or a wad of chewing gum, or a mud puddle or even a carrot.

With a smirk on my face, I backed up a couple of steps and let down my guard a bit, still tired and still hungry. As I stared at this kid a disturbing thought flashed across my mind that I was actually face to face with a resurrected Hector Hobart after a facelift and new identity training. I calmed and collected myself when a second equally disturbing thought flashed that this guy wasn't Hector but one of his cousins or friends and he'd come to see me on Hector's advice for help and companionship. I strained and struggled to regain control of my runaway paranoid imagination and convinced myself that neither could be a real world (non-dust particle planet) possibility. I shook my head in exasperation and started to walk away.

"You're Archer, the marble player, right?" the stranger called out.

"Yeah, so what?" I whined back annoyingly as I stopped and half-turned back towards him to answer.

First he looked left, then right and then left again and then right at me like he was checking to see if it was safe before he tried to sell me a hot watch or stolen school supplies.

"I'm Billy Schoutenlauder from Avenging Grace. How 'bout a match?" he stated with a hint of mystery and flare.

Rumor and remote impossibility materialized into human form right before my eyes. I had no idea what to say, my head was

Keepers Weepers

empty. Although I instantly forgot about how tired and hungry I was my exhausted empty tank couldn't fuel an appropriate or immediate response. Uncertain of the reality of the moment, a moment I'd been certain just hours before was the stuff of daydreams, I swung my marble sock down off my shoulder and let it hang free as it bounced against my right leg, my arm dangling straight down at my side. Billy continued.

"We can play it anyway you want. The only thing is I choose the time and the place and it's winner take all. Fifty marbles each to play and it's just you and me," he plainly stated.

The words just echoed and rolled around in my head. Regaining my mental sense of balance and collecting my scattered and disorganized confidence, I turned straight towards him and re-slung my double sock full of marbles through the air in a wide arc and back over my right shoulder and gave Billy my answer.

"Yeah, I'll play."

Billy stood straight-up and walked for his bike that leaned against a nearby tree.

"Be in the alley between Fifty-Seventh and Fifty-Eighth just north of Nash at two-o'clock this Saturday afternoon and we'll settle this."

I could barely make out the last words, his voice trailing off as he hopped onto his bike with a rolling start and pedaled away down the sidewalk. I stood there motionless, like a small tree planted in the sidewalk. From the second Wilbur Hunt passed on the rumor, the very idea, whether true or not, I wanted to play Billy Schoutenlauder more than anything. The match that I wanted, the match I daydreamed about all school day was going to happen. I was going to get my chance.

The familiar sights and sounds on the walk home took on whole new perspectives as my view of the world had changed and expanded again. Tired, hungry, who cared! The biggest challenge of my reign as school marble champ was at hand. The match would not only determine who was the local best, but it would put to the test my entire philosophy, my dedication, the whole purpose of living with my marbles twenty-four hours a day, day in and day out, the practice and the preparation, for months on end.

    Back at home I found myself pacing back and forth in my room like a captive tiger impatiently waiting for the five-o'clock feeding. On edge again, looking down, looking out and looking up, I felt ready to jump over, jump out and jump up into space all at the same time. It had become disconcertingly apparent that I knew nothing, absolutely zilch, about Billy Schoutenlauder; nothing about his playing abilities, his playing style or what to expect in a face to face meeting alone in an alley blocks from home. All that kept playing over and over again in my head was what Wilbur had said standing at the urinals in the boys' john at school, "the best marble player Avenging Grace had seen in decades." Decades, that was groups of years in tens, right? "Oh shit," I'd thought to myself (a serious and situation appropriate use of the word).

    What if this kid turned out to be some sort of marble Einstein! I started to worry for real. Horrible dark visions flash-punched and glare-slapped across my face from all directions, bleak visions of being cleaned out as badly, or worse, if that was possible, than the time I'd been steamrolled and mugged by Babes Hanrahan. What had I done? What was I in for? I suspected it would be – no, I knew that it could only be – either brilliant victory or the bottomless pit of dark defeat.

    I sat at the supper table in a trance. I hardly laid a fork to my food. Mom noticed and Dad didn't. Robert sensed that something was in the works. My brother would catch me blankly staring in his direction as I wondered if he'd ever faced a similar situation in his years of playing baseball or baseball cards. Managing to only get a couple of small bites of food past my gums and into my nervous gut I excused myself from the table. Mildly concerned, Mom asked if I was sick or just tired of her cooking. As I walked from the table and headed for the stairway to my room, I reassured her that neither was the case. That the weight of the world had just settled onto my shoulders and into my stomach was not a thought I was willing to share at that moment.

    Closing the bedroom door behind me, I knelt down and reached under the bed and retrieved my huge marble cache and with some effort emptied the entire collection onto my made bed. I'd tossed the empty marble box to the side and spread my marbles evenly across the patchwork quilt. Kit Cat, recognizing the sound, arrived and pawed and meowed at the bedroom door to come in. I sauntered over to the door and opened it a crack as the cat rushed in and up onto the bed where he made himself comfortable in the middle of my marbles. With both hands in their respective pants pockets, I continued to pace the noticeably worn path in the carpet around my bed as the real Cat's-Eye's of Kit Cat followed my back and forth progress. I occasionally stopped and shuffled my hands through the little ocean of marbles, scratched the cat behind the ears, hoping to absorb, by mystic or divine vision, the solution and answers to all of the potential, actual and/or imagined problems, questions and doubts that swirled and fomented in my head.

I flopped down into the big high-backed overstuffed armchair that sat in the corner of my room next to and between the bed and the window. I looked out over the backyard toward Robert's tree house which was eye level with my bedroom window. The back door opened with a squeak and then bounced shut as my big brother, having finished his supper, dessert and all, climbed up into his tree house for an evening of quiet and private contemplation. I watched, unnoticed, as Robert steadily and surely placed each footstep and climbed the ladder made from two-by-four sections securely nailed at regular intervals into the broad tree trunk.

I was leaning forward in my easy chair as I watched Robert make his climb. I slid back into the chair's engulfing padding and more lay than sat across its fat and embracing open arms. Billy's face kept popping up in my mind, sometimes at a distance and sometimes disturbingly close-up, just inches from my mind's eye. I sat up, leaned forward again and stared out the window thinking that maybe Robert would be able to provide some valuable advice and and useful insight about the pending match.

I had my reservations, some hesitation. Robert really hit the mark when he helped me deal with the Babes Hanrahan situation but he'd completely dropped the ball on the bum steer he'd provided on Axlerod's junkyard. But being my brother and all, in the final analysis, Robert's judgment and words of wisdom were more reliable than not. I wrestled myself free from the arms of my chair and slid to my feet and pressed close to the screen on my open widow and shouted out across to Robert in his tree house. He stuck his head out of the tree house window and shouted back, "WHAT?"

I shouted again that I had some news, a rapidly developing situation that I needed to talk over with him.

"Yeah, okay, come on over," he responded, resigned to the interruption.

I ran past my marble covered bed, past the then sleeping cat, jumped down the stairs two steps at a time and flew past Mom and Dad, drinking their after dinner coffee at the kitchen table, and sprinted for the back door. As I breezed by I burst out through the kitchen screen door, yelling back that cake and ice cream would have to wait. It was the only time that I could recall in my young life that I made cake and ice cream wait for anything. Mom, perplexed, looked after me as the summer screen door banged and bounced close. Climbing the two-by-four ladder rapidly, not demonstrating the deliberate skill of Robert's climb, I was breathless as I crawled through the tree house door flap and took up a familiar position along the wall opposite my brother.

"Guess what?" I said as I caught my breath.

"What?" Robert queried halfheartedly.

"Billy Schoutenlauder, the champ from Avenging Grace wants a match!" I blurted out.

Robert's reaction was akin to the one he'd come up with two years before when the family Doctor told him he'd have to skip his chance to play in the *Little League Championship Game* because he'd contracted a slight case of the mumps. An open mouth, "I can't believe what I just heard," really bad news, horribly bad surprise sort of look. I'd gone just a bit crazy with the relief of having told someone the news when Robert blew a hole right through the center of my excitement with his negative reaction.

"You didn't tell him you'd play, did you?"

Robert's question wasn't one of casual disinterest as he put aside his baseball cards, leaned forward and impatiently waited for my answer.

"Well, did you or didn't you?" he followed up.

Taken aback I responded guardedly.

"Yeah – well – yeah – I did. This Saturday in the big alley just off Nash."

Robert rolled his eyes up into his head and leaned back against his wall of the tree house.

"Why, what's the big problem?" I answered defensively.

It wasn't the name Billy Schoutenlauder that created his reaction – it was the words Avenging Grace that got his engine all revved-up. He'd pulled himself back to sitting upright and made his feelings very clear.

"Because you gotta be careful, you can't trust those jerks from Avenging Grace, that's why," he emphatically stated.

My hard-won positive anticipation was rapidly fading into a dark and murky uncertainty. What was it about the kids from Avenging Grace that made them so untrustworthy? Being a religious institution you'd think that trustworthiness would be sort of a requirement to go to school there, yeah know, with Jesus and Mary and God and all those Saints they always talked about constantly looking over their shoulders listening, watching and keeping track of and critically judging, second by second, what they thought, said and did. That's why my brother and I were lucky our parents sent us to a public school where you had more privacy in your thoughts and actions without all of the interference that came along with the constant, moment-by-moment "spiritual surveillance" AG kids had to put up with. I put that very question to my brother but in a rephrased, roundabout way.

"Well – yeah – so what? What am I not supposed to trust about them anyway?" had been my attempt at an equalizing retort.

I tried to maintain my cool and hold my own in the face of my brother's serious and unexpected negativity. I tried to convey that he couldn't tell me something I didn't already know, when, in fact, all of it was brand new I-didn't-have-a-clue news to me. What I'd hoped for was something simple, something along the lines of "great, go get 'em little brother. No problem. They're all just a bunch of bozos anyway." Nope, my brother had to go and be brutally honest with me. It was not what I needed to patch and mend my cracked and splintering self-confidence.

Robert went onto further explain that, as far as he was able to figure out, it was all the religious training that the AG kids got in school everyday. They always said one thing and then turned around and did the complete opposite. This made them arrogant and selfrighteous to the extreme. Robert said it was like setting off a cherry bomb in the school toilet. An AG kid would place the explosive, light the fuse, flush the bomb and then turn around and blame the toilet for the explosion and resulting flood in the lavatory. I asked Robert for the source of all this negative information. It was first hand. As a *Cub Scout* his troop played the AG Cubs in a friendly scheduled game of the local *Cub Scout* whiffle baseball league. A lot of the kids who showed up to play for the AG side could have been *Eagle Scouts*. His Cubs took an undeserved beating that fueled his resentment and mistrust to that day.

I wasn't at all worried about playing someone older and bigger than myself. I'd earned my place as champion by regularly outplaying and, on occasion, as necessary, outrunning my share of angry losing upperclassmen on my way to the top. Grudgingly almost all of the older kids I'd bested in the marble ring had accepted and acknowledged that my winnings were honestly earned and rightly deserved. But there I sat, on the verge of having an argument with my brother, when all I wanted was to talk things over and get his take on the match.

I quelled Robert's cynicism and solidified my dissolving resolve by admitting to myself and by telling Robert that it was too late to change my mind, that there would be no backing out. Even if I had the chance to call it off I wouldn't do it. I'd made my decision, poor judgment or not – I'd accepted the challenge and I was perfectly willing, regardless of any actual or potential risks, to put my practiced and seasoned abilities up against Billy or anyone else from Avenging Grace.

Robert relented and made a noble effort to suppress his justifiable pessimism and focused on the real issue at hand which was my preparing for and playing in the match. He'd remained contemplatively silent for several seconds as he commenced the mental exercise of putting himself in my place. Speaking quietly, he arrived at a series of questions and suggestions that he thought would be of assistance.

 First, he wanted to know the rules of the match, if any. I passed along the simple arrangement we'd both agreed to. Robert's first suggestion was not to take or use any of my best marbles because if the match turned out to be a setup of some sort, the loss of fifty marbles, though tragic, would not be catastrophic. Secondly, once the match was over, victorious or defeated, to get my behind out-of-there as soon as it was physically possible, just in case, and especially if I won. Setups, running for your life, oh man - marbles could be... hazardous.

"Yeah, just in case of what else?" I asked.

"Just in case Schoutenlauder turns out to be another poor loser," my brother emphasized, bringing back to full memory fleeing for my life from Rodney Strong.

 I decided it was best, in addition to practicing my shot, to put in some road work to buildup my physical endurance and breathing capacity for any emergency exits and resulting long distance pursuits.

Thirdly, Robert warned that AG kids developed a protective gang instinct early, so I should be prepared to not only deal with Billy but also be ready to put up with a lot of his friends showing up and razzing me during the match. Fourthly, if something like that happened, if things just got too hot, too out of control, whether the match was over or not, with or without my marbles, to get up and leave, get out and, if necessary, without delay and without any hesitation or second thoughts, to make a run for it!

 I listened intently to all of my brother's suggestions. Having departed the tree house and climbed down the tree trunk ladder, it occurred to me that Robert had spent the entire conversation warning me. I felt like I should be preparing for an ambush and hand-to-hand combat instead of sharpening up my shooting eye. Where I sought solace and encouragement I ran into flashing red lights and enough negative feedback to fuel a month's worth of bad dreams. Robert agreed to my request that it all be kept under wraps, to keep everything from Mom and Dad who might have interceded, out of the best intentions, to put the big kibosh on the whole thing. With conflicting thoughts and emotions I stumbled back into the house. If the match deteriorated into a fight, I decided to fight fire with fire and take along a concealed selection of homemade smoke bombs just in case a diversionary device was necessary in the event that Robert's worst fears, that were then my worst fears, came to pass.

I walked back into the house where it immediately became apparent that any skill I pretended to have with regards to concealing my concerns fell far short of my comparable marble skills. Mom noticed my burdened expression and offered the dessert that I'd earlier refused. I said "sure," figuring that I'd take full advantage of any and all desserts that came my way before the weekend.

I'd taken my regular place at the kitchen table as Mom served up a huge piece of chocolate cake with two giant scoops of vanilla ice cream. She flipped her dishtowel over her shoulder as she sat down across from me at the table. I was shoveling in the cake and ice cream like I was a twelve-horse power snow blower cutting through a five-foot deep snowdrift. With her elbows on the table and her chin resting in her upturned palms, Mom asked again if I really felt okay. I mumbled with my mouth full that I was feeling just fine, "right up to snuff" and all that.

Being the Mother that she was, she could still sense that I had more on my mind than the cake and ice cream in my mouth. Of course she was right but I wasn't going to tell her that for anything. Mom wasn't the pushy, intrusive type. She cared and she only went far enough to let me know that the door was open if I wanted to step in and talk. I didn't want to lie to her, but under the circumstances, I made an exception and told a fib, not a whooper, just a convenient little untruth that had the ring of prior truth attached as a rationalizing modifier.

My second worse subject in school, right after arithmetic, was spelling. Manipulating numbers could be like trying to decipher ancient languages, but spelling – spelling was just plain witchcraft. Spelling was such a mystery, such a bugaboo, that I had trouble spelling a word that was written out right in front of me. That didn't even count as actual spelling but only as actual copying; it didn't matter. Mom was well aware of that particular academic deficiency as the numerous progress notes sent home with me from Mrs. Goodchaulks attested to. I told her that there was a big ten word spelling test coming up at the end of the week and the very thought was making me edgy.

Mom eagerly offered her assistance but I turned her down, citing the preference to lick the tough test with a passing grade entirely on my own initiative. Then, like a bolt of lightning on a clear day, Mom reminded me that a long dreaded and overdue visit to the family dentist was coming up that Saturday morning. The news settled over me mid-swallow like a blanket sized black veil that floated down from the ceiling above. Not only would I be putting everything on the line that Saturday afternoon, I'd also have to suffer the added fear and uncertainties of the dentist's chair that same morning.

The cake and ice cream left on my plate took on the appearance and consistency of cold dirty mud just as the ample portions of both that I'd already consumed transformed into a big, cold, indigestible rock in the pit of my stomach. What was left of my greedy and desperate appetite flew out the kitchen window along with most of my hope. I halfheartedly thanked Mom for the dessert and excused myself from the table for the second time that night and dragged my weighted stomach and my weary mind from the table and back up the stairs.

Having reached my room, barely, I resumed a comfortable but unorthodox position in my easy chair by the window and contemplated the coming events of the next few days. The last reds and oranges of the evening's sunset faded into a clear but dark cobalt blue night sky. My head spun right along with my spinning thoughts and tumbling innards which together whirled all around me like the high pitched distorted voices on a phonograph record played at twice the normal playback speed.

My stomach churned and gurgled like roiling and boiling muddy floodwaters as I corralled and collected my marbles off the bed and back into their box by the cupped handfuls. To put a stop to the voices, to damn the rolling flood, I dragged myself across my room to the bedroom door side of my bed, undressed from my street clothes, redressed into bed clothes and crawled into an early bedtime, hoping to sleep away all of the mental stress and accompanying physical discomfort.

It was my personal custom before turning off the bedside lamp and turning in for the night to sort through my boot box full of marbles and pick out the next day's players. My marble box was still on my bed as I crawled up on top of the covers. It was becoming more and more difficult to lift and maneuver the heavy, bulging and increasingly flimsy boot box out from under the bed and then up onto and around the top of the bed. The continuing accumulation of victory's rewards continued to press all of the glued seams of the cardboard box to their designed weight limits. I reminded myself, for the hundredth time, to secure a larger, sturdier box for the safekeeping of my marbles.

I was sitting up in bed, drowning my worries in a boot box full of marbles, when my mom stuck her head through the partially open door for a quick good night look-see. She was surprised to find me in bed so early. I could see the shadow of worry creeping across her face. I thought it best to quickly and assertively answer her before she could verbalize the inevitable question.

"Everything's all right - just tired tonight," was my preemptive answer.

She walked in and sat down on the edge of the bed nearest to me. With a little grunt of effort she lifted my full marble box from my lap and onto the floor next to my nightstand (commenting to herself as much to me that I needed a new marble box) and then gently tucked my blanket in around me. Kissing my forehead good night, she turned off the bedside lamp.

"Sleep tight," was her good night as she roughly folded and then tossed my bedspread up over my coat rack and then closed the bedroom door behind her as she left my room.

There I lay, all alone with my disturbing thoughts and equally disturbed full stomach. Light from the street lamps in the back alley streamed into my bedroom through the open window as I'd tried to drift off to fitful sleep. The cake and ice cream in my jumpy belly were each fighting for the distinction of being the first to make me run for the bathroom. Luckily, I quickly fell into an uneasy sleep before either one could claim the right. Unluckily, my rumbling innards had their revenge not long after.

It was late, middle-of-the-night late, the exact time unknown, but there I was, confused and blinking, with my mom and my brother shaking my shoulders as I sat upright in bed. Robert was standing right next to me and Mom was sitting on the edge of the bed as the light from my bedside lamp glared into my sleep sensitive eyes. I slowly came to wakeful consciousness only to see my brother staring at me in his own bleary eyed fashion with a terrified face that shouted "WHAT THE HELL'S GOIN' ON WITH YOU?"

After my eyes adjusted to the light I discovered that my mom had the same look on her face except that it shouted, "what the HECK'S goin' on with you?" I looked around in my confused condition and discovered that other things were not right, not in proper places, in fact, sort of way out of place. My bedding had been scattered all over the room.

The two bed pillows were sitting upright next to each other in my armchair by the window as if they'd intentionally sat down and were carrying on a conversation. The sheets were piled on the floor at the foot of my bed. My blanket had been removed from my bed and partially shoved under my closet door. I was sweating like an overdressed fat man in a steam room. After my eyes started to work again so did my mouth as I'd managed to ask what everybody was doing in my room in the middle of the night. Robert wiped the sleep from his eyes and caught me up.

"You were having one helluva nightmare, that's what!" he blurted out.

That remark drew a comment from Mom to the effect that Robert should watch his mouth and that, while he was at it, he could leave the room and go back to bed. At least I had an explanation as to why my bedding had been flung around the room. But at that point I still didn't remember any nightmare or recall throwing anything anywhere, much less trying to stuff my bed blanket into the closet via the small space between the floor and the bottom of the door. There we all were, me confused as a newly-arrived babe, Mom half-asleep and frightened with her sleep-head-hair verging on the *Bride of Frankenstein Monster* style and Robert, with his own weird bed-head hair style, slowly walking from my room wondering out loud why he couldn't say "helluva" when the situation called for it. Sometimes a guy just had to express himself appropriately for the circumstances.

With her full attention directed back to me, Mom wiped the perspiration from my forehead with the palm of her hand and asked what I was dreaming about that would result in me face down on the bed moaning, screaming and thrashing about. I hadn't the slightest idea and, in fact, felt lucky to have slept through the whole thing. I felt fine except for being warm and wet with sweat. In my drowsy state I didn't understand what was wrong with me to feel better about in the first place. I was a confused little boy.

The nighttime landscape of sleep and dreams for little kids could be, and frequently was, a mystery. Mom concluded that it was probably the potent combination of the upcoming spelling test and the richness and large portions of dessert hours before that were responsible for my erratic and frightening nocturnal behavior. She asked if I wanted company for a while longer, or if I wanted her to stay the night in my room. I sufficiently collected my wits and assured her that neither would be necessary. My only request was to leave the bedside lamp on and I'd decide sometime later when to turn it off. Mom had collected the scattered bedding and tucked me in for the second time that night. She wished me a better night and left me for her own bed where my dad had slept through the whole thing – what a log.

After Mom left the room, the first thing I noticed was that my uneasy stomach felt much better. I cautiously reached over and snapped off the lamp and laid back, satisfied that I could lie awake a bit longer and enjoy the combination of the dim street light, mild moonlight and the warm breeze that drifted into the room through the open window. I let the hypnotic effect of the soft light and gentle air carry my sleepy gaze through the familiar surroundings of the bedroom. There was my armchair by the window, my writing and homework desk against the wall, the bookshelf by the desk, the plastic model fighter squadron suspended from the ceiling above my bed and the tall black hooded figure standing tall at the foot of my bed. "WHOOOOAAAA – OH SHIT!" (A frighteningly serious use of the word and it wasn't necessary for Russ to be present). "WHAT THE HELLUVA!" (Robert was right, it just had to be said).

My body went from relaxed limp cooked noodle to a snapping, frozen stiff iron rod with a chilling tingle as the temperature in the room instantly dropped to a hundred below zero. I could swear that I felt the ice crystallizing in my veins from the feet up. All the hair on my body stood straight-up, rigid, at attention, and stuck right through the fabric of my pajamas like hard sharp pins. I'd been dunked into liquid nitrogen. The ghostly figure stood silent, faintly outlined by the dim light that flooded the room.

I was too afraid to actually get up out of bed and poke "it" in order to ascertain to a certainty whether the apparition was alive, dead or some in between combination of both. The effect of the unknown, uninvited visitor was immediate and direct. The not-remembered but not-forgotten nightmare replayed in my mind undeleted and uncensored. Petrified in the bed, my eyes fixed on the figure standing in front of me, the full extent of the bad dream came to life in the suddenly too dark and too lonely room. The suppressed images burst forth and flashed before my eyes in extra sharp focus and finest detail as drenching cold sweat dripped from every skin pore of my body, flowed between all of the rigid upright body hairs, soaked through my pajamas and down onto the bed.

It seemed barely a path, hardly visible in direct line of sight, more apparent by turning my head and catching it through my peripheral vision, the way some stars at night are more visible out of the corner of your eye rather than looking straight at them.

With my full and flimsy marble box tucked tightly under my left arm I walked the faintly visible path baby steps at a time. As my dream eyes adjusted to the dark I sensed approaching something big and solid somewhere to my front.

As I cautiously moved forward the dim light increased to a mist-shrouded diffuse glow. The big solid object materialized; a large heavy wooden door in an equally robust wood frame stood alone in the fog. No surrounding walls or supports, just the massive door and its oversized frame isolated in fog-shrouded dark space. A single overhead light shone down on the face of the door, revealing the bulky metal hardware that held the door and its frame together. The beam of light centered on the middle of the door where it illuminated a symbol that hung there: a large crucifix with a lightning bolt shooting through it.

Inquisitively, cautiously, stepping up for a closer look, I discovered that two tall, dark, robed and hooded figures stood silent guard on either side of the door, just barely visible in the mist, appearing and disappearing as the drifting fog became thicker or thinner. They blended equally and perfectly with the transition between the light on the door and the darkness that encroached on the structure from every direction.

As with most dreams, whether good, bad or undecipherable, one's motives for action or inaction often remain a mystery. Regardless of the reasons, whether compelled by meta-physical forces or unconscious psychological motives I did not recognize or fully understand, like a dreamland idiot, I knew that I had to go through that door (that's what dream doors are for, walking through, just like dream windows are for looking through). I turned back to make one final check of my surroundings only to discover that the original path I'd followed had vanished and in its place a vast empty impenetrable darkness had settled in. The only way open to me was through the door. I turned back to face the unknown. The previously closed door stood wide-open and unattended, revealing another equally black and shapeless void. The two silent guards had dissolved back into the mist and darkness.

Dense cool damp air flowed from the dark passage doorway

and silently washed over me and off into dark space. I moved forward with small steps, with steps that were even smaller than baby steps, they were pre-baby steps. I moved slower than a starfish speeding along the ocean floor at the blazing speed of an inch an hour. There were no discernible shapes or forms or any calculable indication of distance past the open doorway. Ten micro-steps into the void, like I stepped on a hidden light switch, there was a silent explosion of glowing light all around me.

I found my dream self in an alley at night, a city alley like the one behind my house, but...different. There were the normal backs of houses, backs and fronts of garages of all sizes, conditions and colors, rows of metal garbage cans and parked cars. It was the concrete, the ultra smooth cement, like the pristine concrete floor Uncle Dave had in the service garage that first caught my eye. Second was the solid blue-gray extremely low rolling cloud deck that drifted rapidly and silently overhead just above the house and garage tops. The soundless wind pushed the cloud bottoms along as they caught and reflected back the soft glowing light coming up from the alley. But just beyond the alley, on all sides, the buildings' constructs faded into empty dark space. As if drawn in by the light, a persistent shallow and dense ground fog rolled in from the surrounding darkness on all sides. The mist drifted up in slow spiraling swirls as if searching for the source of alley illumination. At times the fog was so thick that in the diffuse low light my dream ankles and dream feet disappeared from my dream view, yet I continued to stand firmly on what I assumed to be dream solid alley cement.

From behind came the creaking and squeaking of the ancient wooden door suddenly, heavily, coming to a close. I turned just in time to see the massive door pound shut with a dull THUD that echoed and reverberated throughout the unknown length, depth and width of the alley and surrounding void. The two robed hooded figures had come back to stand watch, this time on the alley side of the door, again just close enough to either side of the structure to be barely visible. I crushed down and around even harder on my marble box with my left arm. The only known escape route had been cut off. To test this fear, I slowly walked back towards the door only to have each guardian slide toward the center of the door with each step closer I took. Just feet from the door the two faceless apparitions closed together and stood shoulder to shoulder in full light and completely blocked the door.

I turned back around to face what apparently, inevitably, must be faced. My eyes adjusted to the light as the details of the alley became amazingly real, more than real, hyper-real, more real than real life. The sharpness in the detail was threatening, verging on dangerous. The darkness all around the alley was a true and infinite darkness, the kind of darkness that you'd walk into and lose and forget everything, a darkness where one would no longer exist in past, present or future time. I knew it, I could sense it and I could feel it.

The walk back away from the door and back into the alley was instant and infinite, simultaneously. It ceased being a quiet walk, as distinctly close by and distant noises; voices and sounds competed for my attention. The nearby whispering, the distant shouting, walking footsteps then running footsteps, doors opening and closing were all sounds that were more felt than heard. In the darkness outside the alley came a sense of movement, fleeting figures crossing the alley to my back and then to my front, figures and impressions that were more of an afterthought than solid in-the-present images. I arrived at the end of the lighted part of the alley and looked back to judge my distance to the door. There, on and across the face of the door, the dark sentries had been replaced by oversized crisscrossing linked iron chains held fast at the center by a giant pad lock. The only way to end the nightmare was to press on and pass through it, whatever it turned out to be. Reluctantly, I prepared to face all of the unknowns that awaited me.

Turning one's back, even for the briefest of moments, was apparently the high sign, the signal to all the hidden unknowns a dream was capable of producing to manifest themselves. Facing front, the bleakness before me gave way to another silent shock wave of light and another section of dream alley appeared. My attention was first drawn to a tall metal pole just off the center of the alley that had two street signs crossed at the top. The signs read N. 57th Street and Nash Street. It was the alley of the big match. I walked on as the furthest reaches of the alley became visible. At the far end I saw, and felt, my reason for being there.

A large closed overhead double garage door slowly creaked and moaned open. The sound of the moving door came from all around me. A flow of brighter light poured out from under the slowly and vertically opening door. Standing in the light of the open cavernous garage was a perfectly formed broad semicircle of robed and hooded figures. Standing separate and alone at the apex of the half-circle was Billy Schoutenlauder. He was clad just like the rest with no visible hands, feet or face but I knew – yes – yes I knew without a doubt that it was Billy. I apprehensively glided towards the menacing gathering that seemed to float upon the fog rather than stand on any solid ground beneath. I entered the circumference of the circle and stopped twenty feet to the front of the figure I knew to an absolute certainty to be Billy Schoutenlauder. He lifted his hooded head; his face still just a bottomless blackness and spoke.

"Ready to play?"

"Ready as I'll ever be," I responded shakily, while giving my boot box of marbles another reassuring pat with my right hand.

"Let's begin!" Billy commanded, spreading his robed arms like extended black wings to the front and then to the sides.

The mist that covered the ground between us blew away and revealed the most unorthodox marble-playing ring that I'd ever seen or imagined. I went down to one knee to get a closer look. After a quick and revealing examination, I discovered that the ring consisted of a series of unevenly spaced concentric circles superimposed over one large spiral circle which converged to a spinning infinity at the center of the playing ring. On even closer, more careful inspection, I further discovered that the entire playing area was riddled with holes, their presence rendered almost invisible by the optical illusion created by the concentric spiraling circle patterns. The holes were of varying diameters yet all were just big enough, surprise-surprise, for a marble to fall through. There were holes of all sizes for marbles of all sizes.

The game was rigged, pure and simple.

"What kind of game is this?" I demanded as I looked up at the figure of Billy.

Billy folded his robed arms and answered in a mocking voice, "A game you can't win."

Billy leaned back and released a howling, screeching hyena-like laugh that echoed endlessly into the surrounding confines of the garage as all the other hooded figures joined in with a chorus of giggled and whispered, "A game you can't win, a game you can't win, no, no, no, you can't win."

Staring back down into the playing rings revealed that more black magic was at play as the entire field of play had became a whirling and swirling mix and overlay of spinning and spiraling lines and rings endlessly feeding into a large black hole at the very center with all the other various sized holes throughout randomly appearing and disappearing, opening and closing, anywhere and everywhere. I jumped to my feet and turned with the intent of running back down the alley to take my chances of escape at the chained and locked door. My dream path was blocked by more of the monkish figures that had completed the circle behind me with Billy and myself at the center. I was trapped - like a rat! All of the ghostly apparitions had the same insignia burned into the chests of their robes, the cross and the lightning bolt. I spun back around and Billy stood directly in front of me, toe-to-toe. With his phantom arms resting at his phantom sides he whispered into my face.

"Where do you think you're going? You will play, I will win and you will lose."

The whispering chorus piped in again, "You will play and you will lose, you will play and we will win."

Standing as close as we were I should have been able to make out some features of Billy's face, feel and smell his breath, something. There was nothing. Only his disembodied voice coming from the black empty space where his head and face should have been. There was only an empty space that reverberated with the echoes of my own wildly beating heart and rapid shallow breathing.

"No way," was my breathless but grinning response.

I bolted for the door back at the far end of the alley.

Bursting through the ring of robed figures, sending several of them sprawling into the fog above the floor, I made my bid for escape and freedom.

"There is no escape, Archer! You must play, you will play and you will lose, there is no choice," Billy bleated in a hoarse goat call.

"I will not play, but, even if I did, I'd win anyway!" I shouted back as I ran through the misty alley.

I soon found that the faster I ran, the harder I tried, the slower my progress became. I strained against the maddening slow motion

The previously stationary apparitions were on the move in a steady and unencumbered pursuit with Billy in the led. My assailants glided in fast as my escape momentum ceased and my forward progress came to a halt. I glanced back over my shoulder at the gaining ghosts when unexpectedly my tortuous slow motion, without warning, relinquished its grip and I shot forward, launched like a marble from a slingshot.

I barely had time to turn my head back to the front when I ran smack-dab into the side of an old rusted junk car which had unavoidably parked itself across the width of the alley directly in my path. I bounced none too daintily off the driver's closed door and fell backwards, landing butt first on the alley pavement. My prostrate body was totally obscured in the thick rolling mist. It took all of my dream strength just to keep from spilling my marbles during the impact and subsequent tumble to the ground. It would have been impossible to recover any of my marbles if I'd lost my grip. They would've rolled away under the cover of the fog, drawn from the alley by the endless darkness into the infinite on all sides.

Looking up to judge the extent of the obstacle, I crushed down hard on my marble box. Before me, sitting in the rusted old junker without wheels, were two human skeletons, both staring down at me. One sat in the driver's seat and his bony companion sat in the back seat directly behind. Both had their bony skulls shifted in my direction as I struggled to gather my wits on the cold damp alley floor. They glared directly down at me. Their stares shot through me like arrows flying at the speed of light, razor sharp arrows that were already five-hundred-thousand miles away before you felt the painful sting and saw the seeping blood from their passage.

In each of their bony eye sockets rested the deepest and most horrifyingly blood red, yet, infinitely beautiful, Cat's-Eye boulders. It was a look of the damned, a vacant gaze down from the hilarously absurd and yet, a gaze of goodbye, of a final parting, with a resigned warmth and bitter tenderness. They each ate from large overflowing plates of chocolate cake and vanilla ice cream which they shoveled into their bony gullets with big metal spoons that they gripped in spindly bone hands. You could see the mixed ice cream and cake, swallowed whole, in large gulps, slip down their bony throats and slop and glop along and between their hard, lifeless bony ribs.

With feeding skeletons to the front of me and robed ghosts coming up from behind, I struggled and fought to keep myself from disintegrating into a pile of disconnected little person parts where I fell. The effortless gliding pursuit of Billy and the gang were bringing them ever closer. I turned back to my front only to find the rusty heap and skeletal occupants had vanished: the head turning thing again.

With marble box tenably intact and in tow, I crawled back up to my feet and ran for the chained door. Mustering all of the speed and momentum I could I ran full speed, head and shoulder down, and slammed into the closed door's massive bulk. It seemed worth the unsuccessful try. Dazed and bruised, I picked myself back up and fell back against the door hard and frantically pulled at the chains and viciously pounded on the lock that barred the only avenue of escape.

Frantically searching the immediate surroundings for another way, any way out, in the few desperate moments I dreamed I had left, I pushed back from the door and, as if heavenly inspired, looked up. There, in plain sight but well above the door on a single nail hung the key to the giant pad lock which held all of the door's restraining chains in place. I feebly tried jumping to reach the key but it was too highly placed. The hooded horde was a scant few yards away. In one last hopeful attempt, I looked about and sighted several old but stackable wooden crates.

Hastily collecting the crates which, mysteriously, weighed several more pounds than they should have, I laboriously stacked them into a swaying pile that I thought would be high enough to climb and reach the key. The plan was to get the key, jump off the pile of crates, kick the tumbling pile into the path of Billy and company to delay their arrival, unlock the lock, open the door and get the hell outta there. "Yeah, that would work," I dreamed.

Just as I made it to the top of my thrown-together tower my would-be assailants reached the bottom of my unsteady perch. I stretched and strained to reach the key to my salvation, my peace of mind, but it remained just fractions of an inch beyond my out stretched hand. Billy and friends were at hand, shaking and pulling at the stacked crates which comprised the hastily assembled ladder, trying to tumble me down to the ground and into their unmerciful arms. As the tower swayed I fought to keep my balance, reach the key and avoid falling into the clutches of the black shadows that had collected below me. Tragedy struck as I lost the firm grip on my marble box. My collected crystal treasures slipped from my grasp and fell into the greedy, waiting arms of Billy. As my marbles disappeared into the black void of his spread-wide robed arms, he growled, moaned and cackled like a starving wild animal devouring its first meal in weeks. "Disgusting," I dreamt.

My marbles were lost. The last and only chance left was to save my marble soul because at that point I dreamt they wanted that as well. I lurched upward in one last gasping attempt to reach the key and come one-step closer to ending my torment and suffering. The final leap used up all of my remaining strength. My eyes were pressed close from the exertion. Success! I made it to the key – I thought. I opened my eyes in anticipation of seeing the brass in my grasp only to find, perched above me, one of the marble-eyed skeletons kneeling on a ledge above the key. I looked at my hand to find it clutching not the treasured key but the cold dead hand of the bony menace.

All hope vanished. My swaying perch started to fall apart and me along with it. Billy laughed from below that I could never win and that my marbles, and everything that went with them, would be his forever. With teeth bared and fists clenched for the final fight, I yelled back that I'd never give up and that what was mine, marbles and all, would never really be his, ever. The piled crates finally gave way. I dove head first, screaming, with my fists flying, into the flailing arms of Billy, his ghouls and the other Cat's-Eyed skeleton.

It was no wonder that I yelled and cried out in my sleep. I fought the urge to scream out loud all over again even though I was wide-awake! My eyes hadn't blinked in minutes. I stared a dry-eyed hole right through the figure that stood motionless and menacing at the foot of my bed. Wide-awake but frozen from fear, I laid on bedding soaked through with my own sweat. Shivering from fear and dampness I mustered any and all of the courage and raw nerve that I had left and, haltingly, contemplated reaching for the corded switch on my bedside lamp to try to pull on the light as quickly as my wooden clothespin-like fingers would permit.

The last time I was that frightened, Robert and I were camping out in the backyard in a tent improvised from a discarded cardboard refrigerator box. It was three in the morning when, just feet from our heads, two stray cats started to fight. I thought the devil himself had stuck his head up out of the ground searching for fresh young souls to drag away to Hades.

I surmised that if the thing standing in front of me was real, the certainty was that as the light went on I'd pee and poop in my pajamas and then die of fright right there in my messy bed. The second possibility was that the thing at the foot of my bed had an accomplice under the bed just waiting for my outstretched arm to grab onto as I reached for the light. Pee, poop and die or lose my arm, then pee, poop and die. That lose-lose-no-win-no-matter-what choice is how I saw my predicament.

Somehow, I summoned the resolve from somewhere deep down inside of my little being, from the unknown depths of my cramped and shivering body, after several minutes of confused nerve-building deliberation, to make a try for the bedside light. My only other choice would have been to spend the rest of the night soaked in my sweat waiting for "it" to move or the "thing" that I was then certain was under the bed to make a move or for the sun to come up which would scare them both away. With eyes clenched closed I reached for the lamp switch cord with a quick lunging stab.

For little kids, having one's eyes closed in such situations, when there were spooks and other entities of the night about, was akin to holding up a crucifix to a vampire or wearing a necklace of garlic to fend off werewolves. Through an extended and detailed process of childhood rationalization I concluded, and several of my friends at the time concurred, that monsters and other assorted beings of the dark night that invaded one's bedroom had a sort of evil creature code of ethics which prevented them from attacking mortal beings, especially small children mortal beings, when those small children had their eyes closed, i.e., as a child you had to see and watch it coming or it didn't count, no exceptions or do-overs for the monsters and spooks. Well, it must have been true because it worked. I found the light switch with my arm intact and heard the light click on and recognized the pink and orange glow as the light filtered through my tightly shut eyelids.

With eyes still clamped shut, just in case, I slowly lay back down onto my bed and shook as my body reconnected with the cold wet sheets and pillow. Clenching my fists and filling my lungs with air for one last final shriek and call for help, my eyes popped open! I almost screamed anyway just to release all of the pent-up tension.

My worries evaporated into the late night's warm air. The stress-compressed air from my lungs passed through my pursed lips with the sound of a deflating balloon in erratic flight. The menacing dark figure was nothing more than my bedspread which my mother had taken off my bed and tossed over my coat rack when she'd said her first good night some hours before. It was just an old quilt, too much hard-to-digest cold dessert and the dim light and dark shadows of the night having conspired to kill me. I checked my wind-up alarm clock on the night table: three in the a.m.. Relieved but exhausted, I moved over to the drier side of my bed, finally ready for sleep. With the light on, I contemplated the first real doubts I ever had about being the school marble champ.

Dreams, good or bad, never happened by accident. Dreams, despite their frequently compressed and confusing imagery, are always direct and honest in their meaning. The imparted feelings, during or after the dream, are always right on the mark. It is the most reliable form of communication your subconscious brain has with your conscious mind.

Whatever is bothering you, whatever you hope for, whatever you look forward to and whatever you are glad is past and behind you, whatever makes you happy or sad, whatever reassures or frightens you, as you sleep your brain will work it out and then spell it out in your dreams no matter what form the visual and emotional code might take. The imagery and emotion of dream speak is the interpretation of what happens, what comes into your life on a daily basis, how you take it all in, absorb and work things out from each day, through that night and into the next day.

There are no incidental, frivolous or insignificant images, meanings or feelings in your dreams. It is always the unvarnished truth if you can just decipher the efficiently compressed and abbreviated psychological shorthand. In my case the message was there, plain and simple, loud and clear. That I was worried about Billy Schoutenlauder was no longer in doubt. My head had decided it and had done its part; the message had been composed and delivered as required and in a fashion equal to the significance in my life. I had worried enough for one night. I drifted off to a less eventful but still restless sleep.

The next morning, a Tuesday, despite the best efforts of my mother to help me wash up, comb my hair, brush my teeth and put on fresh clean under and outer garments, no matter that I shoveled down a breakfast fit for a lumberjack, I barely dragged myself to school. It was my turn to look and feel like the kid who'd spent a cold night on a park bench under a pile of newspapers. There was an exhausted translucent darkness to my complexion, like a six-year-old kid who needed a shave and a percolator pot full of hot strong black coffee. It was marble nightmare hangover and I had it bad.

By Wednesday morning I managed to partially recover. The rest of the week passed uneventfully, by day and by night, to Friday, the day before the big match. The bad-dream-induced rattled nerves stayed with me, just beneath the surface, throughout the week, making for long tough days to get through. The daily schoolwork became a significant and tiresome inconvenience. I chose to play only a few matches and those were only with Russ and then only for funzies. The rest of the time I preferred to practice on my own off in a far deserted corner of the school playground.

On Friday, during the first lesson period after lunch, it was our class's turn to visit the school library. We visited the library after lunch on Tuesdays and Fridays. The practice was to return to our classroom, gather up our library stuff and then, in a silent single file line, walk from the classroom to the far end of the school where we all waited, just as silently, for entry into the library.

Ever since leaving the lunchroom that day Wilbur Hunt had been trying to get my attention. I'd purposely avoided him on the playground in order to get as much undisturbed practice time in as possible. The class departed from the classroom for the library in our silent single file line through the long, quiet, softly lit school corridor. Halfway to our destination the girl ahead of me in line, Caroline Edwards, handed me a crinkled up note from behind her back. "Just what I needed," I thought to myself expecting another untimely declaration of unsolicited devotion and romantic attachment. I looked ahead in the line and in front of Caroline there was Diane, Wendy, Deborah and then Wilbur. I didn't recognize the scribbled first grader style printing so it could've been from any one of the girls.

It turned out not to be from any of the girls as they'd just passed the note along. Fortunately my initial instincts were incorrect as a closer inspection of the note revealed it was from Wilbur and with no chance of an inconvenient romance. Wilbur was a fair piece ahead in the line so I figured that it had to be pretty important information for him to take the chance of passing along a note five places back in a single file line right under the watchful gaze of Mrs. Goodchaulks. As we all steadily marched along I managed to read the simple note that stated, "wEe gOt twO tUaLk." More rumors, no doubt, from Wilbur's neighborhood source who was in attendance at Avenging Grace. I finished reading the note and then crumpled it up and shoved into my pants pocket. As I saw Wilbur look back over his shoulder I nodded my response. We silently lined up outside the library entrance doors.

    The school library was "A Quiet Place - A Place To Be Quiet." It said so on the library entrance doors and signs all over the inside of the library. After being read the library's proper conduct rules which emphasized and included, repeatedly, the library being a quiet place, along with other last minute instructions, pointers and reminders from the librarian and our teacher, we were all dismissed from our seats at the library tables to silently roam among the books. That particular library period was a free period during which we were all allowed to browse and read at our leisure for one hour. Wilbur looked at me and with his eyes motioned to meet in the far corner of the library.

    Having taken different routes, Wilbur and I surely and steadily headed for the far corner near the window and the library's collection of dinosaur books. Mrs. Goodchaulks excused herself from the room, leaving us under the ever-watchful eye of old Miss Bookbender, the school librarian. Old Lady Bookbender viewed the library as her private domain, her personal study, which she reluctantly shared with the students.

    Her pet peeve was students talking and carrying on in her kingdom. There were posters strategically placed and posted about the room that were intended to remind everyone, on a second by second basis, of her constant and unwavering vigilance. The poster was a black and white photograph of Old Bookbender, with her finger pressed vertically against her lips, shushing anyone who looked at the poster. The poster photo had that unnerving quality that her eyes would follow you and stare right at you from wherever you stood to look at it. High or low, left or right, it didn't matter. Beneath the photophotograph the poster read, "Shhuussshhh. Libraries are quiet places."

One of the photo posters was missing, having been taken down awaiting replacement. It seemed that some day prior, one of the upperclassmen had drawn an extension of Bookbender's vertical finger pressed against her lips that went right up into one of her nostrils and altered the printed phrase to read, "Shhuussshhh. Libraries are *'booger'* places."

The particular unaltered copy of the Bookbender poster that watched over Wilbur and me hung just above the bookcase where the dinosaur books were shelved and sat squarely between a portrait of President Lincoln on one side and President Washington on the other. Abe was on the left looking right and George was on the right looking left. Old Lady Bookbender was in the center looking straight down at us, with her finger-plastered perpendicular up against her lips, the eternal "Shusher."

I reached the designated area after Wilbur, who was busily paging through a book on the history of the Tyrannosaurus Rex, one of the most popular books in the entire school library. I joined him and picked out an edition which briefly described the life and times of the Stegosaurus. Wilbur nudged me with his elbow and pointed to a page in the T-Rex book were the Bookbender-photo-altering-artist had visited and left his mark, "Tyrannosaurus *'booger'* Rex" read a caption for one of the book's drawings (we figured the 'booger artist' wouldn't be hard to find; just look for a kid with a big nose, wide-open nostrils and abnormally long pointy fingers).

After we stopped giggling under our breath, Wilbur looked right and I looked left as we checked to see if the coast was clear. Bookbender, as was her practice when kids were in the library, was out and about on the prowl, trailing ensnaring library-violator-catching-nets and trolling long clinging lines with grasping hooks at the ends as she cruised the bookshelf backwaters looking for any easy catch. Wilbur leaned in real close and was about to give me the latest low down when Bookbender popped out from around the corner of a nearby tall bookcase. She stopped right behind us and just stood there looking down over our shoulders with her arms folded, impatiently waiting for us to break down under her hard penetrating stare and fall to our knees and confess that we were just waiting for our chance to break the rules and talk behind her back in her deathly quiet library. She was standing so close that we both felt and smelled her warm humid old lady after-lunch breath as it wafted down over our heads and shoulders from behind.

We refused to break. We knew her game. We'd both been witness to other unfortunate library rule breaking souls who had been put through the 'Bookbender Mill'. We both staunchly held our ground and silently, innocently, continued to page through our books without so much as exchanging glances. Bookbender, thwarted, gave out with a series of irritated little fake coughs as she crossed her hands behind her back and drifted away down the aisle to continue library patrol. Once she disappeared around the distant corner, Wilbur shuffled closer and started whispering excitedly, almost urgently.

Wilbur spit out that he'd heard, through the AG neighbor kid, that Billy had been bragging all over Avenging Grace that he fully intended, and in fact had a plan, to "really pound the shrimp from the Fifty-First Street School" in that Saturday's match – the "shrimp" being me. Billy was telling everyone and anyone who'd listen that he'd forced me into the match with threats because I was, supposedly, too frightened of playing him for keeps. Billy was spreading another story as well and, by Wilbur's pained expression and sudden silence, he indicated that he was unwilling to relate the rest of the story's contents.

I waited impatiently for Wilbur to untie his tongue and finish what he started. I elbowed him hard and silently mouthed "come on." Wilbur choked out that Billy was also telling his closet friends that if, by some remote chance, I turned out to be the real deal and actually won, that I'd still leave the alley without a single marble. So it wasn't going to be a marble match at all, just a marble robbery disguised as a match. So Schoutenlauder turned out to be a lying jerk, nothing more than a thug and a thief in the disguise of a marble player. He didn't care what deities and saints were following him around and looking over his shoulder. The little Devil that sat on his left shoulder had sucker punched into unconsciousness the little Angel that had been sitting on his right shoulder.

I almost dropped my Stegosaurus book on the floor. Looking hard at Wilbur, hoping that he'd stretched things a bit, embellished a lot for dramatic effect, I pressed on and asked if he knew for certain that those were Billy's exact words. He assured me by crossing his heart, giving the *Scout's Honor Sign* all while reciting that "if he lied he died" that to the exact word is what the neighbor kid had told him. My traumatic dream just nights before wasn't just a food-induced bad nightmare, it was a warning, an honest and accurate premonition, as if I'd unconsciously read Billy's mind that Monday after school on the sidewalk.

My previously calm insides did a full three-sixty tumble with a loud gurgle. My partially digested lunch instantly petrified and went dead cold in my stomach. Shakily, carelessly, I returned the Stegosaurus book to the shelf, well out of place from its original required *Dewey Decimal System* position in the section. I placed my left hand over my stomach and my right hand over my concealed marble sock. I whispered to Wilbur that I'd see him later. Haltingly, limply, I walked for my assigned library table seat at the far end of the library.

My almost healed nerves were once again frayed, sparking and raw. I unexpectedly found myself on the verge of a complete, smoky, fiery and explosive short circuit. All I wanted to do was play marbles, not punch it out with Billy Schoutenlauder. What was so difficult about that? I walked with my left hand rubbing my stomach and my right hand held fast to my loaded marble sock that was tied to my belt and concealed under my sweater.

Unknown to either Wilbur or myself, while we were having our private discussion, Bookbender, trusting her library violator instincts, had circled back behind us, taken up an eavesdropping position and spied upon us throughout our entire conversation. I was just about to turn the corner at the far end of the aisle when Old Lady Bookbender jumped out right in front of me. With one bony claw-like hand on her bony hip, her other bony claw-like hand thrust out as she grabbed me by the shoulder. I stopped frozen in my tracks, mouth open for a scream that never came.

Her sudden and completely unexpected materialization was, as intended, a successful surprise attack. As her lunging bony hand found my shoulder I flashed back on the bony hand of the marble-eyed skeleton grabbing my hand in the nightmare. I must have jumped a full foot off the floor, propelled into the air by my vaulting stomach. In the shock, the fright of the moment, my right hand, still clutching hard onto my marble sock, jerked violently and involuntarily out and away from my side. The force ripped the sock knot loose from my belt, releasing all of that day's practice marbles as the upside down open-neck marble sock emptied itself in just a few seconds. The marbles hit and bounced up from the hard tile floor in rapid repeating succession like ricocheting machine gun bullets.

I landed back on the floor bent over and covering my mouth, certain that I was going to throw-up right then and there in front of everybody and all over the sacred ground of the library floor. It would serve Bookbender right to have my lost lunch all over and inside of her clunky librarian shoes. I couldn't believe what was happening to me. Bending over and fighting not to lose it, I helplessly watched and listened as the escaped marbles took full advantage of the free library period as they freely and energetically worked their way to, around, past and finally stopping and coming to rest in front of a wide and varied eclectic selection of nearby subject-by-subject book sections.

I'd flagrantly committed two of the most heinous library crimes and just barely prevented myself from committing an atrociously disgusting third in Bookbender's *'Book of Library High Crimes'*. Everything moved very fast from there on in. Mrs. Goodchaulks joined Miss Bookbender in the library while I was still gagging and even before all of my rolling and book browsing marbles had come to a rest. It became very clear that I wasn't going to get any help, understanding or protection from my teacher. If anything, by the look on her face, she seemed eager and willing to join in on the flogging or whatever they planned to do with me. It wasn't long before I found out.

I was rapidly escorted from the library, held firmly by the arm, to the principal's office. My captor, my escort, my guard for the trip was Old Lady Bookbender herself. Bookbender, Mrs. Goodchaulks and a small group of teacher's pets who'd eagerly volunteered for the duty, led by Holly Harder, had collected my scattered marbles which Bookbender deposited into a brown paper lunch bag that she hung onto as desperately as she hung onto me. We walked in quickstep silence except for the click-clunk-click-clunk of Bookbender's loosely fitting old lady librarian shoes.

She walked with a very unsteady cadence and leaned on and against me as much as she held my arm and walked along side of me. I'd become sort of a temporary but effective moving little boy crutch. She'd become so unsteady, so wobbly, that it seemed at any second some combination of her ankles and knees would give way and she'd careen wildly side to side and then collapse onto the floor face first with a bone-shattering SMACK!

Bookbender had insisted to Mrs. Goodchaulks that she alone would walk me to the principal's office where she intended to personally plead her case against me to the school's highest authority. Mrs. Goodchaulks stayed behind to supervise the rest of the class. Wilbur, thanks to the dramatic commotion created by my scattered marbles, had been forgotten, overlooked and escaped any and all repercussions of our library infractions.

An elementary school student could not attend years of grade school and not at one time or another have reason or cause to pay a visit to the principal's office. The distinction was the type and reason for the visit. There were a lot of good reasons that might arise requiring one's presence in or one's visit to the school office. It might involve claiming some important or valuable personal item from the lost and found, picking up a forgotten lunch delivered to school by Mom or Dad after you'd rushed out of the house late for school on a particular morning, or the rare honor of being selected by your teacher to deliver important classroom materials to the office which involved a solo walk through the school during class time with an official hall pass; that type of good stuff. Then, there were trips to the office for not such good stuff. Being caught committing infractions of school rules and other offenses and missteps that resulted in various disciplinary responses were common reasons for an office visit or even multiple office visits.

I'd never been sent or taken to the principal's office for any good or bad reason up to that point in my young elementary school career. You didn't have to be a bad kid to end up in the principal's office for a school rule infraction. Bad kids with bad intentions in self-created or sought out bad circumstances were the school's familiar models for frequent and repeated trips to the office. At the other end of the scale were the basically good kids, like I was, who were caught up in a set of unforeseen or unexpected bad circumstances – again, like I was.

Sadly, if there was a place in school where unforeseen bad circumstances could pop-up and bite you big time in the backside it had to be the school library. The cleverly concealed traps and intentionally camouflaged pitfalls, something completely out of place, completely unexpected, in a room full of interesting books, were just to numerous to have counted and kept track of. Unknown to me at the time I had a lot of past, then present and would be future, unsuspecting and entrapped school kid company on that list.

Considering the risks I'd willingly accepted and undertaken in my schoolyard marble exploits the likelihood of not ending up in the school office at one time or another for some intended (less likely) or unintended (most likely) rules infraction would have been like asking me to transverse a messy muddy barnyard full of roaming farm animals on a rainy day wearing all white with the unrealistic and ridiculous expectation that I'd come out the other side without a single drop of brown or black slop on the white outfit. It just couldn't be done.

Your parents would drop you off at the gate where you left the protection of the clean and dry covered wagon. They'd wish you well, the best of luck, with hugs, kisses, plenty of smiley goodbyes and reassuring "see you at home later's" as they saw you off on your life's first semi-solo adventure. But once you were down off the wagon and standing unprotected in the rain and you started your treacherous trek across the farmyard (schoolyard) all bets were off.

If it wasn't the broad-body clodding cows walking and bumping by while dropping fresh greenish-brown pies everywhere (most fifth and sixth graders), or the squealing pigs rooting and rolling around in the mud and then scampering between, around and up against your legs (countless third and fourth graders), or the brazen crowing rooster that flies from the top rail of the fence and lands with clawed feet on your shoulder intending to hold fast while repeatedly pecking you on the top of your head (one was one too many Bookbenders) or all the once nice white cute ducks waddling through the mud on their way to walking across and standing, muddy webbed feet and all, on top of your white shoes as they quacked, chattered with their bills and nibbled at the ends of your shoe laces (many second graders and more than a few other first graders), or some combination of all such uninvited attention and assaults including, and not to be forgotten, just slipping and falling into the slop all on your own without any help from anybody.

You also had to keep a wary eye out for the larger, more dangerous animals that would, on occasion, get loose and wonder by. Donkeys, also known as asses or jackasses, mules (the big, dumb and stubborn variety), bullying bulls, cranky chew-on-anything-in-site goats, angry charging rams, preening-scratching chickens and large, honking, bill-snapping gossipy geese, all more commonly known and identified as junior high and senior high students that inhabited larger even muddier and sloppier farmyards somewhere down the road in both time and distance. Those animals had graduated onto those farms of higher education and were already previously and permanently stained by the relentless, unforgiving and clinging elementary schoolyard mud.

Nobody from kindergarten onto twelfth grade – nobody – had a white hanky's chance in mud hell! Before you knew it and long before you expected it those spotless dress angel whites would be rapidly transformed into a broad spectrum of demon browns as if you'd just finished an hour-long round trip ride-along-tour over and across every single plow rut of the deeply furrowed back-40 while seated, unprotected, inside of the farmer's bouncing, towed-behind and fully loaded manure spreader.

All of these required social and educational excursions would take place under the discerning eye of the farmer (Wagermann) who stood secure and clean, high and dry, in the protected open door perch of the barn's second floor hayloft. Leaning against the loft door frame wearing a farmer's straw hat, a farmer's bibbed blue overalls, with his hands buried deep in the overall pockets while he purposefully chewed on long blade of green grass, he'd bide his time. With watchfully focused eyes and attentively tuned ears he stood, with megaphone in hand, and loudly called out, as and when required, words of encouragement, warnings, watch outs, watch your steps, admonitions and other various situation appropriate positive or negative advisements.

We all learned that the pure whites (along with any pure white expectations) were best left behind at the schoolyard gate because everybody showed-up at school – parents, teachers and kids alike – dragging around their own special versions, in ample supply, of black and brown personal slop and glop that they just couldn't wait to share (intentionally or unintentionally) with anyone and everyone they crossed paths with. Whatever personal or family mud that couldn't be carried to school on our own or within us as kids, our parents would be certain to stuff into all available empty pockets and/or safety pin to our shirts and jackets like big yellow name, address and telephone number I.D. Tags in their lovingly misguided efforts to aid, albeit hinder, us on our elementary school travels.

Rare was the kid who showed up at school as a benign blank slate. We all arrived as impressionist paintings in progress (some with damaged frames and torn canvas, some with canvas and stretcher frame intact with most falling somewhere in between). Whether you ended up as a landscape, a still life, some surrealistic modern art masterpiece or an unfinished canvas would remain an open question for sometime. How good or bad, interesting or uninteresting, meaningful or meaningless, mysterious or undecipherable the resulting art work eventually turned out to be would only be determined by where you ended up hanging in the gallery years down the road. Starting as little kids we were all destined, throughout our entire lives, regardless of what we wanted, hoped for or worked to accomplished in those lives, to become and remain full-time, rarely adequately compensated, emotional baggage handlers; our own as well as others. Marbles, like any one's life, could be...messy.

Thus prepared for the first full onslaught of flying educational institution mud and manure I entered the school (barnyard) office, which also served as the principal's (farmer's) reception office, in the firm grasp of the vengeful school (rooster) librarian. We took seats across from the school secretary, who informed the principal by intercom that Miss Bookbender had come to see him regarding a first grader named Michael Archer who was waiting with her. His metallic machine voice came back that he'd be free to see us in just a few minutes. My only prior experience with the school principal was second hand, through my brother Robert.

The year before, when Robert was a third grader, he and three of his classmates were sent to the office for cutting out pictures of old antique cars from magazines and selling them to other kids in school for as much as a nickel apiece. They collected almost seventeen dollars which they stored in three old metal *Band-Aid* boxes.

Their teacher and the principal uncovered their activities through the complaints of irate parents who discovered that their children were spending their lunchtime milk money on worthless pictures of cars cut from old magazines. Robert, Mom, Dad and his three friends and their parents were all called in to a conference with Principal Wagermann and their classroom teacher. Nothing serious came from the meeting other than there'd be no more selling activity of the kind anywhere on or near the school grounds and all the money already collected would have to be returned to the rightful owners. It was further revealed that the entire enterprising idea grew out of a social studies class in which the background and incentives of the *American Free Enterprise System* had been explained. My brother, his friends and I (through my brother) all at very tender ages, discovered firsthand that the *Free Enterprise System* was very free for some and very limited if not completely off limits for others.

   Bookbender sat in the chair next to me. The cool and impersonal fluorescent lighting of the room gave me the feeling of being inside of a slightly-not-cold enough walk-in freezer. My hands were both sweaty and yet cold to the touch. I waited in sheer dread of being put on trial by the old bag in front of Principal Wagermann.

   The principal's office door had been open just a crack and I strained to pick up on any indication of Wagermann's mood. Having never been in his office before I was, nonetheless, more than vaguely familiar with all of the stories that circulated throughout the school. The rumors of Wagermann's dealing with disruptive students ranged from simple beatings with a wooden stick to hours of elaborate torture designed to get any and all desired information and confessions from reluctant student offenders. Having been a first time offender myself, I hoped for and planned to plead for leniency. Looking at Bookbender, I knew without a doubt that she would push for the maximum sentence. Bookbender and her damn library; she didn't even have any good books on marble-playing (NOT that I needed any).

   Wagermann was finishing up with a man who was wearing a plaid sport coat and a sharp, light brown, fedora with a small red decorative feather in the hat band; a real fancy dresser. The stranger with the hot duds also carried a small thin black monogrammed valise. He rose from the chair, the same chair that I was certain to occupy within the following few minutes, shook hands with the principal and then came through the office door and into the reception area.

   The guy in plaid momentarily stopped in front of the secretary's desk and checked the contents of a file folder that she handed him at Wagermann's request. He paged through the folder while exchanging chitchat with the school secretary. I closely watched all this from my seat with my chin buried in my chest and my eyes rolling and darting back and forth in the top of their sockets. The stranger looked back over his left shoulder just as I looked up and we exchanged glances for just a split second. The unspoken communication was instantaneous and prolific. His eyes sympathetically spoke, "That away kid, by the look of that bag of bones that's got hold of you, you're really in for it now."

My eyes had responded immediately, "Is that chair you were just sitting on wired for electric shocks?"

Unfortunately we broke visual contact before he could answer the question. He thanked the secretary, said his goodbyes and re-assuringly winked at me as he walked out of the office. As if the upcoming dentist appointment and the match with Billy weren't enough nerve shattering tension and stress for an entire year of my life, I also had to fight off a senile vindictive librarian who got her control kicks by persecuting school kids when they broke her unreasonable rules. Then – then, the rotten cherry on top of the moldy cake, I had to face I didn't know what in Wagermann's office.

Talk about piling on when you're down! Just wanting to play marbles, working so hard to be good at it for the previous nine months, having put up with anything and everything directly and indirectly related to the game, had brought me all the way to the threshold of that singular pathetic moment in time. I was either going to get through it, barely, or, right then and right there, just fall over – dead.

The school secretary got up from behind her desk and opened a tall metal file cabinet next to her desk. She walked into Wagermann's office carrying a file folder and closed Wagermann's office door behind her as she entered. It must have been my file. Six years old, not even finished my first year in school, never been to the principal's office before or even done anything before to warrant being there, and already I had - *a file*!

A few minutes later the secretary reopened the office door and stuck her head out and announced that Principal Wagermann was ready to see us. I fought the desperate urge to pull away from Bookbender and make a break for it. Out the reception office door, twenty feet to the main front doors and then half a block to the nearest alley and poof, I'd be gone, forever, because after a prank like that I could never, ever come back to school, not to mention ever going home again either: just me, my marbles and the clothes on my back. But where would I go? Nowhere, that's where! Even jumping into the open back of a passing and loaded cattle or hog truck would have been preferable to being hauled into Wagermann's office by Bookbender. I saw myself being chased around in the open streets and alleys surrounding the school by a pack of vicious dogs with Bookbender calling them on, "KILL, KILL!"

There was a minor misstep, some sort of "who's first through the office door" protocol confusion as Bookbender and I simultaneously passed through the office door side by side instead of single file. Each of us had bumped and pressed against each other and the door jam with our opposite shoulders at the same time, just like the *Three-Stooges* as they'd try to squeeze through a doorway all at once. We both pressed forward anyway as our combined forward momentum popped us together into the office and past the secretary who was standing just inside the door which she held open for us. I proceeded into the office with my head down and my hands folded in front of me. I felt like lunch being served up on an old beaten-up and bent-up metal tray pushed under the bars into the hungry lion's cage.

Wagermann had his back to us as we entered; he was filing something away from his seated position in his high-backed wheeled office chair, the kind that would lean way back and be very easy to fall asleep in. I walked in, stopped and stood directly behind, but not touching, the innocent enough looking interrogation chair that had been intentionally and strategically placed in front of the principal's desk. Bookbender had taken up a standing position to my back and left while we waited for Wagermann to finish.

The principal rapidly spun around in his chair, making a full three-quarters turn, oblivious to our waiting as he reached for something in another drawer. From there he quickly popped up, spun one-hundred-and-eighty degrees, scooted across his plastic floor mat in his wheeled chair and started digging around in another drawer to our left. While rummaging around in that drawer, he looked up as just the top of his head and eyeglasses were barely visible above his desktop. He finally acknowledged our presence by asking me to take a seat. He said he'd be just another minute. From his stooping position to our left, he pushed off yet again and rolled all the way back to our right where he searched through the contents of yet another drawer.

With quick and unobtrusive glances I looked around the office to see if there was another seat that I could sit in other than the suspect chair immediately in front of the desk. Sure enough, there were two other chairs, sitting side by side, against the far wall in the back corner of the office. I quietly, slowly walked backwards to my right and silently slipped into one of the most distant seats. Bookbender was getting impatient with Principal Wagermann and all of his shifting, rolling and futzing so she started making with the little fake coughing noises and other strange little sounds that resembled piglet grunts in an effort to focus the principal's attentention on the matter at hand, that matter having been me.

"Yes Miss Bookbender, just a moment more, a little patience please," Wagermann muttered, bobbing up and down behind his desk with every word he spoke.

"Principal Wagermann! Could I have your undivided attention for just a moment? Please! We have a serious problem here which requires your immediate consideration!"

Bookbender was unable to control her irritation with Wagermann any longer. I looked around the room baffled when I realized that the serious problem to which she was referring to, again, was me.

"Come now, Miss Bookbender. There is no need to become overly excited concerning this matter, whatever it is," Wagermann responded from somewhere under his desk.

For all I knew, Wagermann was checking and testing all the connections for the electrical shock apparatus wired to "the chair," making certain that everything was in peak working order before the interrogation had gotten under way. Puzzled by the principal's almost comic actions, I quietly observed all the goings-on from my semi-secluded position back in the far corner of the office.

Wagermann had apparently dealt with Bookbender on several other similar occasions. Once again she started in with the coughing and the grunting. Suddenly, Wagermann bolted to an abrupt upright sitting position while resting his forearms on his desk with hands folded as he dizzily, eyes unfocused, looked up in Bookbender's general direction.

"Yes, all right Miss Bookbender, what is it or who is it this time?"

Wagermann's glasses had come to rest crooked at the tip of his nose and that caused me to let slip a slight smirk despite my precarious circumstances. His face and forehead were flushed red. A tuft of hair had fallen down and across his face and came to rest on the bridge of his nose as the longer strand overflow rested on his left cheek. To further add to his disorientated appearance, he'd apparently sat up too fast with a lightheaded result. He leaned way back in his chair to keep from blacking out and tipping over. Good thing he'd recovered because if he hadn't Bookbender would have probably thought he was falling asleep on her time and she would have grabbed him by the arm and started yelling at him as well (the library rules insidiously extended out from the library for a considerable distance, well into other areas of the school like the creeping root system of a giant man-eating jungle plant).

Up to that point in the proceedings neither Wagermann nor Bookbender had noticed that I'd taken a seat as far from the action as was possible without having actually left the room. They both looked at the empty chair in front of his desk. Bookbender let out with a gasp, fearful that her latest victim had escaped before she had her chance at him – me. Silently, sheepishly I huddled down in the secluded seat as they discovered my reclusive position in the distant corner of the room.

Wagermann politely repeated his invitation to join him by taking the seat that stood just two feet in front of his desk. I reluctantly slid out of my chosen chair and walked to the seat in question. With a deep breath I carefully shifted my way into the designated seat. I rested on the seat fully prepared for a blinding flash and body-shaking jolt. As a precaution, I tried to keep my feet from touching the ground in hopes of preventing inadvertent, fully grounded, electrocution.

Bookbender started the trial with her opening statement.

"Principal Wagermann, this young man created one of the worst disturbances in the library that I've ever witnessed (if I'd thrown up all over her shoes, THAT would have been something to witness). Not only was he talking incessantly, he brought these with him and proceeded to drop them over the entire library floor, disturbing the entire class's concentration. It was disgraceful, really disgraceful. You can take my word on that!"

With her last words, Bookbender stepped forward and deposited my empty marble sock and the brown paper lunch bag that held my marbles onto the principal's desk. Having regained his equilibrium, Wagermann titled forward in his chair to an upright position and reached for the confiscated materials.

With her arms folded defiantly across her chest, Bookbender continued.

"The rules of behavior in the school's library are very clear and very simple. They've been explained to all of the students time and time again, but, apparently this student has taken it upon himself to be above the rules of this school!"

Wagermann interrupted long enough to get a word in edgewise, putting the question to me directly.

"Mr. Archer, do you indeed feel that you are above the rules of this school?" all said with his glasses still cocked on his nose and that tuft of hair still down across his face.

"No sir," I timidly responded, hoping my sincerity was convincing enough to keep him from hitting the 'go switch' and giving me 'the sparks'.

Wagermann paused, contemplated my answer, and then finally straightened his glasses and brushed back his unruly hair with his hand. He picked up the empty marble sock with two fingers by a loose thread. By his facial expression I could tell that he was questioning the sanitary condition of the doubled-up garment, sweaty and stinky or fresh from the wash. The principal turned his gaze back to Bookbender and asked if she had anything further to add.

"Only this, Principal Wagermann," Bookbender cackled, "I feel that we should deal with this matter as we have in the past.

It's the only punishment that seems to work in these cases," (Just as I'd suspected, there were numerous previous cases).

"Yes, thank you Miss Bookbender," Wagermann impatiently responded. "I'll consider your recommendation in this case as well."

I knew it. They were in on it together! Wagermann would run the interrogation and Bookbender would provide the victims and fire-up the shock generator from some adjacent hidden room.

"I can count on you then?" Bookbender verbally jabbed.

"Yes, Miss Bookbender. Thank you for your concern and advice, as always. I'll handle everything concerning this matter from here on in," Wagermann blocked.

With her hands folded in front of her at waist height and a look on her face that screamed, "we'll see!" she glared at Wagermann. With her chin and nose thrust up into the air like the bow of a ship cresting a tall breaking wave, she turned and walked for the door. She condescended to look down at me in passing with her old puckered sour face. I'd seen plenty of old people who had even baggier, more wrinkled faces than hers but they were nicer people whose elderly appearance radiated kindness and wisdom. She looked so angry, so arrogant and vindictive, as if she really enjoyed bringing kids to Wagermann and putting them through the emotional grinder.

It seemed to me, in my limited experience at the time, that I encountered basically two types of teachers and other people who worked in the school. There were the mature adults who enjoyed being in the company of children and enjoyed working with them on a day-to-day basis but continued to advance and maintained their educated adult perspective on things. Then there were those who, for whatever misguided reason, just barely tolerated the presence of children and were more interested in a private agenda that resulted in dominance and control as if they were just still children themselves in competition with their wards to be the biggest, strongest and smartest kids in class all wrapped-up in an artificial candy coating.

Either you got it and cared or you didn't, couldn't or wouldn't. Bookbender struck me as one of the second types where all of the candy coating had completely worn off. I guessed that if she left the employment of the school and its library that a job in the nearest maximum security prison library guard tower awaited her. Bookbender finally left the room and in the process had taken all the stale and choking bad air she'd brought in with her.

Without a word, Wagermann grabbed and then slowly emptied the brown paper lunch bag of marbles onto the surface of his large green desk writing pad and slowly, thoughtfully, started to sort through them. For me it was torture by silence. My head was trying to hide in that part of my shirt that covered my chest when it struck me that Wagermann was completely, utterly, captivated by the spread of marbles on his desk. He picked one up here and there, occasionally holding one up toward the ceiling lights to watch with fascination as the light prismed through the little round glass crystal.

Marble-playing, to most people, was similar to the way most people saw and understood everyday white sunlight. It was something that existed, was necessary and needed, but, for the most part, would be taken completely for granted. If the time and effort had been taken to investigate, white sunlight was actually the result of a combined and condensed rainbow. So it was with marbles. It wasn't just a game. When I played I discovered that it was really a composite of all the different facets of my young life.

Coughing to clear his throat, indirectly announcing that he'd come back to our mutually shared place in time and space, Wagermann, very officiously, but gently, brushed the marbles to the side and placed both of his forearms with hands folded on the top of his desk. Peering over the top of his bifocal rims, he looked me straight in the eyes.

"Nice collection you've got here," he complimented me.
"Yes sir."
"Been playing long?"
"Just this year."
"By the way, uummm - ?" he held up my empty marble socks by the loose thread.
"Oh, my mom makes me use only clean socks for my mar-

bles," I reassured him.

"Good, fine, yes - very good. Is this your entire collection then?"

"Oh no sir. Most of these I won last week during recess. I have about – uummm – anotherrrrr – two-thousand at home in a boot box under my bed," I calculated off the top of my head.

"Really? Is that so, two-thousand? Then you're the one that I've been hearing so much about. You're in Mrs. Goodchaulks class then, in Room 107, correct?"

"Yes sir, 107, Mrs. Goodchaulks," I concurred.

"I've heard you're the best marble player the Fifty-First Street School has seen for sometime. Is that true, Mr. Archer?" he'd complimented and questioned simultaneously.

"Well, I'm the champ all right, but if I'm the best ever in the school I don't know 'cause I'm just a first grader," I responded with my chin well out of and above my chest.

"Yes - of course - you're only a first grader, then?" he puzzled.

"Yes sir?" I puzzled right back.

"You also have an older brother here in school as well, right? Let – me – see," Wagermann paged through a large, black three-ringed binder that he kept on the front left corner of his desk. "Yes, Robert, in the fourth grade. Is that right?"

"Yes sir, Robert, fourth grade."

"I've also heard that he is quite the baseball player and baseball card collector as well, right?"

"Yes sir, he knows everything about baseball. He's the best at baseball cards in the whole school," I proudly announced.

"That good is he?"

"Yes sir, the best I've ever seen."

"Do you and your bother ever play against each other, yeah know, in baseball cards or marbles?"

"No sir, never really felt we had to, or even wanted to," was my matter of fact answer.

"I see – I see. You and your brother get along okay?"

"Yes sir. Robert gives me really good advice most of the time." (Fleeting images of Babes Hanrahan and Warren Axlerod flashed rapidly, one after the other in order, across my mind)

"Is that so? That's good, really good. Brothers should help each other out now and then like that. Yes, that's good."

All the small talk helped me to relax. I completely forgot about the possibility that the chair my keister was parked in was hot-wired. Wagermann paused for a moment, rocking back and forth in his chair. For a few seconds it looked to me as if he were almost on the verge of falling off to sleep when he unexpectedly snapped to attention and lunged forward in his chair.

"Well son, I think we should clear up this library matter right away. Would it be fair to assume that things happened the way Bookbender – er – ah, Miss Bookbender said? I would like very much to hear your side of the story if you'd like to speak up."

"Well," I shifted in my seat, "I was talking like she said but not loud. I was whispering real quiet. I did drop my marbles even though I didn't mean to. It just sort of – happened. I was walking back to my seat when Bookbender – er – ah, Miss Bookbender jumped out at me and scared me really bad and then I dropped my marbles. I'm sorry for being a disturbance. I didn't mean to be. I almost threw-up when she grabbed me but – I didn't," I explained in a slightly pleading voice.

"Yes, well, Miss Bookbender runs a pretty tight ship over there in the library. She's one of the best librarians in the entire school district and I feel lucky that we have her here at the Fifty-First Street School. She's been with the school for over thirty years and she works very hard and she's dedicated to her job. She does tend to go a little bit overboard at times. You're not the first student she's frightened, but, of course all that is just between you and me, okay? You know what 'just between you and me' means, don't you Mike?"

"Yes sir, it means it's a secret just between us," I responded with a smile.

"Good Mike, very good. But, this being your first offense and having heard only good things about you, I've decided, in your case, to be understanding, to be lenient. But, we still have to settle this matter in such a way that the needs, the expectations, of all concerned parties involved are met. Do you understand everything I've just said?"

"I – think - so," I nodded my assent, having gotten the overall gist, the tone and tenor of his intentions.

"So, I've decided that you will lose your library privileges for the next week. Each time your class is scheduled for the library you'll report here to the office instead. For the rest of the library period today and then for the two library periods next week, is that right? Yes, that's correct – Mrs. Goodchaulks will send you back here and then pick you up at the end of the library period. We have a nice little study room right here just off from the reception area where you can read, study, draw for that hour or whatever you feel needs to be done in the line of schoolwork. Seem fair enough?"

"Yes sir, fair enough," I brightly responded.

"Good then. Now that we've sorted this all out and settled this man to man I see no need to tell your folks about this little incident. I'll just make a small note here in your file that indicates the matter has been satisfactorily resolved. What do you think, Mike? Do we understand each other?"

"Yes."

"Fine, fine. I've also decided to give these back to you as well."

Wagermann collected the marbles from his desk and dropped them back into my doubled-up marble sock.

"Yeah know Mike, I used to be quite the player myself once, many years back. There's something, I'd say, almost magical about marbles. Don't you think so Mike?"

"Yes sir, I sure do!"

Talk about preaching to the choir.

"I trust you'll do your best to keep them in your sock and keep your sock tied nice and tight to your belt, and, leave them in your desk when you go to the library in the future, agreed?"

"Agreed, yes sir."

Wagermann dropped the last of my marbles back into the sock. Each marble seemed to hold a precious memory of some special time from his childhood. Standing and leaning forward over his desk, he'd extended his arm and relayed back into my possession my full marble sock. He'd scribbled a quick hall pass and note and instructed me to go back to the library and give Mrs. Goodchaulks the note. She would then send me back to the office study room for the remainder of the library period. I tied my marble sock back in place on my belt, triple knotted, and walked for the office door. As my hand reached out for the office door doorknob Wagermann walked from behind his desk and sat on the desk corner nearest the door with his arms folded and his left foot dangling in the air above the floor.

"By the way Mike, I just thought of a couple of more quick questions before you go, just so I have the whole story, all right?"

"Okay, sure," I answered cautiously, thinking that everything had been settled, man to man and all. I pulled my hand away from the doorknob and turned to face Wagermann and his "couple of quick questions."

"Just what was it that was so important that you had to talk about it in the library?"

"My friend had to tell me something, something important that's happening on Saturday," I admitted guardedly.

"You don't want to talk about it?"

Wagermann sensed my reticence.

"Not if I don't have to. It was just kid stuff, yeah know; between me and him."

I started to feel shaky all over again. Just when I thought that everything had been worked out, Wagermann put me right back on the spot. To that point it had been a conversation "all around the edges" as it were. An awful lot of very little substance or actual consequence had been exchanged for such a long private conversation between a six-year-old boy and a forty-something school principal. The atmosphere in the office had suddenly become heavy with potential positive and negative possibilities and outcomes.

What hadn't been said hung in the air like a large fully fed nervous flock of fat pigeons that filled the branches of a tree right above a picnic table covered with a clean tablecloth that just waited for something to drop. I could see that he could see that the question bothered me. My swerving, dodging answer communicated, in no uncertain terms, that I had about as much on my plate as any little kid could handle at that moment. All I wanted to do was quickly fold up that spotless tablecloth and walk away from that tree full of anxious, over fed, ruminating pigeons.

"Fine, fine Mike, no problem. I'll trust your judgment on this matter as well, okay?" he answered reassuringly.

"Okay," I answered, relieved. I turned back toward the office door and made another reach to turn the doorknob.

"Just one more question, Mike, and then I'll let you go, I promise."

"All right," I answered as I pulled my hand back away from the doorknob a second time and turned back to face Wagermann one more time as the pigeons in the branches of that tree fidgeted, cooed and ruffled their chest feathers.

"What's your best shot?" he queried.

"My best shot? You mean my best marble shot?" I answered, surprised.

"Yeah, your 'bread and butter shot'. The one that gets you through, the one that always works?" he legitimately asked.

"The straight ground shot."

"Just the straight ground shot? You must have a really good eye."

"Yes sir, the straight ground shot is my best especially when my curve and hop-drop shots aren't working the way I want," I confidently stated.

"You've got a curve shot!" Wagermann earnestly gasped.

"Yes sir, but I can't always count on it. Can't seem to get it to work every time I try. I think it might have something to do with the weather when I'm playing," I thoughtfully responded.

"Yeah don't say. The weather? What - what in the world is a hop-drop shot?"

"I shoot my marble in the air just over a closer marble that I don't want to hit and then it drops back down to the ground and hits another marble further away," I explained, having used my right hand in a jumping motion over my left hand to illustrate.

"Is that true? Are you kidding me? You can actually make a marble do that? That's gotta be a tough shot to make?"

"Yes sir, the toughest! I use it all the time," I proudly confirmed.

"Yes, I can imagine. Well – okay Mike, I've kept you long enough, off you go," Wagermann casually waved his arm for me to go.

I turned back to the door and actually grabbed and turned the doorknob and opened the door uninterrupted. I walked out into the outer reception office with Wagermann following close behind. I momentarily stopped at the outer reception office doorway remembering that I'd be coming right back in just a few minutes. The pigeons in that tree above the clean picnic tablecloth had bolted as a flock and flew speedily away leaving behind only a few soft fluffy chest feathers that drifted on down through the air. They'd not rest until they found another perch from which to do their business, someplace else to express themselves, probably all over some unsuspecting but more deserving fourth or fifth grader later that day.

I felt pounds lighter, relieved at the prospect, the certainty, that I would not have to put up with Old Lady Bookbender and that prison compound that she called the school library. I looked forward to walking right back into the library to hand Mrs. Goodchaulks the note from Wagermann and then walk right back out again right in front of Bookbender. She'd think that I felt all miserable and guilty about my punishment when the joke was really on her. I couldn't be more pleased with the results of what at first seemed to be a hopeless, inescapable situation.

Walking alone through the hallway on my way back to the library I concluded, for the time being, that Principal Wagermann was a fair man and that the principal's office was electric-toaster-chair-free.

***

Chapter Seven:
False Start

THE RELIEF OF not having to spend the rest of the library period actually in the library that Friday afternoon was liberating. I'd had enough of Bookbender for the rest of my life. The half-hour I spent in the main office study room was a quiet and calming experience, a welcome interlude from the regular school routine. The study room windows looked out on a tree-shaded, park-like setting adjacent to the school. The very idea, the misguided concept, of having been 'sentenced' to the office study room as a punishment had never once entered my mind. If anything, my confinement was more of an unintentional reward. I used the time well, having cleared my thoughts and mentally prepared for the all-important activities of the following day.

During the school days prior to that Friday I'd started to notice glances and, on occasion, outright stares aimed in my direction from classmates and other members of the wider student body in general. Many kids I never personally met or known but recognized, kids I knew only as passing acquaintances and kids I never had any direct or indirect contact with at all were giving me the eyeball, the veritable once, twice and sometimes thrice over. Something unusual was going on and I didn't have a clue until that Friday afternoon when school was dismissed for the weekend.

As I put on my jacket in the hallway outside the classroom, kids walked right up or passed extra close by and patted me on the back or demonstrated other various supportive gestures and words of encouragement. Perplexed, but touched, I gathered my belongings and exited the school building into the schoolyard where the parting reception was equally effusive and positive.

Unbeknownst to me at the time, word had quickly spread that I'd be facing off with Avenging Grace's very own Billy Schoutenlauder in what was built-up to be the neighborhood marble match of the year. Although no one except the principals involved knew when and where the big showdown was supposed to transpire, everyone seemed to know that it was somewhere nearby and sometime close at hand. Wilbur Hunt sure loved to talk. Admittedly, the unexpected and unsolicited show of support was most welcome. It was just what I needed to help me get through the big day ahead because it had been one "helluva" (thank you brother Robert) week!

That Friday evening arrived and with it some of the best television programs the week had to offer. All of the best, the most interesting shows were on Friday night. *Science Fiction Theater, Dark Hall of Horror Cinema* and the *Late, Late, Late Show of Monster Madness* awaited the undivided attention of any and all science fiction, horror and monster movie enthusiasts. But that Friday night was different. I had much more important, more pressing matters on my mind. I chose to stay in my room to sort through my marbles, lounging in my reading chair and conserving my physical, mental and emotional energies for the next day's big event. The match with Billy was the full focus of my contemplative efforts. The appointment with the dentist had also been annoyingly bouncing around in the back of my mind, but it was more of a diversionary nuisance, something that had to be endured before the day's real business was transacted.

I emptied the marble boot box onto the bed as Kit Cat came running, having automatically answered the call. As I focused upon attaining the maximum comfort in my favorite chair, all spread out crosswise within its warm embrace, the family cat assumed his own familiar position stretched out on top of the expansive spread of marbles. We both settled in for some serious thinking (me) and just as serious napping (the cat).

My brother's justifiably held grudge reinforced all the questions I had regarding the trustworthiness of Avenging Grace students in general and Billy Schoutenlauder in particular. It all uneasily tumbled around in my head. Unable to get physically or mentally comfortable I glanced out the bedroom window into the blue of the eastern evening sky. I flashed on the idea that maybe a long walk through the cool evening air would clear my mind; a long walk to take the edge off the building nervous energy. I calculated that a long walk to and through a nearby alley, in fact, the alley of the next day's competition, would probably do the trick.

The agreed site was a mere five blocks away which, at most, was a ten-minute walk. The evening sun was still an hour or more from setting into night, as it remained light well past eight p.m. as late spring approached the mid-summer days of June. I hoisted myself from my easy chair, grabbed my jacket off the coat rack, left Kit Cat sound asleep on top of my marbles and walked down the stairs for the back door. Mom was seated at the kitchen table peeling apples. She gave me the quick motherly once-over with an upward glance. Before she could verbalize the look of concern invading her face I put her worries to rest.

"Just going out in the backyard for a while," I casually tossed out.

"What, no TV tonight?" Mom questioned as she'd looked back down at her apples.

"Not tonight. Outside is better for now," I answered.

"Okay. Just be back in before dark," she stated still watching the apple peeler do its work as she steadily cranked the handle.

"Yep," I nonchalantly called back over my shoulder.

Bumping open the back door, I hopped out into the thick green grass of the backyard and walked for the jungle gym that was set up under the large tree that held Robert's tree house. Climbing to the top of the metal bars I waved to Mom who watched me through the big windows by the kitchen table. I sat straddling the top bar until Mom got up and left her seat at the table and walked out of the kitchen. When she stayed away long enough to indicate that she'd taken up temporary residence in another part of the house, I slipped down off the bars, slid down the slide back onto the lawn and walked through the backyard gate that led into the alley behind our house.

It wasn't a long walk to 57th & Nash but as I neared the opening to the alley my body started to tense up, like my leg joints were made of rusted iron and needed a thorough oiling. I was only a half-block from the alley entrance when I slowed to a stop. An overpowering apprehension enveloped me. I wondered if it was wise, if it was good or bad luck to visit the site of the match, or if luck had anything to do with it at all. I berated myself for being so superstitious. Besides, the alley was extremely long as I remembered it and I had no idea exactly where within its confines the match would be likely to take place.

My logically rationalized self-explanation succeeded. I took a deep breath, relaxed and leisurely strolled the last half-block, safe in the feeling that I had nothing to fear but the terrifying unknowns that fear could unmask. Slowly, almost reverently, I breached the alley's opening from the south, the Nash Street end. My first impression was that the alley was much quieter than I remembered. Then again, the fields around Gettysburg were tranquil and bucolic the day before the battle commenced as well. The alley surface was a mixed consistency up and down its entire length. Old and new concrete, stretches of paved asphalt and small open patched areas of packed and compressed sand and gravel, a typical, older, urban neighborhood alley. The whole scene seemed so normal, so drastically different from the nightmare alley I'd unwillingly envisioned one night earlier that week.

Putting my hands into my jacket pockets, I softly started down the alley, plotting a rough course for the center-most point of the back roadway. The evening air was cool, refreshing but very still, not even the slightest breeze was perceptible. A barking dog and a nearby church bell chiming out eight p.m. were the only sounds that echoed through the otherwise quiet deserted alley.

As I ventured deeper into the alley I continually glanced form side to side trying to pick out the most likely spots a marble match could be played. The alley started to feel...comfortable. The initial reservations and thoughts of jinxing my chances of winning were quickly laid to rest.

I stopped to inspect the best looking spot I'd come across when the world exploded in a burst of harsh eardrum-splitting noise and flashing blinding lights. A car horn blared out its surprise warning and high beam headlights flashed in my face as I quickly turned and faced the menace. From a scant twenty feet away came the roar of a gunned car engine at full throttle. Almost leaving my clothes behind, I leapt to the east side of the alley and landed face and belly down in the grass and dirt between two garages.

A carload of high school lug heads who'd been hot rodding around, drinking beer and being a disturbance to the general public peace had silently coasted up behind me with the engine and the headlights off. I was so lost in thought that the sound of the rolling tires on the alley pavement never registered. They blasted right past me through the alley laughing, yelling and revving the souped-up car engine as the jacked-up *Chevy* peeled away towards Vienna Street at the north end of the alley. A barrage of empty beer cans flew from the open car windows propelled by the high distorted volume of the latest rock-'n'-roll hit from the car's radio.

I dared a peek up from my prone position lying between the garages just in time to see the rear end of the *Chevy* as it took a hard left turn out of the alley and disappeared in the smoke and squeal of burning rubber. I rolled over on my back with a groan, spread my arms wide on the ground and looked up into the tranquil early evening sky and just lay there, unmoving.

What kind of quiet evening walk would it have been without the added thrill, the brief amusing diversion of demented teenage youngsters, sneaking up on unsuspecting pedestrians and passing out, free of charge, cardiac arrests? How did they even know, how could they have even guessed, that throwing myself down onto the alley dirt and pavement to avoid being run over by a deliberate act of malicious fun had always been on my list of things to do? My young marble life had continued to provide, nonstop, free of charge and without any extra input or effort on my part, one mysterious and entertaining event after another.

I took one deep breath after another until the unnerving bad shock feeling faded from my body. Strength and controlled coordination returned to my muscles as I rolled back over onto my side and got myself up off the ground and back up onto my feet. Cautiously, I shuffled back towards the center of the alley pavement as I brushed myself off while keeping sharp lookout for the possible return of the loaded *Chevy*.

Having regained my composure and adopted a more alert and vigilant posture, I resumed my journey through the alley. I walked the entire length, from one end to the other and then back again until I reached what appeared to be the geographic center of the alley, all without further incident. I looked north to Vienna Street and then south towards Nash Street. I started to slowly rotate in a three-hundred-and-sixty-degree circle, all the while absorbing the feeling of the place as best I could.

I concluded, even with all the uncertainties and reservations I had regarding the trustworthiness of my future opponent, that the place felt good, felt right, like I could win there. It was, in fact, the perfect place for the perfect match. I stood motionless and silent for several minutes. I concentrated on the blossoming sunset that beamed in from the west as the warm yellows, oranges and reds flowed between the houses and garages and filled the alley with comforting soft light and equally gentle warmth.

I heard a noise from behind me, footsteps coming towards me. I turned and faced, ten feet away, an older, thin, gray haired man, one of the local residents, as he walked to the alley to bring out his garbage. He stopped, stood tall and upright with the slightest backward lean. With his chin up and his head ever so slightly tilted to the right he tightly held the garbage bag at his right side. His left hand grasped the garbage can cover by its bent metal handle, as he carefully looked me over.

"You okay there young feller?" he cautiously questioned with a look on his face as if he'd been trying to decide if I was up to no good, some mischief, or not.

"Yeah mister, I'm okay," I respectfully reassured him. "Just out walking – on my way home."

He looked both ways down the alley as he yanked up the garbage can cover and dropped his garbage into the can. Then, shoving the metal lid back down hard and tight onto the garbage can, he kindly admonished my presence.

"You'd best be careful walking here. Those damned hotrod kids go racing through here whenever they damn well feel like it, day and night, throwing junk anywhere and everywhere they damn well please. So – you watch yourself."

"Yeah, I know," I responded with a breathy sigh as I looked back and forth towards both ends of the alley while brushing some more dirt and grass off the front of my clothes.

"All right then, you get on home," he advised as he turned

from the alley and slowly walked back towards the back door of his house.

I started back home, walking right down the center of the alley south towards Nash Street where I'd first entered, with eyes and ears wide-open and my head on a swivel, looking to the front and watching to the back, just in case.

Refreshed and ready, mission accomplished and fully recovered from my near death-by-clown-car experience, I left the alley and walked the few blocks back home bathed in the soft magic hour twilight. I re-entered home ground the same way I'd exited sometime before. I climbed back up and resumed my former position atop the jungle gym's top monkey bar just before Mom reappeared and took her place back at the kitchen table by the kitchen window. I waved. She waved back Situation normal. I felt certain, I was hopeful, I crossed my fingers that Mom had been watching television in the living room with Dad and Robert and hadn't noticed my absence and remained oblivious to the fact that I was several blocks away scouting locations and dodging cars for the past several minutes.

Despite the successful jaunt to the big match alley and the mostly good feelings I had while there, restful sleep remained elusive that night. I laid awake, tossing turning, sitting up and lying back down well into the early hours of the morning. My room was warm so I'd had both the bedroom window and the bedroom door open wide to allow for a cooling cross breeze. Giving up on sleep, I decided to pass the hours, for the third time that night, by fumbling and sorting through the old boot box that housed my marble collection.

The feelings of power, confidence and comfort generated as I rolled those little glass crystals around in my hands was...profound. It didn't help me get back to sleep but it magically removed any lingering fatigue as I settled into a relaxed but sleepless peace. Considering the time of night and the open bedroom door I did not turn on any lights. I tiptoed to my dresser and retrieved my all-weather, all-season *Mountain Trail Master* three-D-cell battery powered flashlight that I saved for just such emergency situations. Before returning to bed, I gave myself a quick cheap thrill by looking into my dresser top mirror and snapping on the flashlight as I held it shining up from under my chin. I had the rosy-cheeked appearance of a well-fed vampire or a much too healthy looking resurrected corpse.

Satisfied that I looked menacing enough to scare away a mean dog, I hopped back into bed. From a cross-legged sitting position, I pulled my bed sheet completely over my head and upright body. I then reached out from under the sheet and half-lifted and half-dragged, with grunting effort, the full marble box from the foot of the bed, over the bedspread, into my secluded chamber and then up onto my lap.

With flashlight and marbles well in hand I was fully engaged in my nocturnal interlude. It was my guess that several minutes, or hours, passed when, from out of the darkness which surrounded my internally glowing bed sheet tent, someone or something tapped me on the top of my sheet-covered head. I went rigid stiff as a chirpy sort of gasping squeak involuntarily escaped from somewhere in my body and out through my mouth. Visions of the mysterious hooded nightmare figure returning for the final kill were my immediate first, last and only thoughts. I waited, frozen in place, for bony, clasping claw-like hands to press my bed sheet in and around my head and throat for the final death grip. Fortunately, just before everything went blank and black forever, a soft gentle voice whispered from outside the sheet.

"Mike honey, it's Mom."

I relaxed with an audible sigh. I pulled the bed sheet from over my head and shined the flashlight towards the soothing voice. There was Mom all right, just as I hoped, no monster diabolically disguising its presence by mimicking a familiar friendly voice. I checked her out head-to-toe with the beam of light which caused her to wince in mild discomfort as the intensity of the light flashed across her sleepy eyes. Putting her right hand up in front of her face to shield her eyes, she lowered herself to a sitting position on the edge of the bed. With her left hand she reached out and across to redirect the flashlight beam. Supporting herself with her left hand on my bed, she leaned above and across my legs and asked why I was up so late, hiding under the covers and digging through my marbles.

"Just too warm to sleep," I sighed.

I'd asked her why she was up so late and she gave me the same answer. To that point it was a typical middle-of-the-night conversation. As she brushed the mussed-up hair that had fallen across my eyes and forehead with her right hand, Mom redirected the flashlight beam that had been lighting the ceiling above the bed towards my face.

"Where'd you disappear to from the backyard?" she asked directly but without demand.

"Just felt like taking a short walk, no big deal," I calmly, casually answered in my most reassuring tone, all the while hoping that she wouldn't ask how I'd done on the big spelling test that had never taken place.

"By the way, how'd you do on that spelling test you were so worried about? Did you make your mother proud?"

"I passed," I lied.

"That's great. Thatta boy. I knew you'd do just fine," she proudly complimented.

The guilt, like bubbling boiling mud, rose up to engulf and cook me. I wondered how many more times I'd have to lie before this was all over and how long it would take for those same lies to catch up with me and ruin my life forever, just like Pastor Crossmann preached they always would. My marbles meant everything to me but the trade-offs were becoming clearer and had started to stack up.

"Are you worried about the dentist tomorrow?"

"Yeah, just a little," I quickly answered, glad to be able to at least give one half-truth for a response but still provide a suitable diversion from the real reasons for my insomnia (and, by the way, thanks for reminding me).

"Now, Mike, you know that if there was anything else bothering you, anything at all, other than the dentist, you know you could talk to me or your Dad about it, right?" She lowered her chin and refocused her gaze on my eyes. "There isn't anything else, anything at all, that you'd like to talk about, that you want to tell me?"

"No Mom, nothin'. Just worried about the dentist like you said. Not my favorite place," I admitted.

"Yeah honey, I know, me neither," she confessed with a worrisome sigh.

Another lie. I didn't care one-way or the other about the dentist. I could see Saint Peter crossing my name of the list of eligible entrants through the Pearly Gates of Heaven. The fanged maw of Hell licked its lips, wagged its tongue and opened wide to swallow me whole. One small gulp, I was just a little snack really, and then, I'd be gone. I thought that I'd better win the damn marble match with Billy Schoutenlauder as a consolation for all of the possible eternal strife I was leaving myself wide-open for. But yet, deep down, I consoled myself with the thought that, "what the hell, I have the whole rest of my life to dutifully reconsider my actions and to spiritually grovel and repent."

Mom affectionately brushed my forehead with the back of her hand one more time as she stood up. She suggested that I not stay up much later as we both had to be at the dentist's office no later than nine a.m. later that morning. We exchanged good nights as Mom left my room for her own bed.

My guilty conscience buzzed around my head like a pesky bug that kept nipping and biting me on the back of my neck. Mom was the one who'd gotten me started, put up with me dropping my marbles everywhere they could have been dropped and cheered me on when I needed encouragement or a kind word. But I figured that if she knew the potential risks involved in the showdown with Billy, she might try to stop the match.

I resolved that no one would stand in the way, prevent me from keeping my appointment with what I thought to be my Destiny. As hard as it was, if destined to sink into the mire of unforgivable sin, I'd go down as the champ or at least as the first runner-up who tried his very best. "Sorry Mom," I thought to myself. If I felt I could have trusted her to trust my judgment and not interfere, I would've confided in her in a second. I wasn't sure. There was too much at stake. The burden was all mine and I willingly took it on and proudly carried it.

That Saturday morning, tired and hungry, I took a cool shower to wake up, downed a light breakfast and then spent a full fifteen minutes brushing, flossing and gargling my teeth to a glossy shine. I stopped back in my bedroom, quickly reached into my marble box and grabbed a big handful of my best right off the top, the size and type did not matter. It was their reassuring presence in my pants pocket as they pressed against my leg that was important. I ran down the stairs and then out to the car where Mom was waiting, ready for the short trip to the dentist's office.

I felt a little off center, not because of the lack of sleep, but because of the lack of my normal ritualistic three hours of Saturday morning cartoon entertainment. But, as it was going to be an all around different type of Saturday, a special Saturday where convention would be willingly set aside, I intellectually and emotionally accommodated the change in routine.

Mom put the car in gear and we rolled out of our short driveway into the alley and then drove out to the street. I was surprised to find myself so calm and in control considering where I was going to spend the next hour or two. The drive was uneventful until Mom, her mind out among the planets, drove halfway through a four-way stop intersection before she'd realized her mistake and slammed on the brakes. She stopped the car just in time for the front wheels to come to a perfect rest on the big white stop line that was painted on the road at the other side of the intersection.

We momentarily sat there, in the middle of the intersection, completely blocking all following as well as all left and right cross traffic. Mom was surprised and embarrassed. Her error and subsequent squealing stop caught me by surprise as well as I lightly kissed the all-metal dashboard with my soon-to-be-dentist-inspected mouth. Just by chance my left hand made it to the dashboard first, cushioning the blow and thus averting a potentially massive dental bill. For the rest of the drive, much to my mother's aggravation, I dutifully pointed out loudly, and with obvious and expressive hand gestures, all of the remaining stop sign and red light intersections that inconveniently intervened between us and our 'dental destiination'. Mom hadn't always taken to driving very well anyway and that morning her behind-the-wheel performance would have you think that it was she who was going to spend an hour in the dentist's chair. I suspected a severe case of dental hygiene guilty conscience. Mom didn't always brush twice a day.

We were lucky enough to find a parking space on the street along the curb directly in front of our intended destination. Unfortunately, Mom had to parallel park the car. That proved to be almost as dangerous and perplexing as the four-way stop intersection which had so inconsiderately snuck-up on her earlier during the drive. With all of the trying, trying again and trying one more time you'd think she was parallel parking a forty-foot tractor-trailer rig along a curved curb in an undersized cul-de-sac.

Finally, mercifully, we ended up sort of parked. Walking from the car I told Mom not to worry about the fact that we were leaving the car parked almost two feet from the curb with the left rear end sticking out into on coming traffic, just daring other passing cars to take a shot. The visit to the dentist's office could not be any more dangerous or adventurous than the drive to get there. We had, after all, made it to our destination alive and undamaged which is the exact physical and psychological condition I expected to be in upon leaving the dentist's office. I had every reasonable expectation that the ride back home, despite possible further minor incidents, would be just as survivable. The serious engagement I had scheduled for later that day required that I be as physically and emotionally fit to perform at the highest level as any six-year-old kid could possibly reach and reasonably maintain.

The vaguely familiar, almost forgotten, smell of the dentist's office hit both Mom and me in the face like surprise buckets of cold water. The peculiar odor, different but just as unique as the doctor's office smell, reminded us both (maybe Mom a little more than me) of all the potentially painful experiences one may be required to endure while obligated to be within its confines. Often the actual minimal pain realized was nothing compared to the nerve-racking uncertainty suffered while waiting and anticipating any potential discomfort. We had a few minutes to spare before zero hour, so Mom and I checked in with the receptionist and made ourselves as comfortable as possible, considering the location and circumstances, by taking a pair of seats in the farthest corner away from the door that led into the actual procedure rooms of the office. A quick surveillance of the surroundings fortunately revealed that we shared the waiting room with strangers, that is, no one from school.

I didn't want anyone I knew to be witness to my screams of terror and/or pain in the event that my visit took a turn for the dark side and became some sort of bloody nightmarish medical affair (a potential image deflator), nor did I want any kids coming up to me and wishing me luck in that afternoon's match. The last thing I needed was someone unintentionally spilling the beans and blowing my cover. It would have put my mother onto my lies and the reason for all of my recent bad dreams and sleepless nights.

With fifteen minutes before my turn in the chair I paged through the latest edition of *Trail Life* magazine. I was reviewing a short article on the recommended personal character requirements of the *Forest Ranger* when the receptionist called my name. I'd just reached "Courage" on the list as I set down the magazine and slid off the chair to my feet. My legs wobbled just a bit as they searched for and then found the strength to hold me upright and walk. The word "Courage" had taken on an all-too-real and immediate significance. I prepared to enter the perfectly legal chamber of horrors and tortures of the dentist's operatory.

My usually creative imagination was no help whatsoever as it ran full speed off the rails. Calling upon my imaginative skills in figuring out the angles and geometry of a tough shot during a match was constructive and inspired. But in the dentist's office it generously contributed to all of my worst fears and inclinations. I couldn't get it to calm down, to back off and to just shut up! It started in nightmare alley, continued into Wagermann's office and followed right behind into the dentist's office. The fear was unsubstantiated, had no basis in fact, because the last time I'd been to the dentist I'd been so much younger that all I remembered was the medicine smell. I walked up to the reception window with short halting steps, all by myself. Suspiciously, my mother remained seated and from a distance, with eyes as big as coffee cup saucers, asked if I wanted any company during the teeth cleaning and examination. That's when I saw it on her face, in those big frightened eyes: IN-HER-SOUL! There it was, the source, the wellspring of all my irrational dentist fears: IT-WAS-MY-MOTHER!

She timidly asked instead of boldly volunteering. She hung back instead of simply getting up out of her seat and boldly walking in with me, automatically insisting that without question, "of course she'd come in with me." Her body language was shouting, screaming the obvious. Mom's fear of the dentist chair was magnitudes above and beyond anything I experienced before, then or later. Transference, good ol' Freudian "passing-it-on and passing-it-a-round" is what it was. It was her blatant, unabashed, in-full-view and shamefully undisguised completely unconscious attempt to pass all of her dental fears onto me: IT-WAS-WORKING!

She had every reason to worry. Mom's mouth looked like a silver mine with dimpled cheeks and pretty red lips wrapped around it. She had an extensive record of one mouth care violation after another. She had a file in the patient records filing cabinet that was an inch thick! If a dental office was a dental hygiene court she would have gotten ninety-days for bad brushing and bad flossing habits behavior! My dental file consisted of one-half of one piece of paper with little gold star stickers all over it. My mouth was fine with a spotless record. I couldn't even figure out what the heck I was doing there?

There was nothing but short neat little rows of perfectly formed tiny pearly whites in my mouth. No silver miner's future fortune hiding out next to my gums, no fertile ground for future fortunes in dental mining and certainly no necessity for confidence building or self-esteem salvaging orthodontics anywhere in my oral future. It became painfully evident that I'd just have to bite the bullet, gently of course, and give my petrified Mom a break. Believe it or not, at that moment, despite all of the implanted fear and anxiety, I was emotionally the stronger one. I decided that there was no need for both of us to suffer as I bravely informed her that I'd be fine, I'd go it alone. Mom wasn't just relieved, it was obviously more than that – she'd been spared.

"That's my brave boy," she shakily encouraged.

Besides, I wanted my mother to be sharp, alert and fully sound mentally and physically for the all-important drive home. I wanted those big scared eyes of hers to shrink back down to normal size. There weren't sunglasses manufactured big enough or dark enough to have covered and protected her fright-blown peepers from the late morning sunlight.

The receptionist met me at the doorway that led to the exam and lab area and then escorted me to one of the vacant operatories. As I walked in I was struck by all of the mechanical insect appendage-like hardware attached to and suspended above and around the chair I'd be sitting in. It reminded me of all the mechanical hydraulic hardware, but in miniature, of *Big Jack's Service Station* where we had the family car locally serviced and repaired. I was left in the care of the office dental hygienist, Miss Ann, whose job it was that morning to give my teeth and gums a preliminary exam, a set of basic x-rays and a thorough cleaning. She quietly and calmly explained all of this as she assisted me into the super maneuverable barber-like chair and then put a large plastic-covered cloth bib around my neck. The bib-thing raised my suspicions immediately. I felt my little body's blood pressure crank up like I just stepped down hard on an accelerator connected to my heart and kidneys. I figured the plastic meant that things were indeed going to get messy!

I swallowed hard and with difficulty as the medicine smell became more intense in the small exam room than it was in the larger, more open waiting room. It didn't help that once situated, I had a more thorough sense of all the strange sounds and a much closer look at all the silvery, spindly, sharp and menacing looking machine gadgets that filled the room and surrounded me in the chair.

Unconsciously, in response to my stressful situation, I reached into my rights pants pocket and pulled out three of the seven marbles that had accompanied me that morning. They were friends who would stand by me, be right there with me through whatever horrific horrors would come my way. They hadn't hung back, they were right there on the front lines with me, holding my hand as I held them in mine. Gripping them tight, I unconsciously rolled them together every so often, tumbling them one over the other, as a nervous but nonetheless welcome release of the continually accumulating tension.

A more thorough and concentrated look around the room revealed large wooden cabinets with many narrow wooden drawers, just like the many big rolling tool cabinets at *Big Jack's*. *Big Jack's* tool chests just brimmed with pliers, wrenches, soldering irons, torches, punches, hacksaws and claw hammers, punch hammers, screwdrivers, chisels; any and all things used to push and pull, bend and break, etc., any of which if not properly handled could be the cause of temporary or permanent severe pain and injury. I must have associated the cabinets in the operatory with *Big Jack's* tool chests as a way to give context to the room and me being in that room. I suspected, I feared, that the cabinet drawers all around me housed a selection of devices not so dissimilar from what I'd seen in one of *Big Jack's* car service bays, but on a miniaturized 'fit inside your mouth' scale.

Lying back in the chair, surrounded by the leering shiny machines with their bug-like protrusions and attachments, my fear and imagination teamed up. I was transported, I was dragged against my will was more like it, away from the admittedly comfortable confines of the operatory chair to being strapped, belly down, onto the I-beam rail of a hydraulic automobile service lift in the repair stall of a service station.

In place of the fine detailed assembly of the praying mantis-like dentist's drill was a large, dirty, vicious looking grease gun. The grease gun hung next to my head, which hung over the end of the lift rail, face down. The soft-spoken hygienist, dressed in clean snow-white medical dress, was replaced by the same girl outfitted in a full-length blue-gray coverall coated with grease and oil stains. Her face was no longer the kind, confident yet delicate picture of reassurance as it also became equal to the new setting and tasks at hand with several dirty smudges of oil and grease of its own. Replacing the low sugar gum that she'd been gently chewing as the hygienist was a plastic tipped miniature cigar which she vigorously sucked on. Her soft brown hair was rolled-up and stuffed into a *Milwaukee Braves* baseball cap that sat askew on her head. She stood by the controls of the lift and worked the levers adjusting the rail height to a working position. The soothing background string music of the dentist's office was replaced, overpowered, by loud and jarring *Polish Polkas* that boomed and blared from a small AM radio that rested on a metal shelf situated just above the used tire rack against the back wall of the garage.

The mechanic in charge, *Annie*, of *Able Annie's Service Garage*, walked up to me while wiping her hands on an oily rag, furiously puffing on her little cigar, and asked me what the problem was. My head rested suspended above hers by a few inches as she looked up at me and I looked down at her as we spoke. Strapped tight to the lift rail with my head bobbing over the end, my face pointed down towards the floor, I answered shakily that there was no specific problem and that I was there for just a quick check and clean.

"Okay, a quick check and a good clean, eh? Want that I should gives ya a quick lube job and oil change too while you're here and while I'm at it and all if ya know what I mean, eh?" *Able Annie* cackled out of the right side of her mouth while the left side of her mouth bit down on the plastic cigar tip.

"Ahhh, no, no – just a clean and check is all I wanted today, thanks," I meekly responded.

"Got just what the Doc ordered, Sonny," was *Able Annie's* brisk and confident answer.

She walked back to her workbench at the back wall by the used tire rack. While digging through her tools she hummed and danced in place to the polka music that blasted from the radio speaker that sympathetically vibrated the metal shelf where the radio rested. She returned, much to my dismay, with a two-handled, two-handed high-speed high-torque drill that had a huge circular wire brush firmly seated in the drill's rotating chuck.

After plugging the drill into a nearby hanging electrical extension cord, she hit the drill switch.

The whine and the hum of the rapidly spinning wire brush was too much. *Able Annie* sauntered towards me, smiling, as the cigar in her mouth flicked up and down like a telegraph key. As she'd closed in with the whirling wire brush, my right hand, strapped tight along side of my prostrate suspended body, rolled the three marbles in its palm so fast that the friction and resulting heat would have soon burned my hand and worn the marbles into dust between my fingers.

"Open wide," were *Able Annie's* last words and Miss Ann's first words.

I came out of the garage and back into the exam chair gripping the marbles so hard that I was surprised that they didn't crack from the pressure. Gruff *Able Annie* was gone and only soft-spoken Miss Ann remained. As *Able Annie's Garage* faded from view there was Miss Ann, up close, looking me straight in the eye. She asked, with a concerned look that beamed right through her nose-and-mouth mask-covered face, if I was all right. My eyes must have resembled two big shiny, multicolored protruding doorknobs. With my mouth clamped shut from the fear of having my teeth wire brushed down to the gums, I mumbled through my clenched teeth that things were just fine, could not have been better.

I started to respond to Miss Ann's kind manor and relaxed my cramped, clamped-shut jaw, yielding just enough to allow my mouth to crack open ever so slightly. The death grip that I maintained on my three marbles left what seemed to be permanent marble shaped and sized indentations in the palm of my right hand; little eye sockets for little Cat's-Eyes.

My left hand hadn't fared much better. It had become numb and frozen in a claw-like, cramped and contorted fierce grip on the left arm of the exam chair. Detecting that I wasn't just a bit on edge but rather that I'd actually arrived and stood with my toes at the very edge, Miss Ann reminded me that I had nothing to worry about and to try to relax at least as hard as I was trying to be frightened. Her logic and the soothing words she used to explain that logic eased my stiff jaw muscles to the point where I was able to answer in understandable English that I was, in fact, a slight bit on the nervous side as the marbles in my right hand scratched and scraped against one another inside of my closed fist.

I felt guilty, bordering on remorseful, for having imagined Miss Ann as the rough-and-tough *Able Annie* who was prepared to reduce my teeth down to a collection of worn-down white stubs. As Miss Ann momentarily turned away to gather and prepare her instruments for the cleaning and exam, I began to loosen up and settle down into the admittedly unusually comfortable chair. Just as the last tense muscle in my body relinquished its grip, the sweet hygienist turned back towards me with a tray loaded to bear with the most gruesome looking little tools and devices that I'd ever seen or could have ever imagined. I wasn't sure if they were going to be used inside of my mouth or under the chair on the hydraulic system. Not even in my worst or wildest imagination could I have dreamed up all the jabbers, sharp stickers, pointy pokers and multi-angle scrapers that she'd gathered and assembled on that tray. What the hell? Miss Ann was more prepared to sculpt a piece of marble than work on my teeth. Suddenly, unbelievably, the wire brush didn't seem so bad.

Miss Ann set her tray of torture tools down on a small platform attached to the right side of the operatory chair. She asked me to "open wide" as panic could not have described the flow of current that pulsed through my body. I was trapped. I was helpless. If I'd called out to Mom in the waiting room she would probably have bolted out of the office, down the stairs, across the street and into the woods of the nearby city park and hid behind a tree. Going it alone took on its all-to-real meaning.

To my complete surprise the initial examine was relatively painless as Miss Ann ran her latex gloved finger around my gums and teeth, stuck a little round mirror in my mouth and looked around. The little suction nozzle she stuck in my mouth tickled as she vacuumed out the drool and dribble being caused by her hand walking around inside of my mouth. The x-ray film holders poking at the inside of my mouth and digging into my gums were about as unpleasant as the whole exam got. At the time I wasn't certain what x-rays were exactly but when that chrome metal cone was against the outside of my cheek and the x-ray whirligig started to "whhiiirrrr" I was certain that I'd sensed, even felt, the invisible rays penetrating and shooting through my head (sort of like that night in August several months before).

  As the hygienist approached my mouth I slunk and slid down into the chair and simultaneously opened my mouth barely enough for air to whistle in and out past my pursed lips. As her hands came closer I slipped further down into the chair. Miss Ann deftly countered by tapping a lever on the bottom of the chair near the floor with her foot which raised the chair, thus neutralizing any thoughts I had about a mutually accepted draw, calling it even and being done for the day. I wasn't the first patient-turned-momentarily-unsuccessful-escape-artist that Miss Ann had faced. There was no place left to slide down to. I looked at her through squinted eyes with my lips going blue from pressing them shut so hard. Miss Ann just stopped, stared down at me with eyes that said, "well, what's it going to be?" I relented. It would be me sitting there with my eyes clamped shut and my mouth wide-open, that's what it was going to be.

  With the pictures completed, Miss Ann had got down to the literal nitty-gritty of actually cleaning my teeth. The more she probed, scraped and poked, the faster and harder I pressed the three marbles together in my right hand. The gnashing of the marbles against one another wasn't noticeable to me at all. It was my body's way of releasing and diminishing all of the internal static electricity being generated by the metal instruments as they raked over and across my teeth. The unrelenting gritting and grinding of my marbles however, in the mind of Miss Ann, was right up there with other intolerable nuisances like fingernails on a chalkboard or biting into a big thick dry fluffy bath towel while gnashing your teeth back and forth until they squeaked (the tooth squeak would vibrate right up through your brain).

  She would temporarily stop with a shiver, then a mild shudder, and take a quick look around, unable to place the source of the irritating, the brain penetrating, sound. Twice she stopped and rolled back on her wheeled exam stool and searched around the base of the chair checking the equipment and mechanical connections in an attempt to locate and silence the nerve-grating noise. Of course, every time she stopped to look around I unconsciously stopped rolling the marbles around in my right hand and started to look around myself, wondering what it was that she was trying to find. Unable to locate the problem, which mysteriously disappeared as soon as she stopped working in my mouth, Miss Ann continued despite her obvious and growing irritation with the aggravating noise. The frustration on her face had been evident right through her face-concealing hygiene mask.

Thanks to Miss Ann's obvious abilities I actually started to enjoy certain aspects of the procedure. Having water squirted into my mouth with the little metal nozzle hose and then spitting into the little porcelain sink with the water swirling around in it located on the left side of the chair was pretty entertaining. The combination of the little nozzle water hose, the little metal suction nozzle, the little pressurized air nozzle and the tiny sink would be the perfect marble washing setup. I made it a point to ask Mom and Dad for just such a setup for my birthday.

Having finished the jabbing and scraping part of the cleaning Miss Ann moved onto the flossing and polishing part of cleaning my teeth. The small polishing machine was not something to be overlooked either when it came to birthday requests. The potential for polishing and buffing out minor scratches and nicks in several of my best marbles was promising. Miss Ann shot water into and around the inside of my mouth one last time and then asked me to turn and spit. Satisfied that I'd done my part, she excused herself for few minutes to assist Doctor Whitebiter with another patient. The plan was for both of them to return in a few minutes to give my choppers the final once over and then, believe it or not, I'd be on my way.

I was sitting alone and unattended for close to ten minutes when it had occurred to me to give my marble washing idea a try. Everything needed was just sitting there, right next to me within easy reach, unused and ready to go. I transferred my three right hand marbles into my left hand and then reached down into my right pants pocket with my free right hand and pulled out the other four. Unfortunately the little water hose was hung up in its holder just out of reach so I settled for using the swirling stream of water in the little sink to do the job.

Working from the cramped quarters of my reclining position I managed to get all seven marbles up onto the grooved rim of the sink. I reached across my body with my right hand and, one marble at a time, started to get the routine of dipping the marble into the swirling water, washing it and putting it back up on the sink rim to dry. My experiment was proceeding successfully when Miss Ann, along with Doctor Whitebiter, returned to complete my exam.

Caught unprepared for their sudden return, I lurched back to my reclining position bumping the tiny sink as I did so. Four of the marbles which were still air drying and resting on the rim, in unison, together, like four little friends holding hands, jumped back into the ol' swimming hole. The three that had been washed and dried didn't make it back into my pants pocket so they remained concealed, hiding out, back within the warm moist confines of my right hand.

I resumed my innocent little patient posture in the chair just as they re-entered the room. The four little Cat's-Eyes that had jumped back into the sink had barely stopped rolling around as they came to a rest four abreast around the drain strainer as Miss Ann and D.D.S. Whitebiter walked up to the right side of the chair. Doc Whitebiter was all perfect smile as he asked how things were going.

"Just fine," I enthusiastically responded, hoping that he would not notice my four friends lying low in the sink.

As he sat down on the rolling exam stool he asked me to open my mouth. Immediately, obediently, I complied, snapping my mouth wide-open like a hungry baby bird. It was my hope that my enthusiasm, my dental exam excitement, would be enough to serve as a sufficient distraction. But it was not to be, as the situation did not go my way. The dentist took the water shooter and hosed down all of my upper teeth and then asked me to spit. I'd leaned over the sink with my mouth full of water realizing that I was about to spit all over four of my very own. I hesitated, trying to think of a way, anyway, to spare the four little marbles the dishonor, the disgrace, of being gobbed on by the very one charged with their care and protection. It would've been just my luck that one, two, three or all of four of them had spent time in the kitchen sink drain and were then on the verge of being humiliated for a second time.

Leaning over the sink, with eyes closed I swallowed my mouth full of gritty water, thus sparing myself, I hoped, any future retributions the marbles might see their way clear to inflict on me as payback when I least expected it. I was certain they would recognize and understand what I'd done for them as I turned back to the waiting dentist. I settled back into the chair when the doctor leaned in with some sort of mechanical gadget which he was directing straight for my mouth. It looked like a larger, more complicated, more sinister version of the rotating tooth polisher that Miss Ann had used just minutes before.

Whitebiter hit the trigger and applied the spinning rubber to my teeth as I simultaneously hit the trigger on the three hidden marbles that rolled and grated within the grasp of my right hand. Doc Whitebiter stopped, looked around and put the power drill up to his ear and hit the trigger two or three times in rapid succession as he tried to detect the source of the unusual noise which, of course, vanished as soon as he moved the drill polisher away from my mouth. He asked Miss Ann if she'd heard 'that' and she replied that she'd been hearing 'that' off and on for the past thirty minutes.

Checking the connections to the motorized polisher, moving the operatory chair up and down and around, Doctor Whitebiter tested all of the powered mechanical instruments in the room trying to locate and identify the offending piece of equipment. Unable to find the problem, Whitebiter turned his full attention back to me and requested that I once again lay back and open wide. He put fresh polishing compound on the rubber-polishing cup and went back to work on my incisors just as I simultaneously went back to work on the marbles in my right hand.

The Doc went over several more of my teeth, sprayed them down real good and instructed me to spit. I was in a real jam. Swallowing a mouthful of water with a little grit in it was no big deal. But swallowing a mouthful of water which consisted of fifty-percent polishing compound, yuck! It would be like swallowing mud and I probably would've gagged and barfed. I placed my full-face over the sink to block discovery of its undetected contents and spit away, hoping that the four undeserving recipients would try to understand and appreciate my predicament and be forgiving of the unintended insult. Having been forced by circumstances to spit gritty glob all over four of my best, I endured several more minutes of the humming, buzzing and bouncing polisher in my mouth and sought release of my persistent anxiety through the only available outlet. The three marbles were grating quicker, harder and louder than ever, like a miniature concrete saw cutting through tiny bricks.

Doc Whitebiter's irritation grew in direct proportion to the speed and volume of my grinding marbles. He rinsed my mouth again as I unloaded with another mouthful all over the four marbles. The dentist put the polishing tool back on its resting hanger and walked around to the rear of the operatory chair bent upon finding the source of the trouble. At first I thought he was going to leave the room but he unexpectedly reappeared on the left side of the chair where the tiny little sink bubbled away. I had the urge to simply reach up into the sink bowl and grab my displaced marbles with a swift rescuing retrieval but he was just too close. It was too risky. I decided to sweat it out and hoped for the best.

According to the laws of *Newtonian Physics* for every action there is an opposite but equal reaction. However, my case proved to be an exception to that universal rule of matter. The three marbles clutched within my right hand exceeded all physical limits as they started twirling and grinding like ungreased bearings in the axle of a speeding racecar. As Doc Whitebiter's searching eyes came closer and closer to the sink, my right hand went mad. Miss Ann bent down along the right side of the chair to assist the dentist in his search. She winced with every grinding marbles gyration.

Like a burglar hiding in a closet as a searching flashlight beam finds it mark, the doctor's searching eyes passed directly over the sink. At first I thought that he'd looked right at them and the strange unexpected sight didn't register in his brain. Then the lights started flashing and the brakes went on as he did a double take and moved his face back over the sink and returned the gaze of amazement that greeted him from the four marbles in the bottom of the sink.

At that second I knew exactly what those marbles were doing. They were wet, their feelings were hurt and they were casting their little Cat's-Eyes gazes right at me, silently whispering my name. The other three, Miss Ann was about to discover, were on the verge of exploding into dust from the friction and pressure. Miss Ann, from her bent over searching posture, her head at eye level with my right hand, looked straight ahead and refocused. There, right in front of her face, was my stressed and cramping right hand working overtime on the three hot, and getting hotter by the second, marbles.

With my full attention on Doctor Whitebiter, Miss Ann stood up. She reached down with her left hand along the inside of the right chair arm, gently grasped my right forearm and firmly raised my right hand into the air while her right hand found a resting spot on her right hip. Just as the hygienist raised my right arm into the air, Doc Whitebiter looked up and over towards my fumbling right hand and the three grinding marbles within its grasp. I was so preoccupied with the Doctor's discovery in the sink that I was completely oblivious to the fact that my right hand and forearm were being held up in the air by Miss Ann. Looking back down into the sink, Doc Whitebiter reached for a pair of long forceps. He slowly retrieved one of the four wayward marbles and held it up to the light for all of us to see.

At that point my attention shifted from my left to my right to find Miss Ann holding my arm up in place, in the air, while my right hand continued to work away on the three marbles as if it had a will and purpose all its very own, separate from the rest of my body. I looked up at Miss Ann who was looking across to Doc Whitebiter who I discovered, when I looked back to my left, was looking directly at me.

There we all were, the Doctor holding a marble in a pair of forceps as if he'd just extracted it from my mouth, the hygienist holding my right arm and hand in the air which held three badly scratched, scuffed and sweaty marbles, all of which belonged to me, the kid in the middle. Slowly, my right hand stopped grinding like a speeding racecar decelerating and coasting to a stalled stop at the side of the track.

D.D.S. Whitebiter politely asked if the marbles he'd just discovered were mine. It was a rhetorical question because the only other patient in the chair that morning had been a seventy year old grandmother whose marble-playing days had been traded in for canasta, bingo and bridge nights at church some years before. I swallowed, with some difficulty.

"Yeah," I sneaked a whisper out from between my very clean teeth.

Miss Ann asked if I'd been holding the other three marbles discovered in my hand during the exam and the cleaning.

"I guess so," was all I could honestly answer because I really hadn't been consciously aware of or responsible for whatever my right hand had been doing after the daydream about *Able Annie's Garage*.

Miss Ann carefully removed the three worn marbles from my clinched, cramped and aching right fist. Doctor Whitebiter extracted the remaining three marbles from the sink, washing all three in a fresh stream of water before placing them onto the clean instrument tray. He assured me that the marbles would be returned to me as soon as the examination was completed. They both smiled and chuckled a bit, which afforded me the chance to relax and crack sort of a half-smile of my own. The remainder of the exam passed quickly and painlessly enough except for my right hand which readily demonstrated it had a marble memory all its own as it would, intermittently, completely on its own, start working away as if it still had the three marbles within its grasp.

Before I rejoined my Mom in the waiting room, Miss Ann presented me with a new toothbrush, a sample tube of toothpaste and a package of brand new low-sugar gum. Doctor Whitebiter handed me a sample dispenser of mint-flavored dental floss and a small clear plastic bag that contained my seven Cat's-Eyes, washed and dried. I immediately deposited the marbles back into my pants pocket, plastic bag and all. I thanked them both for the free samples and the return of my marbles. As I walked through the exam room door I stopped, turned and asked for a favor.

"Would you guys not tell my Mom about the marbles?" was my whispered request.

"No worry young man, your secret is our secret," Doc Whitebiter promised as Miss Ann crossed her heart and nodded in agreement.

"Thanks," I whispered again, smiling with my fresh bright whites.

Doctor Whitebiter and Miss Ann were all smiles as they escorted me through the reception area and to the waiting room door.

"No cavities!" I announced as Miss Ann gave the 'okay sign' with her hand to confirm that it was a fact.

Doc Whitebiter inquired in Mom's direction when they could expect to see her for a checkup. That put Mom on the hot seat as her hopes for a cool clean escape vaporized. No such luck. The searchlight found its mark and pinned her in the corner of the waiting room. I witnessed my frightened mother's impromptu attempt at working it all out in her head. She went all red in the face and halfheartedly, three-quarter insincerely and fully without any actual planned intent promised that her calling to make an appointment was not more than just a few weeks if not a few days if not a few hours if not mere future moments away.

Mom's dental health and her mental health regarding her dental health were incompatible: classic cognitive dissonance. She would say or do anything to get the hell outta there without making any such future commitment. Any excuse up to and including that the family cat had eaten her appointment time and date reminder card would not be below her dentist avoidance radar.

Doctor Whitebiter looked at her like he was about to kindly scold one of his own dentally delinquent children for gross tooth health negligence. In an experienced voice, a voice that had dealt with reluctant patients before, in a tone that perfectly blended kindness and admonishment, he gently chided my mother not to let it go too long before coming in. Mom interpreted this to mean that too long might be sometime longer than never but not any time period sooner than twenty-five to thirty years at the earliest. Yep, she planned to call and set up an appointment all right, sometime within the next decade or two sounded about right, you could count on it (I wouldn't), in fact, you could bet on it (I definitely wouldn't), guaranteed.

Mom was out the door and halfway down the stairs headed for the building exit before the echo of our goodbyes in an echo-free room subsided. This wasn't the exchange of pleasant goodbyes and friendly see-yeah-soon's before simply walking to the car for the ride home. Our departure was verging on a full break out escape and a mad getaway dash before Doc Whitebiter pulled the alarm, hit all the searchlights and ran after my mom ordering her to halt where she stood!

I quick-stepped out after my mom only to find that she was already down the stairs, out the door and in the running car. Running out the door and onto the sidewalk as if I had a sack full of stolen cash fresh from the vault, I fully expected smoking tire rubber as she'd floor the accelerator and pulled away from the curb with a tire squealing U-turn right in the middle of the street, right in front of the building, all the while shouting out to me to run and catch the car and jump onto the driver's side running board and thread my arm through the open windows around the door's center post and hang on, gangster style.

Luckily for me, my mother may have thought it but she did not act upon whatever desperate fugitive flight scenario she might have imagined. Back in the car and driving for home my mother's (Mrs. Al Capone or Ma Barker, take your pick) anxiety driven hard touch on the accelerator eased and diminished in direct proportion to every block of distance we put between us and the dentist's office.

"Well Hon, that went better than expected, wouldn't yeah say?" was Mom's only nervously breathy comment during the drive home, having been completely unable to speak up until that point in our return journey.

She further comforted herself by avoiding even driving past the place for the next several weeks when running her weekly errands. My continuing and unsolicited verbal advice as to the location and approach of lurking and camouflaged-in-plain-sight stop-signed and stop-lighted intersections served as a further reminder that the source of her worries receded further and further into the far distance and that the likelihood of any return to same for that dreaded appointment had been pushed further and further into the farthest unseeable future.

My mom voluntarily going to the Dentist was just as unlikely as a solitary proton accidentally finding the infinite energy necessary to reach the speed of light and thus attain infinite mass. My mom was the proton of dentist avoidance. She could come close to the speed of light during dentist escape velocity but could never quite go fast enough. Universal forces would never be great enough for either event to ever transpire except for the all too real possibility of a really bad toothache. Protons, according to all past and present scientific understanding, do not get cavities (and resulting toothaches) whereas objectively recorded history had proven, repeatedly, that my mom did (don't forget that one inch thick dental file back at Whitebiter's office).

Spending that Saturday morning dealing with and dodging my own fears and then surfing through, around and on top of the mental shock waves of my mother's dental phobias proved more than distracting enough. I temporarily forgot all about the big match that afternoon. We pulled into the alley and then into our garage just before eleven a.m.. That left me almost three hours to physically and mentally prepare for the match. I stopped at Robert's bedroom door hoping to find him available for the benefit of any last minute advice, hints or instructions he might be willing to impart but he'd left to lead his own life for the day.

I was on my own. It was into my room for a change of clothes and the all-important task of choosing the fifty marbles for the match. For clothing I followed Robert's suggestions and choose my oldest pair of everyday pants, my rattiest shirt and the fastest pair of tennis shoes I owned. I also thought it best to carry my marbles in a double set of extra-large, extra-heavy-duty socks, something that could withstand the extra weight of any possible winnings and take the stress of a high-speed chase in the event any rapid retreat, early desperate-departure or life-saving escape became necessary.

Having outfitted myself in the appropriate garb, I arrived at the most important pre-match task, the selection of the fifty marbles I'd use in the fight for the marble crown. I reached down under my bed and with considerable effort pulled out the large, increasingly flimsy cardboard boot box full of marbles. I carefully cradled it in my arms as I hoisted it onto the top of my bed like it was a box full of rare delicate gemstones instead of a really big load of glass marbles. They were my babies, every single one of them. Removing the lid I was amazed, again, how over the previous nine months the collection had mushroomed from a mere one-hundred marbles to well over two-thousand of all colors and sizes. I'd won and personally owned probably more marbles than all the other kids in school combined. With one rolling WHOOOSH I emptied the entire collection across the top of my bedspread but no Kit Cat came running on cue, as expected, – "strange," I thought.

Without the customary feline companion's input, I started industriously sorting the marbles by size, type, color and style. The bedding sagged from the collected weight en masse. The top of my bed had the appearance of a parade ground for a marble army. I stood still and silent at my bedside staring down at the mass formation of marbles. I concentrated on putting the upcoming marble match of my life into a manageable perspective. All the warning flags that my brother had waved in my face ran over my mind like rough sandpaper dragging over sunburned skin. They were not comforting. I tried in vain to visualize the pending meeting with Billy as I recalled and re-experienced the walk through the match alley the night before. I struggled to imagine what the match might be like.

As images started to form, just as a picture started to come into clear focus, it would all blow apart with the remembrance of a blaring car horn, blinding flashing headlights and me diving in the dirt to save my life. Could it have been an omen? I hoped not. Not a single image I could hold onto materialized. There were too many suspicions, too many unknowns. I walked from the side of the bed and went to my closet to hang up my going-to-the-dentist clothes, all the while glancing back at the marbles that covered my bed. Dressed for the match, I bent down and retied the laces on my tennis shoes extra tight and with double knots. I grabbed two sets of sweat socks from my dresser sock drawer and shoved them inside one another like doubling up paper grocery bags for a heavy load. I walked back to the bed and got ready to pick that day's fifty competitors.

I recalled Robert's admonition to not take the best fifty I had, but it was still difficult so I started by picking the most likely looking Cat's-Eye boulder candidates from the various sorted piles and dropped them one by one back into the empty boot box where the chosen would be reviewed and the final fifty selected. I picked marbles that not only looked like they could be winners but also felt like they could be winners. I sought out marbles that felt clean and smooth and could roll clean, straight and true when aimed and launched.

Like a modern day little Houdini I held each selected marble up to the light and then rolled and squeezed them in and between my hands with my eyes closed tight, checking their round surfaces for nicks and cuts, trying to glean any other mystical revelations. Even if a selected marble's appearance was questionable, if it "spoke to me" it was included. The whole game of marbles from the very start, the ability to be consistent and successful depended upon how the little glass crystals felt when I rolled them around in my hand and how they responded when I cocked my finger and pulled the trigger for the shot.

Marbles was a game of practiced physical skill, all right, but your head had to be fully involved in the game. My emotions and how I coerced, prodded and controlled them ultimately determined how well I physically performed. Playing marbles was as much a meditation as a physical exercise. It was a mental process that my body, like a robot, acted out. If my mind wasn't tuned in and in control of the game, I'd never have won a single match. It was a studied process, the conclusion of which became evident after months of marble-playing. It was part of my natural (unnatural) ability, my talent. It was an unavoidable part of who I was and how I played the game from the very start.

If the game of marbles could be adequately, accurately compared to any other type of mind-body skill it would be closest to archery, *Zen Archery*. One's mind guides the arrow to the bull's-eye, guides the marble to its intended target. I selected the choicest of my collection in a manner bordering on a religious ceremony. It wasn't the type of ritual I would expect from the likes of Pastor Crossmann but rather from an ancient oriental warrior monk who was selecting and sharpening his weapons before a life or death battle. It was as if each marble manifested a spirit of its own which, when joined with my mastery, exhibited almost magical qualities.

Before I could decide otherwise, my imagination was in the pilot's seat. I landed in a rural monastery in medieval China. My modern attire was traded for a sash-tied robe, rope-thonged wooden sandals and oiled and braided hair. I became the venerable master of an ancient "marble arts" school. My weapons, my tools, the objects of my focus, meditation and dedication were not swords, lances, staffs or the bow and arrow, but marbles. I trained myself, and my students, in the peaceful use of the marble for peaceful competition and personal meditation. However, the world was not then or now a peaceful place, so I also instructed my disciples, out of necessity, in the use of the marble as a defensive weapon.

The "marble arts" required patience, tolerance and above all restraint in using the marble in self-defense. The true purpose and objective of the school was to train students to be marble competition champions and seekers of truth and life's deeper meaning through marble meditation. It was a long, arduous but honorable and fundamentally peaceful pursuit. Only in the time of greatest need, of greatest danger, was the marble to be utilized as a deadly equalizer and then only in self-defense or the defense of the helpless and innocent. The training took years. New recruits were schooled in the appropriate body tone and positions with emphasis on eye-hand-mind strength and coordination. The training was deeply philosophical as well as physically strenuous. Initiates were instructed and lectured in mind-marble techniques for several months before they were even allowed to actually hold or use a marble in competitive or defensive practice.

On that day, during that daydream, it was open house at the monastery and I was demonstrating to curious visitors from the surrounding villages the use of the Cat's-Eye boulder as a weapon of ultimate defense. From several resting, casual, competitive and defensive positions I masterfully demonstrated how the marble could be used as a deadly accurate projectile against sinister, unscrupulous, physically superior and menacing opponents. How, even against greater numbers and supposedly superior weapons, the marble and the marble master trained in its use could and would prevail when confronted by such challenges. As a matter of course the young masters were also instructed in the importance, arguably the more important, noncompetitive and non-defensive use of the marble as an instrument for deep thought, soul searching meditation and eventual ultimate enlightenment.

Each beginning student up to and including accomplished masters kept one special Cat's-Eye boulder of their personal choice strictly reserved for intense marble meditation and contemplation that was required at three prescribed time periods per day. Sitting quietly alone, cross-legged on a bamboo mat in a private dark cell, the marble artist would concentrate upon the chosen marble which rested atop a slender stone pedestal one-foot to the front at eye level. At the same level, one-foot to the rear of the positioned marble was a small candle that was the only source of light in the cell. Each meditation period would last one hour and consisted of the meditative student gazing at the candle flame through the crystal structure of the suspended marble. The prismatic candle flame could open entire new worlds to the honest seeker, much the same way the world of my bedroom reappeared before my open eyes. I was slowly released from the spell cast by the Cat's-Eye boulder held out in my hand as it caught the midday sunlight reflected off of the bedroom window's metal latch. The reflected light spread prismatically into my eyes, through me and then all over and around the ceiling and walls of the bedroom.

The bedside clock revealed that I'd have to leave for the alley in a few minutes. I looked into the boot box where I'd deposited the eligible candidates and discovered that I'd chosen many more than the fifty I needed. I simply reached into the box and randomly picked out the fifty needed and dropped them one at a time into the doubled-up sweat socks. With the fifty safely tucked inside the socks I gathered the remaining hundreds still scattered on the bed and, handfuls at a time, steadily and surely piled them back into the boot box. I hefted the bulging container from the bed down onto the floor with a THUMP and then slowly pushed it back into its resting place under the bed. My confidence bolstered by the exotic daydream, I tied the doubled-up marble sock to my belt, reached for my jacket, and then stopped, looked around my room and wondered whether I'd return the victor or the defeated. I closed the bedroom door behind me and descended the stairs to keep my appointment with Destiny.

   The match was scheduled for the agreed upon two p.m.. It was one-thirty when I walked out the back door right past my mother, who only noticed my passing presence after I'd already stepped from the house and into the backyard. Having walked around the back corner of the house I headed for the front yard gate. As resolute in my mission as ever I set a direct and unwavering course for the center of the appointed alley, ready to meet the challenge. My steady and sure pace brought me ever closer and closer to the alley entrance on Nash Street. Within just a half-block of the alley my legs, my body, became strangely weary.

    Each and every step forward became a burdensome, heavier task as the wind started to blow hard and fast against any attempts at my continued forward progress. If I were superstitious I might have thought that there were forces at work trying to prevent me from reaching my destination. Any second I expected to be knocked flat by an onslaught of baseball size hail, electrified by bolts of lightning and doused by sheets of pouring rain, all of it from a cloudless blue sky. As pragmatic as I was when it came to the basic logic of marble-playing I sensed something amiss in the world around me, as if *Mother Nature* herself tried to deter me from ever making it into the alley. Frankly, the entire brief episode verged on the ridiculous. I tried to imagine what unlikely stake any natural or equally unlikely supernatural forces present had in the marble match between two mortal juveniles.

I bravely fought my way forward against the elements to get to the opening of the alley. As I stepped from the sidewalk into the alley's protective enclosure it was like emerging from the chaotic storm wall that surrounded the calm eye of a hurricane. All the strong wind and blowing debris gave way to an unsettling, unnerving and immediate stillness. Another dimension of the alley that further added to the strangeness of the moment was that, again, it was totally deserted. Having arrived early the absence of Billy was not a surprise but it was a warm spring Saturday afternoon and that time of year alleys were a big part of yard work activities. That Saturday afternoon it seemed that no one lived in the adjoining houses, as if everyone had been evacuated in anticipation of some approaching disaster. I never thought that a marble match, no matter how important, would be sufficient reason to clear a neighborhood. Maybe, just maybe, Avenging Grace marble matches had all of the horrific magnitude and menacing battle pageantry of a Righteous Destruction football game, and there I was without a gas mask, a crash helmet or a loaded bandolier of flash-bang smoke bombs.

I tightly pulled in the reins of my stampeding fears and uneasily, slowly, grew accustomed to the unexpectedly lonely back roadway. I walked to the center of the alley just like the night before. I calmly sat down on the alley cement, leaned slightly back against a garage wall and, so settled, waited for Billy to arrive. At first I sat cross-legged and then after a bit shifted to a position with my knees drawn up to my chest, held in place by my clasped hands with the doubled-up and loaded marble sock resting in my lap. I changed back and forth between the two sitting positions several times as I waited, and waited, and waited – and – waited.

During my vigil signs of life finally started to appear up-and-down the length of the alley as an occasional someone would bring out and deposit garbage into a trash can or drive a car into or out of one of the many garages that opened onto the alley. But

I could not help but notice that even the simplest of everyday tasks had been performed in unnatural haste, as if it were dangerous to linger too long in or near the alley. I imagined something huge, gruesome, hideous and dangerous lived nearby and frequently used the alley for passage and no one wanted to be caught out in the open when it passed by.

Although I hadn't carried a timepiece with me to the alley I knew from the long wait that it was at least a full hour past the agreed time of the match. Billy Schoutenlauder was nowhere in sight. I was a typical flexible little kid, able to hold a single position for an extended period of time, but I'd been sitting on the alley cement for so long that my legs started to cramp and parts of my rear end went dead asleep. After what seemed to be another hour I struggled to my feet and in the process almost fell over backwards. All of the feeling and muscle control in my sleeping backside were temporarily inoperative, 'on the fritz'. I'd contracted a case of 'fritz butt' as a reward for my patience ('fritz butt', an annoying but temporary and fully survivable condition).

Depressed and confused, I had to reluctantly admit that my long wait was in vain and the match for that day was a dud. What had happened to Billy? It had been a long week of waiting, worrying, sleepless nights, being victimized by Old Lady Bookbender and the terrible nightmares. All of the anticipation and bottled up energy was still there but it suddenly became directionless. My head felt like a tightly closed canning jar full of captive, angry bees, each one buzzing and bouncing madly from side to side, unable to escape. Hesitantly, I slowly started for the end of the alley where I'd entered some considerable time earlier.

Not wanting to rush my exit and possibly miss a late arrival by Billy, I delayed my leaving by weaving back and forth, back tracking, skipping, hopping and other general time wasting frivolities. The bees in my head were going nuts but I wasn't going to walk away from any chance to see the situation through to a conclusion, so I meandered back to the center of the alley. I decided to count to 100 by ones, very slowly and deliberately, promising myself that if Billy hadn't arrived by the time I'd reached 100 that I'd leave the alley for home straight away. 95 –

96 – and then 97 rolled around and I was still the only marble player in the alley. With 100 on my lips I gave out a heavy exasperated sigh, swung my marble sock over my shoulder and turned to leave.

I spun around on my heels towards Nash Street and there, not ten feet away right in the center of the alley, was a little kid even smaller than me, standing as still and silent as a proverbial church mouse. With his head tilted slightly down towards his chest and his eyes looking up at me from beneath his eyebrows, he took a half-step back when our eyes met. His expression turned from curiosity to suspicion and fear as if I unknowingly held his fate and future in my jacket pocket.

"Who are you?" I announced, the bees still buzzing and bumping uncomfortably right behind my eyes.

"Is Billy here or did I miss it?" he sheepishly questioned.

"No, Billy isn't here and you didn't miss anything. Who are you?" I asked for the second time.

"I live next door, by Wilbur," was his quiet answer with a moment's verbal hitch.

He seemed unsure as to whether or not he should be talking to me. With his hesitant and uncertain response he swung to the front of his body what he'd been carrying over his shoulder and against his back. Almost losing his tiny balance and crumbling to the ground in the process, the little stranger produced a bulging sock of marbles that looked ready to burst at the seams. The tiny kid possessed his own weight in marbles as his arms and legs strained under the burden of his collection. Looking at me as if I'd changed from a little boy into a marble eating monster he asked what was wrong as he took a couple of further cautious steps backwards.

I must have been staring hard at his marble sock as visions of not-yet-seen crystal beauty filled my eyes. My peepers must have been sticking halfway out of their sockets, just like the guy named *Bug-Eyes* I'd seen at the *State Fair Midway Freak Show* the summer before. I pulled my eyeballs back into my head and regained my composure by keeping the conversation going with the interesting stranger.

"So, you know Wilbur?"

"Yeah, he lives by my house."

"You know Billy too?"

"Yeah, sort of. We go to the same school, Avenging Grace."

"Yeah? So, where's Billy?" I mildly demanded. The little kid shrugged his shoulders to indicate he hadn't the slightest idea.

"All of those yours?" I pointed in the general direction of his overstuffed marble sock.

"Yeah," he chirped as he clutched them harder and pulled them closer to his body and took another step backwards, apparently fearful that I might take advantage of our seclusion and relieve him of his obviously priceless possessions.

"So, you play too?" I innocently, non-threateningly probed, trying to show by my calm and polite disposition that I meant him and his marbles no harm.

"Sort of, sometimes, when I feel like it – sort of," was his guarded response, his voice trailing off and dropping in volume until I could barely hear him.

By the time he finished his sentence he'd lowered his head so far down that he was talking to the alley cement more than he was talking to me. He nervously shuffled his feet. I had the distinct impression that his marbles had been purchased, not won. He was a marble holder and watcher, not a player. I'd seen it plenty of times before. There were more than a few kids at the Fifty-First Street School who had lots of nice marbles that never faced the uncertainty of the ring. Not being as practically marble skilled as he was imaginatively marble skilled, he'd decided it best to 'watch-n-carry' and confine his play to the living room carpet, content to compete against manageable and non-threatening phantom foes.

I wouldn't, I couldn't and I didn't blame him because hanging onto your marbles, considering the tough and ever-present competition, was quite the feat. Pulling it off, day in and day out, required all the skill you could muster and all of the random good luck you could not. Putting one's best on the line took a sense of willing and reckless abandon. After a match, win or lose, my nerves would keep firing away for an hour or more. Heck, look where my willing and reckless abandon had taken me that day, standing alone, stood-up for a marble-match-date in a deserted alley, talking to a little stranger.

"What's your name?" I asked, hoping to glean as much inside information on Billy as the little kid would be willing to let slip.

"Frankie Hansen," he responded as he looked up and tried to register any positive or negative reaction I might have had to his name.

"Well Frankie, I've been sittin' here for almost two hours and there's been no Billy Schoutenlauder in sight. Only you and your giant sock of marbles have shown up so far. Do yeah think Billy chickened out?"

"Oh – Billy – chicken out? Naahh, he's pretty good. I've seen him play lots of times. He beats everybody."

Frankie seemed in awe of Billy because Billy played for keeps. That was a tough line to cross, that line between the safer make believe marble-playing and the other side thrill of real winning which was almost always fun and the risk of real losing which was never fun. Frankie had marbles aplenty to play but he didn't have "The Marbles," so to speak, to actually play. Where as Frankie was afraid to start, to take that chance and face the risks, I was afraid to stop.

I was an incurable marble risk taker. I had all the marbles I needed, literally and figuratively. Success had made me, on many occasions, lean towards the reckless end of the scale, and on more occasions than that, unabashedly greedy for the spoils of that success. My success enabled me, pushed me, to take chances with my marbles. As time went on challenges were accepted that would've never even been considered just a few months before. If Frankie was trapped by his fear of trying at all I was trapped by my fear of not trying hard enough. Frankie couldn't start and I couldn't stop. I was unable to figure out which of the two of us had it any better or any worse than the other.

So that day wouldn't turn out to be a total waste of time, I decided to offer Frankie my advice and expertise in a quick game for funzies. Suddenly, Frankie's eyes got as big as half-dollar coins as he yelled to look out and jump for it. I turned just in time to hear the glaring car horn and spot the shiny grill and bumper of the same marauding hot-rod *Chevy* of the night before not more than twenty feet from where we were standing. Just in time I dove to my right and Frankie ran to my left. I landed face down at the edge of the alley in a big pile of fresh-cut grass clippings. I looked back to catch a passing glimpse of the same car full of clowns that had almost run me down on that same spot the night before. The empty beer cans flew from the open windows along with the blaring rock-'n'-roll as the *Chevy* squealed its tires and peeled rubber down the alley towards Nash Street.

For the second time I met, face-to-grill, the lurking monster that kept people out and away from their very own alley. The hideous beast that used the alley for passage had almost run me over twice in as many days. I jumped back up to my feet and brushed grass clippings off my clothes while looking to see if Frankie had also made it clear of the hungry monster. My searching gaze quickly surveyed the entire length and breadth of the alley but there was no Frankie Hansen in sight. I pictured the little screaming Frankie, with his full marble sock clutched in his arms, pinned to the chromed front grill of the hot rod as it smoked and roared its way out of the alley.

The color and condition of the car as well as the poor attitude and likely inebriated condition of the occupants suggested some association with Righteous Destruction Driver's Ed. So I reasoned that, as Frankie was a likely future RD student, the driver of the car would've shown mercy and not intentionally incorporated Frankie into the front bodywork of the car. I concluded that Frankie had simply used the unexpectedly dangerous diversion to slip away.

The bees in my head had only been stirred up and aggravated further by the car-pedestrian near miss as they relentlessly crawled, bounced and buzzed themselves into a frenzy. I decided, finally, that enough was enough for that Saturday afternoon. I headed for home certain that Billy was not just waiting somewhere nearby to spring a surprise and pop out and say "here I am!" My body and brain were worn out by the buildup of unresolved nervous tension and pent-up, unreleased excitement. I was a warmed-up, well-tuned marble engine that had been hosed down with ice water. I'd entered the alley purring on all eight cylinders, ready for a fast start. Instead, I found myself coasting along in the breakdown lane with a cracked engine block, leaking coolant and blowing blue smoke out my tailpipe. My growling eight cylinders were down to five and three of those were misfiring. It was putt-bang-putt-bang-bang-putt-putt all the way home. I was one finely tuned marble player headed back to the pits with a full tank of gas, four good tires and a blown engine. There were no strong winds or flying debris that hindered or delayed my walk home. It was just a long, quiet, jerky walk. Putt-putt-bang-putt-bang.

I purposely walked a course for home that took me and my marbles six blocks out of the way in an effort to walk off some of the built-up unexpended energy. When I finally arrived at the back door it was four o'clock in the afternoon and an hour before a supper that I had no interest in whatsoever. Dad was seated in his favorite chair in the living room safely tucked in behind the evening newspaper and Mom was busy humming to herself and rattling the pots and pans in the kitchen. Robert was somewhere as usual and I didn't know where, as usual. Everything was annoyingly normal.

All the little familiar Saturday afternoon routines and rituals that I usually looked forward to, that I relied upon for peace and security in my life, the anchor in the uncertain ebb and flow of daily reality suddenly became just too certain, too mundane, too – expected. That anchor against bleak uncertainty had transformed into an anchor around my neck. I was bitter, angry and in a foul mood. Mysteriously, life went on all around me despite the COMPLETE LACK of integrity demonstrated by some of its questionably human members.

I argued and pleaded with myself, demanding to know what right that arrogant, boastful creep had not to live up to his proud words and turnout to prove his mettle and stand by his big talk. He could have at least shown up with a note from his mother stating that Billy couldn't stay to prove or stand up for anything because he had to come home right away for his Saturday afternoon nap! Absurd – definitely; unlikely – yes; understandable – possibly; better than not showing up at all – absolutely.

I walked straight into and through the kitchen, right past Mom and her "Hello" and ascended the stairway up to my room. I reached the top step with one final gasping effort. I opened my bedroom door just as my tank hit empty and my engine stalled out. Coasting into my room I tossed my marble sock onto the bed with an over the shoulder fling. It landed with a gritty, boingy bounce near the headboard of my bed as I drifted past the foot of my bed and my body landed with a THUD and bounce of its own in the armchair by the window.

I recalled how I'd wondered upon leaving my room just a few hours before as to whether I'd return victorious or defeated. If I'd known that it would've been undecided and deflated, I'd have saved myself the trip. I had a date with Destiny and I'd been stood up. I even briefly entertained the thought that losing would have been a more acceptable conclusion than how I felt at that moment, which was unresolved. But then I looked at my still intact and still full marble sock on the bed and I stopped entertaining that thought all together.

I pondered the possibility that Billy had gotten the full story on my winning ways and had in fact chickened out, and, if that was the case, did he feel a little guilty, did he feel a lot guilty or did the creep feel anything at all? I couldn't be sure either way, so lacking the necessary information I stopped torturing myself. That didn't mean, however, that I was going to throw any undeserved breaks his way. As far as I was concerned at the time the only legitimate excuse for Billy's absence would be a death in his immediate family and, even then, only his own.

Win or lose, show or no-show, Billy was the type of kid who could never be a friend of mine. That Monday afternoon after school when Billy stopped me on the sidewalk and made his challenge, he'd been just too phony cool, too much Mr. Tough Guy to have pulled a chicken stunt like not showing. Schoutenlauder seemed to be a pretty limited, single dimension, character. That was of no real consequence for me except, competitively speaking, it was a convenience. It allowed me a clear uncomplicated field of view of my potential opponent. It made it somewhat easier to play him and a lot easier to not like him. If Billy was unwilling or just unable to display or put forward any deeper or more complex sense of the person he was or wasn't didn't matter. I wasn't going to waste any time or effort digging around inside of his empty head trying to pull out something, anything, of worth or interest relevant to his marble ability and skill. Whether or not we'd have another chance to play didn't matter to me at the time. I was angry with Billy for his lack of respect for a fellow marble player. It was no small matter, no small match that could just be forgotten and left off to the side unsettled. It was big time neighborhood-schoolyard marbles and he owed it to me to take his chances and play as promised.

The relief valve for my silent rage, my exponentially expanding anger towards Billy, was channeled to and through my ever-resourceful ability to fantasize, the only available outlet I had. My soft, bulky, overstuffed armchair became a swiveling, wood-ribbed, wheeled office chair. I's cut a means rug in my's twenties mobster fashion ensemble completes wit' wide brimmed hat wit' dah front of dah brim stylishly turned downs tah just below my's eyebrows fors effect, a black t'ree piece pin stripped suit ands dah latest two-tone saddle shoes wit' full-calf-length stretch argyle socks. I's sat unders a lone, bare, unshaded high-intensity light bulb d'hat hung downs froms dah tall ceiling aboves ats dah ends ofs a long black extension cord, alls ofs which swung ands swayed slightly ins dah drafty space.

My's elbows rests ons a dark wooden desk as I's evers-so-patiently rolls a Cat's-Eye boulder backs ands fort', backs ands fort' 'cross ans imitations alligator skins desk pad. Dah scene was a large back office ins ans expansive abandoned warehouse downs by's dah river, verys lates ats nights likes (eleven p.m., twelve midnight, minimums).

Sittin' noncs to's comfortably ins anutter wooden office chair ons dah utter side ofs dah desk ins fronts ofs me's, alls tied ups likes a rowdy cow ats a rodeo ropin' contest, sweatin' ands puffin' likes ans overcooked greasy jumbo hot dog forgotten ons dah hot grill alls days long was 'Billy Fingers', ones ofs dah deadliest

Marble Sharks ins dah *Glass Ball Syndicate*. Billy owed me's, owed me's big, ands its was time for Fingers tah puts-up, pays-up ors shuts-up, ands jus' maybes, dependin' ons my's moods, alls t'ree ats once. My's twos business associates aidin' ands assistin' me's ins d'his friendly little conversation was 'Sharp Shooter Frankie' ands 'Blabber Mouth Wilbur', twos ofs dah best enforcers ins *Marble Alley*, dah place wheres alls dah actions ins dah *Glass Ball Syndicate* started ands ended. Its was dah place wheres Fingers was supposed tah haves kep' ans important appointment, ands didn't.

Me's ands dah boyz had been pussyfootin' arounds wit' Fingers fors goin' ons overs ans hour ors so's, tryin' tah gets some straight answers likes dah gentlemens we's was, askin' reals nice-likes, whens my's patience ands abundant goodwills starts tah wears t'in likes ans old sock ats dah heel.

"Alls rights Fingers, we's bot' knows wheres d'his is goin'. D'his is dah last times I's gonna asks yous nice likes. Whys didn't yous shows ups likes yous was supposed tah! HA! WHERES MY GOODS?" I's shouted whiles boobin' my's hat covered head backs ands fort' ands sides tah sides. I's jumped tah my's feets ands leans ins towards Fingers 'cross dah top ofs my's stylish desk, d'hat I's pounds reals hard wit' bot' my's fists, "I's gettin' reals impatient wit' yous impertinence, so's yous jus' bedder – !"

"Wheres yous learns a big word likes d'hat, ya jerk? Off a kiddy's cereal box or sump'n," Billy sarcastically interrupted.

"SHUT – UP – YAS – DUMB – MUG!" I's cuts him off.

I's leans ins evens closers.

"Likes I's was sayin', me's ands dah boyz heres has had 'nough ofs yous ands yous lyin' ands yous ands yous smart guy mout'. Whens we's gets impatients, whens we's has had 'nough we's gets upset, reals upset! Ands yous don't wants us tah gets upset, reals upset, 'cause whens we's gets reals upset, we's loses ours heads, sees, ands we's ain't responsible fors w'ats hap'ens tah dumb mugs likes yous whens guys likes us loses ours heads! Ain't d'hat right boyz?"

"Naaah, yous don'ts wants d'hat - we's ain'ts responsible whens d'hat happ'ns - yous wouldn't likes d'hat - remembers dah last times d'hat happ'nd - d'hat was bad - yous means last week, d'hat last times - ya d'hat times - ya, I's remembers, d'hat was bad, real bad, I's hav' tah says even disgustin' - no d'hat - d'hat would be unwise, ya, d'hat's dah words - unwise," Frankie ands Wilbur simutanleously responds talkin' overs each utter wit' big grins ons d'heir faces, shakin' d'heir heads ups ands downs, backs ands fort' ands shufflin' d'heir feets ands rockin' backs ands fort' alls ats dah same times.

"So's, yous heards its froms me's ands nows yous heards its froms dah boyz, so's starts talkin'!" I's succinctly summed up.

For a wise guy alls tied up ins a chair in not-to's-friendly company ands ins insdefensible circumstances, Billy was pretty cocky, alls mout' wit' his wise guys responses.

"I's gots nothin' tah says tah yous Archer, yous ors yous two dumb flunkies. Ifs I's don'ts feels likes showin', I's don'ts shows! Ifs I's don'ts feels likes talkin', I's keeps my mout' shut! Simple enoughs fors yas! But maybes yous ands d'hat tiny marbles sized brains ofs yous can'ts understan's w'ats I's sayin'! Besides, I's ain'ts gots anys ofs yous goods no hows, no ways, ands anyways, I's don'ts evens knows w'ats yous shootin' yous big mout' off abouts anyways ands evens ifs I's did knows sump'n I's don'ts has tah answers tah dah dumb likes ofs yous! It's my's prerogative – HA! Yous likes big words, gos 'head ands choke ons d'hat ones ya dumb mug!"

I's kicks my's chair backs aways froms me's ands dah desk wit' dah bottom ofs my's shoe ands stan's straight-up. I's put bot' my's hands ins my's pants pockets ands starts bouncin' ands pacin' backs ands fort' behinds my's desk, reals cool ands collected, havin' regains my's composures ands alls.

"Okays boyz, okays, maybes we's cans helps Fingers heres wit' his memorys ands learns him somes respect ats dah sametime. Alls right boyz, gets 'em alls out ons dah desk ands spreads 'em!"

Fingers struggles ands squirmes ins his chair likes dah worms ons dah ends ofs fishin' hooks as I's opens dah top desk drawer ands pulls outs dah eighteen inch longs freakin' framin' claws hammer. Fingers started moanin' ands screamin' evens befores I's starts poundin' as my two boyz grabbed his two hands ands dah goods ands spreads 'em wide ons dah desktop.

"Alls right Fingers, d'his is its, yous moment of trut' as d'heys says, I's wants somes answers, straight answers ands I's wants 'em fast ors else I's starts poundin' - gots it!" I's instructs as I's holds-up ands shakes dah hammer ins dah direction ofs his face.

"Ya! Ya! Gos ons yas mugs. Do's yous worst, I'lls shows yous bums d'hat I's cans takes anythin's yous gots!" Fingers growled back.

"Okays Fingers, haves its yous ways, jus' remembers yous asked for it. Alls right boyz, holds 'em down ands keeps 'em spread," I's ordered.

Wit' a grinnin' grunt ands a long, archin', over my's head wind-up, I's swung dah hammer down wit' alls my's might ands smashed ones ofs Finger's best as he's screamed ins agonys. I's decides tah smash anutter ones as Billy Fingers squirmed ands moaned evens more, ands thens, he's starts yellin' ands screamin' likes some madman.

BAM! I's smashed anutter ones.

"Yous readys tah talk? Yous feelin' inclined, yous suddenlys finds yous selfs ins dah moods tah shows somes respect?" I's reiterated breathless but exhilarated froms dah exertion.

"NEVER! Go's stick yous fat heads ins dah toile – "

WHAMMM! I's cracked anutter ones.

SLAMMM! Anutter ones smashed ins tah gritty pulp.

I's starts tah wonders hows much mores ofs 'dah treatment' Fingers was goin' tah takes 'cause its was evens startin' tah gets tah me's nots tah mentions dah squeamish expressions ons dah faces ofs my's boyz. But, Fingers had tah be taught a lesson, he's had it comin' to's him.

"Alls right boyz, d'his creep is really askin' fors it, so's I's gonna gives its tah him. Keeps 'em spread ands I'lls smash every last stinkin' ones ofs 'em reals good! D'hat's it, keeps 'em spread so's I's gots a reals clear shots ats 'em all, ones ats a time!" I's exhorted.

Fingers was howlin' ands screamin' ins delirious agonys as my's two boyz did d'heir best tah keep 'em spread as I's hammered away. Finally, Fingers couldn't takes its any mores ands gives ins ands a good t'ing its was to's 'cause he's didn't haves d'hat many left fors me's tah works overs. Shakin' dah hammer ins Fingers face, sweatin' ands breathin' heavy my's-self froms dah workout, I's loosened my's tie ats dah neck ands shouts in tah Finger's face.

"Yous ready tah gives wit' dah respect, yas-dumb-stupid-mug?"

"Ya, ya – ya sure, jus' puts d'hat t'ing down, puts d'hat t'ing a-ways! I'lls do's w'ats evers yous wants, evens drinks teas ands eats cookies wit' yous bunch of overgrowns pansies ifs d'hat's w'ats yas wants." Fingers grimaced ands breathlessly begged ands cracked ats dah sames times. I's exhaled wit' a loud hard sigh as I's dropped dah hammer down on tah dah desktop wit' a sharp BANG!

I's lets him gets aways wit' dah teas ands cookies wisecrack ands us bein' pansies ands alls 'cause its jus' so's hap'ens d'hat I's was partials tah teas ands cookies ands pansies jus' hap'ens tah be ones ofs my's favorite flowerin' blooms. Besides, I's wasn't dah dumb mug alls tied ups ins a chair wit' several ofs my's best smashed ons dah desk rights ins fronts of me's. Finger's hairs was hangin' down alls overs his sweaty ands red splattered face d'hat was ins sharps contrasts tah his complexion d'hat was as white as fresh colds snows. I's would haves beens several shades whiter my's self ifs I's gone t'rough what I's jus' put Fingers t'rough.

Dah mess was disgustin'. 'Tweens alls dah red juicy splatter, dah red stringy meat, runny red pulp ands alls dah poundin' hammer marks ons top ofs dah desk dah imitations alligator skins desk pad gots alls messed up, permanent likes. Som' times tah gets t'ings straightened out yous had tah breaks a fews ofs d'hose t'ings d'hat had gones alls crooked likes, ya, alls outta whack, jus' likes Billy Fingers had gones alls crooked ands outta whack. We's pounded Fingers right back ins tah a straight line alls right ands he's wasn't goin' tah forgets ours little 'chat' – evers! We's was alls wipin' off alls dah drippin' red stuffs wit' ours hands ands hankies froms ours faces ands clothes.

"Alls right boyz, untie dah louzy bum," I's instructed.

Frankie ands Wilbur did as d'heys was told. Wilbur looked

likes he's was goin' tah lose his lunch ands I's thinks ins dah excitement ofs dah moments ands alls Frankie already had. Fingers ran his shaky, sweaty ands red covered fingers t'rough his mussed up hair wit' a sigh ands louds snooty sniffles. He's trembled likes dah last dead leaf clingin' tah dah bare tree branch durin' dah winter blizzard. Befores him ons dah desk was w'ats was left ofs several ofs his best Cat's-Eye boulders, alls smashed ands crushed tah powder. My boyz had kep' 'em spread reals good so's I's had a cleans hard shots ats alls of 'em.

Alls dah red splatter was dah unavoidin' results ofs alls dah smashed grapes, cherries, ands tiny tomatas d'hat Finger's, out ofs habits, always carried alongs ands mixed ins wit' his marbles fors snackin' ons whens dah moods struck 'em, a dumb mug's healt'y but careless quirk. That's hows we's tracked 'em him down. My boyz jus' followed dah trails ofs spit-out cherry pits ands dah tiny green stems pulled off dah top ofs dah little tomatas d'hat Fingers left lying arounds alls overs town. It was a cinch.

"Alls right Fingers, whens yous supposed tah shows, yous shows, gots it?" I's lectured.

"Ya, ya, jus' lets me's outta d'his joint alreadys," Fingers pleaded.

"Okays boyz, helps ours palzy-walzy Billy heres finds dah door," I's sarcastically requests.

Billy Fingers shakily gad'hered up dah last, dah very few remainin' ofs his intact marbles ands dah survivin' grapes, cherries ands tiny tomatas ands shuffled ands stumbled, wit' dah helps ofs Wilbur ands Frankie, t'rough dah office door ands outs ins to's dah expanses ofs dah dimly lit empty warehouse. I's straightened my's tie, pulls my's chair backs up to's dah desk ands takes a seat. I's put my's crossed feet ups ons dah corner ofs dah desk ands clasped my's hands behinds my's head as I's leans backs ins my's chair. Each ones ofs my's two-toned saddle shoes sported a miniature Cat's-Eye marble embedded ins dah shoes tongues 'tween dah laces. I's sighed wit' satisfactions ofs my's triumphs as I's tipped my's fedora backs ons my's head. Frankie ands Wilbur walks backs towards dah desk wit' big whites-ands-golds-toothy smiles plastered 'cross d'heir big grinnin' mugs as d'heys hankie-dabbed d'heir foreheads dry, dah 'chat' havin' been somes cause fors exertions ons d'heir parts as wells.

"Dats w'ats I's likes, respect ands a little good funs whiles I's collectin' its. Right Boyz?" I's chuckled.

"Yous bet boss – yous cans says d'hat agains boss," Frankie smiled backs along wit' Wilbur as dah boyz ands I's had a good laugh.

It was just luck that no one in my family walked into my room at that moment because I had the biggest, stupidest grin on my face. It was so ridiculously big and so pathetically idiotic that my face and head had completely disappeared behind the abnormally big and unnaturally expansive nothing-but-lips-and-teeth freakish smile that just sat there slightly bobbing and balancing on the top of my neck. My stupid look was the willing price paid for giving into my persuasive imagination and the resulting temporary side effect of the disturbing transformation into a demented carnival game clownish cupie doll come to life sitting in my chair in my place.

My reclining, hands-behind-my-head position in my armchair exactly mimicked the last imagined position at the warehouse office desk as the dimly lit warehouse faded back into my afternoon sunlit bedroom. My revenge on the recalcitrant Billy Fingers had helped, helped a lot, but yet, it wasn't enough. It wasn't enough to stop the running-on-with-the-ignition-switch-off misfiring of my nervous internal energy engine. Something else was needed, something else had to be done, and soon.

I swung around and out of my armchair to my feet and headed for the marble cache under my bed. I harbored the dark possibility on a mental list of possibilities all the way home from the alley. The very idea, which at first was desperate and distasteful, then drastic and sacrilegious, had by now moved to the top of the list as a definite possibility. I'd gained insight and understanding of my brother Robert's outrage, his feelings of anger and desperation when he'd finally given up and shutdown his marble-playing. The potential relief, the possible release of frustration, offered by the very idea alone of what I was contemplating was beyond temptation.

Without reservation, I would've bet the farm, even though Robert might have been unwilling to admit it, that when baseball card flipping competition had dealt him a blow, when he couldn't make those cards fly, spin, tumble or land the way he wanted, in the way he was accustomed to, bottled bees of his own would be buzzing away in that head of his. I pictured Robert retrieving a pair of sharp scissors and, while secretively secluded in his tree house, just start snipping away at those little picture cards which had brought him so much but could, on occasion, cost him so dearly. Without question Robert would have willingly made the sacrifice if it meant clearing his head to reveal an open path forward.

I located the smaller cardboard box, formally a brick-of-processed-cheese-containing box, further under the bed near my regular boot box cache. The smaller box's contents consisted of a few of the overflow collection whose competitive days had ended. They'd been retired from match play due to their battle-scarred condition. They'd been played so often that their once-smooth clear surfaces resembled the badly cratered surface of the moon. Although I'd previously retired those faded beauties with full honors, I decided out of the necessity of the moment to a change in plans. They were to be pressed into service one final time. Fingering through the box, I picked out seven of the old champs and quickly recovered the box and slipped it back under the bed.

My body actually started to twinge, quiver and tingle with the physical manifestation of guilt and regret, much like a grave robber must feel on his first heist of a body. I pocketed the seven chosen and headed out of my room for Dad's basement workshop. Thinking about, anticipating, what I was about to do left me feeling uneasy and relieved – simultaneously. The closest feeling I could have compare it to was when a bunch of the guys went over to Larry Werner's house over Christmas vacation when Larry's parents weren't home and we all snuck into his Dad's basement storage room and paged through the collection of girlie magazines that were hidden there. I'd left Larry's house feeling guilty but yet feeling better for what I then understood about one of life's previous big mysteries.

I walked past Mom who was still hard at work throwing together Saturday night supper while Dad was still busy grunting and groaning behind the evening paper. Opening the basement door created enough noise for Mom to notice my presence as she reminded me that supper would be ready shortly and to stay at home. I responded, without stopping, that what I had to do wouldn't take long as I closed the basement door behind me.

Standing at the top of the stairs the basement loomed before me in the shadows and darkness of late afternoon. Dim sunlight filtered in through a number of dirty basement windows giving the underground space an air of soft-lit foreboding. For as bold, daring and brave as I always was at the edge of the marble ring, standing alone at the top of the basement stairs with the basement door closed behind me I was quite the scaredy-cat with the partially dark basement awaiting me. But as I had serious business to transact any presence of basement bogeymen or lurking who-knew-what's just had to stay the hell out of the way and wait their turn.

Then the thought occurred to me, as I'd slowly, cautiously, descended the stairs, that the darkness I feared most may have been the darkness that unfolded within me, the darkness of the deed soon to be done and not any darkness that pressed in from the surrounding basement. In fact, all the extra darkness that was flowing out from me made the basement darkness look more like a dull, suddenly-not-so-frightening, medium gray. It turned out that the only bad bogeyman, the only troubled soul, determined to do dark things in that basement that afternoon was me.

That dull, suddenly-not-so-frightening, medium gray light spread through all parts of the basement and provided just enough illumination for me to find my way to the far corner were Dad kept his workbench and associated tools and assorted household hardware. I found an old chair to stand on as I reached for and pulled on the light chain that dangled down above the workbench. With a 'clink' and a 'snap' the work area lit up before me with all of its manly hardware majesty.

At the right end of the workbench was just what the doctor

ordered to cure my rapidly worsening condition, Dad's *Midget Mighty Moe* table vise. I climbed down from the chair that I then dragged along behind me as I walked for that end of the workbench. On the way I picked up a large rubber headed mallet and a pair of welder's tinted safety glasses. Climbing back up onto the chair and putting on the safety goggles, I placed the mallet on the workbench, reached into my pants pocket and retrieved the seven sacrificial marbles. I deposited the marbles into a small shallow tin can which had recently held a handful of small rusted finishing nails and which had sometime prior held a full load of "extra fancy" chunk white tuna. I checked the operation of the vise by rapidly cranking it all the way open and then slowly cranking it back closed to a position just slightly wider than the width of the first offering.

Respectfully, reverently, I reached for the first marble. Carefully, tenderly, I placed it between the jaws of the vise with my left thumb and forefinger while winding the device closed with my right hand. With the first sacrifice in place, I thought a moment of reverent silence to be appropriate. With proper respects having been paid, I clamped the marble firmly in place with the protruding crank handle of the vise parallel to the floor and sticking out in my direction. Finding that my angle of attack was not clear for a good shot I climbed back down and repositioned the chair. Having climbed back up onto the chair I reached for the mallet and placed its rubber head against the vise handle to check my aim and mallet head impact coverage. Satisfied that it was all going to work as planned I placed my feet as far apart as the hard wooden seat of the chair would allow to keep proper balance. Everything was set. I grabbed the mallet handle with both hands and raised the rubber-headed hammer up and back over my head for the strike and prepared to send the first marble sacrifice into peaceful oblivion, marble heaven, the eternal marble hall of fame or wherever deceased marble spirits migrated to.

I was set, all ready, to release my swing when my eyes caught a glimpse of the marble trapped between the pressing metal jaws of the vise. That instantly caused my uplifted arms and the suspended rubber hammer in my hands to all lock in place. With my arms starting to waver under the combined weight of the hammer and my arms suspended over my head the trapped marble stared me down, stared me into inaction as it effectively pleaded its case. I fought the urge to relent and grant an unconditional pardon.

I strained with all of my will and fought the reluctance to pull the trigger. I even tried to envision the held-fast marble as one of Billy's own marbles. When that didn't work I visualized the marble as Billy's head about to be squished to jelly. That worked. With my eyes closed tight, holding the image of Billy's stupid face locked between the jaws of the vise as he stuck his tongue out at me and gave me a spit-slobbering *Bronx Cheer* I released my swing and brought the rubber mallet down with all of my might!

I completely missed. I didn't even come close to connecting with the vise handle as the speeding mallet head pounded down onto the top of the workbench. Every loose tool, every tin can full of nails and screws, every lidded glass baby food jar containing whatever, everything that had been resting on the workbench jumped several inches into the air like a quiet stadium crowd had sprung to life, jumping up out of their seats as the home team unexpectedly scored a touchdown. The recoil of the speeding rubber mallet head caused my arms, with my hands still tightly gripping the hammer handle, to fly back over my head. I fell backwards off the chair as the mallet flew free of my tight grip and bounced off the cement block wall behind me.

The unintentional miss created a tremendous racket. Mom rushed to the basement door and flung it open and shouted down asking what had happened and was I all right. I slowly got to my feet and called back that everything was just fine, despite the fact that my hands felt numb and tingling like I'd just quickly grabbed and just as quickly let go of a hot electrical connection. To keep Mom off her guard and from making a follow-up inquiry or even worse, coming down to see what had happened, I quickly changed the subject by asking if supper was ready. It worked as Mom answered that all would be ready and on the table soon.

"Great!" I called back.

Mom closed the basement door and then walked back across the kitchen floor as I followed her creaking footstep progress just overhead. Having retrieved the mallet from between two stacks of old newspapers, I walked back to the chair that had to be lifted up from the floor and back into its properly aligned upright position. I carefully re-examined the scene of the almost execution. Everything that wasn't bolted down on the workbench had been slightly to grossly rearranged and relocated a few to several inches from various original-resting positions. I climbed back up onto the chair seat and reset the crooked pair of safety goggles squarely on my face.

The trapped marble was silently pleading for clemency more persistently than ever. The problem was that either the marble exploded in the vise or the buzzing bees would start exploding in my head. But under the peculiar circumstances, having blundered and missed with my swing and all, I decided to be a gracious executioner and relented. Willing to endure the bouncing bees in my brain for a few minutes more, I spared the pleading Cat's-Eye from oblivion. Like the wrongly convicted prisoner who claimed innocence all along but was found guilty nonetheless and sent to the electric chair only to find that when the signal was given, the switch thrown and the current turned on, nothing happens. The drama, the strain, the emotional torture of the almost execution earns the convicted but innocent captive a last-second reprieve and pardon.

So it was with the first intended marble sacrifice, a full pardon. It had suffered enough, I reckoned, and deserved to continue its existence in one battered but nonetheless whole piece. Putting my left hand under the metal jaws I cranked the vise open with my right hand as the freed and forgiven marble dropped into the warmth of my waiting palm. I dropped the pardoned glass ball back into my pocket for safekeeping.

For just a few moments I bathed in the glory and grace of having bestowed forgiveness but the unrelenting buzzing of the bees trying to burst from my aching head quickly dispelled any visions of sainthood. I concluded that I'd been more than generous enough, thank you, and that I'd suffered more than enough as well, thank you again. To avoid any further weakness of resolve I grabbed one of Dad's red shop rags with the intent of covering the vise head and thus preventing any further disruptive eye-to-marble contact, sort of a marble execution blindfold.

I grabbed the next sacrifice from the tuna can and quickly, efficiently, clamped it into place between the vise jaws. Immediately I covered the captive marble and the gripping metal vise jaws with the shop rag and just as quickly I placed the vise handle into the proper horizontal striking position. I raised the mallet back over my head and let go with a fierce arcing blow. My eyes remained open this time to ensure that I made a direct and solid hit. The vise handle cranked down a full quarter of a turn with a rapid jerk! Simultaneously, with a resounding POP, BANG and shrieking CRACK, the trapped marble exploded into fine crystal dust within the hard fatal embrace of the vise jaws.

A moment of silence for a marble departed...

The glass dust remnants fell and drifted to the cement floor below like freshly falling multicolored snow. I stood motionless with the mallet in hand and tried to judge the effect, judge my feelings, after actually having done it. The bees were gone. They were as dead as stones. It was like an aerosol can of insecticide had been sprayed into each of my ears at the same time and filled my head with bee killing bug juice. Not a buzz to be heard. Relief.

Something else had disappeared as well. The escalating anger, the building rage towards Billy vanished along with the bees. Even the thought of Billy's absence at the appointed place and time seemed unimportant. Something else much more positive had taken possession of my mind. Maybe it was just the euphoric effect of finally releasing, letting go of, all the tension and anxiety. In a trance-like state of being I grabbed another marble from the tuna can and placed it into the jaws of the vise, covered it with the shop rag, properly placed the handle and smashed the mallet head home as the second sacrifice was sent on its way. Intellectually unaware but emotionally all-knowing, an inescapable charge, a wave of brilliant light, blasted right through me – freedom.

It was freedom from all of the self-imposed goals, release from all of the self-inflicted expectations and pressures, real or imagined, that I'd willingly submitted to over the past many months in order to attain and then maintain my position as the school's marble champion. At that moment I wasn't trying to relive the past or anticipate the future. I was alive and breathing only in that moment, standing on a chair in a basement, cracking a few marbles in a *Midget Mighty Moe* table vise. The letting go of those few marbles was no longer a doubt-ridden, painful ordeal, but rather a purging of all of my marble worries. It was self-granted permission to, temporarily, let it all go.

The fresh feeling washed over me like I was standing under the cool clear deluge of a waterfall on a hot and humid muggy day in August. The cement block walls of the basement gave way to clouds of purest white set against the deepest cobalt blue of a never-ending evening sky. The workbench became an altar high atop a rocky plateau on a snow-covered mountain. Before me on a granite pedestal was a *Giant Cat's-Eye* boulder a full ten feet in diameter with the twilight of the sunset shining through it from the back. The *Midget Mighty Moe* vise was made of solid gold and the red shop rag was a sparkling shroud made from woven strands of finest silk. The rubber mallet was a sledge of finest silver with Cat's-Eyes inlaid along the entire length of its dark oak handle. The mountain top plateau was pure white marble stone inlaid with thousands of miniature Cat's-Eye marbles. The remaining four marbles to be offered for sacrifice were each resting on small red velvet covered pedestals of their own in line next to the two empty stands for the already departed. With the dignity and pageantry due the occasion atop *Marble Peak*, at the foot of the all-knowing, all-seeing *Giant Cat's-Eye Marble*, the remaining four marbles were crushed in the embrace of the golden vise to the honor of all marbles and marble players past, present and future. It was an unexpected, unforeseen and surprisingly inspirational moment.

The sacrifices completed, the *Great Giant Marble* lifted and drifted off on the wind as it rose from its pedestal and elevated into the heights of the endless deep blue sky. As the *Giant Cat's-*

Eye disappeared into the clouds high above, I drifted away from *Marble Peak* as well and landed right back in the basement standing on the chair in front of my Dad's workbench. The rusty tuna can was empty, devoid of any marbles. A pile of fine glass dust rested on the concrete basement floor. The clear glass grains and the crumpled Cat's-Eyes mixed into a multicolored soft flowing drift three feet below the empty jaws of the vise.

Stepping down off the chair I put my hands into my pants pockets and stood looking down at the marble dust for a few moments of quiet contemplation. The basement was absolutely silent. I rediscovered the spared, the previously pardoned marble of a few minutes before. I pulled it from my pocket and held it up to the last rays of afternoon sunlight that streamed in through the basement window just above the workbench. The nicked and cratered surface of the old marble prismatically scattered the light as a multitude of projected rainbows spread warmly across my face.

It was fascinating to consider how a new marble would prism maybe one or two rainbows at once, maximum, while a battered, beaten and broken marble was capable of a dozen or more rainbows simultaneously from just one beam of light. As a marble got older and rougher, one type of ability and beauty was traded for another, like a caterpillar transforming into a butterfly.

The ultimate fate and duty of the one spared marble had become clear to me at once. Dad routinely saved small glass baby food jars to use as storage containers for nuts and bolts and the like and many empty spares were strewn near the back of the bench. Grabbing the only one that I could reach I unscrewed the tiny top off the tiny jar. Using a small piece of scrap sandpaper I carefully swept and then shoveled the drifted marble dust from the floor and into the jar. Having retrieved as much of the marble dust as physically possible I sat down on the chair. I took the single remaining intact marble and ever so gently placed it on top of the dusty remains of its six sacrificed companions inside of the jar. I slowly screwed the metal jar cap back in place thus creating a small but befitting shrine to preserve the memory of the moment.

The basement door swung open with squeaking hinges as Mom called down that supper was ready. I was physically and emotionally drained and just as equally relieved. I was free, for the moment anyway, and I felt better than I'd felt in weeks. The food for supper tasted pretty good. That night I slept the deep undisturbed sleep of a carefree little boy.

*

Chapter Eight:
Limbo

THE FOLLOWING DAY, Sunday, was peacefully uneventful. The morning surprise was that I skipped getting up and going to church. I was so dead asleep, so deep in unconscious rest, that I became invisible, non-existent, to the Sunday morning thoughts and concerns of my mother, my father and my brother. Not only did it work at school it apparently started to work at home just as well.

The strange personal ability to disappear right in front of Mrs. Goodchaulks while sitting at my desk daydreaming just a few feet in front of her, completely immune to her searching eyes and pesky questions had hitched a ride and come along home with me. I was rendered totally invisible to the eyes and thoughts of my parents and brother who got up, got dressed, ate breakfast, went out the door, hopped into the car and then drove to church that morning without ever once thinking to themselves or asking each other aloud, "Where's Mikey? Anybody seen Mikey?"

The question was how to call upon the mysterious subconscious talent at will and then produce enough of it to share it with the other kids. The very idea of me along with all the other kids in our classroom sitting at our desks in plain open view to the world and then, when our teacher turns her back to write on the blackboard, en masse, half the class transforms into a wavy transparency and the other half slips into a misty translucence before becoming – *BINK*! INVISIBLE: a neat trick. Watching Mrs. Goodchaulk's surprise as she'd turn back around and wonder where the heck everybody had gotten off too in the minute she had her back turned, while the entire class still sat at our desks right in front of of her, would be – interesting.

When I got up and found that I had the whole house to myself, still in my pajamas, I got myself a bowl of cereal and milk and sat down at the kitchen table for breakfast and a private first viewing of that Sunday's morning newspaper. Just me, my cereal, the paper and Kit Cat stretched out on his back atop the other end of the table waiting for any leftover milk. It was a perfect Sunday morning.

My thoughts drifted to the inevitable concerns regarding all the likely questions I was certain would be asked from well-meaning schoolmates as to how the "Big Match" turned out. I especially didn't look forward to repeating, probably dozens of times, that Billy had been a "no-show" and that the "Big Match" had just been a "Big Fizzle." I devised a plan of action, a standardized repeatable statement of fact for just such an eventuality at school the next day, when the rest of my family pulled up to the garage in the alley back home from church. They all walked in the kitchen through the back door with no visible signs of worry or concern with a "Hi honey" from Mom, like I'd been with them the whole time and had simply walked in from the car just ahead of them. Forget that I was sitting there in my PJ's with the paper, my cereal and the cat, I was still partially invisible, just a light wispy ghost image of myself, someone, something, vaguely familiar. My guess was that sometime later that day, while my mom was going about her Sunday routine, she'd abruptly come to a standstill, stop right in the middle of whatever she was doing and with a puzzled look on her face, take a quick look around and ask herself aloud, "Mikey? Where's Mikey?" A full several hours of delayed affect! Without a doubt I should have found a way to capture, collect and then pass that stuff around!

My predictions proved accurate as Monday arrived and with it a new school day. As a personal arithmetic exercise I'd kept track of how many times the question was asked about the outcome of the match that didn't happen. Through classes, lunch and three recesses I stopped counting after one-hundred-plus inquiries. Despite the repetitive negative news I imparted, the show of interest and regret had been gratifying. I never imagined that so many schoolmates knew or even cared. But each time I was asked I politely answered with the truth. Billy who? Billy where? Billy when? Billy – NO!

It had gotten down to the last few minutes of the afternoon recess before I finally succeeded in locating and then cornering a very evasive Wilbur Hunt who'd been either avoiding, running from or hiding from me all day long. I needed to hear firsthand what he'd heard about Billy from his little neighbor Frankie Hansen. Under direct questioning Wilbur reluctantly disclosed that he knew about Billy's unexplained absence within minutes after Frankie's escape from the alley under cover of the marauding *Chevy*. I pumped, I prodded and yes, even poked Wilbur (literally) a few times trying for any information, any hint which might have provided a clue as to Billy's whereabouts and his state of mind at the appointed time of the match. Wilbur only knew as much as Frankie Hansen and Frankie didn't know anything either so that left me with a whole lotta worry and effort for a whole lotta nothin'. I had no idea whether Billy wanted a rematch or not. The last hour of that school day was just as big a whole lotta nothin' as well. When the final bell signaled dismissal, the big match was still up in the air.

I took my usual exit out of the school building, the predictable path across the schoolyard and out the same school gate onto the never changing sidewalk on my rarely changing path home when, low and behold, leaning in the exact same place as one week earlier, his bike parked in the same spot, was Avenging Grace's very own disgrace, Billy Schoutenlauder, in person. With his hands jammed into his jacket pockets, nibbling on a long blade of grass that protruded from between his lips and bounced up and down with each movement of his grinding teeth, there stood the red-eyed pretender to the throne. I froze in place as I saw him before he noticed me. I did not expect Billy to be so bold as to make so public of an appearance in enemy territory so soon after such a shameful nonperformance as Saturday. Losing was one thing, in a marble match somebody always had to lose, but not even showing up and taking his chances, especially when the whole thing was his idea to start with, that was another matter entirely. It was ten times worse than losing. In losing at least yeah tried. By not showing up you'd lost before even trying. Billy's searching eyes found me as our icy stares met. I realized that I had nothing, NOTHING, to be timid about because, simply stated, I'd been there and he hadn't. If anyone had apologies to make or explanations to offer it was Billy, not me.

Frankie must have told him that I'd actually turned out ready to play. It must have really rubbed it in until it hurt, a fourth grader like Billy being put on the spot in front of his friends by a kindergarten kid like Frankie. His red eyes were indicative of his response to a full school day of the verbal abuse, biting condemnations and sharp stinging retributions he'd been subjected to by his classmates and school chums for his unexcused absence from Saturday's showdown. But, by the way he was leaning against the street light switch box, so damn sure of himself, it became immediately obvious to me that Billy wasn't going to apologize, explain or generally admit to anything, regardless of his less-than-honorable actions. Taking the initiative, I walked right up to Billy and head-on started the conversation off on a tactful note.

"So, Schoutenlauder, I need to see the note from your Mom, you know, the one that says you couldn't come out to play on Saturday!" I sarcastically twanged loud enough for everyone in close proximity to hear.

Billy abruptly lunged forward and assumed a standing position that placed his jacket zipper crowding my shirt buttons. The blade of grass he was chewing on was launched into the air with a spitting gasp as he double-dared me to repeat what I just said. The fact that Billy was a full six inches taller than me, not to mention that he outweighed me by twenty pounds, resulted in a slight adjustment in my course of approach. I rephrased my question in more diplomatic terms.

"Well Schoutenlauder, I was there. Waited for almost two hours. What happened? Where were you? Get lost or just forgot the way? All yeah needed to do was have little Frankie hold your hand and he would have gotten you there no problem!" I stated the fresh set of questions in an understated mix of mocking concern and fake disappointment, like I'd invited him to my birthday party and the rest of the guests and I waited for his arrival while the ice cream melted around the cake on our plates.

Billy's response was equally tactful and full of remorse.

"None of your damn business yeah little jerk! Listen yeah runt and listen good. Like I said before, I'll play you anytime, anywhere, just name it and I'll beat you outta every stinkin' marble you got. Got it!" Billy pleaded more than argued.

I fought the urge to answer in kind, like Billy really deserved, saying something to the effect that I'd name the time and place and he'd run as far away from that time and place as his legs would carry him, or, that the only way Billy could beat anybody out of their marbles was to beat them up out of their marbles. Instead, I held my breath for a few seconds, stepped back one-step and looked down letting my patience and restraint be the better part of my valor and skill at that moment. I looked back up and locked my eyes directly on his and answered with strong and quiet conviction and determination that arose all on its own from the depths of my little person core.

"Sure Billy, sure. But remember this. I don't know how good you are or how good you think you are, I – DON'T – CARE because either way there isn't anything, ANYTHING, you think you can do or actually do with a marble that worries me one bit. When we play, win or lose, I'll show you stuff, I'll do things to your marbles that you've NEVER seen! I'll do amazing, unbelievable things that I've been able to do with a marble from the first day I held one in my hand! I'll do things with a marble that you could never have imagined were even possible in ten, or twenty, or even a HUNDRED of your stupid life times!"

I poured it on and then dug it in really good. I ground it in with my heel really hard right into the center of his big phony ego. Billy stood there like he'd just gotten a good tongue lashing from the head priest at his school. Despite the explosive potential of the situation I stood my ground hard and fast. I'm not even sure where the words I spoke came from exactly but out they came and with stunning effect. A crowd had gathered as Billy and I exchanged our heated words. When I finished my little speech everyone stood silent and dumb-founded and, just like Billy, they were all staring at me like "what the hell, where did that all come from?"

Billy didn't fully grasp what had just happened but the rest of the kids from my school who were standing around did. They heard the verbal exchange loud and clear and then understood unmistakenly why I was school marble champ. As the incident deescalated I caught my breath, stood down and internally fought to maintain the appearance of being Billy's equal in all respects both physical and psychological. I fought the urge to retreat and crumble into a little kid who was scared of being beaten up by a bigger kid, the thoughts of which had crept back into the back of my mind at that moment.

Billy caught his breath as well.

"This Saturday, same time, same place, same rules and you'd better show up!" he elaborated.

That last crack was totally for effect on the small crowd that had gathered and witnessed our exchange. Billy was trying to save face and cast aspersions upon my character by having the unmitigated gall, the nerve to imply, to suggest in public, that I was the one, not he, who hadn't shown up for the match on Saturday. Schoutenlauder was such a mug. But I couldn't let him get clean away after shooting off his mouth like that so I responded with a tenacity and force of my own.

"Sure thing Billy. Same time, same place, same rules and if you want a crayon drawn map of how to get there and a picture book on telling time just ask little Frankie. I'm sure he could handle it and help you out!" I chided back.

Billy reared up like he was about to deliver a knuckle sandwich to the region of my face around my mouth but he held up and backed away, quickly walking to his bike as he tried to get in the last word.

"You bet pipsqueak! Be ready to lose, if you show up that is," Billy bleated sarcastically.

Resolutely, I answered back in a steady tone.

"I'm not worried Schoutenlauder. I'm not worried about anything at all."

It was that voice again as everyone around me stepped back a another half-step and listened intently with slightly raised eyebrows as the unnerving calmness and earth-firm steadiness of my answer even caused a nervous slip-and-a-hitch in Billy's retreating steps.

Having had my say, using the gathered home crowd to my advantage, I'd successfully reached a verbal stalemate with Billy and maybe even a slight edge as he hopped back on his bike and took off down the sidewalk. Several dozen insulting last word possibilities swarmed in my head (including that new favorite word) but only some of them fell through into my mouth for delivery. They all got sorta' jammed up at the door to my vocal cords. The only thing that managed to slip out was a mumbled garbled mess.

"I'll be ready yeah stupid shi – ."

My unfinished garbled response sounded like all my marbles were in my mouth instead of the sock tied to my belt.

I knew, then and there, without a shade of doubt, come hell or high water, that I was ready, I knew it in my bones. Billy's unexpected appearance and his unrepentant tone and attitude started the bees buzzing again. But this time they weren't going crazy. It was just a low steady powerful hum that was in sync with my desires and goals, not fighting against them. They became a source of power and energy rather than a distraction or obstruction. They became something that I would use, something that would help instead of hinder. This time, the only way the buzzing would be silenced permanently was to face Billy that coming Saturday and beat him right out of his shorts, not to mention all of his marbles. I'd clean him out so completely he'd have to beg for his clothes back. But I'd refuse so he'd have to scrounge around for an old cardboard box to wear home, in disgrace.

I swore to myself, then and there, standing in the middle of the sidewalk, as Billy's presence faded into the distance, that regardless of the course of events between then and the upcoming Saturday, I'd play the best marbles of my young life when it really counted. If Billy even played only halfway fair, or even if he turned out to be a total lousy cheater, I'd still take him for every single marble he brought to the match. That stupid jerk didn't have a clue, hadn't the foggiest idea, of what he was in for.

My growing confidence, my determination, tempered but did not eliminate a re-emerging anger and contempt for Billy. I'd fostered a total disregard for any marble-playing skills or abilities that he might have. He could be, in fact, a real marble ace but I'd make him look like an unskilled, rank beginner. I allowed that Monday evening to pass in a reasonably peaceful fashion, all light duty stuff. The buzzing bees were there all right but they were manageable, under control and doing their part to help as much as anything.

Yet, deeper down, below my conscious sensory levels, those little bees were just being what they couldn't help being, energetic little bees. Those little hummers were as busy as ever manufacturing little picture stories that would play out in my head just as soon as I drifted off to sleep, springing their trap on my wondering subconscious. The fact that I'd never played Billy or ever seen him play or even knew anybody who'd played him proved to be fertile ground from which the seeds of paranoia grew and blossomed into one of my nocturnal horror shows.

Monday night supper was tame enough, I thought. Just a super deluxe everything-on-it delivered pizza pie for Mom's night off. I didn't realize that all the spicy sausage and extra pepperoni were also feeding the bees, providing them with all of the energy and ammunition required for a midnight assault on my psyche. Food for thought was one thing (that would be fish) but fuel for nightmares was the unintended result. Pizza Pie was supposed to be a healthy and wholesome mix of all the food pyramid ingredients. But being who I was, in the circumstances I found myself, all the extra everything on that pie made Monday night dreamland a very unhealthy place to be.

With a three-big-slices-full-stomach, a drowsy head, and *Fred's House of Pizza Pie* still fresh on my breath, I fell off to sleep earlier than usual. I awoke trudging through ankle deep sand in an expansive kettle shaped valley surrounded by towering sand dunes. I stood at the center of a naturally formed sand bowl enclosed on four sides by large rolling sand dunes with tops at least one-hundred feet above my head. It was a dry and desolate place with not a single piece of green foliage in sight. Just tan sand and high altitude ice crystal cirrus clouds drifted across the tall blue sky. In front of me, lying on top of the sand, was a thin metal ring exactly ten feet (to the exact nearest thousandth of an inch) in diameter. The precise diameter of the ring stood out as important for some unexplained reason. I stood alone at the edge of the ring, marble sock tied to my belt, as the wind blew transparent veils of sand from the tops of the surrounding dunes. I knew I would meet Billy at some point in the austere landscape that unfolded before me. I waited silently and alone. It wasn't a long wait.

Through one of the higher valleys between the dunes to my front Billy appeared. He dragged a giant white sock behind him over the sand. He gripped the top of the big sock with both hands over his right shoulder and leaned forward from the effort. The sock trailed twenty feet behind him over the sand, it was that big. As he approached I could make out large round bulges in the long dragging sock that rolled and weaved with the sandy terrain. My reaction was that there couldn't be marbles in that big sock, not marbles that big. But, if they were marbles and if they were actually as big as they appeared to be, Billy shouldn't be able to drag even one of them, much less all of them over the loose and drifting sand. They would be too massive, too heavy. When it came to marbles I was always learning, even in my sleep, that anything goes in marble dreamland and especially in the nightmare desert where I dreamed myself to be at that moment.

Besides dragging the big sock full of big marbles, Billy was dressed big for the occasion as well. He resembled a drawing of *Merlin the Magician* I'd seen in a fairy tale book in Bookbender's school library. With a long flowing dark blue robe, a tall pointed dark blue hat, both of which were covered in painted white stars and yellow-gold crescent moons, Billy approached shuffling through the sand. I untied my marble sock and grasped it firmly with both hands, ready for action, as Billy stopped, robe, hat and giant marble sock and all, at the opposite side of the ring.

Lightly huffing and puffing, mumbling strange sounding incantations under his breath, Billy looked up at me with a start, earnestly surprised, as if finding me waiting there was completely unexpected. He looked down and pointed at the full, but normal sized, marble sock clutched in my hands and started to giggle under his breath. I looked at my marble sock as I held it out in front of me and gave it a slow twirl for a quick inspection. Everything on my side seemed to be in normal order so, bewildered, I stared at Billy who turned and pulled a big round thing from his big floppy sock. It was a marble all right, three times bigger than my own head, a marble that floated and bounced in Billy's hands as if it were weightless. My first thoughts and then worst fears were confirmed. The huge long sock was loaded to the brim with abnormally giant marbles on a scale to match his abnormally giant sock, each one as light as an air filled plastic beach ball.

   Billy held his giant marble in the air above his head with his right hand and pointed at me with his left as his face went red from giggling spasms. It was then that I realized that it wasn't only Billy's laughter that echoed across and down from the mountainous dunes, it was laughter that also rolled down from the tops of the dunes. Jesters, the characters you'd see as jokers in a set of playing cards, were stationed in pairs atop of each of the four surrounding mountains of sand. They all danced and wiggled like they were suspended from sets of overhead puppet strings. They were, unmistakenly, the source of all the extra giggles.

   Gazing from dune top to dune top I tried to stare the uninvited jokers into silence. Whether it was my intense stare or, by coincidence, just part of the unfolding nightmare's master plan, the unwarranted laughter subsided as dying echoes carried away on the wind. While I was busy staring down his jester companions, Billy, without creating a sound, without lifting a finger and apparently without moving an inch, emptied his big sock of all the big marbles and spread them in a perfectly curved semicircle behind him on the sand. "Impressive," I dreamed.

   The moment our eyes connected, Billy's face burst into the unnaturally biggest, weirdest, psycho grin I ever dreamed. He startted to laugh and just couldn't stop. He was a big dark blue bag of compressed laughing gas. He could've laughed for days, nonstop, without even getting close to tipping over for the lack of oxygen. I stood there transfixed, trying to divine any clue as to what might transpire next. Then the laughing just stopped and Billy stood silent with his hands behind his back, chin to his chest with his eyes staring at me from the top of their sockets and through his big bushy eyebrows. Billy, the eight dune-top jester jokers and I all stood in a silent standoff.

　　Billy's maniac grin covered his entire face like a bad rash. From behind his back Billy produced one of his large bouncy marbles. Tossing it up and down in front of my face, he peeked out and around from behind the lighter-than-air Cat's-Eye and spoke his first understandable words.

　　"Ready to lose, pipsqueak? Those tiny marbles of yours look so...so pitiful. I almost feel like a thief for taking them from you. But here you are of your own accord."

　　"I'm more ready than you think," was my sure and brave response.

　　"Well then, I'll just roll my marble to the center of the ring and I'll even give you the first shot. Fair enough?" Billy offered.

　　"Fair enough," I nodded as I wondered what sort of trickery Billy had up his two very long and very roomy sleeves.

　　Billy the magician gently, lightly, rolled his oversized marble to the center, the precise geometric center of the ring. It floated over the sand inside the ring so lightly it seemed that at any second it would lift up and blow away on the breeze. The big Cat's-Eye came to rest a scant five feet away from my side of the circle. I knelt down in the soft sand and pulled out one of my best, a multicolored solid Aggie boulder, and assumed a ready-to-shoot posture. I could have hit that big marble with my eyes closed from a hundred feet away. Something was up. I looked up at Billy, whose insane-looking face stared down at me from just above the giant target marble in the center of the ring. Seven of the eight jester jokers moved to scattered positions on the dune above and behind Billy, with the eighth standing above and behind on the dune to my back.

　　I re-aimed my first shot, as five feet in front of me, at eye level, was the biggest marble target I ever dreamed up. All I had to do was hit it, any part of it, with the marble that I held in my hand, the proverbial "broad side of a barn" scenario. I nervously chuckled to myself that it was a cinch. The only potential problem I imagined was that I didn't have a sock big enough to hold all of the oversized winnings I was certain would come my way. Maybe, I dreamed, Billy would be a gracious loser and lend me his big sock to drag my winnings home.

The sand inside the playing circle was smooth like glass and solid to the touch, perfect for playing marbles. Taking careful aim, just to make sure, I fired my first shot. My Aggie boulder rolled strong, straight and true. Four feet, three feet, then two feet, then one-foot from a direct hit when the sand opened up and swallowed my marble whole, just before contact with the target. Billy giggled under his breath. Shocked, disbelieving, I looked up over the big target marble and discovered the chuckling Billy holding my lost marble in his right hand, firmly clasped between his thumb and forefinger, holding it up for inspection like a bug he'd just snatched from the air in mid-flight. He dropped the captured marble, unceremoniously, into the giant pocket in the right side of his robe.

"Looks to me like you missed, pipsqueak. I think you should try again and this time take more care with your aim!" he shouted as his head recoiled backwards mechanically like a cannon after firing his booming laughter.

Confused and uncertain how exactly my first shot had strayed, I retrieved another marble and prepare to shoot again. I fired my next shot, then another, then another and then still more, again, again and again and each time the result was the same. Just as my marble would close in for the sure strike the solid sandy earth liquefied and opened up like a baby bird's hungry beaked mouth and swallowed my marble whole. The marble would then promptly reappear in Billy's hand and then just as promptly disappear into his robe pocket. Finally, inevitably, the game was coming to an end. I was playing on a magic ring, in a magical world, in a mystical time warp with Billy the controlling magician. It was his world. There was no way for me to win. There was only defeat waiting for me as long as Billy controlled the ring.

"You cheated," I whispered in frustration.

"You seem to have lost most of your marbles. What a shame. You seemed so confident when you started," Billy commented condescendingly.

"Confident, nothing. You cheated. It's the only way you could win," I steamed.

As the words left my mouth, my remaining marbles flew from my marble sock into the air and landed scattered on the sandy surface inside the ring. One by one they disappeared into the sand like breadcrumbs being sucked from the surface of a pond by hungry goldfish, only to rematerialize a second later in the hands of the gleeful, maniacal *Merlin the Mystical* Schoutenlauder.

"You lose, you lose, yes, yes, all you can do is lose," Billy singsonged as he picked my marbles from the air as they rematerialized and dropped them into his big pocket.

I tried to get my bruised psyche out and away from the bad dream scene but the magic words remained illusive and out of reach. I stammered and babbled hoping to stumble upon that one special utterance that would led the way out before my dream life led to mortal peril. I turned away from the circle to run but found my way blocked by one of the marble-eyed skeletons that made it for that trip as well. I spun back to face the ring to search for an alternate escape route only to discover the other half of the bony duo sitting atop the big marble in the center of the ring waiting for me with open arms and a ice cold embrace. I covered my face and eyes with my folded arms in hopes that such action was the secret solution, the exercise necessary to make all of the apparitions disappear.

When I uncovered my eyes I was alone. Billy was gone, the marble ring was gone and the giant marble and the skeletons had departed for nether worlds unknown. I stood solitary and alone in the sand at the bottom of the giant sand bowl. While I had the chance, I thought it best (no kidding) to leave. I tried to walk, to lift my feet which had sunk into the sand, but I couldn't move, not an inch. I looked down to find that I had no feet, only solid hard sand up to my knees. The soft bubbling sand that had no trouble sucking in and swallowing my marbles had turned to compressed, rock-hard concrete. I was cemented in place. With a resounding, booming echo, as if each of the four surrounding sand dunes were a giant speaker, a voice called down to me from the top of the sand dune that faced me head-on.

"Going somewhere pipsqueak?"

It was Billy standing next to the biggest marble that I'd ever dreamed or imagined, asleep or awake. It must have been at least – at least – twenty-five feet in diameter: it was gigantic!

"You can't leave now, just when all the real fun is about to begin!" he cackled.

"Fun! FUN FOR WHO?" I shouted back as I struggled to pull my lower legs and feet free.

"Why – fun for you, fun for me, fun for all of us!" came the answer. "Look around, pipsqueak, and you'll see just how much fun we're all going to have!" Billy commanded.

Next to Billy and his giant marble stood two of the jester jokers, one to each side of the giant Cat's-Eye and each sporting an oversized Cat's-Eye boulder where their heads were supposed to be. Looking from dune top to dune top I discovered two identical marble headed jester jokers per dune, each pair with a giant marble placed between them. These four big marbles were not the airy bouncy type that Merlin Billy had dragged around in his giant sock. These big marbles were the real deal. Their weight and mass were evident even at a distance, as they had sunk into the sand where they rested on top of each dune.

"I'm ready for a really good time. How 'bout you, pipsqueak?" Billy shouted down.

"NooOOO," my voice wound upward in a rising crescendo.

"Good! Goodie-goodie-GOOD-GOOD!" came Billy's shouted answer.

Billy's maniac theatrics were equal to the levels of dangerous fun and dastardly good times that he was alluding to. Simultaneous with his signal each pair of marble heads released their respective giant marbles with the old heave-ho. The four giant Cat's-Eye boulders eased forward from their perches, slowly at first, then with a rapidly building force, momentum and speed, aided by the steep inclines of the dunes. Each of the big marbles was released in slightly delayed succession and at slightly odd angles to one another so that each giant crystal could roll over me in their turn without crashing into one another. The marble angle geometry was as clear and precise as any shot I would've worked out in my own head. My estimation of the mass of the big marbles was also exact as they each left well defined and deeply indented rolling furrows in their wakes as they plowed their way over and through the sand in my direction. First I'd be run over from the front and then run down from the left and then roller squashed again from behind and then finished off for good from the right. The old one-two-three-four rolled-over squasherrooo! I struggled helplessly for my freedom from the sand but escape was proving to be impossible. The end was near and getting closer every second. I was about to be turned into little boy mush, crushed four ways from Tuesday as each giant roller was to have a go at the champ.

At the last second, by desperate accident, the key to my freedom was found; a scream, a bloodcurdling dream-scream. It was the old acoustic defense. As each giant rolling marble closed in for the mashing crunch they each drastically shrunk in size. They reduced in size and mass down to the diameter and weight of soft bouncy beach balls. As they made final impact they simply, gently bounced up against my legs and rolled aside on the sand.

I awoke standing on my bed with clenched fists, eyes clamped shut and my mouth frozen wide-open with drool dripping from the center of my lower lip. As to whether or not I'd actually screamed was an unanswered question. There were no other sounds coming from the rest of the house, no Mom or Dad or Robert running to my room with bedpost clubs, ready to rescue their littlest son and brother from some stranger who'd invaded my room or equally and conversely the sound of running feet as they all fled from the house for their lives hoping that what had gotten me would not get them. Not a sound from anywhere. Either everyone was too sound asleep, or I'd never screamed at all, or I had screamed so horribly that I'd scared everyone to petrified stone in their beds.

A quick and cautious look around my room revealed no sand, no marble headed jester jokers, no giant bouncy beach ball marbles and no Merlin's robe or pointy hat, just my room. I needed to walk to the bathroom to take in some fresh water for my sand desert parched throat and put out some used water from my adrenalin-saturated kidneys and bladder. I tried to jump down off my bed in one swift and silent motion but in my sleepy condition I jumped and fell, none too silently or swiftly, flat on my face, hitting the bedroom floor with a resounding THUD and GROAN!

I found that my feet and lower legs up to and including my knees were hopelessly entangled in my bed sheets. I kicked my legs frantically to get free from the clutching bedding but they just wouldn't let go! I lay back down on the floor and calmed myself before I did any real damage to the linens or myself. Mom would not have understood shredded sheets, all thinly ripped and ready to become kite tails.

Walking towards the upstairs bathroom, groping my way through the dark upstairs hallway, stopping to listen at the other bedroom doors, I wondered what had ever happened to all the nice dreams I used to have. Dreams about fishing with Dad (?), weekends with endless cartoons on the TV and floating down rivers of root beer and ice cream in a boat with giant bending straws for drinking and long plastic spoons for paddling. It was encouraging, however, that the bad dream ended on a better, harmless note as there was no chance of being crushed into mush by soft bouncy beach balls disguised as marbles in real or dream life episodes.

I concluded that the deeper meaning of the dream was my subconscious minimizing the conscious hyper-imagined threat that Billy actually represented. He wasn't the tough guy marble master he pretended to be but was actually a rather small, inconsequential and harmless bouncy beach ball type guy. But, nevertheless, I promised myself that if Billy showed up at the match that coming Saturday dragging a giant marble sock behind him in the dirt I'd forfeit on the spot, toss him my sock full of marbles and head for home.

I didn't get much more sleep that night and I looked it the next morning. It didn't matter that I took a twenty-minute shower. It didn't matter that I combed my hair and brushed my teeth three times each. It didn't matter that I changed my pants, shirt, socks and underwear twice. I still looked and felt like I'd spent a cold rainy night without a blanket curled up on the bare hard plywood floor inside of a doghouse. I was six years old and I had bags under my eyes. I learned to accept that the occasional sleepless night was the price to be paid for being the champ. It was life at the top and few my age were privileged or cursed enough to understand just how rewarding and just how tough it could be all at the same time. Feeling like I'd been awake for three days and nights straight, the prospect of struggling through another school day without adequate rest and sleep to hold me up seemed, at the outset, and unbearable task.

My head floated in a haze while my feet stumbled and dragged into school. I drifted through the morning classes in a state of exhaustion-induced euphoria. I was so tired that by the time it was lunch hour I wasn't able to sleep even if I'd had the chance. I had a case of terminal wakefulness. My eyes were too tired to close. Through reading, arithmetic and science my eyes stared straight ahead into the back of the kid sitting in front of me with my peepers locked open. It took all of my effort just to blink. To add to my overtired, confused and miserable state of existence, halfway through the morning it clouded over and started to rain, which meant that we'd all be staying in for noon recess. It was no big loss considering that I'd spent the morning recess aimlessly wandering around the playground without a warm comfortable hole to fall into.

During lunch my mouth momentarily stopped working. The food I was trying to chew just sat there in my mouth, unswallowed. I used a good share of my remaining strength reserves to keep my mouth shut and prevent the food inside from falling out of my drooping yap and out onto the lunch table. Somehow I managed to make it through lunchtime without choking or without drooling food into my shirt pocket. The little bits and morsels of food I did manage to get down did make me feel slightly better (substituting carbohydrates for sleep) despite the fact that the food consumed was swallowed in whole, unchewed chunks.

On the way back to the classroom for indoor recess I asked permission to make a pit stop in the boy's lavatory before returning to a half-hour of checkers, picture books and games of *Old Maid*. I had my ever-trusty marble sock tied to my belt, as four other guys and me pressed through the lavatory door all at once like a clump of soggy dirt being shoved through a pipe. Inside we dispersed and each of us stepped up to a urinal. I was so out of it that I was unaware of the faulty knot that held my marble sock to my belt. It had been a bad knot from the start that had been originally tied at home that morning in my "getting ready for school with no sleep" stupor.

Being overtired, I deduced, made one pee longer than normal. Everyone else had finished, zipped up, washed hands and departed from the lavatory for the classroom. I stood alone at the urinal waiting to finish. As I zipped-up my fly and stepped back from the tiny porcelain shower (as we called them) the loose knot in my marble sock top gave way completely. My one-and-only's fell to the floor with a gritty ringing crunch. Many of that day's selected best took full advantage of the opportunity to pop out of the top of the sock and rapidly scattered to the four corners of the restroom like they were running away from the eyes-covered counting searcher during a game of hide-and-seek. They playfully bounced, crackled and boinged their ways over the hard ceramic tile floor on an indoor recess of their own.

My marble sock lay half-empty on the bathroom floor while I sleepily chased around the lavatory trying to collect the runaways. Luckily for me I was still alone in the john at the time. I would have certainly looked and absolutely felt the fool if anyone had been present to witness the champ hopping around the lavatory like a monkey chasing sweet tasty grapes rolling across the floor. Having collected all of the readily visible marbles I walked back to the spot where the marble sock rested on the floor and redeposited what I'd managed to find.

When I picked up and jostled the far-from-full-sock it became immediately apparent that there were still a good many missing. I checked and re-checked everywhere, all the corners, down the entry hallway and even around the bases of the toilets inside the metal stalls but the missing marbles continued to escape detection. Baffled, I returned to the spot of the original accident and started over from the beginning.

Standing at the exact spot where the marble sock had hit the floor, I slowly revolved in a complete circle, letting my eyes scan the entire visible floor area of the lavatory without a single wayward marble in sight. The mystery of the missing marbles intensified when my turning search circle once again brought me face to face with the little porcelain shower that I'd just finished using.

The unavoidable, the inevitable, the thought of last resort crept into my head. I slowly lowered my searching gaze and took a step forward, hoping that it wouldn't, that it couldn't be true. I peered down into the urinal as my worst fears were confirmed. There, surrounding the drain at the bottom of the urinal that I'd just used, were the dozen missing marbles circled around the drain strainer like a group of scouts huddled round a smoldering camp fire after a rainstorm. My first instinct was to simply, boldly, reach in and grab them as fast as I could regardless of any real or imagined biological consequences. I was still the only one in the restroom and any such drastic action would have been comletely justifiable and would have remained my own scary and disgusting little secret.

    Calm reason took charge. Settling down and thinking more clearly I recalled that the entire urinal system was on some sort of timer and flushed itself with fresh water every few minutes. Seeing how it hadn't flushed since I'd entered and used the lavatory several minutes before, I logically figured that it was due at any second. I took up a standing watch a few feet back from the urinal in question and patiently waited it out. Seconds started to seem like minutes and minutes started to seem like hours as the fresh water flush failed to materialize. I started to feel mildly anxiousness which gave way to severe anxiety which transformed into a sweaty panic which finally broke down and completely collapsed into shear desperation. I was compelled to affect a rescue, fresh water flush or not.

I stepped forward and was reaching into the urinal to put an end to the drama when the entrance door to the lavatory banged open and a crowd of loud second graders crashed their way in. To save face and have my predicament escape detection, I quickly moved to the nearest sink, turned on the water and started to comb my hair while looking into the mirror. Each one of the second graders took a spot at a vacant urinal and did their duty. Luckily, they were all so busy yakking it up that the kid who used the urinal that I'd used didn't even notice that he was peeing all over twelve of my best marbles. I cringed at the thought but I was helpless to act. It was a certainty that the indignity that my marbles were enduring would absolutely be the final insult and that they'd arrange repayment, in full and in kind, as soon as the opportunity presented itself. Little did I know that such repayment was almost at hand.

The second graders walked from the urinals and rushed to the available sinks in a single clumpy group, washed and dried their hands and departed from the lavatory as noisily and tightly packed as they'd entered. I reluctantly walked back to the urinal to find, as feared, that the twelve little crystal scouts had waded their way through another rainstorm.

They were dripping wet. Grabbing marbles from a urinal that were wet with my own pee was one thing but grabbing them from the urinal when they were soaking wet from someone else's pee was pushing the limits. But, that had been it, enough had been enough, as my self-respect regained the upper hand and I reached for my marbles.

I wasn't two inches from the rescue when the lavatory door banged open again and in strolled Henry Hairboni, the school's assistant custodian. Henry was a twenty-nine-year-old teenager of a man whose tall, thin, sharply chiseled facial features and head of jet black greased back hair would have fit in with any junior class at any local high school. In with him came his handy-dandy ready for any eventuality janitor's utility cart that he towed, pushed and sometimes danced with everywhere he went in the building. Henry seemed a good sort whose tough exterior persona was an all-too-transparent mix of momma's boy, grandma's boy, favorite auntie's boy and "hoping to have girl friend soon overly compensating phony cool boy."

One could always tell when Henry passed by the classroom in the hallway, even with the classroom door closed, because you'd hear the latest *Top 40* hit that he was humming to himself. Henry was proud of his work and his personality, his life force, projected school janitor for now, "famous rock-'n'-roller make-out king" any day now. That day, at that moment, Henry sort of quick-stepped into the lavatory pushing his handy-dandy cleaning cart in front of him with his waist as he combed his hair back with his free hands. He danced into the boys' lavatory whistling number seven on that week's hit parade.

All the close calls in the previous minutes proved to be too much and when combined with my physical and emotional fatigue a paralyzing exasperation held my exhausted body in a firm grip. I was unable to decide and, consequently, unable to act. Should I plead for help, should I go back to the sink and stall in hopes that Henry would soon be on his way without noticing the marbles, or should I just walk away from the twelve stranded marbles? I didn't know. There was no decision forthcoming from my tired and tangled brain so I just froze, in place, prepared to face the music, *Top 40* or not.

Henry steadily whistled his way in to find me standing three feet in front of the urinal with my head down and my arms folded across my chest. He stopped whistling and took a few puzzled moments to consider what exactly the situation was with the little silent kid he'd just come across standing in the lavatory. Henry slowly walked along the far wall to my back and kept staring at me as he pushed his cart. He was puzzled that I hadn't done anything to acknowledge his presence in some way. I had nothing to say and no place to go so I just simply stayed put, standing motionless and silent.

Henry parked his cart along the far wall in the corner and walked up to my left side. He bent down and looked at me in profile, stared at the left side of my face, checking me out. Henry was used to seeing and hearing all kinds of weird and unusual stuff that happened to kids, and what kids did, while at school. I slowly looked to my left and reluctantly returned his gaze with my eyes only, my arms still folded across my chest, my body stiff and rigid.

"You all right kid? You sick or something? You aren't going to lose it all over the floor are yeah buddy?"

"No," I whispered.

"Then what is the trouble here my man? Why are you standing here like some sorta' little stiff?"

With my head still down, I sheepishly unfolded my arms and pointed with my right hand to the urinal.

"There's the problem," I stated.

Henry stood upright, shuffled in place, squinted his eyes as he looked at the urinal. At first he didn't see the marbles, so surmising on his own, jumping to conclusions, he figured that for some reason or another I had to take a pee and couldn't. He then extrapolated upon his assumptions further and decided that I was indeed ill or I was, for some inexplicable reason, afraid of using the urinal. He summoned up his concerns and ideas rather matter-of-factly.

"You mean you can't pee?"

"NO – no, that's not it," I loudly whispered back letting my dissatisfaction with his theory show.

"I dropped somethings in there and I can't get them out," I reluctantly confessed.

Henry's puzzled look went curious as he reached into his work shirt chest pocket and pulled out his glasses. His glasses were black frames handed down from his deceased Grandpa: a gift from Grandma for Grandma's boy. Henry had his own prescription lenses put in the frames. It was a twenty-year-old guy's "close but no cigar" imitation of the then current *Buddy Holly* look. There was no mistaking it, these were real Grandpa glasses. These were even more Grandpa-like glasses than my own grandpa wore. When he put on the glasses you'd swear his hair around the edges was turning gray and when he took them off again the emerging gray would transition back to black, all right before your eyes. It was just one more roadblock, just another impediment, on Henry's journey towards rock-'n'-roll fame and real live girlfriends.

He stepped in real close to the urinal in question, adjusted the glasses on the bridge of his nose, "ahhhaaaed," and then stepped back with his hands on his hips and his forehead pointed to the ceiling as he glared at me through the lower half of his lenses.

"Those your marbles?"

"Yes Mr. Hairboni and I'd like to get them back if I could," I pleaded.

"Oh, you would, would yeah?"

"Yes sir. Think we can do it?" I half-asked and half-begged inserting the "we" hoping to imply that I was willing to help.

"Yeah know kid, there isn't supposed to be any game playing in here. I'd like to know how they got in there in the first place. Well – you going to tell me, or what?" Mr. Hairboni commanded.

"Well, my sock here came loose from my belt and then a bunch of them rolled in there, that's all. There was no game playing going on at all, nothing like that at all. They just fell in there by accident," I politely, innocently explained.

Henry started pacing back and forth at my left side and used the opportunity to get his point across and impress upon me that he was more valuable to the school than most people, especially little student people like me, were willing to give him credit for.

"I got more trouble everyday with you guys dropping and leaving all kinds of stuff in the toilets, the bubblers, floor drains and just about everywhere else things can be put, dropped, rolled, tossed and lost. Geez man, you name it and I've found it and in the darnedest places too! I'm thinking I should turn you over to Wagermann and let him deal with you."

Geez, all I needed for a perfect day was for Wagermann to get in on it. Why not run to the library and tattle to Old Lady Bookbender so she could get in on the action too. She was always up for a student flogging on a moment's notice. All the time Henry was babbling, blubbering and pacing away he was waving and bouncing his hands and arms in the air like an orchestra conductor. After he finished blowing off steam and dumping on me that month's accumulated wrath and frustration, he stood up straight and placed his thin bony hands in his pockets. Thus vented and cooling down he stood silent to let his impromptu lecture soak in.

I remained motionless, standing in the same spot that I'd already stood in for close to five minutes as Henry Hairboni stared a hole into the left side of my head. None of what he'd said soaked in. The words from his little speech all just beaded up on the side of my head like so many water droplets on the back of a duck because I was just too damn tired and frustrated to care. All the energy I had left was focused on the marbles in the urinal and on why the hell that damn urinal system hadn't flushed itself with clean water in all that time! Of all the times for the system to take an unscheduled break it had to be that day, that hour, those minutes! I'd spent a sleepless night before running from one nightmare only to come to school and walk right into another one.

As if the whole absurd situation up to that point wasn't complicated and ludicrous enough, the entrance door to the lavatory banged open again. I momentarily envisioned Old Lady Bookbender, not waiting for a formal invitation to the spectacle, inviting herself in on a surprise raid on the boys' lavatory in search of overdue library books with the idea, the hope, of catching the offenders with their pants down, as it were. I could tell it wasn't Bookbender because she didn't have cleats on the bottom of her shoes, but Principal Wagermann did! It hit me like a half-dollar size mud ball, with a big stone embedded in the middle, squarely in the back of the head.

My first thought was to run for one of the toilet stalls and lock myself inside. No chance. I was too deflated and too tired. My legs were solid lead molded to the floor. I entertained the thought of creating a diversion by passing out, fainting, just tipping over out cold on the spot, or, much worse and to Henry's disgust and dismay, losing my lunch all over his clean lavatory floor.

Wagermann entered the open area of the lavatory from the entry hallway, and walked right up to one of the sinks and started to wash his hands. Maybe Henry and I, standing like two wax figures in front of the urinals, didn't seem unusual at first, or maybe Wagermann had a lot of things in his mind and thought we were just using the facilities. As he looked up and into the mirror above the sink, he discovered that Henry and I were not using the urinals and that we were standing too close together and too far away. He realized that we were just both standing there and intently staring at one of the urinals in particular. Wiping his

Keepers Weepers

hands dry on paper toweling he ripped from the wall dispenser, he walked up to us on my right and looked at the urinals, trying to discern the focus of our attention. Wagermann turned to Henry and nodded a what's up look. Henry leaned back and as officiously and as grammatically correct as he knew how, informed Principal Wagermann of the situation as he understood it.

"It seems, Mr. Wagermann, that this young man has gone and carelessly dropped some of his marbles into the urinal. I told him that there was no game playing allowed in here, but he claims it was an accident."

Wagermann looked down at me and then leaned forward and peered into the urinal adjusting his glasses to make certain of what he was seeing as he finished wiping his hands dry. He stood back up tall and straight, looked at Henry and then back at me as we both continued to stare into the urinal.

The three of us just stood there, momentarily and yet eternally jointly connected to that moment in time and space, each in our own place and each one of us for our own reasons, staring into the urinal as the urinal and the stranded marbles around the drain strainer stared back. All of the elements were present for a real high-powered drama just waiting to unfold and play out.

"How did this happen Mr. Archer?" Wagermann inquired.

Why is it that adults, operating in an official capacity, whose job it was to deal with children, choose to call them "Mister" and "Miss" like they are adults too, when from the beginning the outcome will be that they will be treated like children anyway?

"It was an accident, just like I told Mr. Hairboni. My sock came loose, dropped from my belt and those few rolled in by the drain." I explained as I pointed. "I wasn't playing in here at all or nothing like that. It was just an accident," I recounted as a matter of fact.

I hated having to plead and beg to be believed. Whatever happened to innocent until proven guilty, or, was it guilty until proven guilty?

"I see, but I thought we'd discussed being more careful and not carrying your marbles with you everywhere inside the school building," Wagermann countered.

"Yes sir," I answered with the breathy words echoing in the tile bathroom.

"Well, Mr. Hairboni, would it be too much trouble to ask that you secure Mr. Archer's marbles from the clutches of the urinal and, you know, clean them up a bit, aahh, actually, clean them up a lot?"

"Yes sir, no trouble, although I can think of about a hundred other things I could and should be doing," Henry answered as he retrieved his utility cleaning cart from the corner and prepared to go into janitorial action.

"Fine, fine. Thank you Henry, and when you're through, please bring them to me at the office as soon as you can," Wagermann politely instructed.

"No problem. I'll have 'em for you in a minute and as clean as a whistle too," Henry reassuringly responded.

"Thanks Henry. Okay, now Mr. Archer would you follow me. I think we need to talk again." Wagermann instructed.

"Yes sir," I cowered as I followed Wagermann out, expecting harsher treatment than I'd received in our first encounter.

Just as I stepped from the lavatory into the hallway I heard the fresh water flush wash through and down the urinals and over my marbles. A sinister conspiracy, no doubt, hastily contracted between my marbles and the restroom plumbing. Having successfully completed my demise, the insulted marbles had their revenge as they splashed and danced in the fresh water.

Principal Wagermann indicated the way and that I precede him from the lavatory and to his office with a wave of his arm. I thought for certain that this time the chair in front of his desk would be hooked up, checked out and fully functional, ready for the works. Despite my fear of the forthcoming interrogation I was still just as concerned about getting my twelve marbles back. The walk from the lavatory to the school office was only three classroom lengths long but taking into consideration the adverse circumstances, apprehension was building up on my exterior sursurfaces like ice on an airplane wing flying through a snowstorm.

We entered the school office and Wagermann instructed me to continue on through the next open door and take a familiar seat in his office in front of his desk. He stopped at the secretary's desk just long enough to leave specific instructions that he was not to be disturbed for the next several minutes except for a delivery he was expecting from Mr. Hairboni or for any emergencies that might arise. He also requested that a message be forwarded to Room 107 to inform Mrs. Goodchaulks that Mike Archer would be unavoidably delayed until further notice in the principal's office; nothing serious.

I sat down in the designated chair and used the momentary opportunity of my temporary privacy to recheck the chair for wires, concealed restraints, anything out of the ordinary for a regular chair. I discovered nothing, just like the last time I'd sat in it. The chair looked, felt and functioned just like a regular chair. I did everything I could to protect myself, from checking out the chair to being as cooperative and congenial as possible, in order to prevent the meeting with Wagermann from deteriorating to some point of no return. Wagermann walked in and closed his office door behind him. Ceremoniously, he placed himself into his executive style chair with a sigh and leaned forward, folding his hands together and resting his forearms on his desk pad as if he was going to start praying; he spoke.

"I must say Mike (I was just Mike again, no Mr. Archer) that since our talk one of the last things I would have thought or expected was that I'd be seeing you in my office again so soon."

"Yes sir - me neither," was my exasperated response.

"You're telling me that what happened today in the lavatory was just another accident. Are you willing to stand by that story? Is that what really happened?"

"Yes sir, just an accident, just like I said, just like I told Mr. Hairboni."

Wagermann leaned back in his chair and brought his folded hands up to his mouth as he did so and then, silently, contemplatively, stared at me. It wasn't an angry or mean stare, but it was one of those 'truth-o-meter' type stares that sees right through big transparent fibs and causes liars to break down, fall to their knees and beg for mercy. Well, his lie detector stare-down got nothing from me because there was nothing to get. The only thing he registered was the calm, straight indicator ink line of one big truth teller: me. Satisfied that I wasn't old enough or sophisticated enough to lie my way past his experience and intuition, he relaxed a bit.

"Well Mike, I'm inclined to believe you. In fact, I have no evidence, no reason to not accept your version of events as the truth. But was it an accident that you were carrying your marbles on your belt in school?"

"Yes sir, I mean, no, sir, 'cause it was lunchtime. I usually don't carry them around in school, not since I was here last anyway. I just carry them around on my belt at recess time."

"I see, just a technicality?" Wagermann offered supportively.

"Yes sir, just a tac...nor...mailty...an accident, just like I said," I stammered in response.

"Good, good Mike. I see no reason to believe otherwise. Besides, I'm running a school here, not a prison. Am I right?" he offered light heartedly.

"Right!" I chirped back.

"I'll bet you thought you were really going to get yelled at or something, didn't you Mike?" Wagermann smiled.

"Yeah, kinda'," I smiled back.

"Well, the thought never crossed my mind. You know that Mr. Hairboni's job here is not an easy one by any means, no sir. He's always cleaning up one mess or another and fixing things around here all day long, five and sometimes six days a week."

"Yes sir, I know, I see him working on stuff all the time," I sympathetically agreed.

Then came two soft knocks at Wagermann's office door. He asked my pardon as he got up and answered the door. He opened it just a bit and there was Henry peeking in and holding a transparent wax sandwich bag with all twelve of my marbles inside.

"All cleaned and disinfected, Mr. Wagermann, just like you asked."

"Great Henry, thanks for all your trouble."

"Naaahhh, no trouble, no trouble at all," Henry reassured him.

Then Henry leaned in even closer through the slightly open door and whispered something to Wagermann just loud enough for me to make out what he said.

"I know it's none of my business or anything like that but you aren't being too hard on the kid? I mean it was really no trouble, no big problem at all. You know how I like to jazz it up a bit when I get worked up."

"Henry, I hear what you're saying and I've taken that good advice to heart. Don't worry yourself any further. The boy is doing just fine. Thank you again, Hank."

"Sure thing Doug, any time," Henry responded in kind.

At the last second Henry looked back over his shoulder again and then, oddly, leaned in even closer to Wagermann and whispered something only the two of them could hear. Henry handed Wagermann a small piece of folded paper which he immediately shoved into his shirt pocket. Under his breath 'Doug' thanked 'Hank' for the secret information. Henry backed away and left as Wagermann closed the door. With my marbles in hand and a smile on his face big enough to block the sun on a cloudless day Wagermann resumed his seat behind his desk. I silently followed all of his movements with my head down and my chin hovering just above my chest. He emptied the twelve marbles from their wax sandwich bag onto his large desk pad where he rolled them around a bit with his finger.

"How exactly did these beauties end up in the urinal again?" he inquired again as he shifted in his seat.

I shifted in my seat.

"Well, the knot in the top of my sock slipped loose and they fell down on the floor and a lot of them rolled around. I didn't even know that bunch were in the urinal. I saw that a lot of them were still missing after I picked them up. When I found them I was about to get them out of there when Mr. Hairboni walked in."

"I see," Wagermann nodded as he leaned way back in his chair.

He made a quarter of a turn to his right and surprisingly put his feet up on the bureau along the side of his main desk. Wagermann turned his face towards me and floored me with his next words.

"I've heard, through the grapevine you understand, that Billy

Schoutenlauder of Avenging Grace didn't show up Saturday for the big match."

Surprised by Wagermann's unexpected statement, my head jerked up so fast that the bones in the back of my neck made a loud popping sound like a cork being pried from the top of a champagne bottle.

"Surprised that I know?" Wagermann asked.

"Yeah...sir," (to say the least).

"Well Mike, don't be overly concerned. Word does get around you know. Besides, the big match has generated a lot of interest here at school. In fact, I've heard in the lunchroom and on the playground that you've become sort of a celebrity around here of late."

"Yeah, sure, I mean well, maybe. I really don't know for sure yet or anything like that," I mumbled in response.

"Did you ever find out why Mr. Schoutenlauder decided not to show up?"

"No, but we already talked it over and we're going to play a-gain real soon."

"You're a young man of your word Mike, so I imagine that you will, yes, I bet you will."

Wagermann's last words drifted off along with his brain as he talked more to himself than to me.

"I heard about the match but no one seemed to know exactly where or exactly when it was going to take place. Would you be willing to share that information with me Mike?" Wagermann asked as he'd shifted in his seat again.

I shifted in my seat again, and lied.

"I can't really tell because we haven't decided exactly when or where to have it. We're going to talk again and try to set that all up, a time and place I mean."

"Well Mike, I suppose I could press you if I had a good enough reason, although you understand that your meeting up with Billy for a marble match is not a school sanctioned activity. You aren't going to play here on school grounds are you?"

"No, we decided not to play at any school, his or mine. What does 'sanctioned' mean?" I puzzled.

"Well, lets just say that it's not something you would ask permission from me or anyone else here at school to do. You and Billy are doing it on your own away from school, get it?"

"Oh yeah, I get it. It's just between me and Billy, away from school, right?"

"Right Mike, that's right."

Wagermann was proving to be a real down to earth sort of guy but yet he seemed to be trying to get at something else, something just under the surface of our conversation. The atmosphere in the office was changing. A tenser mood emerged. I sensed that Wagermann had some bigger question on his mind. He reached across his desk and pushed a large lighted button on a desktop walkie-talkie type box and requested the attention of his office secretary.

"Miss Longwait?"

"Yes?" the box squawked back.

"I definitely do not want to be disturbed until I call you again on the intercom. Of course, any emergencies that come up I want to know about immediately. Any other telephone calls or office stop-in's please take a message or ask them to wait in reception, okay?"

"Yes sir."

"Oh yes, and Miss Longwait, did Mrs. Goodchaulks get the message that Mike Archer is here in the office and that it is nothing serious?"

"Yes, she got the full message."

"Thank you Miss Longwait."

Wagermann flipped the intercom switch to off.

Wagermann lifted his feet up off the bureau and put them back on the floor under his desk as he turned and focused his full attention on our discussion. For the next several seconds, the principal became strangely silent, occasionally looking back and forth between me and the dozen marbles scattered across the top of his desk. He started to roll the marbles over the desk pad with the palm of his hand. He stopped, refolded his hands on his desk pad and stared straight at me.

"Mike, I'd like the most honest answer that you're able to give to my next question, all right?"

"Sure."

Wagermann was getting all serious and mysterious all at once. He looked almost embarrassed as he continued.

"Mike, how good, exactly, are you at marbles? Are you as good as I've been hearing around the school?"

It seemed to be an honest enough question but it still hinted at something bigger.

"Well, I played at it really hard to be champ. I played and beat a lot of people and I lost a few times too, but I'd say that I could beat just about anybody if they played halfway fair."

"Sooo - you're confident that you'll beat Schoutenlauder when you finally play him?"

"Pretty sure, yes sir, unless he's gonna cheat or does something tricky like that. I'm pretty sure I can beat him."

"Even though you've never played him or even seen him play, you still feel good about your chances in the match?"

Wagermann had done his homework and a lot of eavesdropping in the lunchroom to have picked up on all that, or, he was a mind reader.

"Yes sir," was my confident response.

"Why?" Wagermann pressed.

I pressed back.

"Because Billy is too full of hot air. I got this feeling that he brags better than he plays. I've seen it before. He uses his big mouth and acts tough because he doesn't understand marbles like he should, like I do."

"Is that so?"

"Yep," I chirped.

"But what happened when you got beaten by Miss Hanrahan?"

"You mean Babes?"

"Priscilla?" he questioned with a rising inflection.

"Yes sir, everybody calls her 'Babes'," I corrected.

Wagermann knew much more than I would have ever given him credit for. But I still didn't understand why he'd taken such a keen interest. At the time I figured that maybe he'd played marbles as a kid at school and being a school principal afforded him

Keepers Weepers

the chance to keep up his interest in the game.

"So, Mike, what happened with Priscilla?"

"Well – I sort of walked into that one. I thought she didn't know how to play and that she'd be a pushover. I played pretty sloppy. Babes, er, ah, Priscilla seemed to have played the match like her life depended on it or something. I learned from my brother that marbles are pretty important to me and all but it's still just a game. You can only go so far and then it's not fun anymore. It seemed that Babes was out to get me for something that I'd never done to her. What I'd heard around school was that she was out to get a lot of kids. Winning was more important to her that day than it was to me. So, I guess I played pretty bad even though I tried to play good because I didn't want to lose either. It ended up that I could afford a loss but Babes couldn't."

"And Billy is different then?" Wagermann probed.

"Yeah, different by a mile. Babes was weird, but Billy, Billy is just a loud mouth jerk and I always beat big mouth jerks."

"So – if I were a betting man," Wagermann continued rubbing his hands together, "a bet on you would be a sure thing, a safe bet, if I were a betting man?"

"Yeaaaah - I guess so."

Wagermann, unbeknownst to me at the time was a betting man, a really big betting man. For some crazy reason he was betting somebody that I was going to beat Billy Schoutenlauder. I couldn't imagine why anyone would even consider a marble match between two kids wager-worthy. Wagermann was up to something. He was acting strange enough all right. The very idea of somebody putting real money on the line, on me to win, was a little unnerving. What if I lost?

"So, you feel that sure of yourself do you?" Wagermann continued.

"Yes sir, as sure as I can be. Anyway, Billy not showing up the first time made me mad, so I guess I've got two things to settle with him."

"Two scores?" Wagermann queried.

"Yes sir, to settle the championship and to teach Billy a lesson for not showing up the first time. I waited for him for over two hours."

"Is that right?" Wagermann smiled.

"Yes sir – two hours."

For effect I almost added that I'd nearly been run over by a car full of drunken beboppers, twice, but I thought better of it. Any mention of potential danger might have tempted Wagermann to get officially involved. That would have meant a call to my parents, which would have put the *'Big Kibosh'* on the whole thing and nobody wanted or needed the *'Big Kibosh'*.

"Mike, would you mind giving me a little demonstration of how you play, you know, just so I can get the feel of how you play the game?"

"Yes sir. I don't have any matches setup for the afternoon recess and if it stops raining there's a really good spot by the south backstop that's perfect!"

"Well Mike, I was thinking more like right now, right here, in my office. Do you think we could do that?"

That was a switch. The principal of the entire school asking me, a first grader, for permission to play marbles in his very own official office in the middle of the school day. I looked around the office and discovered that there wasn't exactly an over abundance of space. The carpet was the right type, a low tightly woven flat pile. I knew good marble-playing carpets just as well as good marble-playing dirt. Wagermann picked up on the concerned look on my face that indicated that a larger space would be required. He interjected with a suggestion.

"Yeah know Mike, we could move some of this furniture if you think we need more space."

"Yeah," I looked around, "we need more space."

The whole thing was too unreal to be believed. Me playing marbles in the principal's office with the principal, in the middle of the school day, when everybody else had their eyes and noses in their books. I was worried that I was going to be in big trouble with Mrs. Goodchaulks for playing marbles instead of struggling through penmanship with the rest of the class.

"Excuse me, but maybe Mrs. Goodchaulks doesn't know that I'd be gone this long. Maybe I should tell her that it will be a while."

"Oh – don't worry Mike," he said, even though he seemed worried that I was worried enough to bring it up, "that's very considerate of you but everything is taken care of, all squared away with your teacher, sooo – nothing to worry about. Agreed?"

"Agreed," I said, relieved.

Wagermann removed his suit coat and hung it up on a hook inside of his office closet. Closing the closet door, he clapped and rubbed his hands together in eager anticipation just like my dad when he walked into the kitchen ready to sit down to supper.

"So where do we play and what has to be moved?" Wagermann asked ready to fully engage as he loosened his necktie, unbuttoned his shirt cuffs and rolled up his shirtsleeves.

"Probably – we should play – here," I directed with some authority in my voice as I moved to and pointed at a spot in the direct center of the room which afforded good shooting angles from all around where the marble circle would be placed. Wagermann went to work.

"Okay Mike, why don't we put this chair in the corner over there and I'll move my desk back a bit and we'll be ready to go."

He actually moved the identified furniture as he explained his doing so. I pitched in as we worked like little beavers clearing our stump for dinner. It was my sole responsibility to move 'the chair' to the corner. I realized that I'd have the chance, firsthand, to finally answer 'is the chair wired' question.

Anticipating resistance and a struggle in ripping the chair from its place, held fast by the electrical wires that ran up from the floor and through its metal legs to all surfaces that would have body contact with sitting occupants, I heaved with all my strength to move the chair. I almost threw that chair across the room into the designated far corner. No wires, nothing holding it in place and fast to the floor, just an ordinary chair weighted down by all the years of needless worry and speculation of nervous students present and past.

Our furniture moving was making noise so the thought of Miss Longwait bursting through the door to investigate only to find Wagermann and me playing marbles was worrisome. The sounds of moving furniture was one thing, but the crack-'n'-snap of marbles slamming into one another would have been a dead giveaway. I simply continued to follow Wagermann's lead. He didn't seem to be concerned in the slightest so I just let it go at that.

"Okay Mike, looks good, ready to start? I'll use the dozen that Mr. Hairboni returned for us and you use the others still in your marble sock. We'll play just a couple of quick games."

"Okay, sure," I shrugged and smiled.

I placed a marble in the center of a four-foot diameter circle that I marked in the carpet with my thumbnail. Wagermann got down on his hands and knees and took, attempted, a first shot. He missed by two feet – not the marble, the circle. He missed the entire four-foot diameter circle by two feet and he was right next to it. I "hummed" under my breath and involuntarily scrunched up my face a bit in reaction to his unbelievably wayward shot. I let him keep shooting until he made contact with the circle and then contact with the marble at its center. The first game lasted about five minutes and I missed three times, which I attributed to the fact that I was playing the principal himself in his office during middle of the school day. It was still hard for me to believe that it was all actually happening. I'd dreamed up some weird stuff both awake and asleep, but I'd never even come close to that moment. I had a slight case of nerves to which I readily admitted to after the first game had been completed.

Wagermann complimented me on my fine play despite the three nervous misses. I automatically returned the compliment in kind even though he didn't deserve it, just situational protocol. The truth was that Wagermann could not have hit the long wall in his office from five feet away without a couple of hours practice first. He tried shooting with and without his glasses on but his aim was internally defective. He didn't need better glasses, he needed better eye-brain coordination and that you didn't just fall into or just pick up in a couple of minutes, hours, days or weeks. It was there or it wasn't, period. I revised my earlier speculation that Wagermann had been a child player who followed the game as an adult. Maybe he had been a player and maybe it was just a fact that as an adult he'd lost his touch. Who knew? But whatever 'touch' he'd ever had, if any, had apparently, obviously, vacated his hands and fingers some years before.

Compliments and initial observations exchanged and completed, Wagermann divided up all of the marbles in the room equally between us and suggested we go at it again. It was fine with me. I couldn't have imagined a better way to spend a rainy school day afternoon. Before I left his office that afternoon a few quick matches had turned into a baker's dozen. Each and every match I demonstrated time and again why I was the school marble champion. I finally relaxed and settled into my game. The last nine games I didn't miss a single shot. In fact every shot I made was hard, clean and true, no glancing blows, all direct hard hits. Wagermann was duly impressed.

After the thirteenth and final game and just over one hour of elapsed time the principal was thoroughly convinced of my abilities. I'd made him a true believer. He helped me collect and return all of my marbles to my marble sock and I helped him move all of the displaced furniture back to original-resting positions. When we were done Wagermann asked me to take a seat for just a few minutes more. He walked back to his closet and retrieved his suit coat. He rolled his shirtsleeves back down, rebuttoned his shirt cuffs and neatly straightened his necktie before putting his suit coat back on. With everything back in place, Wagermann sat down on the left front corner of his desk and folded his arms across his chest.

"Well Mike, you've certainly convinced me. You're the best I've ever seen or heard of at the Fifty-First Street School and I've been here more than a few years. I have every faith that you will represent yourself and your school, unofficially of course, as the true champion that I can see you are. Good luck, Mr. Archer."

Wagermann extended his hand for a man-to-man handshake.

"Thanks," I proudly announced as I rose to my feet, took his hand in a firm grip and shook on it.

"I have no doubt that in the very near future you'll be the rightful champ."

"I sure feel I can be."

"That-a-boy, Mike!" Wagermann said encouragingly. "Now

Mike, there's just one more thing I'd like to ask of you before I let you get back to class, one more little favor if I could."

"Sure, yeah," I responded enthusiastically.

"I'd be very grateful if you'd keep our little practice session just between you and me. Can you do that?"

"It's okay Principal Wagermann, I mean – yeah, it's a secret just between you and me," I cheerfully agreed.

Besides, no one in their right mind would have ever believed me even if I told somebody. Playing marbles with the principal, in his office, during school? Yeah, right Archer, how many loose marbles were rolling around in your head when you dreamed up that one?

"Great, great my boy, let's shake on it." We shook hands again.

"Now Mike, if Mrs. Goodchaulks asks, you were with me to discuss some personal matters concerning very special abilities you might have. She doesn't need to know what abilities, in fact, I'm certain that she won't even ask. Does that square with you?"

"Yes sir, special abilities, we're squared," I reassured him.

Wagermann walked to the door and had partially pushed it open when it occurred to me that I should have some assurances of my own. As I walked for the open door I stopped just short of going through. Wagermann looked down at me beaming a smile that would have lit up a dark room.

"Principal Wagermann, I need a favor too."

Miss Longwait heard my whispered request and looked up from her desk with the goofiest expression on her face. Wagermann's smile faded like a cheap colored cloth in bright sunlight as he coughed and signaled to Miss Longwait with a nervous laugh that it was nothing, just a silly little kid being a silly little kid. He stepped back into the office and just before closing the door, stuck his head out into the office to see if there was anyone waiting to see him. Sure enough, there she was, Bookbender with another library violator in custody seated next to her. She must have brought in one or two a day to see Wagermann. It was amazing that there were actually any kids left in school that could get into her library at all. As soon as Wagermann's head popped out from his office door Bookbender jumped to her feet with a demand for an immediate audience poised on her lips when Wagermann saw her and cut her off before she could utter a word.

"It will be a moment longer Miss Bookbender."

Old Lady Bookbender sat back down in a huff, choking and coughing on the words that got all backed up in her mouth and throat, all frustrated, as for the time being all the hot air went blowing out of her balloon. Her latest prisoner looked dejected and frightened. He definitely looked the library criminal type too. For all I knew he'd seriously provoked the old bag by something as drastic as blowing his nose without her prior permission. I had sadistic visions of a library revolt during which Bookbender would be tied securely to one of the little wooden library chairs and forced to watch and listen as four-hundred noisy school children had a "who could talk the fastest, loudest and most out of turn" contest, with the winners being turned loose to systematically desystematize her library book by book. Wagermann closed the door on Bookbender and my vengeful daydream as his words brought me back.

"Yes Mike, what can I do for you?"

"Well, sir, I'd really appreciate it if you would not talk to anyone about the match, keep it a secret. Yeah know, not mention it or bring it up to anyone, like that, because I want to play Billy first before there's any more talk about it, okay?"

"Sure, sure thing Mike. Is there something to worry about when you play Billy? Is he some sort of tough guy, pushing his weight around, something like that?" Wagermann asked, concerned.

"No – no, nothing like that. I just want it to be a surprise besides, he may not even show up like last time and I'll just spend another whole day answering other kids' questions," I'd responded reassuringly.

"Okay – (thinking about it) – sure, fine, that sounds reasonable, it's a deal. We'll keep it quiet until you say so," was Wagermann's measured response.

"Thanks, thanks a lot," was my smiling answer.

We shook hands for the third time and that time it was on my initiative.

"My pleasure my boy, now, off to class. Miss Longwait has your hall pass already to go."

I walked the extra step up to the front of Miss Longwait's desk as she reached towards me with the hall pass all filled out to current, up-to-date, hall pass regulation standards. But as I reached for the paper which guaranteed my free and safe passage back to class my eyes caught her eyes which locked back onto my eyes with a knowing look on her face, stressing, without words, "say nothing, just take the pass and what is in my hand underneath it." I just stared back at her, my mouth slightly open, as she dipped her chin slightly and firmly pressed the pass into the palm of my open hand. Concealed underneath the paper hall pass was, of all things, a marble. I felt it in my palm, plain as day, no mistaking it. She used her hand to gently but firmly close my hand around the crumpling paper of the hall pass and the marble hidden beneath it all with the most casual look on her face. She didn't break eye contact with me until my hand was completely closed around the paper pass and the secured marble surprise. I dutifully accepted the official hall pass and accompanying mystery marble from the office secretary with matching casualness and turned to leave calling out over my shoulder.

"So long."

"So long Mike, and best of luck," were Wagermann's final words.

Miss Longwait just winked and gave with a little 'bye-bye' wave of her left hand fingers as her left elbow rested on her desktop.

"Thanks," I called back to both Wagermann and Miss Longwait as I walked through the door and into the hallway.

Walking past Bookbender her eyes met mine and the battle was on. The air between us bristled with static electricity as hordes of invisible spears, arrows, swords and daggers flew back and forth. She didn't like me and I hated her. It really got under her skin that I, a first-degree library felon, was all buddy-buddy with the school principal.

We broke visual contact and I emerged from the silent confrontation unscathed, the winner, because what she thought of me, or what she thought about anything else for that matter, didn't concern me in the slightest. As soon as I walked past she literally lunged at Wagermann so fast that he didn't have another second to come up with another excuse to put her off. I wished that I'd been able to communicate, in some fashion, to the kid she had in tow, that the chair in front of Wagermann's desk was not hot-wired and that Wagermann, despite all the rumors to the contrary, was a fair and kind man.

The quiet walk alone back to the classroom through the empty hallway was pure joy. I took my own sweet time. I felt like I owned the building. The bees were still buzzing but the lid was on tight and they were working for me, not against me. I was in total control. Even the stares from Mrs. Goodchaulks and the rest of the class when I reappeared back at the classroom door, a full two hours after lunch period, didn't faze me one bit.

I learned two things some days later about my office visit that day that were unknown to me at the time. First, that after Wagermann concluded his dealings with Bookbender and her latest library capture that day, he once again requested that Miss Longwait hold all calls because he had a very important personal call to make. He pulled a note from his pocket, the same note given to him by Henry Hairboni, and placed a call. One Father Sebastian Wagermann picked up the ringing telephone at the other end. He was the Priest and Head Master at Avenging Grace and Principal Douglas Wagermann's twin brother. The bet was ten dollars that Mike Archer, the Fifty-First Street School Champ, would outplay his boy, Billy Schoutenlauder, Avenging Grace's unofficial representative in the 'off-the-record' competition. Father Sebastian being a pretty 'with it' sort of guy, 'hip man of the cloth', responded in kind with just a few words.

"Yes, I've had a little talk with our boy as well; you're on! And oh, by the way dear brother, God Bless you!"

"And pass along a God Bless you to my brother as well, would you Father?" was Doug Wagermann's chuckling response to his fatherly brother.

The second bit of delayed knowledge concerned the mystery marble clandestinely passed along to me by Miss Longwait. Unbeknownst to me or Principal Wagermann at the time, during the supposedly secret office marble demonstration the noise of moving furniture, the snap-crack of marble play and Wagermann's frequent and unsolicited barks and chirps of amazement at my marble-playing prowess had not been adequately muffled and concealed to escape the notice of Miss Longwait as she worked at her desk on the other side of Wagermann's office door. During the marble festivities one of my ricocheted marble hits escaped our attention and passed right next to a kneeling Principal Wagermann and continued on towards the closed office door where its rolling momentum carried it under the door, out into the reception office, through the open reception office door and out into and across the hallway where it bounced against and then settled along side the far wall.

Fortunately the only person present in the reception office or anywhere near the section of hallway outside the reception office at that moment was Miss Longwait. While the marble was still rolling its way through her office headed for the hallway she jumped up from behind her desk and gave chase, corralling the wayward crystal just after it came to rest out against the far hallway wall. Miss Longwait returned to the reception office and tiptoed up to the closed principal's office door and listened just long enough to verify the true nature of the goings-on inside Wagermann's office. With a smile on her face she resumed her seat at her desk just seconds before Bookbender dragged in the latest library offender. Knowing that of the two of us in Wagermann's office I was the only one in school with the marble-playing reputation, she secretly passed the marble back along to me as the opportunity had presented itself. It turned out that she was all right too!

With all of the positive support that poured in from Wagermann on a day that had started and progressed so horribly I found myself riding the crest of a new wave of confidence. I knew then that I could and that I would win the big match that I was certain was finally going to take place. By not showing up the first time

Billy had to have been sufficiently shamed into showing up at the rescheduled match and take his chances. Besides, little did I know at the time that if Billy had another attack of cold feet, Father Sebastian would have been more than willing to light a motivating fire under Billy's chilled extremities.

By the time school let out that day, the word had spread once again and further and farther afield than the week before that the big match was back on. The unsolicited words of encouragement and pats on the back and shoulders were nonstop. Touchingly, surprisingly, some of the strongest words of encouragement came from previously defeated competitors, and some of those were players I'd beaten more than once or twice. Of course there were those who could hold a grudge forever as exemplified by the all time poorest loser, "King of the Slugs," Rodney J. Strong. He was still smoking, smoldering and smelly from the defeat months before. What the heck, I figured; you can't reach everybody, so why even try. Besides, if it hadn't been me, it might have been somebody else, somebody less able to bear the brunt of Rodney's temper and wrath. I was certain that when Rodney finally forgot about me he'd find someone else to burn up about soon enough. Rodney always seemed to leave just enough fresh fuse stringing along behind him, inviting anybody and everybody with a match to spare to light it up and have a go. Ssssss-BANG!

*

***

Chapter Nine:
Marble Madness

THE REMAINDER OF that week slipped by like a laughing fat kid zipping past on a water slide. Before I knew it, Chubby hit the pool with a splash as the sun popped up and Saturday morning said hello. Through the rest of that week I'd gone nightmare free as far as I was aware, as my internal energy engine had been retuned. It quietly, patiently and strongly hummed along, cleanly idling on all cylinders.

I rolled out of bed that morning with a joint-creaking stretch and decided that rather than over concentrate on that afternoon's match, I'd do my best to follow my normal Saturday morning routine. After a bathroom pit stop, still in my pajamas, I headed for the kitchen and an overflowing bowl of *Half-Moon Strawberry Crunchies* and milk. Then it was a seat five feet in front of the television set for three hours of nonstop Saturday morning cartoons.

Relaxed, entertained and distracted by the cartoons and re-fueled by the *Strawberry Crunchies*, I went back up to my room to get dressed and re-select the marbles I'd use in the contest that afternoon. The marbles I'd chosen the week before had been indiscriminately mixed back in with the total collection. So I was faced with the task of picking the fifty afresh to represent me, to represent the rest of the collection left behind and apparently to represent, according to Wagerrmann, unofficially of course, the rest of the Fifty-First Street School.

Having started the day in such relaxed and normal manner I thought it best to keep the new selection process as simple and uncomplicated as possible, putting my energy into the match rather than all the pre-match preliminaries. I dumped the entire contents of my marble holding boot box onto the bedspread and just started picking marbles that appeared suitable, looked good, seemed right and all that stuff. When Kit Cat made his expected appearance I deferred, several times, to his judgment as any marble he pawed at became one of the included.

I drew a circle in the bedroom carpet using my thumbnail and added a ruffled tuft in the carpet at the circle's center as part of the final selection process. Taking the top of my extra-large king-sized plastic pirate treasure cup, I dumped its secret contents into my top dresser drawer alongside of my clean underwear. I filled the pirate cup with the eligible marbles that both Kit Cat and myself had pawed and picked at on the bed. The cat and I, working together, had randomly chosen a balanced and representative mixed selection of Cat's-Eye boulder styles totaling about a hundred marbles. Holding the pirate cup full of marbles about a foot above the center of the circle, the open top covered with my hand, I quickly flipped it over upside down and removed my hand, allowing the marble contents to fall out and into the center of the circle on the carpet. The marbles chinked, boinged, glittered, bounced and jostled for final resting positions on the carpet. Kit Cat could not resist as he leapt down off the bed and batted at one of the rolling marbles, which with his help took off across the bedroom floor, out the bedroom door, and with his enthusiastic encouragement continued along the upstairs hallway and then over the edge of the top step and down the stairs on their way together to continue the escape and chase somewhere on the first floor below. If only all my chasing-after-marbles had been so simple and carefree. I could've learned a lot from that cat.

Once they settled into their final resting positions, it was easy to select the fifty that were closet to the center of the circle. It wasn't very scientific and nowhere near the ritualistic spectacle of the week before, but it was my decision that chance should select the marbles that would best serve me in the match. The various styles of Cat's-Eye boulders were all equally cherished and equally counted upon to do their best.

By the time I finished it was close to noon and time for lunch. I thought it best not to sneak out past Mom without partaking in the normal Saturday mealtime routine to avoid arousing any undue suspicion and inconvenient questions. Like the morning hours, I planned to carry on as normally and close to my typical Saturday patterns as possible. Then and only then, right after lunch, I'd sneak off to the match.

Putting the chosen marbles into the double marble sock that I'd used the weekend before, at the last second, as a clear and certain afterthought, I decided to grab another empty sock just in case any winnings wouldn't all fit into just the one. I grabbed my jacket off the coat rack and tied the double marble sock to my belt. As I closed the bedroom door behind me and walked to the stairs, I could smell the aroma of food as it drifted up the stairway and then right up my nose.

Having been so engrossed in picking out the marbles I'd not realized that, in the meantime, a visitor had come to call. The surprise guest was no other than one-half of the human vise that had squeezed the marbles right off me at Mom and Dad's anniversary dinner. It was my rosy-cheeked Aunt Wilma herself, in person, every last ounce of her. I heard the voices from the stairway but I walked into the kitchen blind as Aunt Wilma lunged at me like a lightning frightened grizzly and squeezed the breath out of me as she bear hugged me right off my feet. She smothered me under a barrage of hugs and kisses as I feared that once again the pressure of her affections would forcibly free the marbles from my belt.

Satisfied that her welcome had convinced me of its sincerity, Aunt Wilma lowered me back to a freestanding position. As she relinquished her grip and my feet found secure footing back down on the kitchen floor, I staggered momentarily and took deep chest heaving breaths to restore my depleted oxygen supply.

As it had turned out, Mom explained, Aunt Wilma had been shopping in a nearby department store and had decided to take a chance that we'd be at home and stopped in to say hello. "Greeeaaat," I thought. It must have been quite the surprise for the neighbors as well if they'd looked out their windows only to witness a big bouncy boulder shoved into a dress and wearing a hat come-a-flittering, hopping and popping along down the sidewalk. Auntie Wilma was exceptionally, unexpectedly, light on her feet for a woman of her mass. She could have, in fact, I thought, been legitimately considered a gravitationally kinematic contradiction worthy of further scientific investigation and study. Weird visions of Auntie Wilma strapped to exercise equipment with electrodes taped to her as she huffed-and-puffed, smiled, ate and laughed her way through a workout surrounded by white-coated lab technicians with clipboards crossed my mind. If I hadn't known Aunt Wilma personally or had never had the chance to make her prior acquaintance, I might have been inclined to make a run for the nearest high ground. She was the kindest of souls but when she walked, skipped or trotted along she bounced, flowed and rippled like a self-contained pond.

You have to understand that I didn't harbor a dislike for my fat aunt – on the contrary, I found her to be, well, delightful! You also have to understand that at the time an era was coming to an end when personal oversizing and resulting girth were socially accepted signs off success and material well being, an old but passing tradition of weight representing wealth. If that tradition had held true, between Aunt Wilma and my other three large Aunts, we'd have been one really big rich bunch of related people!

There were times when Aunt Wilma could be great fun and there were times when she'd be embarrassed by undeserved and unfair criticism and sarcasm. But she had a "tough skin" as they say and "enough extra to go around" as they also would say. Embarrassing moments were hard on all of us, heck, they were hard on anyone, and Aunt Wilma endured her share with a good-natured sense of humor. Aunt Wilma drew her share of attention in public places for certain but a family reunion picnic at the beach of a local lake was a prime example. Robert and I and several of our cousins were playing in the shallow water near the shore while the adults were all laid out on beach blanets talking and sunning themselves. We'd only been out for a few minutes when a bunch of little kids, all strangers to us, quite innocently, started running circles around our four large Aunts, including Wilma, all of which were spread out in their swimsuits on the sand like sausage skins with too much sausage inside. Some of the circling kids took insensitive advantage of the spectacle.

"Whales on the beach, whales on the beach!" the unruly, misguided, insensitive, not to mention uneducated children started calling out (we were on a beach at a fresh water inland lake with the closest whales about 3,000 miles away in the ocean; Pacific or Atlantic, take your pick).

Aunt Wilma took it all in stride with her self-deprecating sense of humor and spoke for herself and our other three fat aunts as she rolled onto her back and started flapping and waving her fat arms and legs and chanted right back, "whales on the beach, whales on the beach!"

As bad as that time was the good times were really good. A Saturday in mid-January Aunt Wilma invited our family to her house for lunch and an afternoon of sledding and tobogganing down a long fast hill in a city park near her house. It was a clear and sharply crisp winter's day as the snow sparkled a brilliant blue-white and crunched under your boots. After what Aunt Wilma called a "light lunch" we all got dressed in our warmest winter's best and headed out for the park in the crisp ten-degree weather.

The fun started even before we left her house as our round Aunt wrapped herself up in several layers of her warmest clothing that included fur-topped pink rubber boots, several scarves and a furry full length seal skin overcoat. She looked like a giant fur covered beach ball, almost perfectly round except for the scarf-covered mound for a head and two pink boot stubs sticking out the bottom. Holy cow! Robert and I ran out first because we could not stop giggling. The walk to the sledding hill wasn't uneventful either as our overweight and overdressed Aunt slipped and fell backwards into a snow bank, crushing the loosely packed pile of snow into a slab of compressed ice. It took Mom, Dad, Robert, two sympathetic passersby and myself to pull her back up to a two-pink-stubs-on-the bottom standing position.

At the sledding hill Aunt Wilma was initially more into watching and shoving us off down the hill as Mom, Dad, Robert and I made several runs together and individually down the hill. The conditions were perfect. The hill was steep, fast and quick with long runs. For the occasion we'd brought a sled, a toboggan and two metal saucers. Aunt Wilma was reluctant to take her chances on a ride down the hill alone or with any of us until she, Mom and Dad had downed a full, piping hot, extra large thermos of whiskey-loaded *Irish Coffee* they'd secretively brought along for the afternoon. Aunt Wilma, with her inhibitions down and her reckless abandon up, decided that it was then the time to brave the elements and venture an alcohol-fueled solo ride down the snow packed hill. At the time Mom and Dad were too potched and Robert and I were having too much fun to consider any possible consequences of Aunt Wilma's compressed bulk hurtling unchecked, without adequate controls in place, down a snow and ice covered hill. The disastrous possibilities did not become evident until it was too late.

The first step in the chain of events was Aunt Wilma's selection of one of the aluminum saucers for her ride. In accordance with our naively eager suggestions she mounted the saucer a few feet back from the lip of the hill, more accurately, a few feet back from the point of no return. She didn't so much lower herself into the curve of the light weight metal disc as much as she fell onto it with a metal bending blow. Robert and I knelt in the snow as we shoved her stubby pink feet in under her and onto the saucer as Wilma, with some amount of effort, reached down and grabbed the lip of the saucer with her mitten covered hands. Robert and I helped Mom and Dad from behind as we all joined in for the final over the edge push, the second step in the chain of events and our biggest mistake. Even with the sliding saucer situated squarely under her weight we all strained as if we were trying to push a sledge loaded with stacked concrete blocks through deep loose sand. After a full two-minutes of grunting, giggling, outright laughing and joint popping pushing Aunt Wilma was finally in launch position, ready to go over the edge.

"You ready Auntie?" Robert and I breathlessly shouted.

"Oh yes boys," was her giggling response. "I feel just like a little girl again!"

At that moment, regardless of how she felt, Aunt Wilma actually looked like several little girls all bunched up and bundled together into one large lump inside of her bulging winter coat.

With a final grunt we all pushed as hard as we were able as Aunt Wilma finally slid over the edge; our third and final mistake. At first she just sort of inched along, almost as if she might get stuck and completely stop. But slowly, ever so gradually, she started gaining forward momentum, which with shocking swiftness transitioned into downhill speed. That's when we realized, in those gut wrenching couple of seconds, what we'd gone and done, what we'd unknowingly unleashed. It was too late. We could only hope for the best as silent "oh no's" simultaneously formed on each of our lips.

The giant hand of gravity had reached up out of the snow covered hill and grabbed Aunt Wilma and her metal saucer and pulled with all of its might. Within the very short distance of twenty-five feet Aunt Wilma had accelerated from a standstill to 25 mph. By the time she made it a third of the way down the hill it became painfully obvious that she was out of control and in all likelihood unstoppable. She passed everyone else going down the hill in a sort of live fast-motion-versus-slow-motion comparison. She raced down the hill as if everyone else was standing still.

We started shouting for Aunt Wilma to try and steer and for everyone else to spread out and get out of the way. Her downhill speed approached 40 mph as Aunt Wilma's bulk bounced, jiggled and quivered on the thin metal of the saucer. Gravity had a hold of Aunt Wilma like a major league pitcher grasping a four-fingered fastball. Hurtling down the hill in record time, flattening out all of the big and small snow bumps in her path, leaving a rounded indentation trail in her wake, Aunt Wilma packed all of the potential impact punch of a three-hundred pound speeding cannon ball.

The sledding hill sloped at a thirty-degree angle for a good three-hundred feet and then slowly leveled out into a snow-covered flat plain for two-hundred feet before ending at a roadway that ran through the park where other visiting winter recreation enthusiasts had parked their cars. By the time Aunt Wilma reached the bottom of the hill she was a free running unguided human torpedo gone rogue looking for a ship to sink. Our concerns were temporarily alleviated when we remembered that one-hundred feet from the road, stretching across the flat snowy plain, was a manmade snow wall about five feet high placed expressly for the purpose of preventing over enthusiastic sledding fans from shooting into or across the road. Our only hope was that she'd flip over on her side and wipe out. Then the only problem would have been digging her out of the five-foot wide, five-foot deep and twenty-five-foot long furrow that she'd be certain to make in the snow.

As our fat Aunt streaked for the wall of snow on the by-then bent and battered aluminum saucer, we felt sure that the end of her ride was at hand as the snow wall was certain to put a stop to her speeding forward progress. We prepared to rush down the hill on the toboggan and dig her and the saucer out of the snow wall where she'd be embedded. But, to our surprise and utter dismay, Aunt Wilma's low to the ground mass and velocity was even too much for the snow wall to restrain. She hit that snow wall with the kinetic energy of a speeding freight train diesel locomotive. At the point of impact the snow barrier exploded into a cloud of fine white powder. She went through that snow wall like it wasn't even there. Aunt Wilma sped unimpeded towards the road. Heaven help anyone who got in her way.

At best, the snow wall impact might have knocked maybe five or ten mph off her speed as she continued to clip along at a dangerous pace. Hell bent for metal, Wilma was a runaway train as she roared towards a line of parked cars at the curb. After emerging from the street side of the snow wall she was hard to visually reacquire as she was covered in white and blended in with the snowy surroundings. All you could pick out at first was a powder white contrail that she'd left in her wake. It wasn't until she was a good fifty feet from the parked cars that we were able to reestablish exact visual contact.

Apparently blinded by the snow Aunt Wilma was unaware that she was about to make a direct hit on one of the parked cars. The human missile had acquired a target and homed in. Whether or not heaven or hell was going to intercede, or whether they'd both just back off and stay out of the way, was a wide-open question. The immovable object was about to be tested by the irresistible force. A simple case of *Classical Newtonian Physics* but nobody needed a slide rule to figure out what the outcome would be.

Meanwhile, inside the randomly targeted automobile, completely unaware of the impending impact, were a Father, a Mother, a young Son and a younger Daughter, the model of the basic American family unit of the late 1950's, all cheerfully warming up with big mugs of freshly poured dark, rich, foamy, sweet and sticky hot cocoa, a family treat after a day in the cold winter outdoors just before the drive home. Just a scant twenty-five feet from the car Aunt Wilma's snow blurred vision cleared just enough for her to realize that she was about to make an impression. Unable to even attempt a stop, she decided, instinctively, desperately, to slam into the selected car with that part of her anatomy which naturally provided her with the biggest impact cushioning effect, her bottom end. She leaned and rocked backwards with her pink-booted feet in the air. What a sight. The metal saucer took point as the seal skin torpedo plowed towards the unsuspecting family all comfy and cozy in their late model *Ford* sedan.

We all saw the impact before we heard it. We were a good five-hundred feet away as the boom and shock wave from the collision rolled up to the top of the hill like thunder from a distant lightning strike. The combined booming thud and crunch of aluminum saucer metal against steel automobile sheet metal of the *Ford's* door panels shook snow off the branches of nearby trees. Just as *Newton* would have predicted, Aunt Wilma stopped dead at the curb, the exact plane of impact, as the car, its human occupants and the four big mugs of hot cocoa absorbed the transfer of momentum.

The *Ford* drifted sideways about seven feet from the curb over the ice and snow-covered road, blocking all passing traffic from both directions. The inside of the *Ford*, including the windows, the seats, the dash and the passengers were all bathed in varying degrees of splattered, sticky and runny hot cocoa. The passenger side of the car at the vertical post which divided the front and back doors as well as portions of both doors bore the contact imprint of the aluminum saucer and the saucer bore the imprint of Aunt Wilma's two oversized cheeks and I don't mean the ones to either side of her nose.

It was later reported that the little girl in the back seat did give indirect warning of the impact having said something to the effect, "Look, mommy, a big snowball!" Months later we learned that Aunt Wilma not only reimbursed the Jenkins family for new right side door panels on their *Ford*, but also paid for a complete professional cleaning of the cars interior and the dry cleaning bill for all of the clothes they were wearing. No one was hurt. The car was fixed and cleaned to showroom standards, the clothes were laundered to like new; it was the poor aluminum saucer that was a total loss. After the 'incident', it looked like a crushed beer can and was collected and then discarded as such.

My concern about Aunt Wilma's presence was that her visits, surprise or planned, often dragged on for hours, resulting in waiting around and delayed departure after delayed departure. There was always one more thing to talk about, one more thing to look at or one more bite to sample. I didn't need any such unplanned holdups that day of all days. I planned to play along and if things started to look like they were going to drag out, I'd take advantage of the first opportunity to unobtrusively slip away and pass any remaining time before the match in some secluded spot, safe from any and all well-meaning relatives.

Having made my kitchen entrance with my jacket over my shoulder and marble sock tied to my belt in plain sight made it more than obvious, I assumed, that I had places to go, people to meet and things to do. Robert, the lucky rat, always seemed to be conveniently gone during such episodes; he'd lucked out again by managing to get lunch at a friend's house. Robert's absence put all the more pressure on me as the sole recipient and center of focus for Aunt Wilma's maternal attention and affections.

Mom was being her tolerant and polite self. Of course she'd invited Aunt Wilma to stay for lunch and of course Aunt Wilma accepted but only after Mom insisted then reinsisted after repeated halfhearted protestations to the contrary by my Aunt. Aunt Wilma was always hungry, even after she'd just eaten. Wilma refusing a meal was as likely as the moon actually turning out to be made of green cheese. If she earnestly refused an invitation to eat it was because she was sick or felt that the spread was inadequate to feed her and the other folks present. Wilma was overweight upon layer of overweight. No matter how dainty, how lightly feminine she acted, the chairs she sat on always creaked, cracked and squeaked their protest, as if begging for mercy or a swift and painless end to their misery. Lunch that day was grilled cheese sandwiches and cream of tomato soup, one of my all-time favorites and a staple of American dinner tables during my childhood. It was one of Aunt Wilma's favorites as well, along with all of the dozens of other favorites, as she ever so daintily yet mercilessly polished off three whole bowls of soup and four whole grilled cheese sandwiches. "Man", I thought, "what an eater!"

Food disappeared into Aunt Wilma like light into a dark cave. Whenever she walked within twenty feet of any exposed food it would start to tremble and shake as if my fat Aunt's extensive and concentrated mass exerted a gravitational pull. She was the only person I ever suspected of being able to open a refrigerator door just by looking at it. She was a miniature living model of the universe collapsing back in on itself as the outward momentum of the inflationary phase waned and contraction took over. I imagined a bloated, rosy checked and smiling Aunt Wilma floating through dark empty space. Suddenly, a lone streaking proton traveling near the speed of light pierces her outer skin. Aunt Wilma explodes and instead of stars, comets, planets and galaxies bursting forth into space it was sausages, pizzas, chops, potatoes, bowls of hot chili, roasted chickens, steaks, tasty hot casseroles still in their oven safe glass dishes, pies, pastry and loaves of bread (sliced and unsliced) flowing out and filling the heavens.

Everything was still on schedule. I helped Mom clear the table as Aunt Wilma announced that she had a wonderful idea. She suggested that Mom and I join her on a little shopping expedition to the local department store to buy me a nice gift. For Aunt Wilma nice gift translated into such interesting items as new underwear, sweaters or a box of handkerchiefs with a matching bow tie. I could tell by her fat rippling smile that she thought it was just the greatest idea ever. So did the chair she was sitting on as it moaned and creaked in anticipation to the end of its torture.

Mom said it was a good and generous offer but that she could not join in because of beckoning house and yard work so they both looked at me. The hot potato had landed square in my lap and was burning its way into my crotch through my pants with nowhere to dump it.

    My decision either way would be all right with Mom because she was really fair and respectful that way. She and Dad both would talk Robert and I into doing things for our own good but with reason, logic and kindness, never forcing or threatening us to do something against our will. Aunt Wilma, on the other hand, had taken on the appearance of a woman who was a finalist in a million dollar drawing. Her eyes got as big and wet as two miniature party pizzas with extra runny cheese as she eagerly, desperately awaited my answer. I wanted to say directly, flatly, "Sorry, no, I've got other plans." But that would've invited a whole line of questioning, propelled by her hurt feelings, as to what plans of mine could possibly be so much more important than her plans for me.

    Aunt Wilma was puffing up with nervous anticipation like a rapidly inflating helium weather balloon ready to set sail for the upper atmosphere. A "no" answer from me would have pulled her cork and she would have rudely deflated right there in the kitchen like a leaky old tire inner tube. Either way, the chair she was sitting on was begging for a decision. The kitchen clock read 12:15 p.m.. The shopping center was a twenty-minute walk from showdown alley. That gave us just over one hour to fulfill Wilma's dream of a shopping excursion without treading on my dream of the biggest marble match of my life.

    Cautiously, I relented and agreed to go on the condition that there were other important things that I wanted to do that afternoon as well. Aunt Wilma was all smiles from the top of her head down past her extra chins and right into her spare tires. She tried to persuade Mom one last time to change her mind and join us anyway. Mom held her ground as Aunt Wilma quickly rebounded at the thought of just herself and her nephew going on an outing together.

    Admittedly, I wasn't very excited. We hopped into her car

which was parked at the curb to the front of our house and in no time flat we were browsing through one of the city's better department stores. During the ride though, I couldn't help but notice how the car tilted, leaned and listed to her side as Aunt Wilma took her place behind the wheel. The steering wheel sort of disappeared into the rolls and folds of the front of her body, as she couldn't move the seat any further back and still be able to reach the brake and gas pedals with her feet.

As a courtesy, she asked what particular items most appealed to me as potential gifts. I didn't feel like I could really tell her the truth because I sensed that she had her own ideas and her mind set on more practical selections of surprises such as pillowcases or packages of new socks, things that would score points with Mom, Dad and her adult conscience, not me. What I really would've liked, what I really wanted, wouldn't have interested her in the least and in most cases would've probably shocked and upset her. I just couldn't picture Aunt Wilma putting out cold hard cash to equip me with a set of authentic rubber *Frankenstein's Monster* hands or a new *Wrist Rocket Slingshot* that had the "power, accuracy and range to break a glass soda bottle at 100 feet." Nope, it would probably be a new dress shirt for church with a pair of imitation gold cuff links to match.

I resigned myself to the fact that whatever it turned out to be, whatever she picked out would be of little or no interest to me. I couldn't remember the last time I took a shirt from my closet and a pair of matching cuff links as objects to play with, much less wear while I was actually playing. Aunt Wilma wasn't in the same league, the same class, as my buddy Russ' Uncle Chester who was in the perfectly acceptable habit of sending Russ all kinds of interesting and useful presents.

I decided to go crazy over the very first thing she suggested and put an end to the outing as soon as possible. Shoe Polish – Yeah! Shaving Kit – I'm ready! New toothbrush – How'd you guess! Much to my dismay my fat Aunt seemed to be in a trance, in a shopping world all of her own, under a witch's spell, as she was unable to decide between a new belt, new shoes or a package of new undershirts. We must have stopped at two-dozen display counters, all of which were overflowing with a multitude of just the sort of boring stuff that Aunt Wilma loved.

"How about this? Would you like this Mikey?" was the standard line each time she picked something up for consideration.

"Yeah, Auntie Wilma, that's great! I really like it and I could use it too! Mom and Dad would like it too!" I enthusiastically responded.

It didn't help and didn't work. Despite the biggest smile on my face that I was capable of under the circumstances, Aunt Wilma would just put whatever the item was back on the counter and walk onto the next item that had caught her eye like I'd never said a word, pro or con. She acted like I wasn't there at all. I even suffered through the public humiliation, the indignity, of her holding up a pair of new briefs against the front and back of my pants, checking for approximate fit at the boys underwear counter.

But it was walking behind my Aunt Wilma that was an experience in and of itself. She really cleared a path. Properly outfitted and attired she could have cleared a way through just about any and all situations and terrains that could possibly, that dared, stand before her. Through a stump-infested swamp, the tall stand of a cornfield, through the deepest drifted snow or through the dense underbrush of an old growth forest or anything else in the direction that her impetus would take her Wilma would've been unstoppable. Aunt Wilma didn't have to dig in and drive her way through any potential obstacle. She just had to ever so slightly lean just a few degrees off center toward the direction she wanted to travel and her kinetic mass and momentum would do the rest. She was a detectable and measurable combined earthly geologic and space-time gravitational force.

It was a good thing that there were no hills or ramps inside the store because only one little trip, one minor misstep, could have put all of Aunt Wilma's tremendous destructive potential energy into motion, resulting in unimaginable damage of property and injury to life. It could have been, it would have been, the snow hill all over again, only worse; it would be on dry land. It would be a very localized interior tidal wave. Wilma would roll along in the slightest of downhill directions knocking over and picking up any and all matter of merchandise, display materials, and other assorted debris and assorted persons in her path and carry it all right along with her to some point and place of final momentum breaking subsidence and containment. The department store did have four floors that we went up and down between repeatedly. It was a day that the mechanical memories of the store's escalators would never forget or recover from.

As the minutes ticked away, irritated with Aunt Wilma for her indecisiveness, I started to get nervous. I caught a glimpse of the store's giant wall clock: 1:00 p.m.. In one-half hour I had to be, I would be, on my way whether Aunt Wilma liked it or not or whether she'd even know it or not. We stopped and looked at the potential solution to the problem, the gift to end the outing, more times than I was able to keep track of when we came across the store's first floor lunch and snack counter. Aunt Wilma was all eyes and nose.

"How would you like a little after lunch dessert Mikey? Does that sound good to you? It sure does to me!" Wilma excitedly perked up.

Before I could open my mouth to express my opinion one-way or the other, I was dragged up to the nearest vacant seats at the lunch counter. I really didn't care for anything to eat, still being full from lunch, but Aunt Wilma was ready for another load. I tried to tell her that I wasn't hungry enough to eat anything but before I could get a single word out of my mouth edgewise she'd already gotten hold of (literally grabbed) a passing waitress and placed her order and mine together. I'd be getting a large hot fudge sundae, ready or not, like it or not. Aunt Wilma would be snacking down on a large hot dog with the works topped off with a super colossal banana split.

While I tried to figure out where inside of her body Aunt Wilma was going to put all of that food she'd just ordered, my gaze settled on the clock above the lunch counter grill, 1:20 p.m.. I had to leave. I looked around trying to think of a way out when I noticed, in the direction of the exit doors, the Men's washroom. Seizing upon the only chance open to me I turned to my Aunt and excused myself claiming an urgent need to use the john, I'd be right back. What a liar! I was learning to lie too well, very convincingly and at a moment's notice too. I twinged at the notion that I'd been able to manufacture and then deliver the 'big fib' on command. But, for that moment, I forgave myself, citing that extraordinary circumstances called for extraordinary measures. I'd brought my marbles tied to my belt and concealed under my jacket. I gave them a reassuring squeeze through my jacket pocket as I walked for the Men's room. All the way to the john I plotted and planned my exit.

"Have a good go Mikey and hurry back, our food will be here in a minute," were the last words I heard from Aunt Wilma.

Walking into the Men's room I headed straight for the sinks where I checked my hair in the mirror, rinsed my hands and took a deep breath before walking back to the bathroom door and peeking out. There was one other guy in the bathroom that brushed by me on his way out. We traded momentary looks as he walked by. He looked displeased by my presence. If I were twenty years older I would have told the stranger to keep his thoughts to himself and mind his own business.

In the few moments I'd been away our food had arrived and Aunt Wilma had already polished off the hot dog and was shoveling away on the banana split. I thought it my good fortune to be sneaking away. Sitting next to Aunt Wilma during a feeding frenzy was like walking in front of the intake fan of a revved-up jet engine. I figured that a clean break to freedom was just a matter of seconds away as Aunt Wilma had completely forgotten about me and would at any second turn her full and undivided attention to the unclaimed, melting and mercilessly enticing hot fudge sundae.

Guilt, like a bothersome little dog that had been left behind in the washroom, nipped at my heels I prepared to kick the yelping little pouch to the side and simply walk out of the store's exit doors that weren't ten feet away from the Men's room door. The thought did enter my mind that Aunt Wilma might be concerned that I'd gotten lost or worse, stolen, you know, kidnapped. But when I looked back at her she was inhaling the last of her banana split.

It became obvious to me that my Aunt's only concern was her position at the lunch counter. I didn't feel one bit guilty. I surmised that Auntie Wilma would fend for herself just fine. I slipped out of the Men's room and walked straight and true for the exit. Aunt Wilma wouldn't have noticed an airplane crashing into the building unless parts of it fell onto her plate. When she ate all of her senses except smell and taste were turned off. She even closed her eyes once she determined the layout of the food on her plate. My final parting glance at the lunch counter clock revealed exactly 1:30 p.m.. That left me all the time required to make it to the match on time. Aunt Wilma had already started in on my unclaimed hot fudge sundae.

I'd gotten free of the shopping diversion which had the unexpected and beneficial effect of preventing me from over concentrating on the match. The twenty-minute walk to the alley was exhilarating as my match play energy started to build. It was a bright and beautiful day as I wondered if Billy would show and, if he did, would he play it fair or cheat and pull nasty surprises. As I approached my destination the thought occurred to me that Aunt Wilma had probably ordered seconds of everything. I pictured my Auntie pouring it in as the waitress tried in vain to keep up. With a smile on my face I found myself at the north end of the alley, which I'd never entered or exited through, the other end, the south end, being closer to my house. It was a different perspective of a now-familiar place: a simple but surprising and refreshing difference. A quick scan of the alley indicated that I was there alone, the first to arrive.

Standing solo, silent and still at the north end opening to the alley, the path to my Fate, the back road to Destiny lay before me as I absorbed the sunlight that warmed my face. With eyes closed I stood motionless just a few steps inside of the alleyway. It felt good, I felt good, I felt sharp and ready and I was going to win no matter what. Slinging my loaded marble sock from my side and over my shoulder I started towards the center of the alley at a slow, steady and deliberate pace. My stride was precise and confident as I mentally prepared myself for the match of my young life. The alley was a full one-hundred yards long and I intended to use the fifty-yard walk to the center to my advantage. I revved my energy engine as the buzzing bees in my head fed the cylinders all of the fuel they required.

    The moment was too charged with anticipation, too emotionally saturated to let it pass without further embellishment from my ever-present and admittedly overactive imagination. I unlocked the door that held my unconscious mind at bay. It burst out of its confines into full view as the visible world was transposed by an alternate one of my own. Any attempt to restrain, to harness, to beat my rampaging imagination back into its locked room would have been in vain as it gushed forth in an uncontrolled torrent of vivid color images. I stood aside and let it have its way and rode the wave as best I could.

A new landscape emerged as a cloud passed over the sun. The bright midday became an early evening magic hour with the sun settled just below the horizon and the sky and clouds softly lit by the fading twilight. A small sheepskin pouch filled with handmade marbles, marbles wrought from lightning forged quartz crystal, hung from my belt where my full double marble sock used to be. The animal skin marble pouch was matched by my calfskin leather tunic and tethered sandals. I was a miniature Jason, a traveler, an explorer, an adventurer and a warrior walking alone through the *Valley of the Troll Twins*.

    Young Jason had no argument, no score to seek or settle with the Trolls, but he had to pass through their valley to pay proper tribute to the Gods who resided atop *Mount Marble* that loomed at the far distant end of the (v)alley. The complication was that the Trolls had property rights to the only place of passable ground that led to the holy mount. Between the foot of *Mount Marble* and pilgrims like myself resided the greedy and magically empowered Trolls. No traveler could pass, night or day, rich or poor, known royalty or unknown peasants without parting with and paying the proper fee, the toll for passage to the Twins; a tribute of several best marbles. Jason had some beauties all right but they were intended solely as tribute to the proper Gods at *Mount Marble* and not for a pair of ugly dwarfs, self-appointed pretenders, who controlled access to the throne.

The fading light of dusk outlined the snow-covered peak of *Mount Marble*, visible throughout the length and breath of *Troll Valley*. Passing through the valley I walked among beggars and stranded pilgrims who'd been cheated out of their marbles by the Trolls. All had been unable to pass as the Trolls' plied their magic con-game, blocking the path to the majesty of *Marble Mountain*. As I walked on I sensed two pairs of beady little eyes, peering out from dark places of concealment, searching my person and checking out my marbles. Working their game in tandem they'd conned and cheated honest striving pilgrims countless times, bilking all and everyone that passed their way out of their marbles and then refusing them passage, holding all back with their insidious boasting threats.

I approached the narrowest part of the alley-valley, a passage way between two garages disguised as large rock boulders, with a clear space of a scant twelve-feet between them. If there'd be an ambush, an attack, a marble shakedown, it would be at the narrowest point of the valley where the obstacles were the highest and a defensible escape almost impossible. I lowered and loaded my sling while steadily and stealthily approaching the breach between the boulders.

Three feet from a clear passage a loud bell clanged, a siren screeched and red and yellow lights flashed intensely as gates swung down from above and more gates rolled from behind the boulders across my path blocking my way and frightening me to the ground. It resembled a really overdone modern railroad-crossing gate except for the sign that hung from the bottom of the structure that read, "To pass this way, the Trolls you must pay. The Management. Established 1005 BC."

Regaining my balance and my composure I popped back up to my feet prepared to defend my marbles and myself against any and all comers, but no comers came. Instead, lounging atop each of the two opposing large boulders to either side of the gate-blocked passage was one of the *Troll Twins*, in person so to speak. The Troll to my right appeared bored. Everything about him said unexcited, distracted, just another day on the rock. His chin rested in his palms as his elbows rested on his knees which were drawn up to his chest as he half-sat and half-squatted on top of his rocky perch. His counterpart to my left was equally frantic about my arrival and proved it by lying on his back with his hands folded behind his head like a pillow while his left leg was crossed over his right leg which was knee-up-foot-down flat on the rock. Both wore red high-topped canvas basketball sneakers and matching monogrammed brown togas with red and gold trim and sewn-in-place marble accents. They were not what I expected when compared to such an elaborate and fancy gate. The Troll to my right was Harrititus and to my left was Larrinitus, both descendants from long ancient lines of various higher and lower levels of accomplished and not so accomplished, distinguished and not so distinguished Titus' and Nitus', both family lines being mongrel mutt amalgamations of *Greek*, *Nordic*, *Roman* and other mixed *Pagan* mythologies.

    Harrititus and Larrinitus posed on their rocks unmoving as they pleaded their case in the form of a poem. They stated quite clearly that a price had to be paid and they quoted what they thought I owed them. They maintained their casual positions with ease as if to imply that they repeated the story, word for word, thousands of times to the thousands of pilgrims that had tried to pass their way. So it was me they planned to prey upon that day. *Mount Marble* was my goal and that night it was glowing in plain sight at the far end of *Troll Valley*. Harri spoke first and Larri spoke second, taking their turns as I'd wished I hadn't found either one of them at home:

> "If you want passage, first you must pay,
> What do you offer? Come don't delay.
> If it is *Mount Marble* you seek,
> You must now know that we own the only
> through street.
> You must pay tribute to use our good road,
> But mind you no tricks or you'll end up a toad.
>> *(Just then a giant rubber toad flew out from behind Harri's rock and landed upside down, lifeless, on the valley floor near my feet)*

There is no other way that you may gain entry,
So show us your offering and it better be plenty.
So shocked, so frightened, such a look of surprise,
Naive young traveler with *Mount Marble* in your eyes.
Could it be fear and doubt that we see,
crossing your face like the waves of the sea?
If you seek fortune, peace and great fame,
you must dance to our tune; you must first play our game.
So empty your pockets and show what you've brought,
let us decide what your journey has wrought.
Be quick, be silent and follow our rules,
do not refuse or we'll set loose the ghouls!
> *(A ghostly white sheet with a black crayon drawn face flew by just above my head on a wire clothes line stretched across the valley)*

They'll chase, haunt and hound you till death,
so give us your treasure, give us your best!
> *(The white sheet ghost flew back across the valley over my head back in the opposite direction)*

Don't try to fight us and don't try to flee,
don't dare ignore us and don't try to see.
For here you must pass, look here is the key.
> *(A giant feather-light painted cardboard key swung down on a rope between me and the gate)*

We demand your attention; to us you'll pay heed,
we require your donation, pay up with great speed;
Remember we warn you; remember we advise,
it would do you no justice to act so unwise.
But if you adhere to the path that you follow,
without paying your duty, life would be so hollow.
It is you who will suffer; it is you who will find,
that life is too short and failure too fearful;

> So hand us your tribute and go your way cheerful,
> through our gate to the foot of *Mount Marble*,
> for a life oh so joyous and unending marvels!
> PLEASE PAY NOW!"

Two large metal pails, each on the end of a long bending stick, one from behind each of the Troll boulders, came lurching out banging into each other and repeatedly bumping up against me in anticipation of the big marble payoff.

My head had been bobbing and swinging back and forth like the pendulum of a clock as Harrititus and Larrinitus recited their canard. The legend was true and it was plain to see that Larri and Harri had tried to stick it to me. I shouldered my slingshot and started to think while Larri and Harri each had a drink. The *Troll Twins* were clever, that was for sure, so I answered their demand with a poem that I was certain would give them a stir. It was a poetry shoot-out, rhymes straight from the hip as I gave back what I'd gotten by giving them some lip. Quietly and confidently and not trembling to boot, I informed Harri and Larri that I didn't give a hoot:

> "Poor Larri, poor Harri, I bring you sad tidings,
>   it seems you've been left alone at the siding.
> I didn't come to offer, I didn't come to bear,
> I didn't come to give; I didn't come to share;
> It is sad and surprising that you have not heard,
> that all the new pilgrims sail to *Mount Marble* on
> the wings of *The Great Bird*;
> Your gate is impressive but small nonetheless
> when compared to the wingspread of *The Great Bird*
> to the West,
> No tributes, no offerings, no tolls must they pay,
> as hundreds fly over every hour of the day;
> All of your warnings will do you no service,
> for I'll turn and leave and it won't be me who'll
> get nervous.
> You rant and you chatter, you rant and you rave,
> of ghouls that will haunt and follow to the grave.
>   *(I reached up and poked at the ghost sheet*

hanging above my head)
A toad in the road I will not become,
    (I kicked at the big upside down rubber toad
    lying near my feet)
for to reach *Mount Marble* this way I needn't run.
So keep your dark road and ghosts at your bidding,
and sleep on your rocks, me pay?, you're kidding!
So shocked, so frightened, such a look of surprise,
poor Larri, sad Harri there's fear in your eyes;
I wish I could stay and soothe your hurt feelings,
but there is nothing to say to stop your heads reeling.
I have to be going and hitch a free ride on the wings
of *The Great Bird* that glides through the skies!
GOODBYE!"

    Larrinitus and Harrititus trembled with fright, almost falling from their rocks with the thought of no travelers alone in the night. Their bluff I'd called and they fell for it good, as their faces resembled two old pieces of wood. I played out my hand with the smarts of a fox as poor Larri and Harri suffered from shock. They came to their senses and packed their bags quick, hoping for a ride, two seats, on the big bird's next trip. They ran right past me leaving two clouds of dust in their wake while yelling and screaming they would not, could not, be late. They slowed for a moment and called back for directions as I shouted right back to keep going and seek the protection at the end of the alley where they'd find *The Great Bird* and the waiting pilgrims rallied.

    The Trolls abandoned their gate in the valley and ran on their way to the nonexistent rally. No giant bird in the sky giving free rides only Larri and Harri and the dream I'd put in their eyes. Larri and Harri were to be disappointed and when they returned they'd find their gate disjointed. They'd plan, they'd scheme, they might even have their revenge, but that day was mine, I had a-venged. I walked to the gate and lifted it slowly as I strode towards *Mount Marble* in all of its glory.

    The sun flowed back out from behind the passing cloud. The daydream played itself out like the empty scratching of a phonograph needle at the end of the record. Exhausted and satisfied that it had done its duty, having for the time being vanquished any lingering self-doubts, my spent imagination willingly, of its own accord, crawled back into its cell and closed the door on itself.

Still alone, my walk-along daydream had carried me to within a few strides of the center of the alley. I sat down on the cement with my back resting against the familiar garage. I cleared my mind and began to meditate, relaxing away any and all extraneous thoughts in anticipation of Billy's arrival. I closed my eyes and turned my face up towards the sky to absorb the warmth of the afternoon sun as its rays beamed down between the newly arrived billowy drifting white clouds.

In the distance, the sound of shoes, more than one pair flopping on the pavement and moving in my direction, refocused my attention to the there and then. From the Nash Street alley entrance to my left, I saw three unknowns heading toward my position. At first I thought the three strangers might just be passing through, using the alley as a shortcut to some further destination. But when they adjusted their course and pace, it indicated that this was the place they were looking for. As they approached they stopped talking amongst themselves and pulled up to a simultaneous halt eight feet in front of me in the center of the alley.

"You the kid from the Fifty-First Street School?" the one in the middle asked.

"Yeah," I answered with my left hand shielding my eyes from the sunlight that was shining from directly behind the three stranger's shadowy faces.

They mumbled stuff back and forth among themselves for a few seconds and then moved to the far side of the alley and sat down against a garage wall directly opposite me. The three guys sat there on the alley cement quietly talking between themselves and staring at me as I occasionally stared back. I'd never seen them before so I assumed that they were from Avenging Grace, plus they had that Avenging Grace look about them. All three of them appeared to be at least third graders if not older. I shifted a little on my seat on the cement wondering if Billy had some dirty tricks planned for that afternoon's activities. The sun passed behind a thickening cloud cover which added to the cool, gray creeping doubt of the moment. We all sat there just trading stares and not exchanging a single word since the initial asked and answered question.

From the end of the alley where I'd entered, two more strangers came walking in our direction. The alley was usually too deserted for the new arrivals to be a coincidence so I assumed they were looking for the three guys across from me. I didn't even have the time to consider, to think through, the new developments when four more guys entered the alley from the Nash Street end and approached the growing throng in the center of the alley.

All six of the newcomers knew each other and the three earlier arrivals. It started to sink in that there were nine whispering strangers sitting, squatting, leaning and standing across from me. I couldn't tell if they were carrying marbles or not because the remnants of the clouded-over sunlight was still partially blinding me. I'd reassured myself, in response to my charging-up fight-or-flight nervous system, that they were all just spectators of the unfolding big event, Billy's cheering section.

I nervously recalled, remembered, with precise clarity, all the warnings and admonitions Wilbur Hunt had explicitly laid out to me that day I got caught by Bookbender in the library. Oh shit! (the fear component of that new word). Suddenly I didn't feel so good. I wrestled with my worst fears, shoved them into an empty closet in the corner of my head, slammed the door shut and locked it tight. I was then certain that they'd probably all do their appointed parts in trying to disrupt and disturb my playing concentration throughout the match.

I could not help but feel disconcerted as I stared across the alley at the collected assortment of potential troublemakers. I knew then that Billy was going to show because he'd be unable to bail out on all of his very own pals. I refocused and tried my best to conserve my energies for the match and put out of mind, but not out of sight, the nine complications loitering twelve feet away. Robert was right; I couldn't, I shouldn't have trusted those kids from Avenging Grace. For all I knew they were all just waiting around for Billy to show up so they could all gang up on me and roll me around on my head until I willingly or unwillingly gave up my marbles without so much as a single shot being fired.

There was one kid, one of the nine strangers, who looked different. His posture was different; he was quiet, really quiet. He stood slightly off from the rest and didn't join in with the rest of the gaggle clucking away amongst themselves. He was trouble and I knew it. There was something wrong with this kid. He wasn't there for marbles or anything else related to the game. He was the only one who scared me. I wriggled anxiously on my concrete seat thinking that regardless of how things were going to play out it wouldn't be too much longer before it was all decided.

Suddenly, the bushes to my right rustled and parted as little Frankie Hansen emerged, bulging marble sock and all. He worked his way clear of the grasping tugging bush branches and stepped into the alley with his baseball jacket partially pulled off and his cap askew on his head.

"Hey, look who's here!" one of the nine sarcastically announced, "it's little Frankie!"

They all giggled like a bunch of little girls, except the weirdo, as Frankie held his own and called back to the taller talker, a guy named Turner, to shut up.

"Shut up Turner!" Frankie looked around as he pulled his jacket back on and straightened his cap. "Hey, where's Billy?" Frankie inquired.

"Keep your shirt on shorty!" another one of the nine replied.

"He'll be here," he said forcefully as he cast a threatening glare in my direction.

"How dramatic," I thought.

To my dismay and growing concern Frankie spoke up again.

"What's he doing here?" Frankie questioned, looking at the weird loner that was generating all the bad feelings.

The guy just looked at Frankie and didn't say a word; nobody said anything. Frankie slunk back a step or two as the weirdo just stared through and past him. Yeah, I knew it then for certain, that guy was so far out of place, like he'd just dropped in from Mars. He was so out of place, like he didn't belong here, or – anywhere. "Ah shit," I thought to myself, "he's trouble." I could just feel it.

With all the lively banter serving as introduction, from the Nash Street end of the alley entered Billy Schoutenlauder. He was cruising in on his *Glider-Rider* bike with an overly casual flair for effect, as if to give notice for everyone to stand up and show the proper respect and attention before he executed his formal entrance. To compliment his dramatic entrance, Billy wore a school jacket from Righteous Destruction complete with official Crusaders insignia, the good ol' cross and lightning bolt. It looked official all right and ridiculous at the same time as the jacket was at least ten sizes to big for him. It hung on him like a wet blanket, probably a reject from an older brother, the *Eagle Scout* no doubt, who'd played in the whiffle ball game along with the *Cub Scouts* from Avenging Grace some years before that my brother Robert so bitterly recalled.

In the meantime, little Frankie had moved to the other side of the alley to a relatively neutral position a good ten feet to the right of the AG goons who were all eyes, ears and tongues wagging like a pack of whipped puppies hoping for a scratch behind the ear from their lord and master, except, again, for that one kid who just stared at me.

Billy, having almost everyone's attention, went into the final act of his entrance drama as he pedaled hard and picked up speed. His cheering section kicked in right on cue as Billy bore down on me at top speed and then slammed on his brakes skidding to a sliding stop not more than a foot from my stationary left leg. Unflinching I held my ground. Score one for the first grader from the Fifty-First Street School. I'd been around long enough to know that playing the big matches wasn't just rolling marbles around in the dirt.

With a sneer on his face so cocky that I thought he'd sprout feathers, Billy removed his hands from the bike handlebars and folded his arms across his chest. With one foot resting on the ground and the other on one of his bike pedals he leaned back on his bike seat.

"Ready to get creamed pipsqueak?" Billy cracked.

Billy made a fast hard left turn to the other side of the alley and jumped off his moving bike just before it piled into a clutch of nearby empty metal garbage cans. Just another staged diversion to impress the weak minded with his toughness and resolve of purpose. The problem for Billy was that we were about to play marbles, not trash-can-bike-bowling. Billy coolly walked from the wreck even before his bike and trashcans had finished falling and rolling around on the pavement. At that moment thicker clouds drifted in and completely blocked the warm sunlight. Even the sun didn't want to watch. I had to do it all on my own.

Billy walked to the center of the alley and chose the flattest area available. From his jacket pocket he pulled a string two-feet long with a piece of white chalk tied to one of the ends, something his mother probably did for him. He silently held up his hand with two fingers raised as Turner and one other guy, on cue, rushed forward.

"Draw it here," Billy commanded.

With his eyes locked on mine he'd pointed down at the pavement. It was Billy's lame attempt to psych me out and put me off my game. I knew then that he was worried. Turner held the string in place as the other guy walked around drawing the circle (two guys to draw a little circle? Reminded me of a joke about how many dumb guys it took to change a light bulb I'd overheard at a family picnic). Billy stepped to the side and pulled out his marble sock. The 'production' for my benefit looked poorly planned and badly rehearsed. The big opening scene did not play out very well. Turner and his pal finished with the circle as they stood up and stepped away and handed the string and chalk back to Billy so he could take it back home to his mom.

"You got your fifty marbles pipsqueak?" Billy interrogated.

"Yeah, Billy, I got my fifty, and, I got something else too."

"Yeah what's that?" Billy mockingly sneered while glancing back at his pals.

"I got just what it takes Schoutenlauder. I got exactly what it's gonna take to clean you of every marble you got. The pipsqueak

Keepers Weepers

is going to leave here with all fifty of your marbles Billy, count on it," I responded with a steady calm tone reminiscent of our last sidewalk conversation.

I'd sprouted a few feathers of my own, just to keep things even. It certainly set Billy-Boy back on his heels that I made no apologies for anything and didn't plan to either.

"You talk pretty big for a runt. Let's just see how good, or should I say," turning back again to look at his gang, "HOW BAD YOU ARE," was Billy's sparkling retort.

Everybody snickered except me, Frankie and the stone faced weirdo who seemed to be slowly descending into some dark place right in front of me and everybody else.

"Hey Billy, I'm over here," I pointedly announced as I walked up to my side of the circle to check it out. "You keep turning and talking to your girlfriends over there. You gonna go off and play with them on the swings or are you gonna stay here and play me?" I calmly taunted.

That ruffled some feathers. Like I said, playing the big matches wasn't all marble touch, marble feel and marble shot geometry.

The playing circle was on perfectly flat smooth cement. The alley from one end to the other, with the exception of our cheery little group, was as dead and deserted as ever. Billy's cheerleading squad spread out in a circle of their own, ten feet back from the playing circle, except, again, for the dark stranger who remained disturbingly silent and off to one side. Frankie Hansen stayed back as well, opposite the weirdo, as a neutral observer. I was surrounded but I didn't panic. They all did their best to look and act tough but I was more determined than ever to keep my cool and see it through wherever it led.

Billy awkwardly removed the Crusaders jacket with all the flare and style of removing a smelly old tennis shoe as he tossed it to one of his friends who in turn put it on for safekeeping. The privileged temporary keeper of the jacket beamed with all the conceited arrogance imparted by its tradition. The other kid looked just as stupid in it as Billy did. We both bent down to our knees as we prepared to play. Billy and I each dropped the five marble ante into the center of the ring.

"I'm gonna shoot first, pipsqueak," Billy commanded.

"Go ahead, let's see what you got," I responded, straight faced and unemotional. Billy prepared to take the first shot. The rules of the game were simple enough. If one of us cleared the ten or what was left of the ten ante marbles from the circle, the guy not shooting would have to keep supplying his marbles as targets until the shooter missed or cleaned out the supplier. Finally, after weeks of waiting, wondering, false starts and all the other stuff, public and private, the match was about to begin.

Billy ran a string of three hits then missed. I ran two out and missed. Billy shot again and missed big time, by several inches, embarrassing. I momentarily stared at him, intentionally, wondering with my eyes, questioning with my facial expression, if he'd really meant to miss by a mile! It got under his skin; I could see it and I could sense it. I shot again and ran out two before missing. Billy ran one out and missed again. The quick exchange left only two of the original ten ante marbles in the circle as my turn to shoot came around again.

The match to that point had been a typical back and forth opening sequence jitters session. Billy and his goons had all gone surprisingly quiet once the match was underway. Far from being obnoxious and harassing, they all diligently paid attention as they murmured their approval when Billy connected and all shutting up when I ran a streak. But I was still the one in the hot seat as the match pressure flowed thick and heavy like hot freshly cooked chocolate pudding.

Billy wasn't really bad but he wasn't really good either. He was really just an average player. His hits weren't solid, they were glancing shots, unconvincing in their aim and execution: I might have almost called them luck. Conversely, my hits were dead on, solid and sure. Even my rare and infrequent misses had a confidence, clarity and consistency of style about them that his even rarer and less frequent glancing-at-best hits completely lacked. I got to my feet for a short stretch while surveying the position of the two remaining marbles that lay near the center of the circle. Billy used the break in the action to slip in another one of his wittier comments.

"Ready to give up pipsqueak?"

Almost everybody chuckled again. That irked me, really ticked me off. There I was being cool, playing well, holding my own and not running over at the mouth, outnumbered and even giving Billy the undeserved respect that he might, just might, have been a capable, competent and comparable player. I felt my anger and confidence blend together and then surge to the surface in a flash of power and heat. The bees went into high gear. I roared on all cylinders clean and hard. Kneeling back down and before taking a single complete breath I cleared the ring of the remaining two marbles with a single ricocheting shot. They all gasped as Billy muttered something about a "lucky shot." I knew better.

Looking to Billy, I faked a cough just to let him and everybody else know, just to rub it in, that he was the first one to pull a marble from his sock as a target, a definite psychological advantage for me and, conversely, a big psychological disadvantage for him. Before the dropped marble even came to a rest, while it was still rolling on the cement, I fired away and hit it solidly from the circle. He quickly dropped another marble towards the center of the circle and I clocked it straight on in mid-air (yeah, that's right, MID-AIR) as it cleared the circle in less than a split second. Dead silence. Billy froze in place, shell-shocked. It was obvious that he wasn't used to, nor did he very much like, having to reach into his marble sock and put his best up as targets. At that point in the match I stood a tall four marbles ahead, eight to four.

Stunned, disbelieving, Billy unintelligibly mumbled and grumbled to match all of the unintelligible mumbling and grumbling that was coming from his pals as he had to reach into his marble sock fifty-seven straight consecutive times as I delivered on what I'd promised. I ran him clean. I was on fire. He never shot again in the match. His friends shuffled in place uneasily. Looks of disbelief were plastered on their faces like wet clay masks. The weirdo just kept staring. Frankie Hansen was silent but smiling. Billy slowly got to his feet as he stared at my bulging marble sock that was full of all of his ex-marbles. He stood rigid, frozen and as pale and discolored as a melting, dripping, pale yellow lemon *Popsicle*, as he held onto his flat, empty marble sock.

Still kneeling on the pavement, I was gathering the few of Billy's marbles that I hadn't yet socked away when appearing directly before me, in the middle of the marble ring, were the shoes of the weirdo. I looked up to find him glaring down at me. He was about the size and build of Billy. It became immediately obvious to me in that sickening moment that by the look on this guy's face that he had checked out to another world, some strange place that other people rarely go to, NUTVILLE! I slowly rose to my feet as I began to tie my marble sock to my belt.

Without warning, without provocation, weirdo threw a punch! I jumped back and to my right as the blow glanced my left temple and scraped across my forehead. I let out with a cry of pain and surprise as I landed on the alley pavement with a THUD!

"YEAH," was Billy's reaction.

"NO," Frankie Hansen yelled.

I rolled onto my stomach and tried to gather my wits as a trickle of blood rolled down my forehead and into my left eyebrow. My reaction was instinctive, automatic and completely without fear or hesitation. I struggled to my feet and, still half-bent over, gathered the long neck of my double marble socks and wrapped it around my right fist. I half-turned to face my assailant who stood over me a scant one-foot away. As I turned my body to face him straight on I swung my loaded marble socks with an upward arc and speeding momentum that caught him square between the legs. His face went blank as the air involuntarily escaped from his lungs in a hoarse blowing groan as he doubled over. He never saw it coming. As the blow connected I fell back down onto the pavement from the effort. Weirdo's face was beet red as he struggled, with eyes closed, to breathe.

From one knee on the alley floor I stood back up and with another arcing horizontal swing my full marble socks came full force across weirdo's face in a smashing right hook. He never saw that one coming either. It connected square and true as well with a cracking, grinding force that sent him to the ground. I stumbled back from the blow but remained standing as everyone, including Billy, moved back several feet and stood dumbfounded, mouths agape. Frankie had gone white as a sheet. I feared the worst as I clutched my marble socks with both hands not sure of what Billy and his gang had in mind.

Quickly looking from face to face, trying to judge the rapidly evolving situation as best I could, I detected only surprise and confusion and no visible resolve to charge and pile-on to finish what weirdo had started. The situation just hung there in silent limbo when Billy made clear what would happen next. While weirdo remained in a fetal position on the ground groaning and coughing, as blood ran down the side of my face, windy words from Billy's big mouth blew into the breach.

"I bet you think you're really hot stuff, don't you pipsqueak? Well, I got news for you runt! You ain't finished yet buddy boy, not by a long shot! You're just getting started! Turner!" Billy shrieked!

Turner had been standing behind and to my right. As he'd walked past he made a point of jabbing me in the right side with his left elbow. I immediately lifted my marble sock, ready to swing for the fence, not knowing whether I'd have to fight again or not. I was by then so ready for anything, so hyped-up on adrenaline, I was ready and more than willing to go down in flames, fighting to the last if necessary. As Turner kept on moving past, Billy stepped over the prostrate weirdo and laid out his version of the new ground rules.

"You're gonna play Turner now, got it? And you're not leaving here until I say so, got that too?" Billy instructed to my face.

"That wasn't the deal Schoutenlauder!" I yelled back through wet eyes and gritted teeth.

"Well it's the deal now pipsqueak! Your gonna play Turner and that's it! Somebody get Weirdo outta here," Billy ordered.

They actually called him 'Weirdo'. I knew I'd been right about that kid. One of the nine walked up and half-picked-up and half-dragged Weirdo down the alley and out-of-sight and out-of-mind.

Billy's facial complexion had been invaded by a rolling molten flush red. Fuming, he turned to Turner and instructed him to clean me out. Turner didn't know it then but he was going to need a lot more than verbal instruction to clean me out. From inside

Turner's jacket materialized a sock full of marbles, my guess that the count was fifty. I was dead on. Checking around at the remaining six on-lookers, I noticed upon closer inspection that they were all carrying marbles; fifty each was my guess.

That was Billy's game, his backup plan and his insurance. He brought along his pals all loaded to bear just in case I turned out to be the real deal. Weirdo, on the other hand, apparently just showed up, having invited himself along for the show. Billy would try to have his revenge right then and there through his goons. Robert had nailed it right on the head; you just couldn't trust those kids from Avenging Grace.

Collecting my battered but functioning senses, getting over the initial shock from the unexpected attack and the change in the rules, I prepared to play Turner, another unknown marble entity. I could have just got up and left as I'd kept my word and proven my point; I was the better marble player by a mile, by a hundred miles. Billy wasn't even close. I could have ran and fought my way out of that alley and gotten home clean and safe. But, just for a brief moment, from deep inside my chest, I felt a reassuring rumble. It had momentarily been a bumpy patch of road but the engine was still purring. I was able, ready and willing to see it all the way through. Heaven help any of those clowns who got in my way because marble hell was about to come-a-knocking!

Turner looked dark and sinister but not crazy. Everything about him was dark. His hair, his eyes, his olive skin, even his wardrobe ensemble was black and dark brown. We each dropped our five ante marbles into the ring as I offered Turner the first shot, it being my prerogative, a benefit of having won the previous match. Turner unsuccessfully tried to hide his apprehension and for good reason too. I looked him straight in the eye, silently promising myself, and him, that I'd give it my all and my full concentration and, without mercy, clean him out too. The resolve must have been dripping from my face like sweat. Funny how determined silence is always louder than empty shouting.

Turner accepted my offer of the first shot which he proceeded to miss by a foot. I then ran five straight before missing. Turner shot and missed again and again by at least a foot. It turned out to be be his last shot and his last chance. My next shot was the first of fifty straight solid clean hits. He dropped marble after marble into the ring as I registered clear hit after clear hit. From the start he never had even the remotest chance, I'd properly seen to that. Turner joined Billy in the land of wacked-'n'-shocked, on his knees with mouth hung open like an empty gunnysack, holding the second flat marble sock of the day. It did not look good for Avenging Grace.

Turner's complete collapse and failure just turned up the heat on Billy's tea-kettle-for-a-head as steam and boiling water spurted and whistled from his ears. Turner slowly crawled up to his feet and stumbled around, still not believing or fully aware of what just transpired. He looked like his dog just died. Keeping tabs to gauge the reaction of the rest of the gang I sensed an increasing unease, a jittery trembling just like corralled horses getting ready to bolt for open ground at the approach of a swirling tornado. I was the twister bearing down on them. Thunder and lightning boomed and sparked from between my teeth. I realized that if things kept up as they were, I'd soon run out of places to stuff and carry all of the unexpected additional winnings. I strained to a standing position under the increased load of bulging marble socks and full pants and overloaded jacket pockets as Billy, trying in vain to contain himself, decided that another spur of the moment deal was in order.

"You still ain't finished runt! It's just beginner's luck, that's all! You're gonna lose and lose big. Tommy! You ready?" was Billy's ranting retort.

Ahhh, there it was, Billy's big mistake, his hopelessly flawed logic. He actually looked at me as if I were a beginner, a novice, when in reality, when it came to marbles I was his senior by immeasurable years.

"Yep, just say when," was Tommy's cocky response.

"I say now!" Billy gasped.

As I turned to my left, Tommy brushed by me even more sure and full of himself than Turner had tried to be. Turner was back on the alley floor again. By that time he'd moved to a sitting position leaning against a garage wall across the alley in the exact spot he'd originally waited for Billy's arrival just minutes before. He looked – well – unhealthy.

Tommy, on the other hand, was Mr. Cool. He acted like I'd better watch out because he was onto my game, my 'gimmick'. The problem for Tommy was that I didn't have a 'gimmick'. I was pure marble magic; it's what I did. Tommy dropped his ante into the circle right along with me. Still kneeling, I again offered the first shot to my opponent. Looking around to the others with a smirk on his face like he was onto my tricks, he folded his arms and cocked his head to the side.

"Naaa pipsqueak. You go 'head. First shot is yours."

Everybody smiled nervously as they all hoped that Tommy was actually onto something. Well, as it turned out, neither I nor anyone else was ever to discover if Tommy had been onto something or not. I never did find out how good or how bad a marble player he was either because starting with the first shot, I ran off fifty-five straight solid hits with the rapidity of machine gun fire. Wise guy 'gimmick' solving 'I'm onto his tricks' Tommy never got a chance to fire a single shot. He did prove to be proficient at one thing however: pulling marbles from his sock as quickly as he could and dropping them into the center of the circle where they were efficiently dispatched. When it was over, he was still kneeling in the same place he'd started with his arms folded. Only two things had changed for Tommy during the course of the match. His once full marble sock was empty and the expression on his face had undergone a radical transformation. Avenging Grace was on the skids. They were striking out in order.

Billy was burning up. Heck, he'd even gotten hotter than Rodney Strong, which was hard to do. During Tommy's maddening passive non-involvement in the last match Billy rapidly paced back and forth and kicked at his bike several times, screaming at Tommy to stop sitting there and do something. Poor Tommy could do nothing but sit there while I knocked him out of the match and into Billy's doghouse one marble at a time. By that time in the extended festivities, I knew that there would be no easy clean way out of the alley until I'd played and defeated the whole damn bunch, the entire, unofficial, Avenging Grace marble crew.

After cleaning Tommy of his prized possessions I simply remained kneeling in my playing position at the edge of the circle and purposefully dropped my next five marble ante into the center of the circle. I'd learned from Kit Cat that when everything around you was going crazy it was best just to quietly sit down and let the dust settle until an obvious and reasonable plan of action made itself evident. So I knelt, motionless, in place, took a couple of deep breaths and mentally prepared (the only things I didn't do was yawn and then lick my fur).

"Who's next?" I calmly, quietly, stated without even looking up to see who would move up to the edge of the ring.

Voluntarily stepping forward, all on his own without any coaxing from Billy or anyone else, was the afternoon's next challenger. His name was Harry. I knew that at once not because he told me and not because someone called out his name but because he had it literally written everywhere on his person. It was sewn on his shirt pocket, on his jacket collar, on his pants pocket, on the tops of his socks and was even written on the sides of the soles of his shoes, not to mention sewn into his underwear waistband that stuck out above his pants. I figured that Harry was either a member of a very large family or that he had some sort of disorder, an identity crisis or a memory defect, and kept forgetting who he was. I guessed that as a fail-safe and foolproof backup Harry had his name tattooed somewhere on his body as well.

Either way, Harry tried to come off as the strong, silent, confident tiger-killer-type as he dropped his five marbles into the ring. I did not have to offer Harry the first shot as he knelt down and announced that the shot was his. Having just witnessed the Tommy disaster, Harry made the wise decision to at least have the first chance even if it might be his only chance. From his side of the ring Harry quietly assured me that all the fooling around was over and that he would, single handedly, square things away for himself and his defeated friends in short order. Harry's secret agent demeanor was infectious as all the wounded and unwounded hounds bayed, bellowed and barked for blood. They were cheering Harry on like he was the jockey riding the hundred-to-one long shot in the last race of the day that they'd all just bet their life savings on.

Harry, in his own sort of clumsy-mixed-with-cool way, leaned down and on his first shot made a solid hit and a successful, albeit accidental, double ricochet, clearing the ring of three marbles in a single shot. Everyone cheered that Harry was going to do it to the runt! The problem for Harry was that he'd even surprised himself with the shot as it went right to his head. His entire cool facade immediately deteriorated into a sloppy goofiness that seemed totally ridiculous but somehow much more befitting Harry's truer character. His glory was short lived. His next shot was a truer representation of his real skill level; it was a total disaster.

His thumbnail got jammed up on his forefinger, the marble-playing equivalent of tripping over your own feet. His marble never even touched the ground until it bounced off the garage wall six feet behind me and came to a rolling rest along side of my right foot. Harry looked as if someone had just slapped him in the face. I casually turned to my right and picked up the wayward marble and redeposited it into the center of the circle. I did my best to psyche Harry out. I stared straight into his eyes with a perplexed look on my face that matched the perplexed look on his face and asked, without words, if he'd really meant, if he'd really planned, such a brilliant move. In just under five minutes and with only one missed shot, I successfully concluded the match with Harry and claimed my fourth successive victory of the afternoon. I hadn't lost a single marble and was, in fact, two-hundred ahead for the day. Harry threw his empty marble sock into the dirt as he got up and sulked his way over to the loser's side of the alley where the bodies were starting to pileup.

Admittedly, the discovery that Jason would end up doing marble battle with the multi-headed *Hydra* besides the *Troll Twins* on his way to *Marble Mountain* was to say the least, unexpected. But I was proving equal to the task, as the beast was no match for my deadly aim.

It was four heads down and four to go. I looked around the circle at those that remained standing as, still on my knees, I dropped five more marbles into the circle for the next inevitable match.

To my astonishment Billy had calmed down and started to laugh as he called for a huddle of all the gang and he cautioned me to stay put and for Frankie to butt out. Billy and his pals bumped heads as they argued back and forth before they agreed on their newly devised plan (the third to that point if I recalled accurately), the final sure-fire plan of action. The huddle broke as even Turner and Tommy seemed to have emerged from their stuporous mental states and they'd all resumed their circular positions around the playing area. Billy leaned in really close from his standing position, his face within inches of mine.

"Well pipsqueak, you seem pretty hot so we figured you wouldn't mind a little stiffer match to cool you down. You don't mind, do you runt?" Billy snidely barked.

Despite his eroding chances of regaining a single one of his or anybody else's lost marbles, Billy still tried in vain to intimidate me into some base act of submission. I did my best to dump a bucket of cold water on what little fire he really had left.

"Billy – I'm ready for any match you got," I stated as an indisputable matter of fact.

"GOOD," he shouted in my face.

Billy stepped back away from me with a big maniac smile on his face, like he'd just spotted death coming for him and was in the process of a complete mental disintegration. He snapped his fingers and not one but two of the remaining untested stepped up to the ring ready to play. Dave and Randy quickly stooped down and dropped their five marbles apiece into the ring. Randy was an average nondescript looking sort of kid but Dave, Dave was from the far end of the scale, the end of the scale that comes from around a blind corner or from up and over the far side of some hill in the far hazy distance. Dave was a short, squat fifty-year-old man in a child's body. That description doesn't make much sense but the physical appearance of the kid standing in front of me didn't either.

Dave was dressed in old baggy blue jeans, army type boots and wore the Crusaders jacket Billy had arrived in, over a dirty white t-shirt. His head appeared to be going bald but he had all kinds of light blond hair growing on his face. At first I thought he was a dwarf. Rumors about Avenging Grace had been varied and fantastic enough that just such an occurrences could have been entirely possible. I surmised that dwarfs had to go to school somewhere, so why not at a church school where God could watch over them? It was further rumored among many outsiders, like myself, that when dwarfs graduated they were talked into repaying God and the church for the watchful care and guidance by going to Africa, Asia or the Middle East (bible land) to be missionaries or shepherds. None of this could be confirmed of course, but if I'd ever seen or imagined a dwarf herdsman, that kid Dave fit the bill.

Randy and Dave took their respective playing positions opposite me. The rules for a simultaneous multiple player setups were basically round robin in nature. It wasn't some anybody-shoots-at-any-time-they-feel-like-it confused melee. There was an order and logic that made such a marble match possible. What Billy, Randy and Dave saw in the setup as being to their advantage was a mystery to me, because, well, no one player or two players working together had any special type of advantage. But, if one player got well ahead in such a match he could take advantage and steer it in a certain direction. Needless to say, I was well prepared to drive that vehicle in any direction I wanted to all day long.

Dwarfy Dave took the first shot and four more as he started the match with a five hit run before missing. Randy then hit seven in a row before missing leaving just three of the original fifteen. Their game strategy and the reason behind all the laughter in the huddle became clear, but so did the fault in their logic. Once the original fifteen were cleared from the circle and it became Dave's turn to shoot he would try for only what was in the circle and then purposely miss before forcing Randy to supply any marbles from his sock. I would then, in turn, have to put up targets for any run Randy would have, Randy seemingly being the better player of the two.

The basic flaw in their plan, the error in their logic, and my counter strategy was that Dave had to put up targets for me if and when Randy missed. That was how the simultaneous multiple player setups worked. If I put a run together on Dave's marble supply when he shot next he'd have to start hitting Randy big time just to stay in the game. So, in fact, for me it was almost easier playing both of them together in this round robin affair than it would be to play each one of them separately. It was all very efficient from my perspective because I'd save both time and effort with a potentially bigger reward. Brainiacs these guys were not.

In that particular instance, it was even easier than I figured because I had the additional benefit, the extra reward of watching Dave and Randy flounder as they tried to execute their hastily and poorly devised scheme; i.e., Randy and Dave didn't work well together. When my turn came back around I put the hit on Dave thirty-eight straight times, depleting his supply to a mere twelve marbles. In an effort to avert the wrath of Billy and stay in the game, Dave put the squeeze on Randy with a run of twenty-six consecutive hits raising his twelve back up to thirty-eight while dropping Randy from fifty-two down to twenty-six before missing. When it came time for Randy to shoot again, forcing me to put up the targets, he was so mad at Dave for doing what he'd done that he missed his first shot and my turn to put the big hit back on Dave came around again! I really started to enjoy their plan.

I ran Dave another thirty-five straight before I missed, a well disguised intentional miss, leaving him with only three marbles left in his almost empty marble sock. In a desperate and confused effort to stay in the game, despite Randy's protestations and outright threats, Dave ran Randy right out of the game with twenty-six straight hits. I'd originally started the match hoping for, but not necessarily expecting the best. Instead I found myself scores of marbles ahead and with Randy, the better player of the two, out of the match having been done in by his own teammate. With Randy sidelined it came down to my turn after Dave who, nervously rattled by Randy's ongoing tirade and uncontrolled outbursts, understandably missed his first and only chance at one of my marbles. He didn't get another shot or another chance as I put together another razzle-dazzle run and cleaned him out. I won the match against what turned out to be the two best players from Avenging Grace that had showed up that day, in an emotionally merciless and strategically decisive manner.

It was six down and two to go as once again, calmly, I dropped another five marbles back into the circle and patiently waited for the next challenge. Billy was blowing his top, cussing out both Dave and Randy who were cussing out each other for screwing up the plan that should have stopped me for sure. While Billy, Randy and Dave argued over who deserved the most blame I turned my gaze to the only two untried players left, Paul and Danny. From the looks on their faces when my eyes meet theirs, neither one seemed all that eager to jump into the fray and willingly put up their marbles in the defense of a losing cause.

It didn't hurt my cause that during the match I'd gotten sweaty, dirty with wild man crazy hair and a long streak of dried blood running across my forehead and down over my face. I looked like a sailor on his first night of shore leave after months at sea who'd spent that night drinking, fighting, falling down a lot and then fighting and falling down some more! But I acted like I looked, like I'd proven myself and that I was ready for battle, any battle that Avenging Grace was willing to launch my way.

    Billy was too frantic to reach any type of reasonable or thoughtful conclusion or understanding with Randy and Dave. He turned back to me and without a word pointed to Paul and Danny and informed them that their turns had come. They were each going to be the next to place their marbles into the sacrificial ring. They both looked at each other, then at me and then at Billy and silently shook their heads, simultaneously, "no" as they stepped back and away from the playing area.

Billy lost all self-control in the face of such rank insubordination but Paul and Danny remained steadfast in their decision. They stated, in no uncertain terms, that I was just too hot, just too good, and they weren't going to throw their marbles away for nothing and especially not to satisfy Billy's loser's grudge against me. Billy went absolutely berserk, a real wild man from the jungle right before everyone's eyes. He ran up to Paul and physically yanked the marble sock from his belt. When he finished with Paul he rushed Danny where he met with stiffer unexpected resistance. They struggled, cussing and cursing as they both fell to the ground, wrestling fiercely before Billy prevailed and jumped up holding Danny's marble sock as well.

Flushed and fuming Billy took a position opposite me for a second time with two socks full of confiscated marbles, prepared to take me on a second time. Paul and Danny were more than upset and didn't hide the fact as they warned Billy that he'd better not lose their marbles or else!

"OR ELSE WHAT?" "You big chickens! You cry babies! You're afraid to play this pipsqueak? You'll get your marbles back, we all will, SO – SHUT – UP! This little jackass can't beat me twice! NOBODY'S THAT LUCKY," Billy screamed back.

If Billy had been in a more receptive, a more rational mood, I would have told him not to bet on it, especially with other people's marbles. As far as beating individual competitors twice, or more often than that, luck had nothing to do with it. I could have provided him with, upon receipt of reasonable written request, a more than ample list of willing references and testimonials from my school.

Turning his enraged attentions back to me, he gave notice that the starting ante was now ten marbles each and that he would be taking the first shot.

"Easy to be bold and brash with other people's marbles," I thought.

For me the increased ante was insignificant considering that I'd acquired an additional three-hundred marbles in the course of the unanticipated marble match marathon. As far as Billy taking the first shot, well, so what, who cared? Unfortunately for Paul and Danny, Billy was too worked up, and not good enough, even when he wasn't worked up, to play at my level. He shot only a total of five short successful sequences. I methodically, precisely, mercilessly, like I'd done all afternoon long, beat Billy out of every single marble he'd forcefully requisitioned from his two certain-to-be ex-friends. About twenty shots into my final run of forty straight clean hits, Billy sensed that it was all over. He never once looked me straight in the eye again for the rest of the afternoon.

Billy was not only defeated, he was finally, thoroughly and completely beaten. On his hands and knees, head down, eyes staring straight down into the alley cement, near the end of the match, he thoughtlessly dumped, en masse, the remaining few marbles he'd taken from Paul and Danny into the center of the circle. Paul and Danny suffered through spastic contortions with every clean crack of marble hitting marble as I cleaned their hard won collections from the ring one marble at a time. When I landed the last and winning shot, Paul and Danny turned their backs, unable to witness the final hit that ended any dreams of marble greatness they'd ever imagined or hoped for.

Billy was catatonic. He was hard frozen through and through, stuck on all fours. Unmoving, unnaturally silent, Billy stared down into and through the alley pavement like it was a window into Hell. I pulled myself upright and, while still kneeling, sat back on the heels of my feet. I looked around at the assembled gathering. Turner, Tommy, Harry, Dave, Randy, Paul, Danny and Billy – not one of them would leave the alley that day with a single one of their marbles; I had them all. There was no one left to play. Before me on the cement and in my bulging marble socks and in my stuffed and protruding pockets were four-hundred hard won marbles, taken fair and square in battle, mine to keep, forever.

Slowly, shakily, carefully, I rose to my feet, thinking it best to collect and gather my winnings and be on my way before Billy entertained any thoughts of trying to rough me up to get his and everyone else's marbles back. All of them having suffered through and shared in a major marble disaster, under the circumstances, all were potentially eligible for immediate and willing recruitment into a ruthless gang of poor and possibly violent losers. The incident with Weirdo an hour before bought me, I hoped, some measurable credibility with regards to my self-defense capabilities.

I was ready to walk away when Billy's head cocked up mechanically, like a robot being activated. He looked toward me without direct eye contact and then, of all people, little Frankie. Billy leapt to his feet and lunged toward me, grabbing me firmly by my left arm. That was it for certain as I thought, for the second time that day, I'd have to fight to save myself. Instinctively, I wrapped the top of my loaded marble sock with a single hand flip and swirl around my right fist, ready and willing to unleash a defensive blow. Billy was a goner, flipped out; all of his pigeons had gotten loose and flown the coop. He'd lost his marbles! The pupils of his eyes were tiny black beads in a sea of bloodshot white.

"You got one last match to play, Archer!" Billy grinned.

"Who? You and your pals are done, cleaned out," I emphatically stated.

"You're gonna play Frankie boy!" Billy whined and mocked like he was ready for a straitjacket. Frankie heard this but he didn't want to believe it. He went stiff from fear as Billy stared at him. I yanked my left arm free from Billy's grasp and took a step back ready to strike.

"I'm not playing anybody!" Frankie half-shouted and half-cried.

"Yeah you will yeah little jerk, so get over here right now!" Billy commanded.

"No I won't and you can't make me!" Frankie pleaded as he made a break for the bushes across the alley from which he'd emerged earlier.

Billy was too quick. He jumped in after Frankie and pulled the struggling and protesting five-year-old back into the alley from the bushes, dragging him by the back of his jacket.

Billy's friends were visibly disturbed by the turn of events, tired of the whole situation. Paul and Danny told Billy to lay off Frankie and that everybody, all of them, were willing to leave things as they stood and go home. Billy wouldn't hear of it, wouldn't have any of it. He made a fist in Paul and Danny's direction with his free hand and warned them and everyone else that no one left until he said so. Still holding the captive and crying Frankie by the back of his jacket, Billy shouted his final instructions to Frankie and me.

"Okay boys, now the two runts here are going to play, isn't that right Archer? Right Frankie boy?"

"Leave him alone Schoutenlauder! He doesn't want to play so I won't play him," I retorted.

"You'll play him Archer or my fists will play with your face!" Billy threatened.

Billy was just too big for me to handle straight on. Besides, I could only move so fast being weighed down by an extra twenty pounds of marbles in my pockets. Further, maybe Paul and Danny might have stepped in to help me or at least stayed out of any physical fracas I'd have with Billy but there were still all of the other losers including the brooding dwarf Dave to contend with. I'd just get killed and then rolled for all of the marbles besides. So what could I do? I played Frankie who, at the time, wasn't even fit to walk a straight line. His eyes were all teary and bleary from crying as his whole body, including his hands, were shaking from being so frightened.

Schoutenlauder viciously yanked the full marble sock from Frankie's resisting but weaker grip and reached in and pulled out a handful of marbles as ante and threw them down into the ring. Reluctantly, but watchful for some advantage to come my way, I knelt down and reached into my jacket pocket and grabbed and dropped a handful of marbles into the circle as well. Frankie still resisted, unwilling to take part so Billy forced the issue even further by knocking off Frankie's baseball cap and then shoving him up to the playing circle as he informed him of the situation as his distorted world view presented it.

"Look yeah little jerk, you're from Avenging Grace just like the rest of us so, if we lose your gonna lose too, GOT IT?" Billy shouted into Frankie's ear.

Frankie responded with a fresh flood of tears. Billy was exposing his true self - cruel and vindictive. To ease Frankie's pain and trauma I quietly offered him the first shot and told him to take all the time he needed between shots as I gave him a big wink. Billy butted in instantly and told me to shut up and for both of us to get on with it.

Billy hung over us like a black cloud. While Frankie wiped his watery eyes and runny nose on his jacket sleeves, I unobtrusively emptied my jacket pockets of their share of that day's winnings. I planned to keep all the marbles I won from Frankie separate from the rest. I guessed Frankie's collection to total about seventy marbles. Every single one of his marbles was as clean as a new marble, not a nick or scratch to be seen, real virgin beauties.

Frankie wasn't too bad of a player despite his tender age. But he was so nervous, so upset and so traumatized by being bullied into playing, not to mention Billy's continuous threats, that he wasn't able play up to any real or imagined capabilities. Throughout our forced match Frankie was sniffling and continuously wiping his wet eyes and drippy nose on his already soaked-through jacket sleeves.

There were several instances during the match, owing to my skill, that I made several intentional close misses just to make things look good for Billy and allow Frankie a breather and regain some sense of composure, but it was useless. Even if I let Frankie intentionally start to win Billy would not have let him stop until I'd been completely cleaned out. Considering Billy's poor attitude and completely corrupted state of mind, even if I lost everything to Frankie, Billy would have probably claimed most of it as his fee for getting everybody's marbles back. No, there was no clean and kind way out of it. I'd concluded it best to get it over with, see what would happen next and try to sort it all out sometime later.

As expected Frankie's water drenched vision and fragile state of mind caused him to miss repeatedly. I refocused and put two quick runs together with Frankie only shooting one more time as I claimed the bitter and hollow victory. It was gut wrenching for Frankie and torture for me. Every time he reached into his marble sock to put out another target it was if he was tearing off and throwing away a little part of his soul. His five-year-old sanity and solution to life was being taken away against his will and and sacrificed one marble at a time. Whenever he was slow or reluctant, unwilling to pull another marble from his sock for the center of the ring, Billy shouted at him and dug into Frankie's marble sock and pulled one out himself.

Frankie's eyes and nose were so red, wet and puffy that he barely looked like Frankie anymore. He was shattered and marbleless. Billy wasted little time in adding insult to injury by throwing Frankie's empty marble sock onto the ground and grinding it into the pavement with his shoes as he relentlessly berated and belittled Frankie for being, in his opinion, a worthless wimp. Frankie sat cross-legged on the alley floor with his elbows on his knees and his head resting in his hands as the full force of the humiliation took its toll. Frankie lost all will, any emotional strength he had left and cried uncontrollably.

"Billy, you damn creep," I'd thought to myself as I stood up. I struggled with the urge to jump on him and wreak as much physical havoc upon his person as I could before he and his goons could regain the upper hand. As if my thoughts had been said and heard out loud, I was saved the effort by Paul and Danny, who stepped forward and announced together that the match was over and done with and that the better player of the day had been victorious. The tone of their voices indicated that they meant business and that they would think nothing of grabbing Billy, tying him up, gagging him and then dragging him away in tow behind his own bike for several blocks over the rough pavement.

The rebellious conduct was unacceptable to Billy. It was his friends, his pals and his subordinates telling him that enough was enough; that was too much for him to take. Billy threw a temper tantrum. He acted and looked completely ridiculous in the eyes of everyone present. The cool, calm, tough cocky facade of Billy Schoutenlauder had been stripped bare and exposed as a false front. He was a phony. He regressed into infancy for all present to witness. Billy had found and was expressing his true level: a poorly behaved two-year-old with an upset tummy whose rattle had fallen from his crib. Even sobbing Frankie had more class, dignity and presence of mind. Frankie looked up in bewilderment as he watched Billy flip out right in front of everybody.

With both hands balled into tight fists Billy started for me with death in his eyes. I'd been watching Billy very closely the whole time, waiting for him to completely snap. I took a quickstep back and with marble sock cocked and ready to fire I prepared to defend myself as best I could for as long as I could. If I was going to go down I would go down fighting to the very last. Billy was about to lunge the final five feet and land on my head with fists flying and feet kicking when, to my complete surprise, the dwarf Dave stepped in between us and faced Billy and told him, nose to nose, to lay off! Dave repeated what Paul and Danny had already said, it was over and he was ready to leave things as they were. Billy started to tear up as he pushed Dave hard by the shoulder.

"You're a disgrace you jerk! Give me my brother's jacket back you – rrraaat!" Billy screamed.

"You got it!" Dave shouted back. "The only disgrace around here, Schoutenlauder, is you!" Dave added as he took off the Crusader jacket and threw it at Billy.

This put Billy back on his heels, it knocked him right out of his hysterical tantrum. He didn't expect Dave, one of his own pals, to face him down and call him out. Billy struggled to regain and maintain his previous level of mania as he mockingly, in an inappropriate baby's voice, told Dave to run along home so he could finish the job himself. I was the 'job' he was referring to, the 'job' being to try and beat me to a pulp. Paul and Danny stepped up and added their blocking weight between Billy and me in support of Dave as they reiterated to Billy that it was finished and that he should stop embarrassing them all and stop acting like an unbelievable jerk. They also used the moment to remind Billy that he had no right to take and lose their marbles the way he did and that they expected to be repaid, in full, for their losses.

Shocked, embarrassed, Billy reacted in a predictable manner. He flung his brother's Crusader jacket over his shoulder and stormed over to where his bike had crash parked. Kicking the empty metal trash cans out of his way, sending them rolling all over the alley, he jerked his bike up to a riding position, hopped on and rode off towards the Nash Street end of the alley as fast as he could. All the way Billy was shouting back at his friends, calling them all a bunch of rat-fink-chicken-bastards along with a few vaguely familiar hand gestures and other unrecognizable cuss words thrown in. Harry, Turner, Tommy and Randy ran after Billy, hedging their bets with the past, unable to accept the change, the new way, the real Billy. You just couldn't have tyrants without people who wanted to be tyrannized. Dave, Paul and Danny stayed behind for a while with their hands stuffed into their empty pockets, each with an expression like, for the first time, they'd seen and experienced the real Billy Schoutenlauder.

After several seconds of awkward silence, Billy and his sheepish followers disappeared from the alley. My heaving chest was relaxing, my breathing rate slowing down, my blood pressure returning to normal.

"Yeah know Archer, you're the best marble player I've ever seen and I ain't kiddin' either," Dave confessed.

"You sure are," Danny added as the three of them turned and started to walk away towards the north end of the alley.

Suddenly Paul stopped and turned back, almost as an after thought.

"Hey Archer, here, your probably gonna need this." Paul tossed me his empty marble sock. "You won 'em fair and square."

Dave and Danny followed suit as they each also reached into their jacket pockets and tossed me their empty marble socks.

"Archer, just remember one thing," Paul continued, "not all of us at Avenging Grace are crazy animals like Billy and Weirdo," as Danny and Dave sighed in agreement.

"Yeah, I'll remember that, and, thanks – thanks a lot!" I called back as they turned and walked away.

I heard them talking among themselves as they walked into the distance, something about a Father Wagermann having a serious talk with Billy, something along those lines.

Well, the showdown was over, history, everything had been decided. It had lasted just over two hours, a personal record, with total winnings of over four-hundred marbles, possibly a world record. The only ill effects other than my frazzled nerves were a slight headache from Weirdo's punch and a cramp in my right shooting hand from the extended workout. Not being a 'switch shooter' did have its drawbacks.

Breathing easier, it finally struck me full force that the big match and the excitement, worry and doubt of the previous two weeks were over. I could have never imagined, even with my wild imagination, that I would have encountered and prevailed against such extreme circumstances. You just couldn't make this stuff up! As I slipped my hands into my near overflowing jacket pockets, it was immediately clear to me that the match had been decided but the business of the day had not been concluded.

Frankie slowly rose to his feet as he wiped his eyes and nose again and again. Without saying a word he looked down at his dirty, empty marble sock that Billy had so cruelly ground down onto the alley pavement. Frankie was in bad shape. He'd suffered greatly from all the intimidation and humiliation he'd been subjected to. He looked up at me for a moment while sucking several tears back up and in through his nose. Having picked up his baseball cap he put it back on, pulled it down over his eyes and started to walk away towards the north end of the alley.

Frankie bore the unbearable weight of his crushed world and handled his loss and disappointment with a dignity and bearing that would never be within Billy's reach. His parting glance shot through me like a hot bullet; just for that second I felt all of his searing pain and anguish. He walked in halting steps like he was being held together by an assortment of mismatched nuts and bolts, all of which were dangerously loose. At any moment Frankie's shaky little body could start falling apart one piece at a time.

I'd thought of it earlier and in fact had even planned on it with my wink at Frankie when our forced match started. But I'd been forced to put the plan on the back burner due to the uncertain and erratic behavior of Billy and his friends. It came back to me as bright as one of my mother's *Instamatic* camera flash bulbs at Christmas time. It was the only logical, the only decent, the only right thing to do as all the dust settled and the whole picture snapped into sharp, clear and undistorted focus.

Being champ wasn't all practicing and competing, all ability and playing perfection. A champ also had to know justice and fair play, when to be reasonable, generous and compassionate. If Frankie had challenged me on his own, knowing full well the risks and consequences, I might have played him or maybe not if

I thought he wasn't competitively competent. As I got better at the game I frequently declined match requests or even stopped a match early on if it was obvious that the challenger was not a true match or anywhere near my skill level.

I'd won plenty of marbles over the school year, probably more than all the other kids in school combined. I didn't have to claim everybody's marbles for myself. I wasn't a needy-greedy marble pig. Fairness and justice in the marble game wasn't just knowing 'how to play', it was knowing 'when to play' and 'when not to play', when not to take unfair advantage. If Frankie had been a serious self-determined player I would have kept his marbles along with all the rest without a second thought and headed for home. Marbles, no matter how intense or threatening the competition, was still just a game, a game more perfect than others of course, but still a game that left a lot to be desired, especially in the way it affected the hearts and minds of the more ruthless, less stable players. Frankie had been through marble hell and I had the chance, the intent, to make it right and pull him back up into the light.

I picked up Frankie's empty, flattened, dusty, dirty marble sock that he'd left behind and repeatedly slapped it against my pants leg, knocking out all the loose dirt and sand. Frankie's stride had become dangerously irregular as he weaved like a speeding car riding on three flat tires. It would be only a matter of seconds before all of his loose nuts and bolts would pop and he would collapse into a little heap of small, disjointed human appendages. After a quick inspection for holes and tears, Frankie's abused marble sock appeared to be intact and after the thorough shaking seemed reasonably clean as well. I started walking after Frankie while, handful at a time, refilling his marble sock with all the marbles I'd been forced to win from him. Just as I caught up with him the last handful of marbles had been redeposited into his sock.

"Hey Frankie, hey, wait up a minute will yeah?" I called out as I tied a good strong knot in his once again bulging marble sock.

Frankie stopped but he didn't turn around, his right hand buried in his pants pocket and his left dangling free for use as his jacket sleeve handkerchief.

"Frankie, I got somethin' here that's yours, wait up!"

He turned around and he looked – rough.

I held out his full marble sock and announced, "These are yours, not mine."

"But you won 'em," Frankie sniffled.

"Yeah, but it wasn't fair and square like it should have been. I didn't want to beat you Frankie, I didn't even want to play you. I was afraid that Billy and those other guys were going to beat me up if I didn't. I had no choice then but I do now. So, here, take 'em back, they're yours, not mine."

Frankie reached out for his marbles as his face lit up like a two-hundred-watt light bulb in a dark room as he wiped his nose with his soppy left jacket sleeve. He opened the top of the marble sock and looked inside just to be sure that they were really his and really actually all there. You could have almost heard all the loose nuts and bolts rapidly tighten up with a "WHHIIIRRRR" all at once.

"They're all yours and they're all there, I kept 'em separate from the rest. They're a little dirty but you can wash 'em up at home. Just soap and water but don't let them get away from you when you do, trust me," I earnestly advised and consoled.

Then, to make his ordeal a bit more bearable and his recovery a little quicker and a lot sweeter, I reached into my pants pocket and pulled out a handful of Cat'-Eye boulders that I'd won directly from Billy and held them out to Frankie as a gift in much the same way Hector Hobart had done for me some months before.

"These are for you too. They're some of the ones I won from Billy. He was a real creep to you. He was a real creep to me too. I want you to have 'em from me to sort of pay you back for all your trouble and all," I said reassuringly.

Frankie cracked a big squeaky, puffy red eyes and nose smile in appreciation.

"Thanks Archer, thanks a lot but I gotta go 'cause I was supposed to be home a long time ago."

"Yeah, me too, I'll see yeah around," I acknowledged.

Then, without a second thought, I grabbed him and gave him a hug, a real hug, like he was a little brother. He hugged me back. Frankie walked away, his steps lighter and tighter, less fragile than before, when he stopped and called back.

"Thanks for giving me my marbles back, Archer."

"That's okay. You gotta lotta nice marbles there. Don't let anybody take 'em away again if you can help it. Yeah know, anytime you wanna play, yeah know, not for keeps or anything, just for funzies, just call me or something, anytime, I mean it."

"Okay Archer, see yeah."

"See yeah Frankie."

Frankie turned away and started to jog his way home. I turned and headed back to the center of the alley and the scene of the match. I hadn't taken three steps when Frankie called back one more time.

"Hey, Archer."

I turned, "Yeah?"

"You're the best player I've ever seen. There ain't nobody at Avenging Grace who could beat you 'cause I seen 'em all play and there's nobody!"

"Thanks."

"See yeah Archer."

"Yep, see yeah."

The extra icing on the cupcake! I felt even better if that was possible. It wasn't just winning the surprise marathon, beating Billy twice in the process; it was squaring things with Frankie. Little Hansen and I were only a year apart but I felt like his much older big brother. It reminded me of an old poem quoted in a weekly grade school magazine that Mrs. Goodchaulks read aloud in reading class. The lesson of the poem being that what we did to and/or for other people, good or bad, when they were young, counted and permanently influenced their lives in some positive or negative way. Positive actions created good memories; a sense of fairness and understanding which in turn inspired trust and confidence. Negative actions and the bad memories that they created subverted inspiration and caused lifelong bad feelings which could be responsible for unsympathetic and hard sharp edges to a person's adult view and approach to the world. From memory the lesson of the poem was that what had been taken from a child unfairly, unwisely, could not be returned to them after they'd hardened into an adult.

After recalling the poem as best as I could remember it, I self-reflected that when little Hansen grew up and people called him Frank instead of Frankie, whatever cold, hard, sharp edges he'd acquired along the way weren't going to be because of anything I'd done, that was for certain.

Frankie, Billy and his gang had long departed and I found myself alone in the deserted alley. Walking up to the faded chalk drawn playing circle I let out a long audible sigh of relief and satisfaction. Before my eyes the inside of the ring became a view screen as the past nine months of my marble life replayed before my eyes.

The first matches, Rodney, Melissa, Hector, Warren and on and on. All the wins, the losses, the chances, the chases and the embarrassments all came together in that one final moment on a Saturday afternoon in late May, 1959. The wider world would never know nor would the wider world have cared that I, Michael Archer, a three-and-a-half-foot tall first grader beat eight guys who were older, bigger, stronger and meaner but not better or wiser, to become the local undisputed marble champion. But I knew it, I cared and that was all that mattered on that warm spring Saturday afternoon.

The world of the quiet alley returned as the view screen in the marble ring dissolved back into blank alley cement. I started for Nash Street at the south end of the alley that would led me toward home. My slow confident gait turned into a slow, bent forward, steady run as I got caught up in the magnitude of that afternoon's success. I wanted to run for home as fast as I could but my bulging marble socks, pants pockets and jacket pockets would not have withstood the weight and strain of my victory.

With a grin on my face big enough to intercept several flying insects, like bugs smacking a car windshield, I half-ran-half-waddled my way home eager to share the news.

Waddle-running through the yard gate, I even got excited about making it home without dropping a single marble and without the weight of my winnings ripping holes in my clothes. The pockets of my pants and jacket would be permanently stretched out and baggy. The thought of enshrining the clothes I'd worn that day in the bottom drawer of my dresser became a definite possibility. I made my way along the sidewalk on the south side of the house ready to burst with all the good news. Hustling up the back steps to the door, fighting to keep my balance and not trip and fall from all the extra marble weight, I yelled out that I'd won even before I actually made it through the door and into the house.

Exploding through the back door and into the kitchen blind from the brighter exterior light I immediately sensed that there were people present, strangely still and quiet people. I flung my arms wide-open and shouted.

"I won!"

Dozens of marbles flew from my stuffed jacket pockets and rolled, bounced and boinged their way across the kitchen floor. With arms raised triumphantly and a big bug-filled toothy smile on my face, my eyes adjusted to the lower interior light level and there, sitting at the kitchen table, waiting to welcome the hero home was my Mom, my Dad, my tearful Auntie Wilma and – a cop. Mom looked like she could have shouted, "I knew it!" Dad looked like he did when he fell out of the boat, except this time he was dry. Auntie Wilma looked fatter than ever as she chewed away on a comforting aggravation consolation sandwich and the cop looked like he was ready to write me a ticket for negligent treatment and abandonment of a relative. Even the biggest day of my life had a price to be paid.

 Fortunately, I didn't get a citation for running out on Aunt Wilma, only a verbal warning. Dad didn't say much, as usual, and Mom was relieved that her youngest hadn't been kidnapped, flattened by a truck, or hadn't run away to join the circus side-show as "The One, The Only, The Amazing Magnificent Michael the Marble Boy."

Aunt Wilma never did decide upon a gift for me and it was years before she tried another surprise visit despite the tasty wholesomeness of Mom's grilled cheese sandwich and tomato soup lunches. As an afterthought I concluded that the plan all along had been for my Aunt to visit the lunch counter at the store and the gift purchase idea was just a pretense. Auntie departed later that day on good terms as Mom and Dad appeased her fat frazzled nerves with an all-the-fix'ns ham dinner. She left teeth marks on the ham bone. Her kitchen chair spent the following three days in the basement workshop intensive care section re-covering after all the wooden joints had been re-glued and bar-clamped to reset.

I'd won, won bigger than I could have ever imagined and yet, wouldn't yeah know it, the world hadn't stopped to take notice. Life, near and far, just plunked and plodded along like always.

*

***

Chapter Ten:
"It" Finishes

THE FOLLOWING MONDAY word spread throughout school regarding the outcome of the match faster than an outbreak of the chicken pox. Kids not only knew that I'd beaten Billy twice as well as each one of his ten friends who'd been willing to try, they also knew about the fisticuffs with Weirdo and my reconciliation with Frankie. Apparently, Frankie, upon arriving home after Saturday's drama and his emotional trauma, ran next door to Wilbur Hunt's house and unburdened himself by giving a threat-by-threat, blow-by-blow and shot-by-shot account of that afternoon's proceedings.

By the time I arrived at school Wilbur had blabbed the entire story ten times over. In the school lunchroom even Principal Wagermann gave me a passing pat on the back along with a big grin and a that-a-boy wink. Unknown to me at the time, it was the least he could do for being ten bucks richer thanks to my derring-do in and out of the marble ring. That particular Monday was the third to last day of school before the start of summer vacation. My first year in school could not have ended on a more perfect note. All things considered it had been a pretty decent nine months.

The last day of school was great fun, more like a day at the carnival rather than a day at school. All three recesses were each an extra fifteen minutes longer, we all got extra free chocolate milk with lunch and we played all kinds of games instead of having academic lessons. All the kids in my class right along with me had been passed onto the second grade and each of us had received a gold star pin to wear which announced to the world that we'd all learned how to read.

The only hitch in the festivities was Melissa Williams and her award for the best penmanship in the class. She certainly deserved the honor but her classmates didn't deserve her incessant bragging. At the noon recess she took her award certificate out onto the playground where she shoved it into the face of "Stinky" Peterson. He responded in his typical fashion to the annoying news with one of his patentable precisely controlled aimed gas releases, something he was well known for, and, in some circles, admired for. That Stinky had a real talent, something all the guys thought could be really useful someday.

   As for me, I spent most of my recess time doing what I'd done at recess time for the previous two days, telling and retelling the story of Saturday's big match and demonstrating, to the best of my recollection, how I'd gotten punched, fought back and then went onto win four-hundred marbles. Admittedly, it started to go to my head. I'd never dreamed that so many other kids, many of whom had never touched a marble in their entire young lives, could vicariously experience such a personal victory.

   Between the last recess and the end of the last school day we all took time to clean out our desks. We all brought paper grocery bags from home, as instructed, to serve as carrying cases for all of our desk stuff, papers, supplies and whatever else ended up unknown and lost inside of our desks. It was quite the experience, full of surprises that in most cases were interesting and in a few cases tragically disgusting.

   My desk was in pretty good order but the guy in back of me by two desks, Chucky Green, had spilled a carton of milk into his desk around the middle of April. It was thought that it had been all cleaned up but the cheese-like substance that had formed and grown in the bottom of his desk indicated otherwise. The ripeness of the concoction of old milk mixed with chunks of white school paste, white school glue, worn down crayon stubs and assorted scraps of paper yielded a clump of stuff approximating a heady gelatin-like delicacy. For two months everyone thought it was Chucky who was the stinker and not his desk.

   Another desk surprise was in store for Glenda Schroeder who'd been crying off and on for weeks in February when she'd lost her new pet turtle right after Show-'n'-Tell. The tiny turtle had eluded several classroom wide searches and rescue attempts. The little critter turned up that day in May in the bottom of her desk under a folder full of scrap construction paper, dead and all dried up like a crinkly dried leaf on the ground in late autumn. Glenda started crying all over again. After Glenda cried her last tear and

Chucky scooped and scrapped the last of the headcheese out of his desk there were only minutes left in the school day before weeks of summer free time.

But, there were some final day surprises still in store as the last day of school ended on a high note. We were all absolutely delighted when cookies and fruit juice were delivered to the classroom door. Along with the refreshments came an unexpected visit from *Mr. Summer Safety*, in person, dressed in a collage of street signs and slogans. He'd peddled his unicycle around the room, rhyming and singing, giving pointers, advice and friendly reminders on the proper ways to cross busy city streets, ride your bike and other suggestions for a safe summer.

None of us in class actually knew who the guy was under all the getup but he must have led an interesting life, going from school to school dressed like a billboard with a big "Stop" sign for a face and a "Watch Out" sign that covered his backside. We all thought that in particular was funny, especially when he turned around, stuck out his butt, pointed at the sign and asked if everyone knew what it was.

"Yeah, that's your rear end!" someone shouted.

We all shouted and screamed with laughter, even Mrs. Goodchaulks cracked on that one.

"That's right, but what does it say?" *Mr. Summer Safety* called back.

"WATCH OUT," we all shouted back.

Mr. Summer Safety was in a generous mood besides being in good humor as he passed out plastic replica policeman's whistles to each student, each one individually wrapped in a clear plastic cellophane pouch.

"Not bad," I thought, "sort of like Christmas with green grass on the ground and green leaves on the trees."

As *Mr. Summer Safety* was leaving the room with loud goodbyes, Principal Wagermann's voice came over the PA System to announce that we'd all had a safe and productive school year and that he was very proud to have been our principal for the past nine months, that he looked forward to seeing us all again in September and to have a safe and happy summer.

At the very end of the day, just minutes before the last dismissal bell of the year, everybody got sorta choked up. Mrs. Goodchaulks held us back for our own miniature graduation ceremony. She told us how wonderful we'd all been ("even Stinky Peterson?" one of the girls had mumbled; guess who?) and to show her appreciation for our cooperation, hard work, and reasonably acceptable behavior, she presented each one of us with our first grade graduation cards; a small individual diploma with our name written on it, and then, to each and every one of us, a brand new retractable, blue ink, ballpoint pen, for most of us our first. We each, in our turn, thanked her as she called out our names and we walked, skipped and trotted to the front of the class to collect our cards, diplomas and pens to the applause of Mrs. Goodchaulks and our classmates.

At the conclusion of the private ceremony the last bell of the school year rang out and we were dismissed. Our entire class along with every other class in the school poured into the hallways carrying our paper sacks, some kids blowing on their plastic whistles and others nibbling on the last of the cookies and sucking down the few remaining cartons of fruit juice. *Mr. Summer Safety* was riding his unicycle up and down the hallway weaving between the exiting students saying goodbye and be safe as a final announcement came over the school wide PA System from old lady Bookbender reminding, demanding, threatening, that all overdue library books were to be returned immediately, at once, or else.

"Or else what!" one of the older kids mingling in the hallway called out in response.

Nobody listened. Bookbender might as well have been talking to an empty school building.

Mr. Summer Safety, on the other hand, distracted by Bookbender's loud PA warning, failed to notice a large tightly packed gaggle of honking and clamoring fifth graders hogging the hallway right in his path. He noticed the impassable blockade only at the last second and took a hard, sharp, unicycle tire squealing, evasive right turn. Fortunately, his hard right didn't lead straight into an unforgiving concrete block hallway wall. Unfortunately, his hard right took him right through the open door into the short hallway that led straight into the school janitors office and workshop where he apparently met, head-on, with Mr. Hairboni and his "handy-dandy always loaded and ready to go" cleaning cart.

It was about a second after he disappeared through the doorway that the resounding crash could be heard up and down the length of the hallway. A large portion of the resulting crash debris (which included the detached unicycle tire and Mr. Hairboni's favorite black comb) made its way back out into the hallway where students bustling for the exits had to take evasive action to avoid becoming entangled in the accident's fallout. Nearby teachers hopped, skipped and jumped over and around it all as they rushed to the scene of the collision.

While many of the kids leaving school that day knew well in advance how and where they'd be spending or would have liked to spend all or parts of their summer break it was more than likely that *Mr. Summer Safety's* immediate summer vacation plans had to be canceled or put on hold. His immediate future would most certainly involve spending a good portion of his vacation time back at *Mr. Summer Safety Remedial Summer Safety School* for a required refresher courses and instruction where he'd be subject to stringent and mandatory re-testing and recertification in order to keep his *Mr. Summer Safety* title, approved official issue uniform, costume signs and his *Mr. Summer Safety* badge (yes, he even had a badge).

Forget the damaged unicycle which had to be towed away by the unicycle towing rig. It would be back onto the really big learners-level tricycle pedaling his way around and through the red cone-marked safety track for our disgraced *Mr. Summer Safety* before he'd be allowed to even look at an official issue unicycle again. That guy really had to love his job to go back through all that tedious and demeaning re-education. It was a good thing that everybody got their plastic police whistle before, you know, the big accident. It would have been interesting to witness the *Mr. Summer Safety Accident Investigation Squad* later that day with the accident scene all roped off and all the *Mr. Summer Safety Accident Investigators* doing their work taking pictures, measuring with big long tape measures and writing pages of big-lettered coded notes. I wondered what kind of *Mr. Summer Safety* uniforms/costumes they'd all be wearing and what kind of signs they'd have attached to their costumes ("Ooops!", "should've turned left!", "didn't see that one coming!") and if their emergency response unicycles would have been equipped with special reflector kickstands, flashing red and yellow lights and loaded with multi-tone horns and sirens.

 I walked toward the school gate, waving, saying goodbye to all of my school chums, some of whom I'd see during the summer, others I would not. Russell ran up and invited me over to his house after school to show me another neat present he'd received in the mail from his favorite Uncle Chester (must have been delivered in the dark of night to get it past his mom). I volunteered, as an added attraction, to bring along my entire marble collection, altogether, all at once, allowing Russ to be the first living human being, besides myself, to see it first hand (the first and only other living creature to have seen it all on a regular basis was the cat). Russ thought that was a great idea and we parted, agreed on that afternoon's plans.

 I was a free boy. The uneventful walk home seemed much shorter than usual as I popped into the backyard and into the house through the rear kitchen door. I noticed that the barbecue grill had been set up meaning cook out time for supper later that evening. Mom was busy making hamburger patties and potato salad as I dumped my bag of school goodies all across the vacant kitchen table.

 "I passed! Look at all the neat stuff I got!"

 "Well, that a boy!" was Mom's answer along with a big hug. I showed her the whistle, which I tested out for her, my graduation card, the diploma with my name written on it and the ballpoint pen, my first. I told her about the cookies, the fruit juice, the chocolate milk and the "Watch Out" sign stuck to the rear end of *Mr. Summer Safety* as she laughed too but in a way as if she'd gotten something completely different from it than I had. Anyway, Mom told me that dinner would be a bit late that night which suited my plans with Russ just fine. With all of the school memorabilia back in the bag and back in hand I bounded up the stairs as I passed Robert who was bounding down.

"Hi Robby," I acknowledged.

"Hey Mike," he responded.

That was all: just brothers passing on the stairs.

Anyway – I ran into my room, quickly changed clothes and then reached under my bed and pulled out my bulging marble box. The large cardboard boot box had served me well throughout the year as it had taken on, week after week, without complaint, the ever-in-creasing burden that bore testament to my success. It was understandably flimsier than months before as the collection had grown and filled it to the very top. But it was a tough old box, just like the tough old boots that came in it that my dad wore to work everyday. It would certainly be strong enough for the trip to Russ' house and back in one secure piece. The sides of the box were so bowed out that I had to press them in just to get the top snuggly in place. I decided that a little extra insurance was called for; some extra heavy-duty rubber bands placed around the box at certain strategic points would be all that was necessary.

I lifted the box of marbles onto my bed and retrieved several of the extra-wide, extra-long rubber bands that Dad had brought home from work. I studied the problem and figured that two stretched the long way round the box and five stretched and spaced around the narrow width of the box would be just right. When I pulled on the two that went long way around the box they both snapped in half simultaneously and savagely whipped across the tops of my hands with a loud CRACK!

"YEEOOOWWWW," I yelped in surprise and pain.

Not only did it hurt like you wouldn't believe but there were also long red welts that immediately puffed up along the backs of my hands. Thoughtfully, I chose two more bands and carefully test-stretched them first and then guardedly pulled them around the long circumference of the marble box as they tightly snapped into place and then promptly broke again, this time brutally whipping across my right forearm with a stinging burn and with another long red puffy welt left in its wake. It hurt even worse the second time as I danced around the room clutching my injured forearm against my body with my face contorted, distorted and my voice choked with pain.

Having been seriously wounded twice in as many minutes I looked for two rubber bands that were longer than the rest. I found two but they were narrower and lighter than I would have liked. They snapped into place without attacking me. On my guard, like I was handling nitroglycerin, I cautiously stretched and placed the other five rubber bands without any further painful replies.

Satisfied that all necessary and sufficient precautions for the trek to Russ' house had been taken, I walked to my coat rack and put on my jacket. When I turned back to the bed, to my surprise, Kit Cat, the trusty family cat, had taken up comfortable residence right on top of my marble box, all stretched out and ready to nap. He was a great family cat, friendly and affectionate, but when I tried to ease him off the marble box he wouldn't budge. He just lay there with a "leave me alone, come back when I wake up" sort of look and attitude. Gently I eased my hands underneath him and lifted him to the side and laid him on the bed. As soon as I pulled my hands out from underneath him he jumped right back up onto the box and resumed his prior "I'm here to stay, get lost, come back later with treats" position.

Well, enough was enough so I scratched him under the chin to distract him and gave with a firm but gentle shove that dislodged him along with the promise of treats, maybe, later on. Just before he jumped down off the bed he turned and looked at me with a soft squeaky "meeooowww", scratched his right ear with his right rear paw, licked his right front paw, used same to wash his ear and then just stopped and stared at me. What he was getting at I couldn't decipher.

Gingerly, I lifted the heavy marble box off the bed and into my caring and cradling arms. Walking wasn't difficult but the weight and bulk of the entire collection limited my forward vision, especially that area right in front of my feet. But I thought that a surmountable problem and any worries were quickly laid to rest as I successfully navigated and transversed my way out of my room, down the stairs and into the kitchen without incident.

Mom was surprised to see me carrying what appeared to her to be most if not all of my marbles at one time. As I usually only brought out and carried around a smaller, representative selection, I'd assured her and reassured myself that I felt confident I could go to and from Russ' house without collapsing under the weight of my nine months of cumulative victories. So, off I went on my way to my best friend's house, slightly staggering under the load but proud, nonetheless, that it should be such a heavy responsibility.

Glorious is the valiant knight, whose life is lost on the battlefield, fighting to the very last against unbeatable foes, after many previous battle victories. There is no shame in such defeat, only fond and honorable memories of a vanquished hero. But ridiculous and cruel is Destiny when our knight in shining armor falls, not in battle, but upon his own sword during a drunken stupor, while his senses are clouded and muddled with illusions of indestructibility. Thus bloated and gloated with just such visions of invincibility I strode none too humbly onwards towards my best friend's house.

As Fate would have it, the *Troll Twins* were to have their revenge after all as a tragedy equal to or greater than any from *Greek Mythology* struck when I took an unfamiliar shortcut to Russ' house through a short, narrow, steeply inclined and seldom used utility alley on the way. I was about to experience, firsthand, the failure end of the success-failure spectrum. Owing to my limited field of vision directly in front of my feet because of the way I cradled my marble box, I failed to noticed a small chunk of dislodged alley pavement ever so slightly jutting up directly in my path.

Life, like marbles, could be a game of tiny fractions of inches. Death could be called the arrow launched at the moment of your birth that falls back to earth and strikes home at the instant of your passing. The marble launched into space at the moment of my discovery of the game in the school playground dirt months before had succumbed to gravity and vacated its high orbit as it streaked back down through the atmosphere, about to strike.

There are moments when you hang on by the thinnest, the barest, of threads. Sometimes you know it and sometimes you don't. When you don't know you inadvertently pull with all of your might, pull with all of your weight on the stretched slender thread with every careless yank, thoughtless tug and neglectful pull.

My path, unwavering and unvaried by fractions of an inch in a five block long walk, took my left foot directly to a meeting with the jutting piece of pavement. One-half square inch at the front of my left tennis shoe caught the one-half square inch of the exposed chunk of cracked pavement dead on. That high-orbit marble of my marble life had become the falling, the plunging, marble of my death as it hit home as hard and true as any one of my best aimed shots. I carelessly trailed out all of the reserve line of that thin thread on my walk toward Russ' house and when I reached the last forgiving length it snapped as I inattentively severed the last and only tie to my marble life. With all the grace and elegant form of a large plastic bag full of mud tumbling down a stairway – I tripped.

In tortuous slow motion agony my forward momentum pushed me into gravity's firm and relentless grip as it pulled me down. As I fell I tried to twist onto my side in an attempt to protect my marble box which, from my failing effort, glided out from my protective arms and into the air in a long floating arc. I hit the pavement hard and fast as my overstuffed, flimsy, rubber banded boot box loaded with every marble in my life hit the alley floor four feet in front of me like a twenty-five ton Coach Bus dropped front-first from a thirty-story building. The boot box shattered on impact with the sound of popping, snapping rubber bands and ripping, shredding boot box cardboard as my entire collection burst out in all directions like an exploding marble-packed land mine.

I fell down hard and flat onto the pavement like a soaking wet swim suit thrown down onto the locker room tile floor. Scraped and stunned from the fall, momentarily held in place against the alley cement by my downward momentum, I helplessly watched as all of the rewards of my hard won success bounced, rolled and raced at high-speed down the steeply pitched concrete towards a large, gaping, waiting storm sewer grate at the far end of the very short alley. A chilling recollection of Hector Hobart willingly feeding his marbles to the storm sewer at school intruded into my panic. Never had I felt so helpless as my marbles, my beautiful marbles, rolled unimpeded, like lemmings on the mythical journey to willingly, instinctively, jump off the cliff and into the sea.

Frantically, I fought against gravity's firm hold, scrambled to my feet and raced back and forth in an attempt to recover what I then was realizing to be irretrievable. The first marbles had already reached the end of the alley and were disappearing through the sewer grate as overwhelming fear hampered my efforts. What few marbles I managed to save were once again free and rolling as in my uncoordinated panic I tripped and fell hard a second time like I had lead for bones. What I'd worked for, what I'd fought to protect and hold together for months was unraveling before my eyes, just beyond my reach, in only seconds.

Two girls who'd been bouncing a tennis ball off the side of a garage in the alley watched curiously as I wildly raced to salvage what I could of my boyhood. It was at this point that Fate had once again intruded its ugly head. If it had been a poker game for my soul with the Devil I would have found myself holding only a pair of deuce's while the horned beast flashed a full house and prepared to take me along with the rest of the pot. The two girls close at hand were none other than the earlier scorned Melissa Williams and her best friend and confidant Jennifer Connally.

I feared, I expected, that at any second they would join in the chaos laughing and sneering with delight while doing everything possible to assist my lost marbles on their way to the waiting sewer. Fortunately, six-year olds weren't inclined or adept at holding personal grudges long term. Surprisingly, Melissa and Jennifer offered their assistance, with a condition. Unfortunately, Melissa hadn't completely forgotten or forgiven our earlier disagreements as she ungraciously offered their services for the price of keeping a portion of what they'd collect and save from the sewer. I was in no position to take a time out and negotiate as the sewer was claiming my marbles at an ever-increasing rate. There was nothing I could do to prevent Melissa from having her untimely revenge. I hastily agreed to their offer, as I was willing, at that point, to do anything to try and save what I was in the midst of losing forever.

It was a tearful, frantic, hopeless five minutes as I, Melissa and Jennifer collected what the storm sewer hadn't. After reluctantly keeping my word and paying off the two girls in accordance with our hastily contrived agreement, I had pitifully little left to show for all of my hard won success over the past nine months.

As Melissa and Jennifer went on their way I stood alone for an indeterminate amount of time, staring into the sewer, sorrowful and shocked at how everything, my whole life, had changed so drastically and so suddenly. It was not more than an hour before that my world had been a peaceful and beautiful place. Any and all of the world's most solemn secrets and cleverly disguised mysteries all became empty, formless and meaningless. I could barely breathe.

There'd been no recognizable or readable premonitions of approaching disaster. There'd been no disguised but decipherable hints of impending doom. No unexplainable gale force gusts of wind holding me up or steering me in a different, safer direction and, most certainly, no intervening *Marble Mountain Magic* that would have saved the day; that would have saved me.

It had been the thoughtfulness of the planned and mindlessness of the unplanned, the obvious brightness of the seen and blinding darkness of the unforeseen, the random compilation of the most significant and the relentless accumulation of the most insignificant actions taken over all the accumulated seconds, minutes, hours and then days, weeks and months of my marble life all compressed into one single pivotal moment of one kid's shoe meeting up with one tiny chunk of cement, one piece of out-of-place pavement that took up less than one square inch of the multi-million square mile surface of an entire planet.

What were the odds of not altering the passage of time by just one second – one second of delay or one second of earlier departure in any of the previous seconds, minutes and hours. What were the chances of not altering my step, lengthening or shortening my walking gait, by one inch in the tens of thousands of inches, thousands of feet or hundreds of yards of my path prior to that moment. Any slightest change in one or the other, or some infinitesimal combination of the two could have, would have, changed everything – forever. The mathematics of my personal tragedy could have provided years of study to any number of interested and advanced students of the subject.

Careless Fate, cruel Destiny, the random indifference of exisential happenstance, call it what you will, on that day, I lost almost all of my marbles and those who offered to help had greedily claimed their shares of the mere pittance that remained. It was the painful, gut wrenching, immediate passing of the initial seconds, minutes, hours and then the subsequent agonizing reflection and recollection during the dreadfully slow passing of days and weeks that I crawled, head down, on hands and knees, into the confusion and uncertainty of my life after marbles.

It would be by the smallest of bits and pieces, by the slowest assemblage of emotional odds and ends and the reaching for the safest and closest of familiar here's and the cautious and reluctant stretching for the furthest of uncertain and unfamiliar there's, by the littlest of steps at a time into my life after marbles, that I would struggle to stand back up and raise my head with face to the wind and rain before I started to fully grasp and understand the meaning and implications of that day in my young life because - when it all happened - I was just a little boy.

*

***

Epilogue:

Swimming Trunks

FARMERS HAVE ALWAYS said (and still say) "just give us a good gentle soaking day-long rain every seven to eight days from the end of April through the middle September with plenty of sunshine in between and everything will be just fine." That summer they got their wish with more than a few extra big cold-front thunderstorms in between.

I liked the rain. I liked the big summer storms even more. The wind, the lightning and thunder, the hail and heavy rain really mixed things up, cleaned and freshened the air and, little by little, storm by storm, drenching downpour after drenching deluge, started to wash off the burden of distressing memories. Where the local farmers wanted the rain to soak in I wanted it to hit me hard and rinse me clean of any and all painful residue that came from within and clung to my surface.

There were things that I'd never forget, things I'd not want to forget and there were things best let go of and left behind for good. In my darkest moments I temporarily comforted myself with the overly optimistic, the unrealistic thought, that I could always just pick up where I'd left off. But to start up fresh, as if what I'd experienced was a untimely misstep, a minor inconvenience that could be left behind without a second thought, was very far away from where I found myself. The time and distance passed and traveled from hurting to healing had, by then, already been long and far enough to keep me from ever going back. It was painful to walk away from what was lost but, somehow, less painful to keep moving on and away from what and who I was just a few weeks before.

It wasn't just marbles that had been lost. Part of me went down that storm sewer in that alley, a part of me that could not be recovered or rebuilt. The fall not only ripped the marbles out of my arms (and out of my life), it cracked, crushed and removed the protective marble world cocoon I'd painstakingly constructed and maintained over the previous nine months. The marble portal had closed and the illuminated path that led to and through it had disappeared. The marble state of mind had receded into the distance and became barely recognizable. The only way open was the unfamiliar and uncertain path forward.

Through June the numbness started to subside and I started to feel like a little human being again. I wasn't exactly happy-go-lucky but not exactly walk-out-in-front-of-a-moving-car depressed all the time either. I spent most of my time wearing swimming trunks. Not that I went swimming all the time or went swimming even now and then. But as soon as the sky started to darken with building storm clouds and the distant rumble of thunder could be heard I could be found sitting out in the backyard on the lawn in my swimming trunks waiting on, hoping for and expecting, a drenching downpour.

The chosen wardrobe for my long emotional recuperation was a pair of swimming trunks that a few years prior had been my older brother's swimming trunks. They were just a bit too big for me but if I tugged and pulled hard enough and tied the waistband string tight enough they would stay up even when wet and heavy. But owing to my depressive state of mind my string tugging and knot tying skills and abilities left a lot to be desired. After sitting for long periods in the backyard during downpours I'd, on occasion and out of necessity, struggle to a standing position to stretch and exercise my cramping legs.

On one such occasion when I stood up my wet heavy hand-me-down trunks strayed from my waist and had stayed behind down at my feet. At first, owing to the warm, wet and humid conditions I did not notice that my naked all together was out in the world until I noticed a puffy-cheeked rabbit who'd been snacking on clover under the apple tree and a gray squirrel with cheeks packed full of bird seed sitting in the backyard bird feeder had both stopped mid-feeding, motionless, and stared at me. There I stood in my wrenching emotional pain in the pouring rain bare ass naked to the world from the ankles up. It didn't matter. I had the physical strength to pull them back up but I completely lacked the emotional will and resolve. It was all just part of the ongoing overall humiliation of my loss. Not only was I to be marbleless for the rest of my life, apparently I also had to adjust

Keepers Weepers

to being the backyard naked savage nature boy of the neighborhood.

I don't recall exactly how long I stood there like that in the rain but at some point I heard a rapping sound from behind me. I turned and there at the kitchen window was my mother, tapping on the glass and giving me the high sign to put an end to the show and pull up my trunks. Yes, believe it or not, there was actually a non-verbal hand-gesture high sign that indicated that you'd lost or were about to lose your pants. You'd see the gesture or variations of it at the public pool where it was not at all uncommon for non-celestial sightings of crescent moons, quarter-moons, half-moons, three-quarter moons and on rare occasions, full moons, to make appearances, day or night, when swimming, splashing and otherwise cavorting human bodies entered and exited the pool. If a lot of swimming trunks happened to vacate the bottoms of their owners at the same time, looking around the concrete patio that surrounded the pool, you might see any number of parents, siblings and/or friends calling out and making high signs akin to first and third base baseball coaches signaling in elaborate coded instructions to batters and base runners.

I summoned the will and slowly bent down to retrieve the wet and heavy apparel. Just as I bent over and grabbed hold of the waistband there was a nearby lightning strike along with the corresponding instantaneous and deafening loud crack of thunder. Startled, I pulled up my trunks so fast and hard I almost lifted myself up off the ground with the worst, accidentally self-inflicted, wedgie of my life. There wasn't going to be an end to my pain – ever.

The cold winds of loss had blown through my heart and soul, morning, noon and night for weeks. The room in my mind that had undergone the redecorating quantum cascade of that August night ten months before had been emptied and stripped down to the bare studs for reconstruction and stood eerily silent and vacant.

I began to heal. I started to allow myself, just here and there, every now and then and only in the smallest measured bits and pieces, to look back at it all with a smiling fondness, a gentle regret and a reasoned introspection that did not cause a heaving chest, unstoppable tears and choking unbearable pain. Everyone close to me in my young life had done their part to soothe and comfort me. With the greatest kindness and affection they'd all encouraged me on and sympathetically promised better days and brighter times just ahead. But even as a little kid I knew full well what was lost and what I'd likely never have again.

As with most tragedies it was the passage of time and not dying in my sleep from the initial unrelenting grief that got me through. A few unfortunate minutes had become days, then weeks, of a painfully slow, involuntary dismantling and unraveling of my marble life, a life that had become thoroughly entwined, externally and internally, with who I'd willingly become and who, to a certainty, I'd never be again. What I believed could never be forcefully wrenched from my arms had been coldly and cruelly torn away and the raw wounds left behind stung, bled and burned. What had been forever inseparable had, in fact, separated. As it turned out, marbles could be...heartbreaking.

There was, unbelievably, unexpectedly, miraculously, a life emerging for me after marbles. The drenching rain helped. I just sat there in the backyard, in my swimming trunks, on the grass as the sheets of warm summer rain washed over me from head-to-toe. In the beginning, if it was an all-day steady rain, I just sat there all day, unmoving, not eating, not drinking anything except rainwater I caught in my mouth. A couple of times, admittedly, I peed in place, no kidding – who cared? If it was raining cats and dogs and I was in my swimming trunks, it was just like peeing in the pool, you weren't supposed to but as long as the rain kept falling and the water kept moving there was no harm done, to me or the lawn. In my whole life I'd never be as clean as I was that summer.

As I started to feel better about myself, better about my life, when the rain came I ventured out from the backyard and started walking around the neighborhood in my securely tied swimming trunks. Going for a walk in regular summer clothes on a regular sunny summer day just wasn't in the cards. I just wasn't up to it. I avoided and would hide from the sun. I needed the rain. I needed to get soaking wet. I also needed to get out of the backyard as I became certain that the rinsed off residual pain and suffering had started to leave a coating on the grass where I might have accidentally soaked it back up. Walking in the rain allowed all of it to cleanly flow off of me, down onto the sidewalk, then down onto the street and then down into the storm drains where it would disappear forever.

I had to be emotionally patient and vigilant at a time when it was the most difficult. It was a struggle. If I'd let them, the negative feelings that hurt and held me back could be very convincing in a dark and empty sort of way. Conversely, the positive emotions that comforted and helped move me forward were more fleeting, elusive and lacked a certain level of trust and confidence. Any distressed human heart could find a temporary or even a permanent home in the deepest, darkest, and saddest of places. Fortunately, I only temporarily passed through the far outskirts of that ville having decided, under the protection and with the help of the rain, to get out and about again. Besides, if my emotions caught up with and overwhelmed me at any point the rain falling on my head and flowing down over my face would adequately camouflage and disperse any tears that might make an untimely and uncontrollable appearance.

It was on one of those neighborhood excursions during a pouring rain that I walked as far as the sidewalk that surrounded my school and adjacent playground areas. I decided to start exposing myself to all those places that had played their part in my past marble glory as a way to vent and clear any residual emotions attached to those same places. I started to think ahead a little too because in the autumn I had to go back to school and I wasn't going to walk around the playground crying all the time from the memories that hadn't been properly exorcised. Slowly plodding along barefoot, I stepped into and splashed in the big puddles, as a hard steady rain washed me clean of any negative thoughts that had manged to surface that day. At the northeast corner of the playground, the asphalt paved section where Hector Hobart had blown his fuse and dropped his marbles into the storm sewer; I saw something sort of bunched up on top of the storm sewer grate as I walked by the school fence on the sidealk.

At first I kept on walking but also kept glancing back at the 'object' situated above the sewer grate. As I walked on and my visual perspective changed I recognized the 'object' as a person, a real little person kneeling down huddled up under an oversized dark gray rain poncho that covered the kid and the immediately surrounding asphalt pavement. I stopped and walked up to the school cyclone wire fence to get a closer look. With my hands intertwined, grasping the fence wire, the rain falling hard and straight, I called out to the figure. The densely falling rain hit the schoolyard pavement so hard that a water droplet mist had formed for almost two feet up from the pavement and into the air.

I called out again. The figure changed its posture slightly and a small face looked out at me from under the drenched rain poncho. It was Frankie Hansen, no shit! Blocks from home, in the middle of a rainstorm, sitting on top of a sewer grate in the schoolyard of a school that wasn't even his. He lowered his head and his face disappeared back into the shadow of the dripping poncho hood.

I ran for the school gate and then through the pooling water of the playground and came up on Frankie just sitting there. I squatted down and reached over with my right hand and lifted the rain poncho hood and there, sure enough, was a tearful and soaking wet Frankie Hansen. It was then that I also saw his soaking wet marble sock with what looked like a couple dozen marbles inside. Nobody ever played marbles in the rain, ever. It didn't make any sense unless your purpose was not to actually play, but to do an experiment or something like that. So Frankie wasn't playing, he wasn't practicing and he was way too protective of his marbles to be doing any type of risky experimentation. He was, it turned out, there for something else. He was there for me.

"Is it true Archer, did it happen?" he said in a loud little boy voice, loud enough to be heard above the pounding rain while still looking down through the sewer grate where torrent streams of rainwater disappeared.

I slowly stood up, arms hanging down at my sides and looked straight-up, face first, right into the rain, letting it pelt my head and shoulders. It all came back to me and started to hurt all over again, but only to a point. The rain washing down over my face immediately flushed away the few tears that managed to escape.

"Yeah, Frankie, it happened," I responded in a matching loud voice as I looked back down at him and the sewer grate.

"Was it bad?" he asked as he looked up at me.

"Yeah," I whispered.

"How bad?" he whispered back.

"Bad enough," I sighed back.

We both remained there in our respective positions; silent for a few moments as the steady hard rain was the only sound in the world. I ran both of my hands over my head wringing rainwater from my hair that was immediately replaced by the downpour.

"Frankie - what are you doin' here?"

"I had to find out," Frankie stated.

"Find out what?"

"How it felt to lose 'em like that," he stated sympathetically.

"It was crap, complete and total shi-, – real crap." I caught myself (Frankie would have to experience the fun of discovering that word with a best friend, just like I had).

"You did your best to save me from Billy. I felt I owed you, to know what it was like," he clarified.

"Frankie, you don't owe me nothin'," I assured him. "What do yeah think you owe me?" I really didn't know.

"I owed you to lose some marbles down the sewer too, to help you." He tried to comfort me.

"I didn't need any help doin' that Frankie, (I'd done a pretty thorough job of it all on my own) and, you doin' that won't help me or you," I tried to convince him.

I knelt down in the puddle building up around the sewer grate and went nose to nose with Frankie as I'd reached inside his poncho and twirled it around so that I was partially covered too. We looked like the wet poncho covered humps of a camel that was half-buried in the schoolyard. We conferred.

"I don't know what to do," he confided.

"I can't tell you what to do – I won't. But if you have to know what it was like, if it was me all over again, and I had a choice, I think – I think I would've picked just one. I don't know exactly how I would've done it, just havin' to pick one out of 'em all. Pickin' just one to lose, just one to give up on like that, to lose forever – I don't know. I think that it would've been just as hard sayin' goodbye to two of 'em, or to some small bunch of 'em or, to – all of 'em..."

I used both of my hands to press and then wipe away the external and internal moisture that had built-up in and around my eyes.

"It would have been one of my best 'cause every one of 'em was my best. It couldn't have been one of the worst 'cause not a single one of 'em was ever close to bein' 'a worst'. But, it would have been one that mattered just as much as any other. How I would've chosen one that wasn't everything to me when each and every single one was everything to me, I don't know. How would yeah say goodbye to one that by losin' it, would become the best one of 'em all? I'm not sure how but you'd find a way 'cause you'd have to, just have to – no choice. That one...more than any of the rest...would be the one I'd never forget – ever. I think – if I could go back and I knew I'd have to give somethin' up to change what happened, that's what I'd do," I thoughtfully put forward.

Healing a deep personal wound that proved almost impossible to heal in yourself, by yourself, was best accomplished by lending aid to someone else in the same situation and helping them to find a better solution, a more healing outcome than you'd experienced. That was my best advice. It was all I had. Frankie and I stared at each other for several seconds, face to face, under that soaked through rain poncho as we knelt in a deep puddle in the schoolyard as the rain steadily poured down.

"You don't owe me this, you don't owe me nothin'," I reassured him as he stared at me and thought it through. "You don't have to do anythin', but if yeah gotta, that's what I'd do. Whether you do or not – thanks anyway – see yeah."

With a dripping-wet half-smile on my face, I pulled out from under the poncho, stood up and made my way back towards the school gate.

Walking back onto the sidewalk, I headed for home with

Frankie still huddled under his poncho over the storm sewer grate. What he decided to do, if he did or if he didn't, I never found out. But it didn't matter because I'd done what I had to do. I told him the truth as clearly as I could see it at the time. What he did with it, then or later, was up to him.

By the end of July I was finally able to walk around the neighborhood in regular warm weather clothes and saved my swimming trunks for actual trips to the public pool and only the biggest rainstorms over the rest of the summer. I'd rediscovered a personal resilience, an unexpected carry over from my marble life. It turned out that I hadn't left it all behind, lost everything, after all.

The cleared out spaces in my head were being filled with other aspects of my daily young life. By late summer that special room in my brain was ready for another makeover, fresh paint, redecoration and new furniture as, on a warm, breezy, beautifully clear and cobalt blue twilight of an August evening, I gave in to an irresistible urge and stuck my head out of my bedroom window and looked up into the unfolding nighttime sky and watched – and waited – and wondered...

*

Made in the USA
Columbia, SC
21 September 2017